In the World of the Outcasts

ANTHEM SERIES ON RUSSIAN, EAST EUROPEAN AND EURASIAN STUDIES

Anthem Series on Russian, East European and Eurasian Studies publishes original research on the economy, politics, sociology, anthropology and history of the region. The series aims to promote critical scholarship in the field, and has built a reputation for uncompromising editorial and production standards. The breadth of the series reflects our commitment to promoting original scholarship on Russian and East European studies to a global audience.

In the World of the Outcasts

Notes of a Former Penal Laborer

Volume II

By Pëtr Filippovich Iakubovich

Translated with an Introduction by
Andrew A. Gentes

ANTHEM PRESS
LONDON • NEW YORK • DELHI

Anthem Press
An imprint of Wimbledon Publishing Company
www.anthempress.com

This edition first published in UK and USA 2015
by ANTHEM PRESS
75–76 Blackfriars Road, London SE1 8HA, UK
or PO Box 9779, London SW19 7ZG, UK
and
244 Madison Ave #116, New York, NY 10016, USA

First published in hardback by Anthem Press in 2014

Cover image: 'Scheffer. At mines of Kara. Tried in Kiev with Molafski'

British Library Cataloguing-in-Publication Data
A catalogue record for this book is available from the British Library.

Library of Congress Cataloging-in-Publication Data
The Library of Congress has cataloged the hardcover edition as follows:
P. IA. (Petr IAkubovich), 1860–1911, author.
[V mire otverzhennykh. English]
In the world of the outcasts : notes of a former penal laborer / by Pëtr Filippovich Iakubovich;
translated with an introduction by Andrew A. Gentes.
volumes ; cm. – (Anthem series on Russian, East European and Eurasian studies)
Includes bibliographical references.
ISBN 978-1-78308-111-0 (hardcover : alk. paper)
1. P. IA. (Petr IAkubovich), 1860–1911–Exile. 2. Exiles–Russia (Federation) –Siberia–Biography.
3. Prisoners–Russia (Federation) –Siberia–History–19th century. 4. Prisons–Russia
(Federation) –Siberia–History–19th century. I. Gentes, Andrew Armand, 1964–translator,
writer of added commentary. II. P. IA. (Petr IAkubovich), 1860–1911. V mire otverzhennykh.
Translation of: III. Title. IV. Series: Anthem series on Russian, East European
and Eurasian studies.
DK770.I2313 2013
957'.07092–dc23
[B]
2013043691

ISBN-13: 978 1 78308 418 0 (Pbk)
ISBN-10: 1 78308 418 9 (Pbk)

This title is also available as an ebook.

CONTENTS

VOLUME I

VOLUME II

CHARACTERS

Political Prisoners

Dmitrii Petrovich Shteinhart (Shtengor, Shteingor, Mitrii Petrovich)
Ivan Nikolaevich D. (Nikolaich, Mikolaich)
Valerian Mikhailovich Bashurov

Criminal Prisoners and Exiles

Andrei Busov (Andriushenka)
Andriushka Povar
Andriushka Vodianin ("Iron Cat")
"The Angry Cockroach"
Aziadinov
Bulanov
Bykov
Chinaman
Dasher (real name: Ibrahim Nureddin Sarafetdinov)
Diudin
Dubasov
Egor Rakitin
Evgraf Efimov (Egrashka, Egraf)
Gandorin
Goncharov
Gribskii ("The Amateur")
Iasha (Iashka) Pervanov ("Marmot")
Iukhorev
Karpushka Lipatov
Kolpakov
Komlëv
Koshkin
Krasnoperov
Kuzma Chirok
Letunov
Lunkov

Malaika Kantaurov
Mikhail Ivanovich Nogaitsev ("Bruin," Mikhailo Ivanych [Ivanovich], Mishenka)
Mikhaila Burenkov
Mishka Birkin ("Astrologer," "Postal Hound")
Mishka Shuster
Moisha Borukhovich ("*V*orukhovich") and his wife Entale (Enta)
Nikifor Burenkov (Mikishka)
Ogurtsov
Osip (Oska) Nepomniashchii
Palchikov
Paramon Malakhov
Pavel (Old Man) Nikolaev
Penkin
Perminov
Petin ("Elk")
Petrushka Semënov (Petka, Petkin, Petia, Penkin)
Ravilov
Roman (Romashka) Pestrov
Shah Lamas
Shemelin
Shmatov ("Buzzy")
Shooter
Skoropadov
Tiupkin
Tropin
Usanbai Marazgali (Usan, Usanka, Usankin)
Vaska Kos
Vladimirov ("Bear's Ears")
Zhebreek (Zhebreik, Zhebreichik, Zhebrei, "Prickly Weed")
Zvonarenko ("Leather Tack")

Officials, Administrators, and Guards

Andrei Semënovich (Semënych) Monakhov (mine superintendent)
Bezymënnykh (guard)
Kostrov (warden of Kadaia Prison)
Luchezarov ("Six-Eyes," commandant of Shelai Prison)
Pëtr Petrovich (Petrukha, duty officer at Shelai mine)
Petushkov (Ilich) (guard; later, mine duty officer at Shelai)
Prokofii Filippovich (Prokopii, Pron, Pronia, Pronia-the-Living-Dead, guard at Shelai)
Second Lieutenant Lomov (Luchezarov's assistant)
Sholsein ("The Finn")
Snake Head (Vasilii Andreevich) (a guard at Shelai)
Zemlianskii (Shelai's medic)

Female Characters

Anna Arkadevna (Cossack officer's wife and helper to the political prisoners)
Avdotia Finogenovna (Duniashka, Duniakha, Dunka)
Poduzdova (Poduzdikha)
Tania (Ivan Nikolaevich's sister)

IN THE WORLD OF THE OUTCASTS

NOTES OF A FORMER PENAL LABORER

VOLUME II

WITH COMRADES

I. IN THE MINING SMITHY

One freezing March day, when the crowd of miners issued as usual into the watch house, the duty officer turned out not to be there. For around an hour we waited for him in vain. Finally, the driver Burmakin came with instructions from Monakhov to proceed with the usual work.

"But what're we gonna do here?" indignant voices resounded.

"Whattabout the borin'?"

"I daresay you'll be borin' with yer long tongue! Sharpen yer augers first, then get to borin'."

"Go o'er to the smithy there," Burmakin said. "Palchikov, what're you buildin' yerself there? Go to the smith 'n' give 'im yer business."

"No, you do it yerself, if'n yer so clever!" biliously objected Palchikov, taking a little nose-warmer out of his mouth and spitting as if indifferent onto the ground. Evidently, everything was now boiling and steaming inside his tiny, nervous, and, even in normal times, always excitable frame. At the beginning of this scene he'd been standing quietly and immovably at the threshold, and had already managed to don his smith's leather apron and to smudge his pale, scantly bearded face with coal, but now he suddenly ran with quick strides to the trunk where augers and hammers were kept and, probably to emphasize his bilious mood more impressively, sat down on top of them in a most comfortable manner.

"What's this?" Burmakin asked in bewilderment.

"So is you standin' in for the duty officer?"

"Long time ago, boys, we was sittin' back-to-back together in prison, but then he went to the free command, his boots kicked off some mud, 'n' he put on a free command cap—'n' became mis-tah no mis-tah! He's suckin' up to the duty officers as well, 'n' wants to order his own brother round!"

These indignant expressions were approvingly taken up by the whole crowd. Burmakin became embarrassed.

"What you're sayin', lads! There's the duty officer… The gentleman told me go 'n' give an order—'n' I went. What's it to me! As for me, today, I'm servin' as Monakhov's driver, but the com'dant gives an order tomorrow—'n' I'm back to prison again. I'm a subordinate fellow."

Everyone fell silent.

"Well, so whaddya tell the boss man? Palchikov, you gonna tell me, huh? You goin' to the smithy?"

Palchikov was quiet a certain while.

"But why'm I weldin' the augers?!" he suddenly burst completely loose, leaping onto his short legs and menacingly advancing toward Burmakin. "Where is it, huh, your steel? How many times have I told Pëtr Petrovich 'n' Monakhov hisself? Always, day after day, the prisoners curse someone, 'n' who do they blame? *Me*! But I'll chop off my finger so's the fallin' sickness[1] gets you, huh? No, you won't answer me, huh? What're you drinkin' behind them doors? I'm a smith, 'n' so you think I ain't a *man*! You're annoyin' the life outta me, you vipers, so there! All my blood's pourin' out, you barbarians, damn you to the fallin' sickness!"

"'N' really, boys, why're we bein' bullied?" sympathetically ranted the mare, in normal times always at daggers with Palchikov, whose interests went against theirs. "Ain't we people? Don't mention the augers, 'cause they're no good to us at all, but we're asked to complete full quotas. The hauler goes time 'n' again to the smith; Ivan Nikolaevich there has worn hisself out completely, 'n' he's refused to start borin' again… No steel, they say, but where's it got to? If the duty officer or you yourself needed it for work, it'd most likely turn up!"

"Well, hold on a minute, fellas," the old watchman interrupted the conversation, "a new duty officer'll be here in days. Pëtr Petrovich was dismissed, y'know."

"Dismissed, how so? What're you sayin'?"

The old man bit his tongue, but after Burmakin left the watch house's threshold for a little while, he suddenly blurted:

"He was dismissed 'cause of Ivan Mikolaevich, that's why!…"

"Because of me?!" I asked in bewilderment, approaching the old man. "What does that mean?"

The old man chewed his lips silently, as if still trying to decide to tell everything, but the mare encircled him in a dark crowd and began pestering him.

"You minin' spook, since you've started it, tell it to the end! What're you hidin' there?"

"But what's hap'nin' is my life's been tough lately. I'm guilty as well, see, I leave, 'n' a third of youse is all loafin' 'bout in the watch house, drinkin' tea 'n' dawdlin' 'n' not workin'."

"Well, but what's this have to do with me? Why did Monakhov dismiss Pëtr Petrovich because of me?"

"'Cause you can't hardly do half yer quota, 'n' lookin' at you, the other boys is loafin'. But, y'see, you complained to Monahkov, 'n' he wrote a report to the minin' 'ministration. They had an argument right there with Pëtr Petrovich. Petrukha says: 'You talk with 'im yerselves, my tongue don't change 'im—he just flops down, I daresay, 'n' stares at me!' But Monakhov told 'im this: 'You, as they say, is the duty officer, 'n' you're responsible for talkin' to the prisoners.'"

"What are you saying? That I'm not boring seventeen inches?"

"Well, accordingly… You're also lazy, they say!"

"Ekh, you Razgildeev's seed! You're ready to flay a man twice, you Asmodei! Well, but if'n he don't got the strength, if Ivan Nikolaevich just *don't*, then whaddya say he should do. Hit hisself in the head with a rock? Tyrants!…"

"Why're you rainin' fire on me? Why's there a machete in yer hands? Was I ever the commandant? I'm sayin' what I heard… Sin to you comes, if'n yer tongue comes undone."

I walked off to the side, deeply afflicted that I hadn't earlier suspected this underhanded suspicion of me, and resolutely decided to speak openly with the boss man. The mare was still ranting among itself, when suddenly the door flung open and on the threshold appeared the fat-bellied, red-faced figure of Monakhov himself. Talk ceased, though the prisoners, as always, continued to be carefree in his presence, not doffing their caps and pacing about the watch house. Monakhov, having nourished an unsustainable fear of any sort of "dawdling," not only did not inspire *katorga* with respect but was actually scared of it now and then, and allowed the most informal relations. However, today he was puffed up and obviously displeased by the meeting's lack of respect; he even stopped at the threshold with a certain commanding look. But after a minute, he said straight out:

"Greetings, boys!"

Few responded. Then Monakhov, shivering from the cold and rubbing his hands, went to a corner of the hut and silently settled himself on to the steps that led to the building's upper floor—the carpenters' workshop. But he could not maintain his austere silence very long there and, giggling, began joking with the prisoners.

"What's this, Nogaitsev, you gotten thin? Is it the bad Shelai skilly?"

Offended, Nogaitsev walked away, grumbling loudly:

"I daresay you could lose that fat gut o' yours as well!"

Monakhov started jiggling with contented laughter.

"And you, Palchikov, found your apron, ready to get cookin'?"

Palchikov, boiling inside since that morning like a water kettle on a hot flaming stove, had probably simply been waiting for this address toward him. He flew immediately toward Monakhov, stood comically before his knees, and, agitated, choking, and cowering, began to vent before him all his injuries and claims. Monakhov tried to respond to this with his usual jokes and laughter.

"But if you're a true smith, you're smart enough to weld an auger with a pin! He-he-he!"

"No, Andrei Semënych, you jus' laugh, but I'm talkin' real serious to you: I can't do it no more! Call another smith, but I ain't gonna go if you don't gimme some steel."

"Don't e'en send a hauler," railed the borers, "you tries two times on the rock, 'n' he takes the augers 'n' up top he goes! 'N' they say they're mad at us, too, that we ain't workin' enough."

Monakhov instantly took on a serious look.

"Be patient a bit, chap. Not tomorrow, but day after tomorrow, they'll probably bring steel from Algacha. And there'll be a new duty officer."

"Yes, 'n' what's a duty officer to us? Without steel, we can't hold out two days; you ain't really gonna demand we fill the quotas?"

"What kinda smithy do you got?" Palchikov continued complaining. "At the other mines, the smiths always got a striker. But I'll be goddamned if you gimme a helper some day in some era… I'm the bellows-man, the striker, 'n' the craftsman. Don't hurt you if there's no one to weld, nor if there ain't no iron. May that job get took by the fallin' sickness! No, Andrei Semënovich, today you send me to bore 'n' put another in my spot."

"Patience, Palchikov. Perhaps I'll be givin' you an incentive soon."

Everyone in the hut momentarily quieted down: such was the magical impact always held by this word "incentive," or, as prisoners pronounced it, "intenchive." Slowly, out of some sense of propriety, prisoners began leaving for their usual work. The smith left. Monakhov remained sitting on the steps.

I approached him.

"I heard, Andrei Semënovich, that you're dissatisfied with my work?"

"How is it I'm dissatisfied?" flashed Monakhov.

"You think that I'm lazy and that if I wanted, I could bore more?"

Monakhov tried to chuckle, but, having seen by the expression on my face that I wasn't joking, said instead:

"Who tattled this to you, the headman?"

"No, not the headman."

"Well, then, it means it was Pëtr Petrovich. That bastard! Don't believe it, he's always dronin' on to me that the prisoners are lazy thanks to your example. But I ne'er said that e'en once… On the other hand, it's true I dunno what to write in my reports…"

"That's your business. I might just say that if you want to ask me to bore more, just tell me—don't deny me any job."

"Well, mercy, why so… Yes, we'll do that. Palchikov's complainin' he don't got a striker—you yourself heard. True, a striker ain't exactly needed in our little mine, but all the same, I could answer him with one. It'd be more convenient for me to hide you in the smithy than in the mine… He-he-he!"

"But what will you tell Palchikov about the helper you've found? A striker needs a lot of strength."

"What strength! To sharpen augers? That's jus' women's work. You'll simply work the bellows… Let's jus' go to Palchikov—I'll introduce you. He-he-he!"

We set off for the smithy—I, not so convinced by my new assignment, and Monakhov, laughing cheerfully and jiggling his fat belly. In the smithy, the bellows was already roaring. Palchikov, however, barely glanced at us when we appeared at the doors of his domain, and only after grabbing a handful of coal and ardently tossing it into the blazing furnace. His face was dirtied with soot, illumined by flame, and appeared absolutely evil. In the prison, a small bird had been calling out its mockery from all sides, but here, before his work, having barely thrown on his apron and stoking the fire, Palchikov was somehow suddenly transformed, and, as something more than a prison laborer, able to inspire in even the duty officer and the boss himself a certain kind of respect (for everything was depending on him). He'd instantly assumed a powerful and extremely independent appearance, grumbling with terrible curses about fate, God, the administration, what he felt, and how he involuntarily shrank before all those he hated and came into contact with.

Before "introducing" me Monakhov, turning toward me, attempted a joke at Palchikov's expense:

"I've always noted I don't have many smiths: soon as they get into the smithy in the mornin' they cover themselves up to their noses in soot… Y'know, it's said that those I'm talkin' 'bout are a baptized people! He-he-he-he!"

The response to this laughter was a grave silence; the bellows droning over the coal crackling in the furnace simply went on. I was beside myself, and shyly stood near the bench on which the striker normally sat after he fanned the flames.

"Well, Palchikov, here's your striker," Monakhov finally indecisively explained, shifting from foot to foot. "He's yours from now on."[2]

Glancing at neither Monakhov nor me, Palchikov erupted with terrible curses.

"What law might this be? Were that I be slaughtered sooner, damn me lock, stock, 'n' barrel! May you get a hunched back, the fallin' sickness, you accursed creature!"

"Who're you to swear like this, lad? You should quiet down a bit!" Monakhov somewhat raised his voice.

"But am I cursin' *you*? You don't see—I'm cursin' the damp coal, it don't burn at all, the damned crap, may the fallin' sickness take me 'long with it! An ulcer strike you! What sort o' striker you givin' me, Andrei Semënovich? Mightn't he know somethin' 'bout strikin' iron, or do I give 'im instructions?"

"Well, he'll hammer all the same for all that. Why're you so quick? Watch him first. I need to hide the man somewhere…"

And Monakhov left, leaving me alone with Palchikov. I'd pretended I was extremely indifferent toward his relentless cursing of Monakhov's assigning him an excuse-for-a-striker, and began looking around. I'd been in this smithy many times in the capacity of an idle spectator or impatient borer, but it was now appearing to me in quite a different light, imprinting upon my memory all its minute details. It was a tiny shed, knocked together by a quick hand out of some old boards, with huge gaps everywhere through which blew cold wind and swept drifts of snow. The bellows was also old, entirely blackened, and creaked and inflated with reluctance when its rope was pulled. The forge ("*forgê*") was made of bricks by a quick hand, and the iron pipe (the "driver"), through which came air from the bellows, had been poorly cemented to the stove and fell off time and again, summoning forth the smith's curses. Also summoning forth curses was the anvil, situated on a post poorly planted in the frozen ground with its so called "nose" insufficiently long for the smith's various odd jobs. In the opposite corner stood a trough of freezing water used for tempering steel. On the ground lay scattered a pile of augers that needed sharpening. I gazed intently into the face of the smith himself, in which at first there lay practically no inquisitiveness at all. This was a small, pencil-thin man with an impassioned snub-nose, hazel eyes that never looked people directly in the face, and a scraggy beard that at especially pathetic points of speech he wagged in a comically threatening manner. Having noticed an auger lying on the forge, I began pulling the bellows' rope to excite the fire.

"Stop!…" Palchikov instantly snapped, not looking at me. "The iron's been heated a while, so don't blow it… Oh, that the asps drinkin' our blood be slaughtered!"

He grabbed the auger from the fire and, nearly poking me in the mouth with the sparkling iron, laid it on the anvil.

"Strike!…"

Perplexedly looking here and there, I grabbed the small blacksmith hammer out of his hand and began pounding the auger with it… Palchikov spat, dropped the auger on the ground and, nearly weeping from fury, shouted terrible curses which, I assumed, were not directed at me as a formal insult but nevertheless—I felt—did not hold me in good stead. I stood dismayed, thoroughly embarrassed, and completely at a loss as to what crime I'd committed.

"Oh, that the fallin' sickness condemn us all! May his guts fall out, his fat belly burst! May you all give up the ghost!"

"What are you angry for, Palchikov? You know I'm not doing it on purpose… This is my first time… Later, maybe, I'll get the hang of it, I'll learn," I sheepishly muttered.

Then my eyes fell on a large hammer lying near my feet, and I remembered that I'd seen more than once exactly how a striker used this hammer, whereas the small hammer that I'd taken out of Palchikov's hand was always the inalienable property of the smith; having remembered this, I realized that my offense had not so much spoiled his work as offended his craftsman's dignity… Picking up the hammer, I was trying to laugh, but that was even worse. Vulgar curses rained anew to an even greater degree. I finally lost my patience and gave Palchikov a sufficiently sharp rebuke, requesting he hold his tongue. Then, having quieted down a bit and gone silent, he suddenly stooped toward me, made a quick, crooked bow, genuinely reverent, and, for the first time looking me directly in the eye, said in friendly confidence:

"But can you yourself, Ivan Nikolaevich, believe how them yellow-beaked *cheldony* won't stop tearin' our guts out? They puke 'n' spit on our brother like we ain't people!"

"But we *are* in *katorga*—what can you do?"

"Well, excuse me, them things ain't right! Razgildeev times is gone… In my view, it'd be better if he thrashed me or put me in the isolator, than wear me out with his chuckles 'n' exhaust me with all this disorder. Ev'ry time he's pokin' his snout at me with all this 'a real smith' he's offendin' me, 'n' there jus' ain't no excuse for this offense he's givin' me. Ask anyone who knew me on the outside: they'll each tell you that Palchikov weren't the worst tradesman! It's 'cause o' my trade, may I say, I came to *katorga*, but here they've made me the lowest fellow. They say that Palchikov dunno how to sharpen an auger! The hell with them, the cholera take 'em, who else is there in all the prison who gots the know-how I do? Vodianin? Not a bit! Don't push your snout at me with Vodianin. If I want, I'll show you a hunnerd dif'rent types o' know-how!"

"How is it you say blacksmithing brought you to *katorga*?"

"It was jus' I couldn't let General Zavialov bully me round, 'n' so I almost unstitched his belly, that's all."

"This means you were a soldier?"

Palchikov didn't respond to this question. Prisoners who've served before *katorga* as soldiers ("spooks") are generally ashamed of their pasts for some reason, and don't like to talk about them; besides, in a moment of friendship and readiness to be open toward me, Palchikov had managed to relax. He heated the auger again and crossly ordered me to blow the bellows. I obeyed. The bellows started groaning and willy-nilly the conversation ceased. At the point when the time came to use the hammer, I grabbed the real hammer, but then pounded the auger with it so zealously, regardless of all Palchikov's significant raps on the anvil (he considered that saying the word "stop!" would belittle himself), that the auger turned into a pancake. At that point Palchikov however limited himself to a bit of spitting, and placed the degraded auger in the fire once more; but I felt far greater embarrassment from this than if he'd expressed his wrath with some choice Russian words. By the end of this first day of work in the smithy, Palchikov had become a pure horror for me: I jumped in terror at his smallest bark… Many days were needed until I stopped taking so close to heart his constant seething at my evil influence!

The bellows groans and roars beneath my desperate efforts, cuttingly wounded by the sideways looks given me by Palchikov, indefatigably throwing damp coal into the forge which then noiselessly breathes deep in precise, undulating breaths, the breaths of some fantastic monster on the point of awakening and opening its ravenous jaws wide. Pulling on the rope, my hands begin to grow numb with fatigue; my back is also terribly tired and bows with each motion of my hands; my eyes gaze unremittingly at the blazing furnace, my brain stupefied by boring, monotonous ideas soon passing into some gray, disconnected dreams—and I want terribly to sleep, to stretch my limbs, stiff from cold, to close my eyes, to plunge into darkness and oblivion.

"Blow!…" comes Palchikov's shout, and my exhausting dream runs away with alacrity: my eyes open in fright, and my hands begin energetically pulling the rope.

The coal is already aflame. The furnace burns so brightly it can no longer be looked at. A fiery column of sparks rises upwards, flying through a hole in the roof instead of a chimney. How innumerable these bright specks' multitude! Thousands, myriads of them circle, float, tear along in a wildly insane gallop. Now, with an uproar and a whistling, a single, dazzlingly bright shaft of sparks that danced with unusual rapidity a kind of fantastic dance and whirled upwards has broken loose, but pushing it down is another still brighter and more cheerful swarm, and behind this, more and more, a whole series of them that, in an instant, has flowed into one large current of blue-red flame and, with savage joy, rushed into the enormous frozen sky to be instantly extinguished there, leaving behind merely soot and smoke. My eyes ache, but I don't have the strength to tear them away from the fiery spectacle, and these sparks now seem to me not simply dead sparks leaping from a burning stove but conscious, animate beings: because they cling to one another so greedily, because their joy is so rabid, so enlivened by insane dance! Everyone living, you know, enjoys life, and this life is but as brief as a moment—they take from it their portion of fate and then die without anger or complaint! Oh, go, go, new myriads of bright, tiny gnomes, enjoying yourselves, swallowing with great gulps your joyous moment! What matter that there is no discernible goal in this perpetual destruction and rebirth of these one and the same forms—life exists for life's sake, you know! Indeed, I now distinguish the unique features in each of these millions of tiny living spirits: certain of them are tearing along, radiant, full of joy, like Maytide elves spun out of ether and gold, others, by contrast, are sad, dolefully drooping with crushed wings, pale, as if thirsting for extinction and submersion in Nirvana… Why burn? Isn't it all the same—one or two moments?…

"Stop! Strike! Chop!"

And Palchikov takes from the fire a long, white-hot bar of steel from which fiery arrows shoot in all directions. They seem about to go into my eyes, and I instinctively try to cover my face with my mitt; however, fear of the terrible Palchikov surmounts my selfish apprehension and I, having quickly grabbed my hammer, begin striking it against the anvil with all my might.

"Strike faster, faster, you're lettin' the burn slip away!... Argh, the fallin' sickness, you let it go, it's gone cold... They're fiends, the goddamned asps, why do they wanna annoy the soul outta me, why'd they damn me with such a striker? Curse my eyes, they've emptied my belly! May the fallin' sickness, the Siberian plague, curse youse all!"

But, next time, my fear of the smith turns out to be unfounded: the "burn" is caught in time, and my desperate hammer blows along the "chisel" achieve their goal; from a large lump of steel is chopped a smaller piece, which is again immediately put into the furnace, while Palchikov, incessantly looking with suspicion at the smithy's door, dexterously thrusts the large lump into the cold ashes at the side of the fire. Only now do I perplexedly ask myself: wherefrom this steel, when just a short time ago its absence was being bemoaned? Meanwhile, the heated piece is again being taken from the fire and, to my surprise, beneath the smith's expert hammer gradually turns into a small heel, one of those kind fixed to the shoes of dandyish soldiers. I'm getting suspicious about this business. There soon appears in the smithy the heel's future owner himself, a mustachioed officer, a senior guard.

"Well, now, is it ready? Well done, chap, outstandingly made... So, I'll pay you later, no money now... Gave the last of it to Liubka last night."

"But I've already lost so much to your brother," Palchikov grumbles discontentedly, "Burtsev's gone off with so much I made. I made again for Koretskii—'n' got jack! Looks like the boss'll e'en catch us 'n' we'll suffer 'cause o' you... They'll say me 'n' Ivan Nikolaevich is thieves!"

"Well, don't get excited, brother, it ain't bein' charged to me."

And before I can gather my wits the officer leaves, having put the heel in his pocket. I then assume a very fierce look and say to Palchikov:

"How could you say: 'Me and Ivan Nikolaevich are thieves'? Don't you very well know I don't know what goes on here?"

For no evident reason Palchikov forcefully tosses some coal into the furnace with an iron spade.

"What'd I say? How might this be stealin'? You work 'n' work like a sick jade, but can't take a little lump o' steel? Would that the fallin' sickness take 'em all! The profit's great, you're thinkin'. You saw—the damned spooks is takin' a lot from us."

"Large profit or not, just don't you dare get me tangled up in this matter!"

"'Don't you dare'... What're you tryin' to prove to me? Where's it been seen that a prisoner informs on his own brother? What people, what a pair o' ruffians we are!"

"Don't talk nonsense, I'm not about to report you, but I simply repeat: don't dare involve me further. I'll understand absolutely nothing I don't see, so don't tell me. Whether it's official or another kind of work you're doing is none of my business. You hear?"

"Blow!"

I see a small auger lying on the furnace and once again resume the undoubtedly official work.

Following this minor dispute the state of affairs did not, however, change one iota. Palchikov continued thieving before my eyes and lied to the boss and comrade prisoners in the most impudent way. I stood off to the side and acted as if I saw and understood nothing. However, when in my presence Palchikov, as it were, vowed and swore to God that all his steel down to the last bit was gone, but the boss or duty officer both jokingly and seriously called him a thief and a defrauder, I each time could not abide myself, precisely because I was a silent accomplice to his lies and thievery and because this side-work in the smithy was most unpleasant for me. All the more, because I didn't possess the character to have a scene with Palchikov again and he, apparently, had soon forgotten my wrath: his carelessness reached such an extreme level that, while working with his back to the door, he often told me:

"Look-see through that crack, Ivan Nikolaevich, 'n' make sure no one happens to come by."

And, absolutely hypnotized by this carefree impertinence, I silently and submissively looked through the crack…

The new duty officer soon showed up, but although a sufficiently un-stupid man, he didn't suspect me of collaborating in the smith's thieveries. This was the very same guard Petushkov, toward whom Bezymënnykh had earlier composed the murderous epigram:

Like a skeleton, dry 'n' brittle,
He's a poet, a poet o' words none,
'N' so has been suitably laconically
Named: Petushkov!

Petushkov was literate and, according to him, reasonably well-read, but he was in the main too ambitious a fellow to have endured for long under the authority of a despot such as Luchezarov, and as soon as a vacancy to be the mine's duty officer opened he exchanged his guard's position for it and was now, horrifyingly, playing the liberal throughout the prison administration's quarters.

"Well, 'n' how're you gettin' on, Prokopii Filippovich?" he ironically turned to an older acquaintance, a prisoner recently assigned to the watch house as our associate. "Have a lot o' new pencils 'n' quills been found in the prison? Com'dant rippin' you to shreds?"

Prokofii Fillippovich's pale, bearded face looked at Petushkov with severe, gray eyes, and not a single muscle twitched with laughter.

"We're gettin' on as ordered," he dryly and sententiously fired back, "we're proceedin' as the law directs."

"Ha-ha-ha-ha!" howled Petushkov. "'N' what does the law tell you when a rascal's torturin' you to give a long, drawn-out salute, when he's steppin' on your toes for neither this nor that?"

"But didn't you serve in the military?"

"Tsk, tsk, what an eccentric you are, my service was as a citizen o' the Fatherland; but're you really servin' for money now?"

"You yourself served."

"I served, 'n' I got out. No, I won't let you to step on my feet! I'm an independent man, brother!"

Prokofii Filippych, or Pronia, as the prisoners called him among themselves, became discontent and stalked off, whereas Petushkov, having appeared the victor, craftily shot him a sympathetic look from the side. Clearly, he tried with all his might to be on the friendliest terms with everyone, though he bandied with me quite straightforwardly. After all the prisoners dispersed according to their jobs, he'd look in the smithy and jabber with me for entire hours about all possible matters senseless and significant.

"Oh, rascal, it's freezin' out there!" he at last could not restrain himself. "Palchikov's managin' by hisself, so run o'er to the watch house 'n' I'll tell you sumpin', Ivan Nikolaevich."

"Maybe later, if it's not so important?"

"No, it's a very serious matter."

I went with him to the watch house. There, having settled himself down on a trunk and seated me beside him, especially if none of the guards were warming themselves at the stove (he wasn't shy in front of the old watchman), Petushkov began, with a dancing voice, repeatedly using the familiar "you":

"It's your wish to live such a fate, Nikolaich! Pronia alone is the Livin' Dead 'n' he deserves it, y'know; I can't stand his kind! Indeed, the other guards are good, too. Well, but the com'dant again? The prisoners? Well, but is there really a brain in that chest o' yours? You should be sittin' somewhere writin' a book, or maybe in Pitenkhburg[3] servin' 'longside big bur'crats, but now… you gotta blow the bellows for some Palchikov, the rascal!"

"But what can be done? In for a penny…"

"No, I know what you should do."

"Escape? And are you going to help me, Ilich?"

"Well, why escape!" Ilich frowned. "No, but go 'n' put a petition in! In your place, I'd be writin' twenty petitions ev'ry God-given day, so's any of 'em might save me quick… So 'tis, I tell you: I heard from Luchezarov hisself—'ministration's jus' waitin' for you to ask for mercy. 'N' often we, us guards, say 'mongst ourselves: y'know, seems that devil would go free if'n 'e jus' made a bow! Well, why dontcha do it?… But Luchezarov said 'bout you: 'That's a cliff wall,' he says, 'not a man!'"

"But you know what a cliff wall likes to be, Ilich. Isn't it time to boil the tea and call the workers together?"

"Go on 'n' call 'em together if you like," Petushkov drily retorted, clearly dissatisfied that I had diverted the discussion according to my wont.

In secret, away from prisoners and even the watchman, he often proposed I join him for the breakfasts his wife or daughter brought him and which consisted of cheese curds or Siberian biscuits, and he was each time very distressed when I, as it were, point-blank refused these sumptuous victuals. In general, I realize, I was never able to decipher the true intent behind all of Petushkov's friendly gestures toward me and that now and then bore a sentimental quality; from time to time I myself felt deeply sympathetic toward, and completely believed in, this man, but I was also from time to time suspicious and ready to see him as no more than a cunning politician possessing a soul filled with nothing except selfish and ambitious means and ends. Thus, despite all his wordy liberalism about things, he was a big coward, since he didn't prevent the watch house's watchman and guards from secretly selling the prisoners free food—meat pies, potatoes, and so on—and he rarely, and even then with great reluctance, spied these forbidden snacks through his fingers, scaring even the watchman into giving up his spot behind the scenes.

"Why should I go 'gainst my authority, boys?" he said to the mare in a heartfelt, friendly tone, "what harm comes from food? Why should people starve on meatless skilly? Just 'magine: well, can you smell it all of a sudden? A brother such as yourselves shows up… 'n' then, what good'll it do me 'n' you?"

"Don't worry 'bout us, Ilich. No, suffice to say, you're way too cowardly, 'n' it's all fer nuthin', y'know, 'cause that's the guard's problem, not yours."

"You ain't judgin' right, boys. You yourselves know how the guards hate me… This Pronia-the-Livin'-Dead is alone simply ready to devour me, curse that rascal! Now they're sayin' I'm indulgin' you. Well, they can laugh at me, they can appoint another duty officer, but you really think it'll be better? You yourselves can see I got a heart 'n' I'm always ready to respect a man whene'er possible. Only, I always gotta be careful."

He maintained these same politics with regard to the issue of work, kindly and unctuously persuading prisoners to work harder and better for the sake of his heartfelt qualities…

It was a Saturday, a cold, nasty day in that same month of March. A piercing wind blew through all the chinks in our beggarly smithy, spraying snow on our faces, and our threshold was framed by whole snowdrifts. The bellows droned with a kind of especially malevolent noise, belching from the glowing furnace a column of madly dancing sparks; Palchikov belched forth his no worse streams of usual damnations, whereas I, huddling under my cold prisoner's sheepskin, luckless and silent toward everything in the world, leaned incessantly and blew the bellows. My feet were unbearably cold, and in those hours it seemed to me that my very brain was beginning to congeal, that I was gradually returning to a lump of soulless rock, lying for ages in one spot without goals, without thoughts or desires… On that day I was for some reason especially gloomy and not paying the slightest attention to Petushkov, who had several times already been suspiciously fidgeting about me, wanting absolutely to communicate something but at the same time hesitating. Finally, after Palchikov had picked up the basket and gone out the smithy's door to get a new supply of coal, he quickly leaned over and whispered to me:

"Today!"

I looked at him indifferently.

"Today, I say…"

"What?"

"They'll arrive."

"Who will arrive?"

"You really dunno?… Two… o' your comrades. One, they say, is a dokhtur, such a dokhtur, 'tis said, as we ne'er seen in Siberia. But he's still very young. Only, I jus' can't 'member who he is, the damn rascal… His surname is difficult, not Russian-like… Wait, I 'membered, I 'membered: Shtengor! 'N' the other is Bashurov. I dunno 'bout him, only, as should be, he's also from the big nobility 'n' served in an anniversity. Well then, in a word, the pair ain't like our mare, but I'm tellin' you straight—they're your comrades. But, please tell me, jus' how're such people endin' up in *katorga*? Akh, it's such a mockery of you all!"

"Are you really telling the truth, Ilich?"

"I'm 'bout to stand here 'n' tell lies!"

I choked up and my vision dimmed… I quickly lowered myself onto the bench. Palchikov returned with a full basket of coal. Seeing what a powerful impression his information had made on me, Petushkov frittered about the smithy. Behind the smith's back he stared fixedly at me and made pleading gestures. I understood him to be asking for the news to be kept strictly secret, and nodded my head in agreement.

"Akh, the scoundrel!…," he gave vent to his feelings with his favorite expression and hurriedly left for the watch house.

I had in the meantime been seized by an indescribable sensation. I counted the hours and minutes until the mining work would be finished, and ran time and again to the watch house to see whether the workers had returned from the shafts; during this, Petushkov tried not to look at me and carried on an animated discussion with the Cossacks about something. He'd evidently become thoroughly frightened and repented of having involved me in the prison's great secret… When prisoners finally formed ranks and, as usual, carried themselves headlong in the direction of the prison, I felt my knees shaking and a pleasant chill running throughout my body. I had always been internally angry at this haste, but today it seemed to me, on the contrary, that we were certainly not running fast enough. I soon got hot, so I undid my sheepskin. My frozen brain began to thaw—bright, cheerful ideas filled it, absolutely scorching sunrays beaming out of a nocturnal fog… Just a short time earlier I'd felt almost old, a helpless, pitiful cripple, but now I was young and strong once more and, once more, I wanted to live, to hope, to believe!

I passionately loved anew the world, where all of several hours ago I'd seen only the pointless and thoughtless hubbub of phenomena—I loved life and people, whereas not long before I'd truly despised as pitiful the laughing marionettes striving on behalf of their own pitiful existences!

"We shall survive, we shall overcome…" I whispered to myself, quickening my pace so that I almost stepped on the feet of the guards leading the way. "Life will now be easier… with comrades!…"

II. DESIRED GUESTS

As the mining party approached the prison, it did not escape notice that standing among the Cossacks at the gates were two or three new, "not-from-around-here" individuals, and also that there was some sort of activity in the guardhouse.

"Boys, could a party 'ave arrived?"

"Well, lookit the cart o'er there! Well, 'n' as should be, there's one 'n' a half men pokin' round… Doin' a search."

The most vigilant, having known not only to look through the window but even, as the mare said, to tell by the bayonet, recognized at that moment all the details of a search.

"There's two!… A young 'n' an ol' one… Young one's white-haired, the ol' one's black… Well, they're goin' through ever'thin' piece by piece, m'boys—I can't make 'em out. I should think 'cause o' their gentlemen's clothes they ain't simple folk. Lookee, look, they got a gold watch offa one of 'em… Them rogues was thinkin' they could take ever'thin' into the ward, like in another prison, 'n' be allowed to go round in freemen's clothes… No, ain't gonna happen! Six-Eyes levels ever'one! So you'll be livin' offa Shelai skilly, 'n' he don't give a damn 'bout your things, thank you!"

"Boys, they also got books! Mightn't these be comrades o' Mikolaich? Glory be. Maybe they brought Chichikov again?"

With such expressions the prisoners loudly bantered among themselves until the guard searched us, as always, beneath the window of the guardhouse where the newcomers had made their entrance. But the herd's curiosity was not overly strained, and as soon as the gates were shut it flowed like rain into the wards, hurrying to dinner.

I alone stayed at the gates. The guard who'd closed them grinned.

"What're you waitin' for?"

"Who's got the newcomers?"

"What newcomers?"

"Well, why deny it? I already know everything all the same. Is it the commandant?"

"No, just the senior guard. They're comin' this very moment."

And, indeed, after several moments a whole group of people emerged from the guardhouse, and the figures of the two newly arrived prisoners appeared at the prison gates. I ran up to them with words of welcome… But, to my surprise, the senior guard—an absurdly hissing fat man, red as a brick—behaved like a steward, jumping between us and loudly protesting:

"Nope, no can do! Com'dant's pleadin' wid us to git goin' *now!*"

Raising a hue and cry, the other guards supported him. I unwillingly withdrew. The newcomers were looking around in confusion and perplexity. The search's vulgarity had evidently had an effect on them, and both were glowering around like hunted wolves; the baggy prison clothes they'd just put on gave them a pathetic, comical appearance. I gazed greedily into their faces, searching out intelligent, friendly qualities in them… The mare had not been mistaken: one, an absolute youngster, was blond, the other, significantly older, a brunet. The blond appeared stocky and broad-shouldered; he had a beardless, childishly pink face with large, utterly kind eyes; his initial impressions of Shelai had agitated and patently shamed him… His comrade, a tall lean man with a silky black beard, was by contrast rather exasperated; his dark eyes glowered angrily from beneath thick eyebrows nearly sprouting from his forehead; he stared at me in distrust and did not smile once… "Well, he probably won't get along with me," I bitterly imagined, "he must be the doctor."

As the guards were taking the prisoners up the prison steps through the main corridor the young man turned in my direction (I was walking a certain distance behind) and, smiling, blew me a kiss; but his comrade, completely immersed in his thoughts, did not even glance at me. Both were then concealed inside the orderly's room, in which they were locked pending Luchezarov's arrival. After this, the guards left and I rushed up to the locked door where the first hurried, fragmentary, but ardent exchange of questions took place between me and the prisoners.

"What's your name?" came a stern voice, evidently that of the older of the newcomers.

I told him.

"So! You're Ivan Nikolaevich? Is this the truth?"

"Why are you surprised? Were you imagining I was someone else?"

"No, I immediately suspected it had to be you," answered the young voice.

"But for some reason I thought you weren't here," said the first, "and that we'd be completely alone with the prisoners."

"Ah, so that's why you seemed so terrible and unfriendly!"

"Your prison inspires terror!"

"Wait a bit, this is just the beginning…"

"Luchezarov, they say, is a wild beast?"

"Gentlemen, I still don't know your names, you know."

"Yes, yes, of course; I'm Shteinhart, Dmitrii Petrovich Shteinhart, a fourth-year medical student."

"And I'm Valerian Bashurov, a first-year law student."[4]

"But you're still very young?"

"Well, of course… Twenty-two…"

"And it seems the mare has mistakenly christened you an old man, Dmitrii Petrovich?"

"Has it really already christened me? I'm twenty-eight, though have some gray hairs already…"

We then exchanged several words about things to be found in Shelai, and touched again on the given state of affairs. One quick question feverishly followed another.

"What's the worst thing here? The banner issue?"

"Aha, you've already heard!"

"How are your relations with the prisoners?"

"And with the leadership?"

"Stop, gentlemen, I can't answer so many questions at once."

"You've not answered: is Luchezarov precisely the type of beast they say he is? How do you recommend we deal with him?"

"Is it possible to survive here in general?"

"As you see, I've been surviving… But now, with your arrival, I'll begin surviving so much better!"

"But will it be possible to be put in the same ward as you?"

"If Luchezarov is predisposed toward you—I'll ask him about this."

"Can you stay with us and him? If so, we'll respond to him with silence. What do you think?"

However, before I could gather my thoughts regarding this proposal, in the yard the piercing, disturbing whistle blew announcing the commandant's entry into the prison, and I hastened to depart for my ward. However, I was so excited that I didn't touch dinner. The reception ended earlier than I had expected, and a new whistle announced Six-Eyes's departure. Then I ran into the corridor once more and saw Shteinhart and Bashurov, sacks of regulation items in their hands, now coming to meet me. Here we embraced and kissed for the first time… Having spilled out of the ward, the mare watched this scene with sympathy and curiosity.

"Well, how did it go? Which wards have you been assigned to?"

"Just imagine, Luchezarov was unusually kind, even a gentleman! He gave a little speech about his humanity and his prison experience and advised us to only be: patient, patient, and patient! Moreover, he expressed great joy that I'm a medic and might be useful in the prison."

"Indeed, your renown as a wonderful doctor was trumpeted here earlier."

"I got that title once I reached Siberia, during the march into exile, from grateful patients. In fact, I already told you, I'm just a fourth-year student…"

"Did you speak with Luchezarov about the ward?"

"Indeed. He agreed with great pleasure to settle me together with you, though he assigned Valerian to another ward. 'I have,' he says, 'a general rule: as possible, to break into small parts any cabals there may be among prisoners—Tatars, Skoptsy, schismatics…' 'Pardon us,' we ask him, 'but are we Tatars or Skoptsy?' 'You,' he answers, 'I include among the group of educated persons.'"

I ushered my new comrades into my ward and prisoners, without waiting to be asked, immediately took the sacks out of their hands and ran to clear a space next to mine on the sleeping platform, but expressed great chagrin when they learned that only Shteinhart would live there.

"Why can't them barbarians settle all three together! What, there ain't 'nuff platforms?" My friend Chirok grew indignant. "Where's the harm if'n they wanna squeeze in anywheres!"

I brought to the newcomers' attention my old cohabitant Chirok, with whom I was good friends.

"Is it likely that he ended up here wrongly?" Valerian Bashurov asked. "It's quite evident from his face that he's an honest man!"

"Well," I broke out laughing, "I'll tell you what the prisoners say about his honesty: the Devil tried to comb him, and he broke the combing machine."

"See whatta liar this Mikolaich is!" Chirok began clawing his head with both hands. "How he punishes me in front o' his comrades! Don't believe 'im, don't believe 'im—he's the worst slacker in the prison!"

"Like Ivan Nikolaevich, you can teach us, too," Lunkov, smiling querulously, approached the newcomers. "You dunno, but we got a whole grammar school, gentlemen, 'n' I'm its best pupil."

In his corner Elk snorted disdainfully, but remained quiet.

"It was quite terrible," Lunkov continued, "sometimes Ivan Nikolaevich was tired, but he learned us ev'ry evenin'."

I told Shteinhart and Bashurov about our school; it interested them greatly. And when I talked about having at one time read aloud in prison, the prisoners seconded me with sympathetic outbursts, and even those who had been little interested in the books began maligning and cursing Six-Eyes.

Chirok had in the meantime run to the kitchen to brew us some tea. I gave him my kettle in which to pour the tea, and myself brought my comrades to the ward assigned as Bashurov's residence. Prisoners living there greeted us with the same hospitality, and moreover approximately the same exchange of ideas, as in my ward. Here lived, among others, the communal headman Iukhorev. He instantly appeared beside us and, casually and kindly shaking the newcomers' hands, sat them down beside him and struck up a conversation. Iukhorev's imposing appearance, open, intelligent look, and gigantic size evidently made a deep impression on them, and for a long time they were nonplussed by what they had to deal with. This man really did make quite an impression. He seemed to consist entirely of muscle, strong and powerful as steel; his large gray eyes looked around courageously and decisively, and to withstand their direct, penetrating gaze was difficult; his long mustaches set off his energetically defined lips. By the same token, his round chin was somewhat protruding, though his cheeks were always carefully shaved with the assistance of glass or prisoners' hidden razors. His forehead was prominently high, and into its midst jutted a rectilinear triangle of wiry black hair. This endowed his long, dark-complexioned, stern face with an almost fierce look, however lessened by the impact of an indisputably great intelligence that was apparent in this powerful man's each and every feature and gesture. Completely illiterate, Iukhorev spoke so intelligently, mellifluously, and even beautifully, interspersing his speech with a collection of unique epithets and sayings, that had he not been so candid, you might have conversed with him a good hour and even then not guessed you were dealing with a simple, uneducated peasant and not some mid-level baron, land councilman, or landowner. An inflexible willfulness was apparent in the whole of this iron, heroically chiseled physique, in its impetuous yet at the same time restrained movements, in its quick, forever hurrying, but easy gait. Having sketched Iukhorev's exterior physique, I will even say that once, having seen in the bathhouse his naked back covered with thick, shaggy hair, I was not a little surprised… "Here's rich pabulum for Lombrosian deductions!" I involuntarily thought.[5]

To a man, prisoners respected and feared Iukhorev, yet by no means only because he was the headman, and I never saw an instance in which anyone seriously tangled with him or on any occasion engaged him in a slanging match. On the other hand, Iukhorev did not suffer opposition. With the merest ruffian who happened in some way to irritate him, he sorted things out as follows: the giant quickly bounded off the sleeping platform and, saying not one bad word, began kneading and pummeling him with his sinewy hands (resistance was, of course, inconceivable), so that the victim was left only to turn the argument into a joke or to beg for mercy. By the same token, with "serious" prisoners Iukhorev restrained himself most diplomatically and carefully.

"Your things, gentlemen," he turned to my comrades, "will be put in the *shtorhouse.* I'll put 'em there meself. If you need somethin', jus' gimme a whisper. Y'know, I often go there to take from that thick-talkin' devil what won't be missed. 'Iukholev, weesh watchin' youse, 'n' nuthin's gonna be took.' I see 'im jus' gogglin' 'is eyes at me there, the red-haired lout, but I've already managed to get back inside twenty ways. Bing! Bang!—'n' that's it, got what I needed. I saw some ink, quills, 'n' postal paper in one o' the chests next to ya there... Jus' wink yer eyes at me!"

We thanked Iukhorev for his generous offer, but declined it.

"I'm friends with Luchezarov 'swell... Y'know, I bring a sample dinner to 'is office ev'ry day—'n' we 'ave all sorts o' talks there. I pour it out for him, I meself, so's that the fat's floatin' high... Once, I hear Ivan Nikolaevich here clamorin' 'bout this: why I gotta do that? On the contrary, as they say, ya need to show the com'dant the best sorta food... But, gentlemen, here's why Ivan Nikolaevich—'n' I won't be 'fendin' 'im—could live ten years in prison 'n' still not unnerstand a thing 'bout our bastard life! Our minds ain't all busy, as if they're thinkin' how to reach the final truth. But I know by experience 'ow the com'dant cares 'bout our brother—that's only one test'ment of 'is view. 'Cause we're penal laborers to 'im, *varnaki*, 'n' so we'll be till the end o' time! I tried showin' 'im the real skilly, y'know. 'E stamps 'is feet 'n' shouts: 'Ah! youse a thief indeed!' Mercy me—a thief. Should 'e get rich from thievery in this or that world as I do here! 'E'll go to heaven without 'is trousers. I won't argue—I steal, jus' not from me own brother; it's enough for me if 'e misses 'is steward when I go with 'im to the 'thorities. So, gentlemen, after such nonsense, I decided to bring Six-Eyes a sample o' jus' the best fat. 'N' now we's live in friendship. A pity our bathhouse ain't cookin' today, they're fixin' its stove. Well, but next Saturday, gentlemen, I'll personally steam, really steam, youse, prob'ly like the gov'nor hisself don't steam... Ha-ha! You might say the bathhouse's my specialty."

"But Chirok's probably brewed our tea already," I rose from my spot, "let's go, gentlemen!"

Iukhorev courteously stood up as well.

"This means I'll be lyin' wid you on the same platform, livin' in comradeship," he turned to Bashurov. "Outstandin'. Ne'er worry 'bout the tea: I got a hunnerd devils here who'll run to the kitchen to serve me. 'Ey, you, you Finnish Chuvash!" he suddenly bellowed at a prisoner lying on some bedding next to Valerian. "Git yerself a good ways outta here, I'm lyin' there!"

"But what harm am I doin' here?" the Chuvash muttered.

Like a cat, Iukhorev sprang from the platform, and before the prisoner knew what happened he and his bedding went flying to a different spot and Iukhorev's bedding ended up next to Bashurov's. The mare began rumbling approvingly; and after thinking a bit the victim, having decided it was much more prudent to suffer his unwelcomed *salto mortale* humorously, began to laugh ... We laughed, exiting the ward.

"Who *is* that individual?" Shteinhart asked me.

"Headman for the whole prison, the second little tsar here, after Luchezarov.

"That is clear. But do headmen really exercise such authority?"

"Not every one, of course, but as you can see, he's not commonplace."

"He seems very friendly. What do you think?" asked Bashurov.

"It's none of my concern… Anyway, I hardly know him, and haven't happened to live in the same ward."

Chirok had already arranged his business, and the kettle, with tea prepared—it turned out—with milk from God knows where, sat wrapped on all sides by a cassock on the sleeping platform.

"So's it wouldn't cool off," said Kuzma, grinning and obligingly unwrapping the tea.

"Very well, then, let's celebrate, gentlemen!" I invited.

But just as the celebration was about to begin, the door banged open and into the ward came, in a cap askew and a cassock foppishly slung across his shoulder, broadly grinning and rather hilariously genuflecting side to side, the prison buffoon and fool Karpushka Lipatov. His hair, orange as carrots, his likewise little orange beard, hanging beneath his cheeks and leaving his chin bare, his homely freckled face with small pug nose and cunning gray eyes, his contrived grimaces and simply can-canesque body movements—everything about Karpushka was unique and amusing. Certain prisoners considered him absolutely insane, others, by contrast, to be a clever rascal who played the advantageous role of the fool. To decide this issue was difficult, all the more so because Lipatov did not try to do what prisons' typical fakers tried to do, that is, to get out of work and get committed to hospital. Sometimes, having ended up there, he very quickly began arguing to return to the prison, and on the job he was more excessively hardworking than lazy or calculating.

"Greetin's, 'steemed gentlemen," Karpushka began, sitting down beside us, "didn't I catcha you noticin' me? I, too, got noble blood, y'know, 'cause e'en though my mother was a townswoman, my father was a bureaucrat."[6]

"But, Lipatov, didn't you say you never met your father and that you're illegitimate?"

"Now, I ain't sayin' I was *legitimate*, 'n' anyway I don't mean my noble blood's from that side. I'm tellin' the truth! I possess a real aristocratic look, y'know… Can his or his mug over there compare with mine?" Karpushka nodded toward some prisoners. The latter began laughing.

"But, y'know, I came to you for a reason, gentlemen. Which o' you here is, as they say, a dokhtur?"

"Well, let's say it's me," responded Shteinhart.

"'N' may I know your patronymic?"

"Dmitrii Petrovich."

"Well, Mitrii Petrovich, I gotta talk with you, hand in hand."

As he said this, Karpushka gave a variously meaningful wink.

"What's the matter? Are you afraid of strangers?"

"No, I ain't 'fraid o' nuthin'! Ain't ne'er 'fraid! Ev'ry roll call I speaks my mind to Six-Eyes hisself. Here I'm hopin' for, but ain't anticipatin', a district dokhtur with whom I'd like to share a few friendly words."

"Do you have some illness?"

"There's a real sickness inside me. Y'see, Mitrii Petrovich, I'll tell you, I don't got one little bone in my back. But the medic here, Zemlianskii, says: 'You're lyin', you sonofabitch, you got a bone.' But how can he say this when I know very well I don't."

"You know what, Lipatov," I suggested, "you can consult with Dmitrii Petrovich some other time: he'll give you a thorough examination then. But, you see, he's with friends now, so give him some peace. We still haven't been able to talk with each other as we'd like."

"That's right, buzz off, Karpushka!" the prisoners shouted at him. "Why're you makin' such a fool o' yourself? Beat it back home!"

Karpushka spat to the side indifferently and continued sitting there.

"Clever you, Ivan Mikolaevich, wantin' to get rid o' Karpushka. I'll let you talk 'mongst yerselves in your group 'n' slake your thirst with tea, but it could be said mine's a matter o' life or death. I'm tellin' you, I ain't got a bone in my back! I tell the medic: 'Gimme some real *khananiia*, 'n' that'll drive the sickness outta my bones.' But he, with his Gypsy-snout, keeps stuffin' me with *kalidat* after *kalidat*! But, I know what this *kalidat* is. This sickness is inside, y'know, killin' the bones..."

"What do this *kalidat* and some kind of *khananiia* mean to him?" Shteinhart appealed to me in bewilderment.

I was already reasonably familiar with the Karpushkin lexicon, and understood that by *khananiia* he presumably meant any sort of medication in general and that *kalidat* was *kali iod*—potassium iodide.

Shteinhart and Bashurov began laughing loudly, and Karpushka himself joined them.

"That's what's the matter... Now it's certain there's a real dokhtur here—you unnerstand ever'thin'. Now I know I'll get 'scribed real *kalidat*. You're now marked as a good man, 'n' not like Ivan Mikolaevich: 'Buzz off, Karpushka Lipatov,' they says! 'You can't join *my* group...' 'n' why can't I? I gots noble blood, too, y'know. Gentlemen, you should gimme a little noble tea to drink. Baikov tea[7]—indeed, it strains very well through your tendons, specially with milk. Better'n any *khananiia*."

We gave Karpushka a cup of tea.Thus we were unable to carry on our discussion: soon came the orderly's whistle and his anxious shout in the corridor:

"Out for roll call! Hurry to roll call! Com'dant'll be here!"

For a long time now, Luchezarov had not been appearing at roll call, but today an evidently solemn ceremony had been prearranged for the newcomers' arrival.

"He was ever so courteous toward you, but will nevertheless want to put a scare into you," I mentioned to my comrades as we were going to the prison yard, and I hastened to apprise them regarding what went on during roll call.

We bid farewell to Bashurov, thinking we wouldn't see him anymore before morning. He turned toward his ward, which "had been made" at the other end of the long prison row. There, Iukhorev immediately placed him under his protection, as confirmed by his own sturdy back. Shteinhart and I went to where our ward-mates were bestirring themselves. Chirok, my usual match, was already standing in the first row, peppering me and energetically abusing anyone who absent-mindedly tried to occupy my spot behind him. The giant Petin moved in front of Shteinhart, who stood next to me.

A guard worriedly bustled around the prisoners' ranks taking a preliminary count. Only now did the alarm for roll call sound; we froze there for around five minutes, but still Six-Eyes did not appear.

"He's makin' us stand like good steeds," unrepentant prisoners caviled.

Finally, there was a movement behind the gate's grilles, and before everyone's eyes there appeared a stately figure in a huge, shaggy papakha and broad, flowing greatcoat. We three had now been standing there without hats for a long time. The gates were flung wide open. Stiff as a poker, a guard delivered in a preternaturally shrill voice the command:

"At-ten-tion! Caps o-o-off!"

Instantly, there was the sound of hundreds of heads being uncovered.

"Caps on!" Luchezarov entered hurriedly, almost before the guard's cry ended.

"He'll continue being courteous," I whispered to Shteinhart, and looked at my comrade with interest. I noticed his face had darkened and was now and then twitching with nervous spasms… Luchezarovian courtesy had evidently consoled him little. The rest of roll call proceeded in the usual pompous format already established and, fortunately, without any unpleasant incidents. Work orders were not read out, since it was a Saturday.

"Ma-arch to the wards!" the concluding order resounded, and pairs of prisoners moved with precise rhythmic steps toward the prison. Shteinhart walked in front of me, pale and gloomy, hanging his head. Valerian Bashurov came running up to us in the corridor.

"Gentlemen, this is horrible! What humiliation!" he whispered, compulsively clenching his fingers. Agitation flushed even more his childishly rosy face. Shteinhart remained silent.

"Had you really expected better?" I said in a soothing tone. "Look at these things philosophically. If possible, even shore yourself up with humor…"

We shook each other's hands and parted. Meanwhile, the prisoners in the ward had again formed ranks. As before, Shteinhart and I stood near our sleeping platform behind Chirok and Elk.

The door burst open, five guards flew in like a hurricane, and one of them screeched the usual:

"At-ten-tion!"

With impressively slow steps Luchezarov entered, casting his inquisitive gaze at prisoners' faces and clearly looking for someone. His well-nourished, ruddy face was as usual smiling just barely ironically; since I, as a teacher, had last seen him, there had been no alteration whatsoever in the brave staff captain, albeit with this exclusion: he now wore a full captain's braids and this circumstance, of course, endowed him with still greater imperiousness and majesty.

He finally noticed Shteinhart and, after moving close, silently gave him a letter that he pulled from a side pocket. He then whirled round and angrily said to the guards:

"Do you smell that? What's that smell?"

"We can't tell, Mister Com'dant," someone indecisively answered in a sort of terror.

"What can't you tell? Don't you have a nose to smell with! It's a vile, disgusting smell!"

"Yes, 'tis indeed a finch-catcher's stench,[8] Mister Com'dant," agreed the same guard.

The difficult smell in our ward had for some reason lately become an object of constant irritation and fixation for the brave commandant. He smelled it even on those days when our window vents had long been open and when other wards' atmospheres were likely twice as noxious, and he was bawling out the guards and wretched headman over this and that. Now, he dashed behind the partition where the ward's waste tubs were located. His entire retinue followed him.

"Open them!" we heard the commandant's imperious voice from there. "Smell!… No, smell well and truly!"

One after another the guards could be heard approaching and sniffing. The mare, laughing quietly, looked at each other.

"That's it!" announced Luchezarov, appearing in the ward once more. "The headman and cleaners understand their responsibilities poorly. There's not enough cleanliness and order! Watch, I'll call them strictly to account."

And with quick steps he practically ran into the corridor; his retinue followed him with a banging and crashing, the door slammed shut, and the padlock clicked. Prisoners began whispering and laughing and resumed their usual conversations and diversions.

Shteinhart, having hunched over the table, was reading by the lamp's dim light the letter he'd received, and his gloomy face and heavy frowning brow reminded me of the first moment we met. My heart winced painfully… I again felt alone, and reflected jealously that this man would always possess his own special world that I would never penetrate and in which he would suffer and feel joy singly, exclusively, and silently. I lay down in my corner and gave myself over to these bitter thoughts; for a long time my comrade sat over the letter that he'd obviously finished reading much earlier. Then, having risen, he began walking back and forth throughout the ward in deep contemplation. Lunkov and Elk, having put away their notebooks, were sitting at the table swearing at each other.

III. SHTEINHART'S STORY

It was already quite late. The prisoners, not excluding my pupils, had for a long time been snoring punctually when Shteinhart, after climbing onto the sleeping platform, began making up his bed next to mine.

"You're still not asleep, Ivan Nikolaevich? Do you know whom I received the letter from today?" he suddenly said to me in an undertone, having noticed I wasn't asleep; and, after looking at his face, I started joyously: it was bright and friendly once more and his dark eyes were beaming like two stars from beneath his smooth eyebrows, unmasking me with warm, affectionate rays.

I, of course, didn't know whom his letter was from. His mother? His sister?

"No, my fiancée," Shteinhart said with a deeply moved and sad voice. "She's lost all hope already! Today, during Luchezarov's reception, he directly told us that he would deliver letters only from verified closest relatives, and that all others would be held right up until our release to settlement. He said it's a law impossible to disobey. Then suddenly—he brings this very letter this evening… For this magnanimous act, Ivan Nikolaevich, I confess I'm quite prepared to forgive Luchezarov and reconcile myself with very much in his regime!"

"Yes, I saw what an impression roll call made on you."

"It was terrible! But… do you know what my fiancée is asking about? Besides, I want to tell you our whole sad tale. Of course, these are personal torments and joys, and perhaps they won't interest you…"

"Listen to you, Dmitrii Petrovich! I simply fear I haven't earned your confidence in me yet."

"No, I feel I can confide in you… Everything you've said and observed is from the heart. For me, this is… I'm so tired of hiding my thoughts and torments!"

"But what about Valerian Mikhailovich? Aren't you friends with him?"

"You see… I like Valerian very much, but he's not my friend. He's still too young, and has characteristics that are disposed towards expressiveness. Well, in a word, you'll get to know them soon. In any case, he knows my personal life in only the broadest terms. First of all, did you know I'm a Jew?"

"You're Jewish? I never would have guessed! Yes, your name…"

"Well, a name means nothing. In actuality, I'm not a Dmitrii at all but a Mordecai, and not a Petrovich but a Pesakhovich, but you know how beastly that sounds in Russian… However, tell me openly, Ivan Nikolaevich, are you at all Judeophobic?"

I began laughing.

"Fortunately, no. I can say this with hand on heart. I was born and raised in the deep north, where there are almost no Jews. So, when I entered Petersburg University, for a long time I thought every country yokel saying 'filf' instead of 'filth' was a Jew. Later, several of my closest comrades and friends were Jews."

"I'm very glad. You've lifted a heavy stone from my heart. You won't believe, Ivan Nikolaevich, what scandalous things are going on now in Rus! Seemingly educated, intelligent people are not ashamed to say the word 'Yid' loudly and openly and to express disdain and hatred toward Jews. The more a man like myself, being Jewish, sees and hears all this, essentially nothing save birthplace seems to connect him to the native tribe. And when those wretched folk hurl spittle and stones from all sides, it may then be asked, how should I feel and whom should I love?... Yes, this damned Jewish problem has damned my personal existence!... Are you hearing me?"

"I'm paying complete attention."

"So, I'll tell you my story.[9] I was a second-year student when I got to know my present fiancée. I was twenty-three, Elena twenty. We were both full of that 'blessed discontent' that Nekrasov speaks about[10]—mutually rapturous, naïve, youthful souls... It was on this proverbial basis that our romance developed. Do you recall Petersburg's vernal nights, those magical white nights with their fantastic coloring and sickly melancholy, simply spilling around you in the air? Do you remember night-boating on the Neva, and the company of friends or likewise enthusiastic dreamers at the seashore? Or—students' winter evenings with loud dancing and boisterous songs? However, I personally love now to recall a most different picture. Appearing before me is Elena's little room in Peski,[11] a small, cozy little room... The samovar on the table would have gone out long ago, but we'd sit up half the night and talk for ages in the lamplight. About love? Oh, no, most rarely and least of all about love! All the issues were serious and important: we'd reconstruct human life, decide the world's future, and prepare ourselves to go on a great exploit in the service of the people... It would happen that Elena would finally remember she had to deliver a lecture and that I should not be prevented from thinking about similar things; she'd then undertake to coax me homeward. We'd begin saying goodbye, but, saying goodbye and still holding hands, would for a time again be carried away by serious conversation, that purely childish chatter. I'd be standing on the room's threshold the whole time, already completely dressed, but we couldn't part at all, and would ten times hold each other's hand and ten times resume the conversation. Back then we talked about everything, thought about everything, and forgot only one thing, that I was Jewish and she Russian Orthodox... Everything in our relationship seemed so plain and simple: we loved each other, and this meant all our life would steadily proceed hand in hand, 'without afterthoughts, without struggle, without fatal notions'...[12] To us, the notion of a legal union did not seem the sole reason that our hearts, beating in unison, were at that time soaring too high to worry about egoistical personal fates; but perhaps we were suppressing the disturbingly unwelcome problem... A break with her faith, not out of conviction but out of the joy of love, seemed to Elena a blasphemy against her race; moreover, I feared having to deliver the cruel blow to her old mother, who loved me insanely, albeit according to the precepts and traditions of the Old Belief. Yet, life between us did not tarry and decided the problem by its own accord. When, one beautiful morning, I was arrested and imprisoned in the fortress,[13] not only was Elena unable to get a message to me, but was herself arrested and exiled to her hometown.

Correspondence between us was even prohibited… I went into a frenzy, went crazy, not knowing what had happened to Elena, whether she was alive, whether she was free. You know, of course, the feeling when you're ready to pound your skull against cold stone walls!…

"But, Ivan Nikolaevich, man is an infinitely patient, disgracefully hardy being, and I, too, endured all, did not lose my mind or smash my head, and I remained alive and healthy. In the meantime, two whole years passed. At last, I was sentenced to *katorga*, and during my removal to Siberia was taken to the House of Preliminary Detention. After my complete isolation in the fortress it seemed I'd landed in a racketous maelstrom of life: the footsteps, voices, living voices of living people resounded in the corridor continually; prisoners communicated through the walls from all directions just like indefatigable woodpeckers… Well, it was just as you yourself know—there's nothing to say about this. But, I admit, for a long time this noise irritated me terribly, and I recalled my former silent crypt with a profound desire. Upon transfer to preliminary detention I could have, of course, quickly written to Elena—and I knew this—but I didn't think of writing. For some reason, I had decided long before that she'd stopped loving me and probably already gotten married. At first, when such ideas entered my head, a fury possessed me and I became jealous, wept, and vowed revenge; but, over time, I reconciled myself to the 'unavoidable law of woman's nature,' as it's bitterly called. 'This man here,' I thought, 'is another matter! If I have to wait twenty years, I'll find enough love and strength in me to carry on!'

"Then, one day, the ward's door opened and a guard gave me a dispatch. Not believing my eyes, I read: 'Telegraph the warden of Tomsk Prison to learn how soon you'll be deported. I am loving and thinking of you. Your Elena.' The telegram was from Tiumen.[14]

"I nearly fainted with joy… The icy crust shattered and the corpse beneath it revived. Spring! Spring! Resurrection!… That same day, I sent an answer in which, unfortunately, I could not precisely specify the time of my deportation.

"At first, I wasn't even distressed that Elena was being exiled to Siberia or that she'd lost her freedom. I hadn't been forgotten, and I was beloved! We would be seeing each other again—only a day before, reunion had seemed possible only beyond the grave! I read the telegram an endless number of times, and, forgetting that the handwriting was another's, kissed its precious lines…[15] So, I went about in a blissful haze for several days… Sweet one! Faithful one! My recent reproaches and suspicions made me feel petty and commonplace! I now feared only one thing: what would happen if my telegram was late and did not find Elena still in Tomsk? I imagined a thousand instances that could sunder our reunion and turn it again into an unrealizable dream…

"My deportation encompassed only two weeks at the end of July, yet not until mid-August did our barge finally sail to mysterious Tomsk. I don't have the strength to express how nervous I was that unforgettable morning. For me, the routine worries that so troubled my comrades—how would their new commandant receive them, what kind of search would there be, and so on—simply did not exist. I departed with all of one thought: would Elena be there? What would it be like meeting after a two-year separation? Not waiting until the party was led into the prison yard, I ran toward the warden as he was walking outside. The sullen, unwelcoming old man told me with evident reluctance that

Elena wasn't in the prison—she'd received my telegram on time but had presented no request at all to remain in the prison.

"'Is she healthy?'

"'Completely… Indeed, a very cheerful lady!'

"Crestfallen and embarrassed, I walked away from the warden, and it seemed he was watching me from behind with mock sympathy… The old demons awakened in my soul: 'Certainly, I've been forgotten, I've been forgotten! And so quickly!'…

"In the meantime, I encountered stories about the cheerful lady prisoner at every step.

"'Well, she weren't sad at all… A truly good soul!' some old vagrant who'd seen her warmly told me. 'She'd greet anyone, snuggle up, laugh 'n' joke with anyone.'

"This family characteristic had even struck me on the outside: among others, even in a moment of sadness, Elena could appear cheerful and carefree, and her silvery laugh rang out so loudly and often that no one could at that moment ever imagine she was suffering. A unique, familiar characteristic! But I now forgot all this and simply repeated: 'Cheerful, joking, laughing, when…'

"From Tomsk, as you know, begins the real deportation, the voyage on foot… And here, not even a few steps from the first stall, there came floating to me from a small group of escorting officers who were walking ahead the sound of Elena's surname. I flinched and began listening to the conversation I'd till then ignored.

"'I'm tellin' you, gentlemen, you gotta keep a sharp lookout with these folks. You're there jus' gawkin', 'n' suddenly it's "wham in the head!"—'n' the knives is flyin'. Look how that beautiful, innocent girl suffered!' thus was orating a fat little officer with a simple-minded face and already grizzled beard.

"I was beside him in the twinkling of an eye.

"'For God's sake, Captain, what happened to her?'

"I watched his comrades earnestly blink their eyes at the officer and cough, but he paid no attention to this and, with great courtesy, agreed to repeat his story to me.

"'You really didn't hear the story 'bout what happened at Khaldeev Station? It's the second station from here.'[16]

"'I've heard nothing.'

"'Some Circassians in the party rioted 'n' went after the Russians with knives. One hit Elena N. in the head with his iron manacles—so hard, they say, he sliced off half her skull!'

"The whole world started spinning before my eyes, and I floated to the ground like a leaf. When I regained consciousness, his comrades and the ingenuous captain himself, having just realized he'd told me about my fiancée, began soothing and consoling me.

"'But you didn't listen to me fully,' the nonplussed little captain explained, 'I didn't tell you she died… Indeed, I reckoned it was half her skull 'cause that's how I was expressin' greater picturesqueness, so's to speak… Well, much of her skull was there! Only a little bit o' the bone got scratched… I assure you she's alive 'n' well.'

"But it goes without saying that I was not so easily assured, all the more so because the mare, which had also heard about the Circassians' riot, told me an entirely different story: it seemed the Circassians burst into the women's ward at night and the women were only saved by the appearance of the guards, who killed several of the Asiatics on the spot; apparently, one of the women was injured during the mêlée…

"Understandably, such a version could only disconcert and frighten me all the more. For endless hours there appeared in my dreams and daydreams Elena, pale and gushing blood…

"During our two full days at Khaldeev Station I was able to dispel myself of exaggerated alarm and danger. The friendly captain who had alarmed me instantly brought the commander of the Khaldeev detachment, and he personally assured me that my fiancée was alive and completely fine. This is what had happened. One of the Circassians squabbled with a Russian prisoner and so powerfully stabbed a knife into his stomach that the man died after several days, though at the same time the Circassian was wounded in the head. Elena went to bandage his wounds, and at that moment the enraged mountain-dweller, having raised both manacled arms, tried to smash the head of my girlfriend Elena, who was standing near him. She was barely able to withstand the blow. The wound caused great pain but presented no danger, and Elena continued on with the party.

"Soldiers from the Khaldeev detachment and the old ward attendant confirmed this story; it was impossible to doubt its veracity.

"'Such a cheerful lady, y'know,' all the storytellers invariably put in, 'e'en laughed after that! She got told: "Don't get within a hunnerd paces o' that animal." But she goes: "It's alright," 'n' says, "the poor man's obviously very irritated now. In his place, you might've struck out at the first person you saw." 'N' whaddya know? After that, she secretly goes straight to the door where the Circassian's bein' held 'n' asks him: "Why did you hit me? I wanted to bandage your wound." Well, he's an animal, 'n' an animal eats: he's lookin' at her from under his brows like he's gonna eat her… They're *"poor"*! They should all be hanged from the nearest aspen—then we'd be done with 'em!'

"But the old captain who'd alarmed me rubbed my hand cheerfully and just told me:

"'Well, now you see… There's your half-a-skull! Ooh, dear man, what a lovin' 'magination can picture! He-he-he… forgive my bluntness.'

"He'd obviously forgotten the imagination that had pictured this was not mine but his own.

"Only in Achinsk[17] did I receive the first news from Elena herself, a telegram from Krasnoiarsk: 'I'm healthy, I'm waiting.' For me, those days were filled with a sort of blissful intoxication. Regardless of my heavy chains and unfamiliarity with walking, I hardly sat in the wagons through the last stations and would go on foot for twenty versts without feeling tired; if I did sit down, it was to rest, and then I'd quickly be on my feet: it absolutely seemed the wagons were moving far too slowly, and I'd hurry to the front of the party where the best of the penal laborers were marching.

"We arrived in Krasnoiarsk on a bright sunny day. As if through a fog, I recall my farewells to comrades from the previous party, standing at the prison gates and in that final hour getting ready to embark upon the rest of their journey. Almost every one of them smilingly shook my hand and congratulated me that I'd finally see Elena. But I was now trembling with a fever and simply responded mechanically to all questions given me. I simply can't remember how I found myself in the prison yard as the last of the party was beyond the gates; I ran up the prison steps someone indicated to me, stumbling and tangling my clanking chains, and there, at the doors, I collided with a pale, thin, young woman who embraced me… When I came to, we were already sitting and conversing in the very small room in which Elena lived. That said, this first conversation after a three-year separation soon turned into disconnected childish babble… I recall being for a long time too ashamed to remove my prisoner's cap and show Elena my shaved head…

"Was it Dante who said that it's more difficult to remember a day of blessedness in a moment of grief? Now here I am in torturous pain. I'll therefore be brief. The whole time we imagined I had only to be christened and we'd be permitted to wed and be separated no more. How shocked we were when we learned that penal laborers are allowed to marry only upon conclusion of a probationary and correctional term, and that for me this term was seven years! Irkutsk was the last point before which we would be traveling in the same party, and our new separation, a separation of seven whole years, was to commence in all of two months… Those months, when we always felt a Damoclean sword hanging over our heads, were blessed and also terrible. In Irkutsk, we were as is customary put in different sections—I in the men's, Elena in the women's, which was somewhere in another yard. We could look at each other only during strolls in the prison garden. About our impending separation, everything had been said, in gloomy meditations and resentments, everything had been endured. The separation happened quite suddenly. One evening, in mid-December, a troika drove through the prison gates and I was invited to the prison smithy to be shackled in chains (before this the physician had ordered me temporarily unshackled). It cost me much to persuade the warden to have Elena brought there so we could bid farewell, and while I was sitting on the smithy floor and the smith circled me with a hammer riveting me tightly in fetters, I heard the familiar hurried steps… We seemed to exchange roles that evening: beforehand, I'd always been despondent and taciturn and Elena hearty and cheerful in aspect; with regard to our future her eternally sylvan and seemingly trouble-free laugh actually sometimes annoyed me… Now, faced so unexpectedly with this unanswerable calamity, I, by contrast, felt strong and courageous and spoke words of consolation and hope, but the whole time there welled heavy glistening tears in her darkened and dimmed eyes… Up until then, I'd never seen her cry in my life… She left the smithy to accompany me outside the prison gates—for some reason the warden found it unnecessary to protest. I'll never forget that freezing, solemnly quiet evening; an enormous number of stars burned in the dark sky… After I had finally sat down in the vehicle beside a pair of mustachioed guards, the chilled troika almost instantly burst into a mad gallop and whirled into the snowy distance. Turning around, I for a long time shouted something to Elena that I can't recall: it utterly seemed that something unspoken, unexpressed, and, at that time, highly unusual, remained between us… I must have shouted all kinds of tripe! For a long time, it seemed I could make out in the dusk of the starry night, as if standing beside a lantern near the white prison wall, a familiar, grievously wilting figure…"

Shteinhart fell quiet, and I sensed he could not refrain from bursting into tears at that very moment. I myself could find no words of consolation. I simply asked:

"You knew, as you were parting, that you wouldn't officially be allowed to maintain a correspondence?"

"Yes, of course we knew, though, in any case (he, as you can see, had indeed imagined), Elena promised to write from time to time. In general, we arranged to communicate through an aunt of mine, an educated woman long familiar with our relationship. She lives in Minsk. And so, Ivan Nikolaevich, can you imagine how long it's taken for me to receive news about Elena, and she about me? The letter took no less than five months to complete this circular route! Indeed, I'm terribly grateful to Luchezarov for giving me this letter; it must have moved him… But I, Ivan Nikolaevich, feel that everything in me has changed… In the name of our love, Elena demands that I endure everything here and just that it not injure my human dignity—and I will fulfill her wish."

"So that's your secret, that Luchezarov gave you this letter!" was my not-cutting declaration.

Shteinhart pondered.

"You're probably right… Well, it's all the same! I will bear everything that does not injure my human dignity. You've really been bearing everything? *They* are bearing it!"

"Well, about *them* we'll yet be able to speak, though not now… and not here," I emphasized in French. "Lunkov over there doesn't seem to be asleep."

We continued chatting for some time. Shteinhart expressed aloud his surprise that he'd been so immediately candid with me.

"But do you regret it?"

"Oh, no! Not at all!"

He shook my hand vigorously.

"I've felt," he sincerely said, "more a corpse than does a corpse, and have been unable to laugh… Understand, Ivan Nikolaevich, all this time there's seemed to be this so called 'other world'—the world in which I'm now living with you. Today, I told you about my earthly existence, far away and never to return!"

After this we became quiet and decided to try to sleep.

But sleep still did not come for a long time. A story I'd heard long ago and had forgotten awakened my dozing soul… I was seized by a profound, searing melancholy… Shteinhart also turned from side to side on his own hard bed until late in the night.

IV. STARTING OVER

The guard's whistle interrupted my dream at a most interesting point. I was dreaming that I was still a student in high school, a youth of fourteen, and that I was sitting by myself with comrades I disliked. They're all looking at me and laughing with evident disdain, although the reason for this laughter eludes my comprehension. I am aggrieved and infinitely hurt by my comrades' unfair treatment of me, but I must be disdained by all, must endure everything, if I and he whom I observe with all the ardor of tender youth, whom I regard as an unobtainable object and ideal of intelligence, heroism, and talent, are not to be in concert with them. Who, strictly speaking, this favored comrade is, I cannot clearly tell: his face bears features I'd long forgotten, the features of some other fellow student who had actually existed, as well as entirely new, mournfully familiar, features. Here is the profile of a severe, pale face with knitted black eyebrows… Akh, why doesn't he want to look at me, why is he turning away? Can he, like everyone, so misunderstand me, not knowing that I alone divine his soul, I alone truly and passionately love it. Beneath my fixedly staring gaze the youth suddenly turns toward me… I am ready to meet his strong dark eyes, to read the anger in his severe face, and instead of that—God! Before me, a face inundated by tears… Gentle, loving eyes look at me with touching affection, trembling hands reach for me.

"Dmitrii!" I exclaim, throwing myself into his embrace and suddenly remembering his name.

But he avoids me, and presses a finger to his lips, urging silence… A terrible danger threatens us both. One sound could ruin both of us… And I suddenly remember that we're in a *katorga* prison and both of us are wretches, abandoned by everyone… The surrounding nighttime gloom is a kind of high stone wall behind which lives Elena and from where we shall kidnap her, so as to escape together… We move quietly, holding hands and quivering by the second… Suddenly—savage laughter bursts from behind, keys bang, a rifle rattles… We are utterly ruined! We've been discovered, found out, with nowhere to hide! I've recognized the angry voices of Luchezarov, the guards, Iukhorev…

"Take them to the isolator! Put them in chains!"

I'm spilling into horror.

"Get to roll call, go!"

The guard is coming down the corridor with his whistle… I grab my head, trying to remember something neither very stupid nor very good.

"Yes, I'm no longer alone among this horror. I'm with my comrade…"

Oh, how fortunate I am! What invigorating strength suddenly courses through all my veins! Gone are doubt and despair! Life now has a purpose—to ease the suffering of other people just beginning a hard *katorga* career, people weakened and neither accustomed nor hardened toward ordeal…

"Dmitrii Petrovich!" I call to Shteinhart. "Are you awake as well?"

Shteinhart is sitting on his bedding and nervously, hastily, dressing. But he does not quickly answer and turns toward me neither angrily nor in shame.

"Where are you off to in such a hurry?"

"But what about… isn't roll call now?"

"In the mornings, roll call's in the corridor. This concession was won a long time ago… After the whistle, it'll be twenty minutes before they open the wards' doors. We can throw our cassocks on then: but seeing as today's a no-work day, there might still be another hour and a half to sleep. Well, how did you pass the night? What did you dream?"

"I slept very poorly and dreamt all kinds of rubbish. Luchezarov appeared as a teacher of Latin in my high school and gave me a failing mark!"

"Yes, he'll be in your dreams fairly often now."

However, after roll call we slept no more, and, after lolling in bed for a bit, dragged ourselves to Bashurov's ward to see how he was getting along. We ran into him in the corridor—he, for his part, had been coming to see us. Strolling three abreast down the corridor, we began relating our nocturnal impressions.

Bashurov complained about the deadly air in his ward, roll call procedures, and the overall burden of the prison regime, but was on the other hand in great rapture over the prisoners and the composition of his ward.

"I'd considered them as being far worse, judging from my impressions during the march," he said. "But there, on the road, conditions of life are so abnormal that, strictly speaking, you can't ask much of people. Everyone there is a stranger to one another, today walking together, tomorrow going on separately; it's really difficult to figure out a man's true character. But things are different here. People live together for years and become friends unwittingly."

"Well, you probably won't see exceptional friendship here," I noted in a dampening tone. "But which of your cohabitants do you like most of all?"

"Most of all, as a humorous character, Karpushka Lipatov."

"I just recommend you not especially encourage his chatter, because if he's breathing down your neck you'll never get rid of him."

"Akh, Ivan Nikolaevich, you certainly are a… stern man! I noticed yesterday that you were too strict with him. He's sweet, that Karpushka… Just imagine, Dmitrii, what he was quarreling about with the whole ward yesterday. I asked for a window vent to be opened and the headman opened it, but he was standing in a pose in the middle of the ward and protesting: 'All you peasant types was raised in a horse shed, 'n' so's you need fresh air, but noble blood's flowin' inside me, 'n' I don't need fresh air.' And then, he pronounces these words for fun: 'nobleman,' 'Dvinsk'[18] (where he was born), and so on. How he made me laugh! He finally began asking for my sugar and tobacco, but then Iukhorev (that Iukhorev's a powerful man!) jumped off the sleeping platform and started shouting at him… Then my Karpushka goes to a corner, to his own spot! The whole ward in general makes a good impression, most of all by their self-possession in manner, respectability, and reasonableness. You simply forget you're dealing with *katorga* and not average Russian folks. And what a thirst for learning, for knowledge. Imagine, yesterday we put together a whole school, and nearly half the ward were pupils! It's interesting, Ivan Nikolaevich, how you view these people! Lombroso's theory seems disgraceful to me, in essence, a heartless theory! In actuality, most of our worst criminals are just the same as all Russian people, and get pushed onto the criminal path only by some sort of happenstance."

"Actually, I don't know, Valerian Mikhailovich. I've been living here for two and a half years now, but for the time being can't make any generalizations at all."

"Well, needless to say, I'm not having an academic dispute with you, but all the same, first impressions are very important. For example, take Iukhorev. Now, he regards himself as a penal laborer and a brigand, but you cut to the heart of the matter and you say: under other conditions wouldn't he be the leader of some Garibaldian band fighting for a higher principle?[19] Given his appearance, he'd even sooner be a social activist than a criminal offender!"

"His appearance, it's true, is impressive, but all the same, it's hard to say what would be, if it were so… For now, he's a brigand and nothing more."

"Not entirely. You really don't know why he was sent to *katorga* from the Olëkminsk gold fields? He was a gold smuggler. Of course, God knows this isn't a lofty occupation, but all the same, it's nothing terrible. Cossacks tried to take his and his comrades' gold and he put up a courageous armed resistance…"

"But why had he been sent from Russia to Iakutsk District?"

"His commune exiled him to Siberia,[20] and if his story is to be believed—and he, it appears, is no liar—this commune was made up of dissolute swine. He was defending the interests of the poor. In any case, this man is undoubtedly remarkable. Imagine yourself, Dmitrii, an essentially illiterate peasant who knows by heart the huge defense speech that one of the Iakutsk exiles wrote for him.[21] Iukhorev was to have given it in court, but he wasn't allowed to. The speech actually isn't foolish but is very courageous. And how energetically, how articulately, this brigand—as Ivan Nikolaevich calls him—delivers it!"

I remembered that Iukhorev had several times been ready to recite me this speech, but the right moment never arrived.

"Valerian!" suddenly resounded from the other end of the corridor the loud shout of the Iukhorev in question. "Tea time, ever'thin's ready!"

"Right away, right away," a rather befuddled Bashurov shouted back, and hurried to his ward.

Shteinhart noticed me slightly wince.

"You're evidently not overly fond of this Iukhorev?" he asked me.

I explained that I regarded it inconvenient in many respects for us to permit too great a familiarity with not only Iukhorev, who was performing the duties of the collective's headman, but with the prisoners in general, with people of an utterly different moral cast. Shteinhart turned thoughtful.

"I fear that Valerian will give us trouble in this regard. In general, he has a weakness—first, he has without reason forged a too friendly, almost intimate, relationship with the people, and without apparent reason he's now suddenly distancing himself from us.

Of course, he's doing this not because of anything stupid, but simply out of youthful simplemindedness… And, furthermore, he's rather arrogant and conceited. Here he's just today given you an easy lecture regarding your supposedly cruel attitude toward the people and, probably, he sincerely thinks about himself that he's not that way, that he's able to love without exclusion all these people like a brother, forgiving them all their shortcomings. But he's already forgotten that you've now been living here without us for entire years and we've found you liked and respected by the whole prison; we're just starting out on our career and who knows what we'll do, how we'll get along with these folks?"

Afterward, we went to our ward to drink tea as well. It was a Sunday, and the whole day prisoners were here engaged in deep sleep, there taking tea for the twentieth time. In places they were throwing cards at each other, in places they were carrying on sluggish conversations about long exhausted topics. Our conversational topics were inexhaustible. Unable to settle on a single subject, we were now flinging ourselves into a second and a third and so on without end. Then again, I at first found myself listening more, since, having lived apart from the living world for so long, I was impatient to know what had been happening in this world during the years of my absence… But my imagination was just barely being satiated in general terms when the storytellers' legitimate and understandable curiosity regarding the details of the lives they would lead in Shelai's mines took over completely and I, for my part, also turned from listener to storyteller. Arms linked and strolling three abreast through the prison corridors, we spent the whole day this way in most lively conversation. I asked my comrades about, among other things, their financial means. It turned out that they both calculated on receiving twenty rubles per month from relatives.

"Outstanding!" I shouted. "Almost as much as I'm able to receive. But while I was living here alone this money meant little to me, since such an insignificant sum could not help the whole prison and it was difficult and unsatisfying to spend it on myself. Now, if you'll agree, we can arrange things so that the whole prison will live tolerably in material terms."

"Is this even conceivable on a budget of sixty rubles?"

"But, judge for yourself. The prison population normally doesn't exceed a hundred and twenty men, and in rare instances reaches a hundred and fifty or so. Prisoners suffer most of all from an absence of tobacco. A pound and a half of *makhorka*[22] per week is absolutely sufficient for one ward, as a supplement to the tobacco prisoners may order for themselves. Taking the kitchen into account, there are ten wards, and so we should buy half a pood of *makhorka* per month."

"But how much does *makhorka* cost?"

"Forty kopeks a pound. This means half a pood is twenty-four rubles… This is the most expensive article of purchase. Then, if a pood of meat is added to the cauldron on fast days,[23] then the skilly will certainly be splendid. Mutton here costs two rubles per pood. Therefore, improving rations on fast days will each month (with eight fast days) cost us sixteen rubles. With the remaining twenty rubles we can have for ourselves Baikov tea, sugar, and tobacco, and still occasionally arrange on holidays for completely sumptuous meals for the entire prison, adding, for example, half a pood of meat to the government ration."

"But, excuse me! What will you say to Luchezarov about all this?"

"Nothing. He himself has repeatedly made clear in public that improvements in the general ration are decided by law. In this regard, it's just unfortunate that prisoners have their own particular opinion: the law doesn't seduce them into communalist theories, and not a single such prison benefactor has turned up so far. But there are wealthy people among them…"

"So, Ivan Nikolaevich, our general collective will unanimously elect you as our headman. You know about these matters so exceptionally. Indeed, you're already on certain terms with Luchezarov."

Not disagreeing, I took the reins of government, soon had a talk with the financial officer, and showed him the tobacco and the meat for the upcoming fast day. Having heard out our desire to feed the entire prison with our money, the portly official chuckled, obviously considering me and my new comrades to be perfect idiots, but neither did he oppose it, and the very next day he acquired fifty pounds of *makhorka.*

"Com'dant's laughin'," he reported regarding this, smiling broadly, "says no one 'cept youse allowed to 'stablish a *maidan* in priso*m*."

I went around all the wards and divvied up among the headmen shares of half a pound of *makhorka* each. Accepting the tobacco, the headmen expressed neither great surprise nor especial curiosity. Having after this returned to my ward, I was unable to observe the impressions this unusual phenomenon of prison life made on each cohabitant. Old Shemelin, our ward's headman, carefully wiped off the table and began laying out the tobacco in sixteen piles, precisely in the same way he did the meat every day. I hurried to whisper to him that he not take Shteinhart and me into account. Shemelin courteously listened but gave no reply. Two piles instantaneously disappeared from the table and were redistributed in precise pinches among the remaining fourteen. Then, with the same efficiency and diligence, the old man flicked his own pile into a little piece of paper (even though I distinctly knew he did not smoke) and went with it to his spot, having loudly announced to the ward:

"Go git it, boys!"

The boys did not crowd together, indeed, as if they hadn't heard him, none of those present even budged at his shout—each continued to be occupied by the merit of his affairs. Only those prisoners who'd entered the ward straight from the yard and knew nothing, after spotting the tobacco, asked in surprise:

"What's this tobacco for?"

"Take a pile," Shemelin curtly answered, and it was astonishing that this answer proved completely satisfactory, so that only those very few who looked at it last of all still asked after this:

"Where's this from? Whose is it?"

The majority accepted this gift silently, almost indifferently, as if it were something long understood, correct, and completely appropriate. Moreover, some of the piles remained until late in the evening, and I then imagined their piles' owners were not taking them out of a sense of pride, perhaps because they themselves were of means and were embarrassed to take along with the paupers—however, in the end, all the tobacco irrevocably vanished from the table; those who didn't smoke and those who'd freely donate it to a comrade took their share.[24] The same occurred in the other wards. It is possible, of course, that during this some prisoners were motivated by a fear of offending me and my comrades.

The next fast day, when a delicious skilly with meat appeared on the table instead of the sickeningly made gruel with a chimera of fat, curiosity once more forced me to observe the mare: How will it regard this? What will it say? But, for a very long time, I simply saw only cold silence and outwardly negligent indifference there. Moreover, many—apparently completely and honestly—didn't even notice they were eating forbidden rather than fasting food. There had probably been talk in the kitchen, behind our backs, but we hadn't heard it. Only much later did rumors of separately expressed opinions begin filtering through, mostly on the part of devout and loyal old-timers like our Shemelin:

"If there weren't gen'rous people you'd die in this prison! Without tobacco, without meat, you'd just sit around… God bless the gen'rous, we're grateful!"

The degree of this "blessing" actually strengthened and grew: now and then the head-spinning sums that we were to be spending on the prison were identified. But the "Ivans" and all those who considered themselves true, professional penal laborers were prideful and independent in this regard, greeting old-timers' outward praise of us with, if not scorn, obvious indifference (they all took the tobacco and ate the skilly dished out on fast days). Only when each lost his self-control did they argue among themselves, and such people spread rumors of the same spirit and intention.

"You ain't seen a thing in the world, you rotten scum," the lanky Petin shouted at young Lunkov. "You e'er been in *real* prisons? Where else would they regale you with a gift o' tobacco or stuff you fat with meat?"

"Ah, so you've been in Heaven?"

"You compared me with yourself, you ass! D'you really deserve such people's attention? D'you got as many brains in your lazy noggin as Ivan Nikolaich or Dmitrii Petrovich does in his little toe?"

Of course, it was interesting to learn how prisoners explained to themselves the material assistance we gave them and what motives they ascribed to our actions. Later developments proved that many even chalked them up to some egoistical rationale on our part, as if they, for their part, were showing us a certain magnanimity by accepting our gifts… After several days happened to go by without any improved rations, one for the most part not-stupid prisoner was extremely surprised by me apropos this, after having asked:

"But, Ivan Nikolaevich, what's happened to all your's reputation?"

"What kind of reputation?" I asked in surprise.

"Indeed… by which *it's up to you* to buy meat 'n' tobacco?"

Having seen my surprised look, the prisoner stopped short, and so I didn't learn what he meant by my reputation.

Six-Eyes had given the newcomers several days' rest, but they were then assigned like me to the mountain. Having arrived at the watch house, I immediately led them, in expectation of their assignments, to the gallery. They ran ahead in the dark corridor with noise and merriment, and stopped far from me behind the lantern.

I've mentioned a certain difference in general between my then comrades' moods and those I went through and experienced myself. I remember for a long time I felt just like a hunted animal, every minute anticipating injuries and insults from everywhere, fearfully and suspiciously viewing each guard as my natural enemy, and even now this suspiciousness has not quite left me; indeed, even now I consider it better to speak as little as possible, and to have as little as possible to do with those who appear to my eyes even slightly like authorities. Even Petushkov, who offered himself in friendship, was not excluded. The newcomers, like me, had during the first moments of their sojourn a depressed and frightened look, but this didn't last very long. Owing either to a more naturally cheerful character, or to circumstances for which they paved the way by not appearing in the capacity of pioneers and by greeting everyone at the right moment, as if they'd been living in Shelai mine for years, they were cheerful, relaxed, and spoke freely not only with prisoners but with guards, and for their part the latter, who'd been frightened by my stiff mien, responded to them readily and even with obvious joy. It was as though some kind of dark charms had spread themselves about and the ice formed long ago was thawing… I won't hide it: during these first days I actually caught myself being dissatisfied with the newcomers… I became convinced something very foolish was on the verge of happening as a result of their tactlessness, as it seemed to me, their too-free behavior, and from the side I timidly looked on like a wild cat who had drawn my cubs from the lair into open light and was looking all around so no danger would come to them. But no danger at all threatened, and little by little my wild-rendered and ice-bound soul thawed out and spread tired wings as well…

We'd barely climbed down into the gallery's depths and caught fleeting sight of it when Bashurov, after not much thought, began singing so that I flinched from surprise:

The knock of the hammer from age to age,
The heavy noise of rusty chains…
Friend! Did you see a human gnome
In the pit of the cold mine?

The young, sonorous tenor's bracing notes resounded off gloomy stone walls that had for so many years heard nothing save the despondent clanking of chains, the monotonous pounding of hammers, and the labored sighs of exhausted, wretched people.[25] My tormented heart, at first rather frightened, now responded joyfully to these bracing sounds…

There is another world, a world of hard, bitter fate…

Shteinhart's beautiful baritone joined in:

There is a realm of endless sufferings.
Half of life a day of labor and bondage,
Half of life a night of terrible blizzards.
Torture and death rule the world there,

And each hammer-blow declares
That feast gives way to feast
For the pleasure of fat lords.
When fortune's offspring feast carefree,
A question grows in my mind:
Are not these goblets filled with a wine
Of blood and tears?[26]

The sounds soared higher and higher, accompanied by the noise of actual chains gripping the soul, casting bitter reproach at someone calling something courageous and great…

"Gentlemen, where did you get those words and melody from?" I inquired after the singers ended their improvised duet.

"One of the vagabond-singers taught it to us on the road. He assured us this is a *katorga* hymn, or a 'Kara hymn,' as he put it."

"Well, gentlemen, this 'hymn' was hardly composed by an actual penal laborer! He who considers, for example, 'rusty chains' to be an attribute of especially difficult ordeals knows *katorga* poorly."

"How so?"

"But you'll see for yourselves whether your chains rust during their wearing. On the contrary, they'll sparkle like glass!"

In the watch house, after we'd returned there, the assignment of workers was already nearly finished.

"Ah, gentlemen vagabonds," Petushkov greeted us, "I'd most certainly thought you'd made your escape! Well, please advise me, Mikolaich, where to assign the newcomers. Borin' prob'ly won't smile on 'em, y'know! This borin' needs a rascal!"

However, the newcomers expressed a desire to try boring straightaway, and I led them to the upper shaft. Shteinhart, like myself at one time, had difficulty on the mountain slope and constantly stopped to rest; by contrast, Bashurov walked freely and easily: a native Crimean, he was used to climbing mountains. Without especial difficulty, he learned to bore reasonably well, while this art came hard to Shteinhart. He continually hit his hand with the hammer, distorted the blasting hole, and became very upset at these setbacks. But when the work subsided somewhat, he instantly began singing along with the other prisoners' hammering:

The knock of the hammer from age to age…

Bashurov joined in. And when in the dark depths of the cold, unwelcoming tunnel the harmonious sounds of the "*katorga* hymn" resounded, arising first in the form of a bitter plaint, next in an angry threat, something terrifying and sweet happened in my soul…

Especially the line—

Torture and death rule the world there

made a strong impression, each time evoking a shudder in me…

Suddenly, the naturally cheerful Valerian switched to a happy ditty by Béranger:[27]

Our glasses sparkle with wine,
Onward to happiness,
Our girlfriends shout
"Fortune, pass us by!"

And, as the hammers quickly beat time on the augers, we all joined in the chorus:

"Knock! Knock!" Who's there?
"Knock! Knock!" We're waiting for Liza.
"Knock! Knock!" Fortune's here.
"Knock! Knock!" We won't open!

Soon, of course, as Petushkov prophesied, boring was not "smilin'" on the weak and nervous Shteinhart, and he assigned him the sharpener's duties. Needless to say, his shortness of breath soon passed and he became an outstanding runner. All the same, this did not hinder Elk from cursing and calling us, not "borers," but "bearers," imagining by this that wind and storm might sooner carry him up the hill than he could lug the heavy bundles of augers on his shoulders. There was also much food for the barbs and various jokes everyone tossed at Shteinhart when, one day, he'd shown up at the prison at the end of work and, as became clear during the search at the gates, was absentmindedly carrying two shortened augers against his chest… The guard who made this discovery was at first astounded, as if pondering what to do on the basis of this evidence, but he soon gave in to the overall merry mood and began laughing as well.

"Wanted to bore through the prison wall!" joked the mare, noisily dispersing among the wards.

A certain time passed before a more important occupation than boring or carrying augers was found for Shteinhart, an occupation that in not only prisoners' but the administration's eyes suddenly more than doubled our previous stock. Late one evening, our ward's lock thundered and the door swung open, sending fear into the card players sitting in the corner, and a guard entered and asked my comrade to attend immediately to the financial officer's wife who had taken ill.

"The com'dant himself asked for you," he ingratiatingly explained.

Shteinhart, having quickly dressed, went out. He returned only after two or three hours, not only having examined the patient but having personally prepared with the medic's help the necessary medicines for her. This first instance of medical practice by Shteinhart proved very fortunate: the patient felt completely healthy the very next day, and his glory as a remarkable physician resounded far and wide. Guards, their wives and children, began turning to him, and all Shelai's *beau monde*—the Cossack officer and his family, his assistant Monakhov, the prison office clerks, and, finally, Luchezarov himself—felt themselves enormously friendly toward the young physician; he was given permission to visit the hospital pharmacy at any time of day or night and, upon patients' summons, to exit—needless to say, under guard—the prison gates. Shteinhart began to be frequently summoned directly from the mine, torn away from work, and was sometimes not ordered to the mountain for entire weeks.

The prison population thronged toward him. Although the drunken medic remained on the staff and performed to the extent that he merely officially released prisoners from work or assigned them a hospital bed, Shteinhart did everything in actuality. Over time, this began to annoy the narcissistic Zemlianskii and he became our desperate enemy. But in the meantime, I was thoroughly delighted that circumstances were so favorable for my comrade and his sojourn in *katorga* might be a practicum for him, "a fifth academic year," as he himself put it.

I saw him cheerful, gladdened, and utterly absorbed by his new duties, having not even sufficient leisure time to be depressed and tortured by his personal grief and sufferings.

Roses and laurels, it's true, are in due time followed by thistles and thorns, but I will talk about this later.

Only late in the evenings, when life in the ward had calmed down and our cohabitants were already loudly snoring, would we have our first chance to converse from the heart, and these conversations lasted half the night. Lying on our bedding and leaning our heads toward each other, we spoke in whispers sometimes right up to daybreak, especially when it was on the eve of a holiday and there would be no work. What did we not say during those quiet prison nights!…

One day, little red-haired Zhebreek, one of our nearest neighbors on the sleeping platform, accosted me in the corridor and conspiratorially said:

"Unnerstand, Ivan Mikolaich, that I been wantin' to ask you: where'd you put them books you used for teachin' yourself?"

"What do you mean, 'teaching myself'?"

"Jus' so. Now, I very well unnerstand what them there books you read to us are—to me, they's silly little books for simple folk like us, for fools. Well, to speak plainly, the *white* books, since they're white, is paper 'n' nuthin' more. They're all written for ol' women 'n' babies. But you 'n' your comrades read the real—*unnerstand?*—the *black* books… I really wanna see *them*."

"I don't understand you. What do you mean by 'black books'?"

"Well, so's you ain't gonna tell me. I ain't some Lunkov or Elk, y'know… I'm a new[28] prisoner with a mind new as a baby's… Well, I've survived fifty years 'n' I knows a thing or two as well. Had meself a woman—I'll tell you straight, no meltin' away—'n' she was a *hag*!"

I looked into the eyes of this old-timer who'd lost his mind: he was, as usual, comically serious and magisterial.

"I hear your talks, y'know… You think I'm sleepin' at night? I don't close my eyes to what's around! I'm lookin' into it carefully—well, I'll tell you straight, I'm fixin' all ears on your talks."

"Let's assume it's not very polite to eavesdrop, but what have you understood of our conversations?"

"But what's been unnerstood is that each of youse gots the Devil!…"

"The *Devil*? What nonsense! Where have you gotten that from?"

"Certainly, that's what I got. The Devil's in ev'ry five or ten words o' yours, y'know. One says: 'Such is *my Devil*,' 'n' the other answers: 'No, that's *my Devil*!'"

I burst out laughing, though for a long time still didn't understand the sense of Zhebreika's words. Shteinhart, with whom I shared this conversation, simply called them a lunatic's ravings. But after a certain time passed, he told me, laughing:

"But, you know, I've understood what 'Devil' Zhebreek was talking about. You'll probably never guess: it's—'ideal'!…

V. THE "STOLEN" MANIFESTO

Spring began many more times… Every year it awakened in the prisoner's soul a sweet, forgotten pain and torments of hopefulness and despair.

All the people are living
Like flowers coming to bloom…

—complains a prison song, composed, in all probability, at no other time but spring:

But my head withers like grass!
I'm going nowhere,
Will come to misfortune.
I trade advice with those
In whom there is no truth.
I shall throw off and abandon the world,
Run to a monastery!
Where I'll survive
And be a monk!

The singer's vow to go to a monastery sounds of infinite and touching sorrow, and casts a bitter irony over me when, following these lines of the song,[29] it is said, changing not only the meter but the meaning of the lyric—showing all one's cards, so to speak—:

Sing, sing, lark,
Sing of spring on a little thawed patch,
On soft silky grass!
Offer your voice through the dark wood,
Through the dark wood beyond Moscow River,
To the stony prison beyond Moscow River…
Beneath the window sits a cold little man,
A cold young man, ah, a little brigand.
He's not been there for one year or two,
He's been in prison exactly eight years.
In the ninth year he began to write a letter,
Began writing a letter to his father and mother,
Father and mother didn't recognize him,

Did not recognize but rebuked him:
"There are no thieves in our family,
There are no thieves and no brigands."

The jaunty singer Rakitin would add to this song one more line that other prison singers didn't know:

The young wife wept tearfully…

But he'd stop himself at this, and in vain I asked him to give me at least the sense of the rest of the lines, about what exactly the young wife had "wept." Nonetheless, the wagger had no compunctions about giving his own answer to the question:

"Ekh, Ivan Nikolaevich! What else does a low-life cry 'bout, if not that her dear vagabond-thief'll return, 'n' yet, in the wink of an eye, she's already got another chap, a better one?…"

I myself was now encountering a third spring in Shelai Prison, and each time, I experienced this especially sweet, especially aching, pain. However, this third time, when again the surrounding hills greened and springtime's vivid sounds and scents were carried from the depths of the awakening taiga to the prison, a thirst for life, liberty, and good fortune awakened with hitherto non-existent strength inside my soul, which had long been slumbering but was now swelled by my comrades' arrival and conversations with them… On those days when Palchikov didn't have enough work in the smithy and I undertook the responsibilities of a borer in one of the mines, I avidly listened to prisoners' endless escape stories while drinking tea in front of the fire, sympathizing in my heart's innermost recesses with their crazy dreams of freedom. Below, under our feet, stretched out the green, strong-scented taiga full of magical secrets and enticements, seductive, young, and beckoning, yet the way to it was blocked by Cossack guards pacing with rifles in their hands. However, there were all of only two men, one at each opposing door of the cap; the rest, having leaned their rifles in a circle, were like us sitting at their own fire, and prisoners often spoke laughingly about these guardians of the law, boasting that if they should just up and run the "dear little Cossacks" wouldn't be able to get a shot off at them… In this regard Elk, who was actually renowned for courageous escapes, especially loved to brag.

"I 'scaped from Irkutsk Prison, so's it's no problem from here," he haughtily snarled, opening his calf-eyes wide. "Real soldiers there, not bumpkins, not like these spooks here. Four of us jumped from the wall one after another, me first… I fell, got onto my feet—still remember my knee banged a rock good—'n' I ran straight to the city. Soldiers couldn't shoot 'cause houses was close by. Then he, that damned spook, raised the alarm, whistled 'n' shouted—'n' presto, them three comrades o' mine was right behind me… So's they got away."

"But you got caught all the same, Petin."

"That was later, not in Irkutsk, but what I'm talkin' 'bout is how cleverly we got outta prison."

"I daresay, your feet ain't so fleet now?"

Petin snorted contemptuously.

"You still dunno Petin-the-Elk! He ain't 'scapin'—means he still don't wanna. But if he wants—then Six-Eyes won't be holdin' him one more day!"

It seemed to me at one time that Petin was indeed considering doing something. He became angry, pensive, and threw away his student notebooks. And once, during a search (this was in early May), a guard found behind the timbers a sack nearly filled with rye bread husks. The administration now began to imagine that an escape was being planned; the Cossacks sharpened up, added sentries, and refused to allow prisoners to move even a foot from the cap without a strong guard. Of course, the husks could have been saved up by someone from the herd for other, less nefarious purposes, but Petin snorted so very knowingly when prisoners brought up this discovery in conversation that he unintentionally pointed the finger at himself. Later, he even directly confided in me during intimate conversation that the escape had been a completely decided matter long before the guard found the husks, but was held up because of comrades; he spoke with indignation about two or three prisoners who'd acquired a fearsome reputation in prison as "thugs" but, however, hesitated and backed down at the decisive moment.

"There ain't no way to 'scape alone!"

"Why?"

"Alone, you get caught sleepin' your first night in the woods… There'll be a stirrup,[30] y'know. You gotta keep your eyes sharp there. Can't go on any o' the roads again, e'en if you're starvin'. 'N' how're you gonna get provisions without comrades?"

"But it seems to me, Petin, that if you escape now, you'll have to be prepared to starve. You can starve for ten days—you won't die, but during that time God knows where you can go."

"See how smart you are. No, I don't agree I'll starve…"

"So that's it. This means Lunkov speaks the truth about you being no good."

"I'll tear his head off, the bastard! Ain't he that way hisself? What can he unnerstand 'bout these things? He's a forever resident o' prison."

One day Elk, flashing his teeth, conspiratorially turned to me. "But whaddya think 'bout this, Ivan Nikolaevich? You ask so curiously 'bout ever'thin'… I could prob'ly take you 'n' Shtengor as my comrades."

"But what use could you get from us? We have bad eyesight, and that means we'd be poor stirrups; and our legs are even worse… In a word, wouldn't we just be obstacles for you?"

"Then again, youse got some money… We could get some freemen's clothes from a trader."

"Aha, that's what you need from us? But then, in that case, wouldn't you turn around and run off into the taiga somewhere?"

"What're you thinkin' 'bout me, Ivan Nikolaevich? Thank you very much! You're simply mistaken: The Elk's as dependable as a stone mountain. No chance he'd give up his comrades. But you always prefer some scoundrel, some prison bastard who can suck up to you."

Petin made a face that showed I'd seriously hurt him. But he very well knew, of course, that I'd spoken with him about joining the escape only jokingly; along with their comrades, he and other prisoners had said to me more than once:

"You ain't like us, Mikolaich, you ain't our brother. You're either gonna die in prison or get out of it in some legal way, 'tain't otherwise. How is it you'd run off? E'en if you dress up like the Devil, to say nuthin' of a *cheldon*, any newborn baby could tell what you are. Your words 'n' manners—ever'thin', ever'thin's dif'rent from us, y'know!"

My prisoner friends were probably right in this regard. I'd either die in *katorga* or leave it by legal means—nothing else would present itself to me!…

The whole prison world, not just in Siberia but even in Russia, lived through the spring of the aforementioned year with unprecedented agitation: there took place an event of truly unimaginable importance for its existence. At first, there were rather indistinct, fragmentary rumors, coming for the most part from sufficiently lackluster and lightweight sources. Karpushka Lipatov went around the barracks and "blathered":

"Well, you Orth'dox peasants, lissen to what Karpushka's gonna tell you. You're there laughin' 'n' laughin' at Karpushka, but he's bringin' you such news that your jaws'll jus' drop! Now, the medic weren't bein' so cozy with me. I tell 'im: 'Gimme—ya ugly Gypsy's mug—the real *khananiia*, the kind that hits yer nose 'n' bones, indeed, what floods yer spirit, but not so as…'"

"What your red mug does say!"

"But the point is, the sov'reign emp'ror's gonna let us all *go*."

"Ha-ha-ha! Outrageous blather, you've gone completely to hell! 'N' how might you know this?"

"No, ol' men," some hitherto silent figure suddenly emerged from a corner. "No, ol' men, the fool's a fool, but this time he's speakin' a fact. When I myself was still on the road to Shelai, one o' them convoy guards come up to us 'n' says: 'Boys, don't be sad! Soon the sov'reign emp'ror's gonna have mercy on youse.' There it is!"

"You, my brother, the sun'll be up soon, so's it's time to shake the mornin' dew outta your eyes! They been talkin' 'bout this great *manafesta* a long time, but it ain't gonna be."

"Wait a minute, the synod shoulda gotten together a bit ago to make the reg'lation. Whaddya you know, ya fathead? Is it an easy business? Jus' sit on a stool, take a piece o' paper, scratch-scratch-scratch, 'n' it's ready?"

For a long time now there'd been such gossip and talk, but no one had credited them much significance. But then one day, in the middle of May, the tailor Bulanov came from the Cossack officer for whose family he tailored and shared some truly sensational news: the manifesto, that "big" manifesto that everyone had been awaiting so many years, had at last been issued, but for the time being the Siberian leadership was hiding the paper from prisoners because of the clemency's frightfully unprecedented scope and because it didn't know what would happen: if all penal laborers are suddenly released, wouldn't there be an uprising?

"What're you say-*in*'?!" one of those habitually silent prisoners who'd regained his voice suddenly paled from excitement.

The discussion went on in the shop where shoes and prison jackets were mended but where, in addition to the tradesmen, a bunch of extra folks was steadily gathering. Cobblers dropped their boot-trees, tailors tossed away their needles. Everyone was standing around the pushy Mordvinian whose always smiling face was at this moment serious and almost stern.

"Boys, they's freein' ever'one? But who told you, Bulanov?"

"The officer hisself. 'Bulanushka,' he says, 'I'll tell you in secret from the master, 'cause for now they're hidin' it very strictly. You'll make your comrade shoemakers happy: a manifesto's gonna throw two-thirds of 'em off the line!'"

"Two-thirds? So that means they ain't freein' ever'one right away?"

"You little pig's head!" the mare, accosting its disappointed comrade, suddenly jibed, jibed like it had awoken from a heavy stupor. "A few ain't e'en enough for you?"

"But you forgot a rightful third?" Shmatov (that is, Buzzy), breathing laboriously and brokenly as always, gesticulating wildly and twirling his long cockroach-esque mustaches, approached (among a number of others) him. "You forgot a rightful third? It can't do without *you*? Well, so's the tsar's manafesta's gonna free two-thirds completely, 'cept for the long-termers!"[31]

Prison "heralds" raced with mad joy and impetuous haste through the wards, and soon the prison's entire population knew the news and was discussing it from all angles and in every detail. Having returned from the mine, I heard about it from my comrades, but we began laughing at its absurdities. Though not a single one had a steadfast belief, the prisoners actually took some offense.

"I'm a-gonna go to the finance officer," Iukhorev declared, "'n' shake the mother-lovin' truth straight outta that lispin' devil."

Having returned from this reconnaissance, he accosted with utmost vulgarity Bulanov and all those who'd believed his story: the finance officer had crossed himself and sworn that Luchezarov had not received any kind of paper from anywhere and that all this was just prison fabrication. The mare pulled its nose. When universal indignation had been vented at the tailor who'd disturbed the usual peace, the prison quieted and became, apparently, both sadder and gloomier than before. Thus passed a day or two.

Then some whispering in corners began anew... "Manifesta," "two-thirds," "clemency"—the rumor reached us again, without generating, however, significant interest on our part. However, we were suspicious when Iukhorev came straight from the finance officer and declared:

"But this is really somethin'... That tongue-tied scoundrel is deceivin', cov'rin' up!"

And that very day, they began speaking everywhere as if Six-Eyes himself had already informed many of the free commandees about a large pardon, about what in coming days would be a service in the prison, after which the two-thirds would be publicly named.

That there really was "something" to this was impossible to doubt; but skepticism lingered toward this rumor of such a large reduction.

"Is it possible?" we said. "Can the government suddenly decide to free some ten thousand people, whom a day earlier it held in chains and considered an element endangering society?"

"But, why not?" Bashurov fired back. "In the first place, those who'd be freed would all stay in Siberia, which has come to be looked at as a cesspool of social sewage; in the second, I think if they take the trouble to give folks some work and a crust of bread, then there'll be absolutely no trouble."

"Where are so many crusts going to come from?"

"What do you mean 'where from'? Don't penal laborers in prison have to be fed? But, gentlemen, you're primarily forgetting about one characteristic of the human soul: it's criminal but also humanitarian… Such a 'pardon,' you know, would undoubtedly produce in people such a burst of enthusiasm, such a high raising of spirit, that—who knows?—these people could be morally reborn… You laugh? Well, if not completely reborn, then they'll open themselves to moral influence. You just can't let the moment slide, government and society must take the trouble to sow a good seed in this softened soil. As for seeds, it seems to me it's most important to demonstrate faith in an unfortunate, a man outcast!"

Such were the kinds of theoretical disputes we—wavering first toward belief then doubt—had regarding the sensational rumor.

A conversation in the mine with Petushkov thoroughly confused me. He crossed himself and swore he'd read with his own eyes the paper, that it spoke directly about a two-thirds reduction.

"I heard yesserday," added Petushkov, "how Luchezarov himself told the military commander: 'According to calculations, all o' seven men shall remain in prison.'"

"This means they'll stay in any case? Who are they?"

"Anyone who's a lifer, who already could ne'er get released."

"But we imagined the whole prison would be closed and all guards sent away from the place."

"Get that outta your head. 'How's there gonna be instruction now?' he says. 'Who for?' Well, I sure consoled him; if there won't be one prisoner left in the prison, then, I said, the guards should stay! They can guard each other 'n' in the meantime won't be hustlin' in a new mare… Ha-ha-ha! Watch that scoundrel!"

That which could only be dreamt in the most unconscious sleep now came to pass during the day. We at last came to understand that "the voice of the people is the voice of God"… A stormy joy of willfulness enveloped the soul, intoxicating it with bright hopes…

May 22nd, for when the service was assigned and, by this happenstance, work was canceled, was a clear spring day. Early that morning a table covered with a clean white tablecloth was set up in the prison yard. The finance officer laid a bundle of wax candles on it. With joyfully beaming faces the mare crowded into the yard. Many had donned clean shirts and slicked their hair with lard. Neither cursing nor the usual arguments were heard. Yesterday's sworn enemies were today conversing peaceably and amicably. Iukhorev, with two or three of his friends, the prison ringleaders, walked his usual heroic way along the prison façade, and here and there I picked up distinct phrases from his conversation:

"So I'm bustin' outta Olëkma again! Start livin' in Transbaikalia with a devil or two!… Girls is sweeter 'n' the booze is stronger there, in my view."

My friends Chirok and Nogaitsev, both ceremonially reliable and smiling casually, came up to me.

"Well, Mikolaich, ain't we awaitin' a holiday?"

"A dream, jus' a real dream! Time 'n' again you're rubbin' your eyes, scared like you might wake up."

"Well, what are you going to do now, Nogaitsev? Return home?"

"I'm goin' back, goin' back right away. Got a woman there… A woman loves me lots."

"How will you survive there?"

"Truly, you're strange to be askin' how… What, don't I got hands? Or do you s'pose if once in life I killed a coupla bastards I'll waste away in jail again? Mikolaich, you yourself know I ain't lived in *katorga* like a loafer. Well, if I'm a tub o' lard, what can I do? It's an illness. It's sickly fat; I began *katorga* a sick man… But gimme some freeman's food 'n' I'll be a real man again!"

Chirok had been attentively listening to Nogaitsev's speech, and his face grew very serious and significant.

"Nogaitsev's speakin' the honest truth," he declared in a persuasive tone, "how can you be a real man in prison?"

"And can you, Chirok, please lighten up on the Cheremisi?" I automatically asked—remembering that before prison this man had been incomparably less of a man—and almost immediately regretted my question.

Chirok's face took on an extremely afflicted look.

"Ech, Mikolaich!" he raised his cap and energetically scratched the back of his head, and this "ech!" sounded more like a bitter imprecation.

I was reminded of Valerian's arguments about a propitious moment for moral regeneration: in point of fact, was there not a bit of truth in these arguments?

"At-ten-tion!" a guard's deafening voice suddenly resounded, and everyone jumped. Prisoners formed ranks in less than a second. The gates flew open, and through them came with powerful strides an entire company of local Cossacks with a young cornet in the lead. An order was given, and the Cossacks formed precise lines to the right of the prisoners. Obviously, an impressive and grandiose ceremony was imminent.

Hardly had the guard quieted, than through the gates came the mining works' senior cleric with a tall, imposing deacon, the Cossack captain, a throng of guards and office scribes, and, at their head, Six-Eyes with a paper in his hands, the sight of which made everyone's heart leap then sweetly freeze. In conclusion, the free commandees entered and formed a separate platoon on the left flank. All this happened quickly, with unusual pomp and great precision.

"Blessings, Sov-e-reign!" bellowed the portly, broad-shouldered deacon, suddenly interrupting the reverential hush, and the divine service began. Like one man, everyone noisily crossed himself with a large gesture. Even those prisoners who didn't believe the words, who were, as they say, not taken in, who offhandedly blasphemed and proclaimed themselves the most egregious atheists, crossed themselves devoutly. Was this a sincere emotion, a legitimate readiness to rehabilitate? Or was it partly influenced by the presence of so many officials?…

Prior to the proclamation of many long years of life, the brave captain solemnly approached the table, slowly unfolded the secret paper he'd been holding the whole time, exultantly cast a gaze over the ranks of prisoners' shorn heads, and loudly announced:

"So here it is, boys, the great pardon you've been looking forward to!… Listen to the proclamation I've received from the military governor."

Had at that moment a gnat flown through the prison yard, its buzz would probably have been heard by everyone. Somewhere far away, beyond the prison gates, someone couched; high in the sky a swallow chirped…

Luchezarov read loudly, unusually distinctly and expressively, emphasizing the following words not only with his voice but with looks and gestures: "According to standards of good behavior, sincere repentance, and the commandant's favorable opinion, the terms of prisoners under punishments assigned them by the judiciary may be *lessened to two-thirds*!!!"

It was as if a heavy stone had fallen from everyone's shoulders: now everyone had heard with their own ears that what had earlier been believed only on the basis of rumors could, however, be completely trusted. The mare heaved a deep sigh, crossed itself, and began swaying joyfully…

"Glory to you, Sovereign!" sounded the old timers' cries.

Luchezarov had in the meantime continued reciting the governor's paper point by point, though no one heard or understood him.

"Well, there it is: you're lessened *to two-thirds*!" he grandly proclaimed yet again, having finished his recitation and raised the paper high in the air.

It was evident the brave captain was himself sincerely exulting. The purplish-red face with long yellow mustaches did not this time seem terrible, but beamed with tenderness… Indeed, all of Luchezarov's imposing physique had seemed to become smaller than its usual size, had changed into a physique characteristic of the deceased… After having gazed attentively at both sides of the prisoners' ranks, Luchezarov came up to me with quick steps and, extracting the paper, courteously said:

"Look in the wards and explain this once more, in case they haven't understood it."

This was the first time he'd spoken to me plainly during so official a situation, without the formal "you."

In the meantime the head cleric, a handsome old man with long white hair, also spoke tenderly:

"So there's a pardon for you, laddies! Perhaps some of you haven't earned it, and will lose that two-thirds off your term. Well, pray harder and warmer next time."

And fervent praying began anew.

"Bruddersth, who wantsth to buy some candersth to light?!" the fat and brick-red finance officer, bundles of wax candles in hand, blurted out to the ranks of prisoners. They snatched them from him (he distinctly noted who did so). They were taken not only by pious old timers but "youngsters" indifferent to religion, not only by well-off people but those the control officer reckoned were worth no more than ten kopeks. The deacon, infected by the universal enthusiasm, simply let himself go proclaiming the call for a long life, and when his powerful bass boomed "many years" to the imprisoned, the confined, and then to their commanders, the prison choir bellowed in reply so earnestly, so thunderously, that it could probably have been heard in the distant hills: suddenly, my view was obscured by the sight of a small kite sailing far up into the heavenly blue…

The stormy willfulness of the exultant mare flowed into the prisoner corridor, encircling me and loudly demanding the precious paper be read once more.

"We'll mem'rize it by sound, by sound! Read, Mikolaich, read!"

Only now did Shteinhart and I exchange glances, and I saw that one and the same thought lay deep in our souls.

"Steady, boys," I turned to the throng, barely controlling my own agitation. "A huge mistake, a misunderstanding, is taking place… Not two-thirds at all, but just one-third of our terms is being eliminated, and that surely not in every case. They may reduce it less, they may not reduce it at all."[32]

"What're you sayin'?! You jokin' wid us?!"

"I'm not joking at all; but the commandant, the cleric, and all of you haven't understood the paper as you should."

After a minute of stunned silence an unimaginable row erupted. Frenzied voices shouted:

"What's he spinnin'? He wants to cloud us!"

"Don't lissen to him, boys! We heard for ourselves, with our own ears!"

"Take the paper from him, read it yourself. Who's literate?"

"*These* people are always sowing discord, always trying to sully the leadership!" I detected in the rear of the ranks the voice of Bogodarov, a penal laborer from the nobility who at one time had completed the sixth level at the Irkutsk public school, ended up at Srednekolymsk[33] for forgery, but then came to Shelai mine for committing murder while drunk. He was a consumptive, a bitter and terribly vain man opposed to everything in the world, who thought himself highly educated (though in fact could not write grammatically) and deeply resented me, another former nobleman, possessed of an authentic education.

"They're not pleased that the government's showing humanitarianism!" Bogodarov continued shouting, loudly and unashamedly, and a sympathetic mumble could be detected here and there. After this, Bogodarov hid himself away somewhere. It later turned out that he ran to Six-Eyes to report that my comrades and I were inciting the prisoners to riot, explaining to them that there wouldn't be a two-thirds at all and that it was only a deception. He later told the mare that Six-Eyes had supposedly become terribly angry and shouted:

"Tell him (that is, me) that I've considered him an educated man until now, but it turns out he's simply… an ass!"

I don't know if the brave captain spoke so forcefully, but my opinion contradicting everyone (including Luchezarov) extremely annoyed him—this much I knew.

In the meantime, prisoners continued to fuss and get angry. The more those who were literate read the paper, the deeper their conviction in a calculation of two-thirds. The lines: "According to standards, etc.… the terms of prisoners under punishment assigned them by the courts may be lessened to two-thirds"—had hardly been read than the listeners went into boundless rapture and, waving hands, shouted with fervor:

"Well, what's there to argue 'bout? Ain't it written there? We ain't deaf as well… Or do they reckon we're all jus' idiots? Them there, the brainy ones… They've studied 'n' studied so, that now they're at wit's end!"

Many prisoners actually completely stopped talking to me during those days, walking past without greeting me as they had earlier and turning their heads away, though some, on the other hand, brazenly looked me in the eye with an undisguised expression of hatred and contempt. During that time comparatively few maintained previously warm relations. Thus Chirok gently reproached me:

"I grew up 'mong tree stumps, Mikolaich, 'n' am myself nuthin' more'n a Permian stump… What the people is sayin', I believe. Well, like ever'one, it must be said, you let one slip this time! What's written on that paper's quite well known—e'en I unnerstand it's two-thirds, but you're mistakin' it for one-third!"

"Listen, Chirok. Let's assume I don't have any bread but I see you have a whole thick slice, and I go and ask you as a friend: 'Kuzma, give me some bread, reduce your portion to two-thirds.' How much bread will you have left and how much will you give me?"

"Well… I'll give you a third part, but I'll keep two!" Chirok replied without thinking.

"So. Well, if two-thirds is not to your advantage, why are you giving away just one?"

In great perplexity, Chirok scratched the back of his head and even his belly.

"Ah, Mikolaich, Mikolaich! Don't trouble my heart, be quiet!"

Among the few other "contrarians" and worldly prisoners, Iukhorev had also not changed one iota regarding me and my comrades. As always, he presented a penal laborer's disdain toward any sort of clemency.

"But, curse me," he said, wagging his powerful head like a lion. "They give a third, take away a third, from a pack o' wild dogs… 'n' anyway, that's the best I can hope for!"

And having uttered a strong word, he hurriedly sped his usual easy way about his business. It seems to me, however, that had I not cast doubt on it, he would have believed as deeply in the paper as everyone else had.

Upon the conclusion of one of my heated arguments with the prisoners that involved that day's duty officer, Lunkov conspiratorially called me to the side and said:

"Ivan Nikolaevich, I'm ready to trust you completely. O' course, not only we, but Six-Eyes hisself disagrees with you. But I'll simply advise you: keep what you think to yourself… What if the high command suddenly catches wind of it? All of a sudden it won't give us the two-thirds… Be better for us, y'know, if they dunno the truth…"

While enunciating he looked at me so beseechingly and movingly that I did not have even the strength to laugh at this. In the meantime Luchezarov, enraged from the very first, necessarily began to reflect. When, during an evening roll call, one of the prisoners specifically asked him whether penal laborers would be given a two-thirds reduction, the brave captain, after casting a sidelong glance at me, responded with some embarrassment:

"I've sent an inquiry to the *katorga* director… There are actually several unclear phrases in the governor's paper regarding this… In any case, the issue will become clear very soon."

Petushkov also undertook to argue more than once with me in the mine. Like everyone, he interpreted the paper in favor of the prisoners and, half jestingly, half seriously, reproached me in the conceit, the desire, that everything be other than it was:

"I know well that you're learned people 'n' we're taiga stumps, well, but all the same, do we unnerstand any less'n Monakhov 'n' Luchezarov?… They've also learned somethin'… And how! The director himself, it's said, explained two-thirds is bein' knocked off… No one 'n' nuthin', darnit, is sayin' what you alone is, 'n' none of us in Siberia can read?"

"They're unable to read, Ilich, but they've all concocted a full two-thirds—this is how they think. But you tell me: let's say you're getting a salary of ninety rubles a month."

"Okh, wouldn't that be comfy, darnit!"

"Now let's say your salary is reduced to two-thirds because of some violation. How much would you then be getting?"

"First you said 'twas ninety? Well, certainly, there'd be sixty rubles left!"

"Well, now you see for yourself what I'm on about."

"How so? What's this? Where do your thoughts go, 'n' why're you tormentin' yourself?" Petushkov broke loose from his spot and continued the argument, agreeing to wager his favorite horse, Blacky, against fifty rubles on my part…

The talk about what three educated prisoners had dreamed up flew just like a snowball through Shelai's environs, and soon even those in the factory knew and were talking about it. Public opinion was not on our side, and everyone anticipated with obvious malicious glee the top leadership's decision, a decision that would of course finally humiliate and disgrace us!

"But, Ivan Nikolaevich," Shteinhart sometimes jokingly said, "wouldn't it now be enormously unpleasant for us if the leadership does indeed give us two-thirds? Or is it perhaps better to remain in prison as the victors?"

"Well, no, I disagree," I responded, joking as well, "in my opinion, it's better to be shamed but to receive two-thirds!"

Meanwhile, time passed. To the very end, most prisoners anticipated they'd be released from prison. Several days went by and some became disillusioned when, after the service, they were not immediately set free and the guards, as always, organized roll call, read out the roster, and locked the wards. Another day someone spread a rumor that all the prisoners in Aleskandrovsk Zavod's[34] almshouse had long since been released, and that the toothless mouths of the septuagenarian mendicants wandering among taverns were boastfully mumbling:

"We're on a roll again, lads!…"

But this rumor was soon proved wrong. Day followed day. Roll calls, assignments, the whole regimen of *katorga* life followed its course; the sympathetic feelings of the guards and Six-Eyes himself gave way to the previous seriousness and severity, and the mare quickly began losing heart. It continued to believe in secret in the two-thirds, but most often, voices were clearly heard to be saying:

"Ivan Nikolaevich is right, right: they ain't givin' us a whiff of a third! What might the law be in Siberia? In a word—it's a rigged jury!"

By the middle of summer no one was even talking about the manifesto anymore. There had been neither sight nor sound of its implementation. Finally, in September, word went round that a pair of prisoners in Zerentui mine had had their terms reduced two-thirds.

"*Two*-thirds?"

"Yes, we talked with reliable messengers."

"Is it really so?… If it's that Malyshev, who I know, then he had all o' several months left, 'cause he got sentenced to twelve years."

"'N' I know Sukhopiatov—he got sentenced same day as me, but got caught by a dif'rent witness, only they gave me more'n a year… If I got two, that means he's already finished, 'n' I reckon his term's done!"

"What about this two-thirds?"

"Well, yes, maybe it's a dif'rent Sukhopiatov."

But then one beautiful evening at roll call, Luchezarov announced that three prisoners assigned to Shelai's free command would also be released to settlement by the manifesto. With regard to them, everyone already knew perfectly well that one had stayed in his settlement a month and the other just two months! After this, each notice brought similar reductions for prisoners, mostly from the free command, whose terms would have ended very soon even without them, and one time there was an order giving a year off to a prisoner who was on the verge of completing his entire sentence!…

The disappointment was complete. *Katorga* was loudly indignant. "Ivans" boasted more than usual, declaring they didn't care about whatever pardons were given, but the petty-minded herd grumbled that the Siberian administration had "stolen" their two-thirds.

"They wouldn't give e'en one, let alone the whole thing!"

They decided to appeal for clarification to Six-Eyes: the brave captain responded more than ever before with grandiose aplomb:

"It was childish to imagine that a full two-thirds would be taken off! I told you at the time: don't hope too much, wait for clarification."

"But will there e'er be a third knocked off, Mister Com'dant?"

"Not a third right away. You just have to wait your turn. It's impossible to apply the manifesto to everyone right away, there are whole thousands of you, you know…"

The *katorga* director himself later told prisoners about the same practical impossibility. But I never understood it, just as I don't understand it now. Whole dozens of officials of all various ranks and salary levels worked in the Nerchinsk *katorga* administration; in the meantime, I imagine, within about a month two or three well-trained and -supervised clerks could have, without any especial difficulty and through using a manifest of sentences for all three thousand men assigned to Nerchinsk *katorga*, reduced them by a third. Bureaucratic red tape managed to stretch this relatively simple matter out from one to two years…

Life went fully along in the usual rut. Rosy illusions were dashed. Over the course of an entire year, "through tablespoons of hours," as prisoners acerbically said, the reductions were for the short-termers. Long-termers seemed to have been completely forgotten. Of course, having a third knocked off their shoulders still left quite a few years' *katorga*, and there was probably no particular need to announce their "pardon," but the long-termers' dissatisfaction had its own, not unfounded, reason. Namely, they hoped (this seemed to me a legitimate hope) that not only would all sentences be lessened to one-third, but that by the same measure the term of the "probationer"—subject to sitting inside prison walls and therefore to serving the most difficult portion of *katorga*—would be reduced. This hope, however, collapsed like many other hopes, and after a year had gone by, Luchezarov explained to us about having received from somewhere a clarification that probationary terms should remain exactly as they had been before the manifesto.[35]

For long-termers, this was the single bitterest disappointment… The lifer to whom the manifesto applied became a twenty-year penal laborer, the twenty-yearer a thirteen-yearer, but this abbreviation had little bearing on the distant future, when at the given moment the former had first to face sitting in prison for eleven, and the latter seven, years, with a disgraceful shaven head and legs shackled in irons.

But there were still other aspects of the manifesto's application to *katorga* that led it to imagine local authorities had "stolen" the tsar's pardon from it. The truth is that good behavior, repentance, and other conditions were mentioned in the manifesto as conditions for its application, and everyone heard this mentioned with his own ears, but each took it to mean that his behavior would be apprised only close to the time of the manifesto's promulgation and by no means would an account be made of violations logged and contained in the record book[36] three, four, or even ten years ago. What was the universal amazement when, in fact, *all* such prisoners were excluded from the manifesto, and most of all the so called fugitives, that is, those who had at some point tried to escape *katorga*. The latters' disappointment at their removal especially struck me, since I'd already noticed more than once how strict and at times unfairly our escape laws are applied, and how dark was *katorga* runaways' complete hopelessness regarding their fate.

"The Siberian leadership stole our manifesto! It's a rigged jury!" said the mare, waving its hands in despair. "Ekh, there's no end for us!…"

During those days many strong words were spat at the commandant's residence, but perhaps more were directed at the old cleric, on whom for some reason they flung all the blame.

"Long-haired devil!… 'Well, now, laddies,' he says, 'pray harder'"—they mimicked him, boiling with inconceivable rage—"''cause there's those o' you ain't deserved it, 'n' those gettin' two-thirds!…' Oh, it's nuthin' to you, ya stinkin' shag-head! We got it!… Two-thirds!… Ooh, a horsy sort!"

Mercilessly ridiculed as well were those prisoners who could be seen before a burning candle at prayer time. For their part, the guilty were revealed and exhibited to the rest. Some blushed with shame, others snapped fiercely.

Thus passed not a few amusing, yet at the same time pathetic, scenes.

VI. A STAND-OFF

Later, irrespective of the manifesto, the Nerchinsk mines' population greatly receded owing to the frequent dispatch of healthy prisoners to Sakhalin, and principally because the arrival of fresh parties from Russia practically ceased (probably also thanks to strong demand for them on Sakhalin). Shelai Prison's population thinned out not by the day but by the hour; there were no healthy prisoners to carry out even those simple functions by which daily life goes on. Particularly felt was the lack of craftsmen of any sort. Very few folks were being sent to the mountain, and Monakhov closed operations in one of the mines. In the meantime, for some reason, not one man from the small parties that did nevertheless occasionally arrive to Nerchinsk *katorga* was assigned to Shelai: prisoners blamed this on the brave captain's "barbarous" reputation and the *katorga* director's stupid attitude toward them. It was suggested that Six-Eyes couldn't survive and was "unable to sleep soundly without our brother," and that his prison might come to a worse turn because of this disregard. They said that he had in fact sent a "request" for new people, and occasionally we were sent, really as if it were a joke, two or three stooped and lame old men who were unsuitable for any sort of work, ignorant of any trade at all, and should have been put in an almshouse long ago. Luchezarov then ranted and raved and instantly returned the "new" party, insisting he had no free space in the infirmary.

With the strong and healthy element's diminishment their hard work in the prison was taken over by the so called "domestic" workers—the ward headmen, cleaners, medical attendants, and other service personnel whom Luchezarov didn't trust, and so all the frail old men and truly sick, syphilitic, and consumptive got worse and worse. The giant Iukhorev alone somehow managed to keep his spot as collective headman, thus allowing him to lie on his side the whole day or loiter about the prison without a care. Six-Eyes was evidently quite disposed toward him and, according to Iukhorev's own account, told him:

"A man such as you, with a powerful throat and meaty fist, should without fail be given a headman's responsibilities, so that discontents can be quickly squashed! So there'll be no grumbling over food or hard labor. Don't complain to me, straighten out the brawlers yourself."

"But let the sonofabitch bark whate'er he wants!" Iukhorev piled on to the brave captain's exhortations. "I lissen, 'n' I keep quiet. Don't matter what he spews 'n' bawls out like a soldier's wife: 'I'm listenin', Mister Com'dant!' Curse his soul."

So Iukhorev continued to be the prison tsar and took into his hands more and more power over the collective. He was in general a despotic character. Only for form's sake did he sometimes walk through the wards and ask: "Boys, you want this or that?" But from the very tone in which he asked the question it was immediately clear that what was desired was the answer the herd always provided. As it were, they disapproved of Iukhorev behind his back and even said that he puffed himself up so he'd be chosen among others to be headman, but this was not said seriously, since everyone distinctly knew that no one else in prison was in a position to contend with Iukhorev either in intelligence or especially in exterior presentation. A crowd of prisoners had only to appear before Iukhorev's mighty physique and, like everyone, the most mediocre herd began looking like little gnats in his presence. There also existed a growing conviction that the collective headman was taking advantage of his enormous influence over the finance officer, tricking him regarding the use of the collective and in general ruling it with an iron fist. I myself actually happened to overhear in the kitchen how Iukhorev openly called the finance officer a lisping devil, and how that one only meekly shriveled and laughed it off. For his part, the "lisping devil" was a sufficiently concupiscent rogue that he could concede something to this most clever and adroit prisoner; the mare's rapture over the headman's intelligence was purely platonic, and the prison didn't see any of the presumptive fruits of his political victory; by the same token, the cauldron's skilly was every month becoming more watery and tasteless and the meat less and less; and lard for the kasha was missing for entire weeks on either this or that pretext. All this the mare saw and felt, but Iukhorev's personality was too charming and overwhelmed everyone too much for there to be any loud protests against him.

In the meantime, Iukhorev, by nature sinewy and lean, began to glow from the lard and an abundance of health; he drank no tea save with milk, smoked only good tobacco, ate a lot of meat, and sometimes even got drunk on liquor supplied by the medic Zemlianskii, with whom he was great friends. Following a prison search he himself boasted that had his jacket been properly gone through, a whole twenty-five rubles would have been found in it. From where did he get such money? From where did he get milk and meat? Continuing silently and submissively to feed on slops, the mare tried not to think about such ticklish questions.

One Sunday, Shteinhart, Bashurov, and I were strolling three abreast down the corridor as usual, when Iukhorev suddenly shouted from his ward's threshold:

"Valerian, come, old chap, breakfast's on!"

"What does he mean 'breakfast'?" we turned to our comrade in surprise.

Bashurov became flustered.

"Yes, you know, there… Iukhorev often treats… It's somehow not easy to refuse."

"What does he serve?"

"Well, there are various things, potatoes, sometimes meat…"

"And you don't know where he's getting all this from? You know he's robbing the collective, and if we participate in his binges, how will the prisoners start looking at us? They'll forgive Iukhorev, but not us."

"Oh! They all do it, you know… Hardly anyone in our wards is surviving on just a potato!"

"That's exactly it: 'hardly anyone'… I doubt Karpushka's being given anything? Your ward is having breakfasts only because it happens to be filled with Ivans, but others are going hungry."

"You're a petty rigorist, Ivan Nikolaevich! It's a measly 'tater or an onion… It's rude to refuse, you know!"

However, Shteinhart came down decisively on my side and shamed Bashurov into refusing that time. But several weeks passed, and I again had the chance to be made certain that, through lack of character or an absence of delicacy, Valerian was participating anew in Iukhorevian binges. Knowing Bashurov's enormous vanity, I didn't think it possible to undertake new debates regarding this and preferred to wave my hand, having pensively told myself that, in the end, each of us answers for his own actions only… But I was mainly quite unhappy that his friendship with Iukhorev grew, apparently not by the day but the hour, and that he was also continuing to enter into familiar and in any case unnecessary intimacy with other prisoners. They allowed themselves to slap him on the back, call him by just his first name, and make rude jokes at his expense. I myself was never touchy or kept apart from the prisoners: on the contrary, many of them even called me "The Dawdler"… But, having undertaken such "dawdlings" (with Chirok, Nogaitsev, Elk, et al.), I tried never to cross a boundary of reserve and self-respect with them. Shteinhart was even more self-conscious in this regard. But now, when an indiscreet comrade was practicing a completely new personal politics, we both instinctively shrank back and began treating prisoners more reservedly and dryly than before. The observational mare soon noticed this situation and in our presence sometimes took to emphasizing (whether with a joke or seriousness) that here, as they said, was Valerian Bashurov—a regular fellow, a fellow spirit—and there was the two of us—haughty people abhorring the dark folk…

But, as Shteinhart predicted, Valerian was unable to remain in one and the same mood for long, and now and then had bitter clashes with prisoner friends. One such clash with his favorite "pupil" Bykov was talked about by the whole prison. Among his kind this Bykov was a prominent figure, and I should say a few words about him. A close friend of Iukhorev, he however owed his notoriety not to any kind of internal, but rather to almost exclusively external, qualities. Obtuse and a bit dull-witted, he stood nearly a head taller than Iukhorev and Elk, but was as dry and skinny as a match; he had an enormous square skull, deathly pale face with deep-set brown eyes and a barely discernible yellow beard, and long bony arms endowed with phenomenal strength—such was the appearance of this terrible living skeleton possessing, in addition to everything else, a vulgar, unpleasant voice with a cutting laugh… Bykov had come to *katorga* for overpowering a woman, though he himself deemed his conviction a scandalously cruel and unfair matter.

"Ha! The law!" he said in his wicked, irate bass. "What's the law? They send a man to *katorga* for some ol' streetwalker…"

"But didn't you injure her, Bykov?"

"Where was the injury? Well, if'n it was a young girl or a man's wife, that'd be another matter. But that ol' widow had the face of a witch's witch!"

"All the same—she *was* a woman…"

"Yeah, but you, Mikolaich, will certainly always stand up for this filthy category! But lissen to what happened. I was livin' in a mine, 'n' this ol' woman was livin' somewhere nearby there, too. Some boys 'n' I met her there, in the woods… 'twas was a holiday affair—well, ever'one was right drunk. Could such stupidity have gotten into a sober head?

Did we have any money or willin' girls? Well, but she, the witch, was gettin' courageous… Another woulda reckoned it was to her honor… ho-ho-ho, to go strollin' with young fellas… But she sticks her snout in the air! Well… well it came down to force."

"How did she later report you?"

"They found witnesses. Two of our comp'ny got drunk… We was e'en warned… Well, but then this bitch told on 'em, 'n' they couldn't keep from talkin' 'n' fingered me 'n' my comrades. I got eight years' *katorga* like gettin' a drink, 'n' that was that! Well, what's this law? I tell you straight, ain't the law, but *rob'ry*!"

Besides his already mentioned dull-wittedness a quite undiluted asinine stubbornness and sickeningly developed vanity, as well as an ability to see injury even where there was not a shadow of it, were evident among Bykov's internal qualities. Thinking himself not a very stupid man, he didn't allow for the slightest objection in arguments, and would start grousing. One time, during summer, enjoying from the prison yard the lavender flowers spread beautifully across the hills, I asked Bykov as he was passing by what he thought of the flowers.

"Well, yes, they're scarlet, o' course, scarlet," he categorically declared.

"But they seem violet to me," I expressed my opinion, "not quite scarlet so much…"

Bykov had now been offended.

"You a numbskull? I ne'er knowed there was such a numbskull… Why you askin' if'n you know ever'thin'? We ain't aimin' to be a priest, y'know! Ho-ho! Numbskull!"

And, chest puffed out, he strode off.[37]

Valerian Bashurov soon had a decisive clash with this person. It's no wonder that Bykov, under the influence of the previously established familiarity in relations, told his teacher in response to some rudeness by Bashurov (like, "get out of here, don't bother me!") to go to some not very ambiguous places… Not having anticipated any such thing, Bashurov boiled over with rage and demanded that Bykov immediately apologize. Bykov, instead of an apology, began obnoxiously laughing and added to this rudeness several more vulgar words. Friendly prisoners such as Iukhorev hurriedly exited the ward as if they'd not heard the argument; the rest of the herd maintained a silent neutrality.

"I kept warning you, Bashurov," I opined to my comrade after he told me this story, "since we can't respond to prisoners' vulgarity with the same vulgarity, we should in general not have too close relations with them."

"Akh, this Bykov's certainly an exception! He's such an ass…"

"Well, all the same, there's nothing to be done," Shteinhart decided, "don't let yourself fight with him."

In my soul, I was greatly irritated by my comrade, sooner blaming him than Bykov, with whom I'd refused to quarrel many times; nonetheless, I officially regarded it necessary to somewhat deceive the latter, usually by responding dryly to his chatter. After this incident Shteinhart and I were generally even more cautious; now, in the mare's presence, each of us three ceased saying anything superfluous or, as it seemed to the others, tactless, such as the warning that had already issued from our clique: "*Noblesse oblige*, gentlemen!…"

Educated by his run-in with Bykov and a whole series of other, pettier skirmishes with cohabitants, Bashurov himself began to regard suspiciously all prisoners with whom he'd earlier allowed unfettered intimacy. He began all the more rudely to snub informal addresses towards him and to receive in response, needless to say, the very same rudeness. His popularity in the prison began to plummet as quickly as it had first risen. Finally, his relationship with Iukhorev began to cool. Unfortunately for him, Bashurov was too open and reckless in loudly proclaiming his ideas about the collective's practices and organization. At first, when he'd held himself on equal footing with his cohabitants, his sharpest observations on this account were apologized for or turned into a joke; but now, when under the influence of wounded vanity he tried sharply to change his initial behavior, retaining, however, for himself the right to play the role of moral censor, prisoners didn't want to grant him this right. It was owing to this that he had his first argument with Iukhorev, two weeks after the manifesto's declaration in prison. Going into the kitchen one morning for boiling water and noticing kitchen workers sitting behind some breakfast, he laughingly said:

"Gentlemen, you're getting along well with the current headman! He's fattening you right up!"

These words seemed to be taken as a joke, but after Valerian left, an entire drama played itself out in the kitchen. Upon appearing there, Iukhorev was told that Bashurov had spoken in the kitchen about putting together a gang under his command. Like an enraged lion, Iukhorev ran into the ward and grandly told Valerian:

"I didn't expect this from you, Valerian. We've lived as friends so far, but I now see you're keepin' a stone in your chest. I jus' shoulda shown you from the beginnin' that I'm ataman of any gang robbin' the collective!"

Bashurov tried to justify himself:

"I was joking, and they're not being honest…"

"Well, we don't joke like *that*," Iukhorev stood up impressively, and added: "Anyway, I know well where all this is goin' 'n' who you're organizin' against me. You're liftin' your noses too high, gentlemen!"

"Who am I organizing and who's lifting his nose?" Valerian challenged.

"We all know *who*!" Iukhorev said, as if snapping his jaws, and flew out the ward.

Having observed this conversation, I didn't doubt for a minute that he'd chiefly decided it was me. Even before the newcomers' arrival I was always extremely reserved towards him, as if instinctively sensing in his conspicuous power a lack of any moral element quite removed from prudence; from the beginning of the friendship between Iukhorev and Bashurov, I (perhaps quite unconsciously) had become not just reserved but even cold towards him. I'd felt that this vibration in my attitude had gone unnoticed in the prisoner's mind. He was from the first impeccably polite with Shteinhart and me, but within this courtesy a suppressed hostility could be sensed. He had evidently been deeply wounded and offended that he'd not encountered on our part the same comradely faith and desire for intimacy as he'd received from the expansive Valerian.

For several days on end Iukhorev's friends found themselves greatly agitated and always talking about something, pacing through the yard in their hours free from work. Upon appearing in the kitchen each of us three met with funereal silence. The head cook, the Tatar Aziadinov, who had at first laughed at Bashurov's joke, now pouted most of all and even refused to answer our questions. When arrived the next fast day on which the skilly was prepared with our meat, it turned out that Iukhorev, Bykov, Aziadinov,

Shmatov, and two or three other fellows had cooked their own, separate, fasting skilly, and during Saturday's distribution of our *makhorka* among the ward they refused their portions. This was an obvious protest. The struggle assumed a sharp and sufficiently unpleasant character…

The baker Ogurtsov, a quite young and unusually easygoing chap, had so far been very friendly with me, but now, when I showed up in the kitchen, he nervously turned away as if not noticing me. Yet, early one evening, as I was brewing some tea for myself before roll call, he came up and quickly put a note in my hand without being noticed by the other prisoners. Upon returning to the ward I read the following ungrammatical lines: "ivan mekalaech Our gang says that you also got a gang that you its ottoman that you wrongly turning prison against ivans. But I unnerstan Got I like you that you bought me tobacco your honest treater of Ogurtsov and I fear iukhoref says theyll knock stuffing out of you."

I should say here that the story of this "honest Richard" is not without interest. Ogurtsov showed up with me in Shelai as practically a boy, a dim-witted chubby lad with fresh round cheeks and an athletic build—but principally with such a naïve, innocent soul that it was simply a pity to see him clothed in a gray jacket with a pair of black *katorga* aces on his back. Not without reason did the mare call him "Grass-leaf"—he, it seemed, was a leaf of grass without any flower or scent, a blank slate on which life could write what it wanted. With level shoulders nearly seven feet wide, a fat, round head (which, prisoners quipped, could not be got round in less than three days), and enormous fists heavy as one-pood weights, the eighteen-year-old Ogurtsov was unthreatening and un-malicious as a dove, and in response to every slight managed only to laugh and grab his belly, and so it was rather difficult to believe that this young and dim-witted Hercules had come to *katorga* for killing a man. On the other hand, he committed this murder without any premeditation or purpose, almost by accident. One day, comrades invited him to a tavern, and when he refused to drink vodka, a sergeant-major who'd been sitting in the tavern and was drunk as a lord proposed to the honorable company that they hold him down while he poured a glass of liquor in his mouth. Defending himself against this witty proposition Ogurtsov tried, in his words, to "smash" the drunken soldier's mug, but he punched him in the temple so recklessly that the unfortunate man's skull cracked and he instantly gave up the ghost.

Ogurtsov and I befriended each other at the beginning of the general arrival to the prison and, though he did not live in my ward, he studied in fits and starts the grammar that came very slowly to him; he also, like Kifa Mokievich,[38] had a great desire for "scientific" conversations, asking me, for instance, why man has only two legs but is nonetheless smarter than a rooster. If such an important topic was being discussed, he for some reason continually covered his mouth with one hand and rested the other over his belly, sat himself down, and shook with reedy laughter; thus was his surprise usually expressed… Like Lunkov, Ogurtsov held the mare in very low regard morally as well as intellectually, was indignant at prisoners' attitudes and behavior, and kept apart from general prison life.

One day, a new baker was needed in the kitchen. Luchezarov cast his gaze over the prisoners' ranks and for some reason chose Ogurtsov. The latter was in great distress.

His heroic physique demanded fresh air and healthy labor, whereas the hot and stuffy kitchen atmosphere only stewed a man, weakened his muscles and filled them with laziness and fat. He was ready to scream from the terrible headaches he began to suffer, but the brave captain simply rebuffed all his requests to be sent to the mine:

"Nonsense, lad, nonsense! You'll get used to it. Indeed, a baker should be a strong man. And it's not for nothing that your surname is Ogurtsov: you're as healthy and fresh as a young cucumber.[39] You're just what a baker should be."

Ogurtsov actually became inured to the kitchen. He got terribly lazy and heavy; delicate, sanguine tones were quickly lost from his face and gave way to a clear-white, bloodless color of sickly puffiness. He was no longer spoiling for hard work and was sufficiently content with his new position; but because the kitchen had always been the center of prisoners' various swindles, Ogurtsov turned into a "weed," a fellow without any moral foundations, and in less than a year there began emerging in him the most unlikeable qualities and attributes. Money began jangling behind his belt, there was always milk following his tea… As for Iukhorev, the "lisping devil" had been his object of exploitation at first but, over time, rags fleeced from the herd of *katorga*'s mare came flying in. Before my eyes Ogurtsov, who was soon being rude toward people even in his casual relations, became corrupt and decadent: like all the Ivans, he began vulgarly shouting and making a show of his meaty fists in squabbles with the petty herd; and when I tried by old memory in the capacity of instructor to teach him manners, he, as was his old habit, crossed his arms over his belly and laughed in his deep bass like a drunken deacon, but it was clear my words had already fallen from his soul. After each such conversation I received merely a written note minutely enumerating all the dirty tricks by his kitchen comrades. During the time about which I've begun speaking the spoiled and fattened Ogurtsov retained only a shadow of my former respect for him, yet continued signing his little denunciations "Your Faithful Quicksand."

Heavy was the moral atmosphere of the kitchen, this prison clubhouse where Iukhorev ruled entirely. He also ruled over the hospital, thanks to his close friendship with the medic Zemlianskii. The headman would have hardly hurried over there than Zemlianskii would also run into the hospital, always drunk and with bloodshot, swindling eyes on a black, Gypsy-like face. By himself, Zemlianskii was barely able to keep any of the regulation prison alcohol, and he used his funds to buy wine and pass it off as medicine, and I often saw Iukhorev, Bykov, and other Ivan-prisoners fairly tipsy. Among the hospital's Iukhorevian agents was the infirmary attendant Mishka Birkin, nicknamed Astrologer, a young, passionate, unusually dim-witted good-fellow and dandy and former soldier. Incidentally, Birkin clung to me, and was suddenly running up to me ten times a day inside the ward asking some rather scientific question:

"But tell me, Ivan Nikolaevich, is there any end to the stars in Heaven?"

Or:

"Is it possible, Ivan Nikolaevich, to dig through the Earth?"

It was presumably because he was most interested by questions about the universe, stars, etc., that prisoners gave him the comical nickname Astrologer; but when he offered any such questions I well saw that he, like Ogurtsov, was essentially little interested by them, and that while listening to my answer and gazing dim-wittedly into my eyes his thoughts were drifting far away and a phrase about something completely extraneous to astronomy or geology was falling from his lips.

"D'you know what a lie Zemlianskii told today? 'Well, Mishka,' he says: 'I'll wring their necks if any patients come today! I don't got no medicine, but I'm 'fraid to re*rease* them from work!'"

And Mishka, without having finished what he was saying, shot out of the ward like an arrow. He was always hurrying somewhere, always worrying about something, and his ruddy face with tousled mustaches always seemed anxious and agitated about something. Because of this restlessness and fussiness, Birkin also bore the nickname "Postal Hound."

Notwithstanding the fact that Iukhorev not only offhandedly called Mishka the worst and most sinister epithets but often soundly thrashed him, Mishka literally scraped before him, nurturing some purely disinterested and self-sacrificing canine affection.

In the prison, the same sort of devoted dog toward Iukhorev was played by Shmatov (i.e., Buzzy), who, owing to terrible asthma, had been completely freed from labor by the physician and had a bunch of free time for all sorts of slacking, intrigue, and gossip. Six-Eyes nevertheless tried several times to assign him to the shops in the capacity of repairer of prisoners' old shoes, but after two or three days Shmatov left work again and, puffing like a steam engine, began straightaway to loiter idly about the prison, spreading through the wards, kitchen, and hospital all kinds of prison news and *bumó*. Another such herald was the cobbler Zvonarenko (Leather Tack), also a consumptive, loud and unusually cruel of tongue; but he was of independent character: an intransigent unmasker of all kinds of untruths and violations of the collective's interests (though in a moment ready, of course, to grease his own palms at the collective's expense), he poked his nose into everything, discovered "irregular practices" everywhere, and, pacing through the prison, loudly shouted about this in his reedy woman's voice, hacking constantly and wrapping his arms across his sunken chest. In reward for his "love of truth," Zvonarenko often received vicious beatings from prison bigwigs. Before us, he was always fawning and trying to ingratiate himself.

Then a long-awaited new party of sixty-four men appeared. There was unimaginable bustling and noise in the prison; not only Six-Eyes but all the guards were rejoicing and celebrating something. For the newcomers they freed up three of the far wards, removing from them old prisoners, who were distributed among the other six wards. For some reason, they didn't hurry to mix everyone together, and for several days the newcomers lived completely separate lives in a separate corridor, even having their own special headman. I, too, faced the prospect of abandoning my familiar nest and transferring to another ward. Shteinhart suggested that I take advantage of this opportunity by checking into the hospital for a certain time, so that the more nutritious food there would improve my rather broken health. However, the prospect of lying in a dark stuffy infirmary completely full of patients, including those from the newly arrived party infected with typhus, and minute by minute awaiting the deaths of certain of them, did not appeal. We were especially jarred when we learned from Birkin that hospital linen smeared with excrement had lain in the infirmary's storeroom for three whole days. An indignant Shteinhart immediately told the medic it had to be removed instantly. Zemlianskii, for a long time now looking askance at the fact that a "prisoner" was freely entering the pharmacy and dealing with it as he saw fit, very rudely replied:

"When you dig up some more, then I'll order it tossed!"

Shteinhart flew into a rage:

"Kindly clean the storeroom *now*! If you're going to be spreading disease here, I'll complain to the physician about you."

Immediately following this skirmish, though still without knowing of it, I went to ask Zemlianskii to check me into the infirmary. He was in the pharmacy ranting and raving and smashing phials in impotent fury, throwing cotton wadding and paper on the floor.

"Ain't no space in the infirmary!" he curtly spat.

"Not true, Shteinhart says there is."

Zemlianskii's black, thieving eyes, sparkling with a vicious fire, shot in various directions. He seemed to be devising a battle plan.

"Well, there is. And what benefit will you get from this place?" he finally said, trying to be cool. "You'll get better rations, bread 'n' milk, 'n' 'three servings,' all o' good quality. You can prob'ly lie in a bed, if you want, 'n' stand up only to get the ration that's in the prison. The commander gets angry when I prescribe you more'n the three servings I hafta."

Having pulled some sort of answers out of the cupboard, he quickly began enumerating to me all the fiscal means at his disposal, the "second" and "third" portions, etc. These portions, about which the medic, headmen, and hospital cooks continually spoke, were always a stumbling block to my understanding: even Shteinhart did not completely understand the arrangements for their assignment, and so I simply preferred to ask Zemlianskii:

"So, this means if you give me a serving of milk you're afraid of the commandant?"

"Yes, the commander… Whatta terrible business! Shteinhart's pest'rin' me o'er the linen as well… But what can I do, if the leader orders it kept in the storeroom?"

I immediately went to the gates and asked the orderly to tell the commandant I wanted to see him about an important matter. As always, Luchezarov called me into his office without delay. When I reported to him that the medic cited his authority in refusing to remove the typhus patients' excrement and to accept me into the hospital, he flew into a terrible rage and promised that very minute to order an "investigation." Indeed, a clerk from the office appeared in the prison within an hour and, inside the orderly's office, began interrogating, one after another, me, Iukhorev, and several patients who'd been in the infirmary. At this time the clerk posed me a question: had I heard anything about Zemlianskii bringing vodka into the prison or giving Iukhorev the regulation medical alcohol?

It was evident from this question that Six-Eyes already possessed some information about this. Of course, I told him I'd heard nothing. What Iukhorev and the other interrogated prisoners said, I don't know, but about the medic, most said he was carrying out his business outstandingly and that prisoners had no claims whatsoever against him. As such, mine was a solitary complaint and the "investigation" yielded absolutely no beneficial results at all.

But in the meantime, a serious disturbance had begun in the prison. In the kitchen, Iukhorev was giving a whole speech against my comrades and me.

"Here they is, the vaunted do-gooders!" he roared, shaking his powerful head. 'We, yes, *we*!… We's for the people, we hate informants…' But who, you say, informed 'bout the alchohol? Why'd the clerk suddenly shoot at me: 'Is it true, Iukhorev, you're buyin' Zemlianskii's alcohol?' There ain't one honest prisoner who ain't bothered by denunciations… Akh, you mangy sneakers, you scribblers! Now I know your real aim!"

The accusation of sneakiness, even coming from Iukhorevian mouths, was, I confess, like a knife to my heart. Shteinhart was outside the prison visiting one of his many patients, and there was no one to consult with. My spirit had been so sickened during the past days, my nerves so rattled, that under the influence of a bitter feeling of insult I lost my head and did a very stupid thing that could have ended unpleasantly for us in every way: in the heat of indignation, I went to all six wards where the old prisoners were living and invited them to my ward for a meeting "on a very urgent matter." The mare evidently quickly guessed how delicate a topic was to be broached, because most didn't even budge from their spots, and out of seventy men no more than fifteen to twenty gathered… Among them were very few persons who absolutely sympathized with me, yet, by contrast, all of Iukhorev's friends—Bykov, Aziadinov, Shmatov, Birkin, and, in their lead, he himself—had shown up. With an as yet uncooled feeling of indignation, I asked the assembled on what occasion during my several years among them had I given them cause to call me a sneak… I was unable to conclude this little speech because Shmatov, standing on the sleeping platform, began shouting me down:

"They think they can buy us with their tobacco 'n' meat! That we won't dare open our mouths!"

"They bought us! *Ha*!" the lanky Bykov ironically assented. Several other men snorted.

"I tell you right here," Buzzy continued to hiss, "I'll quit smokin' completely, I'll starve to death on Six-Eyes's broth, but on the other hand I'll be a free man… That's that!"

"Shut up, you damn little flea!" Iukhorev, who was favored by all circumstance and wished to maintain civilized forms of debate with me, suddenly stamped his foot at him. He boldly forged ahead. "Lemme say a word to the people first."

"But I'm sayin': I'd rather die!…" Shmatov hissed one more time, pathetically pounding his chest.

"Why're you still both'rin' me?!" Iukhorev, beside himself, shouted and aggressively moved to grab Buzzy by the scruff of his neck. Buzzy scampered somewhere into a corner and shut up.

"I will now speak, ol' men," Iukhorev began, and, I admit, he was at that moment picturesque, proudly drawing himself up in all his enormous height: his dark-complexioned face, as if sculpted from bronze, had been paled by agitation and seemed terrible and majestic; his fierce gray eyes glowered with enmity; his iron arm extended forward—and in this motionless position he vividly reminded me (at the risk of seeming comical, but it was so) of Antokolskii's awe-inspiring statue "Peter the Great"…[40] Against my will, I nearly fell in love with my antagonist.

"I will now speak, ol' men. Ivan Nikolaevich's complainin' I called him a sneak. That's exactly what I called him. Well, how can you think 'n' not say so? Ivan Nikolaevich runs to the com'dant 'n' informs on the medic. 'N' our mare don't adore informin'!"

"Yes, on our brother!" I interrupted, giving him short shrift. "But Zemlianskii is part of the leadership."

"Allow me, Ivan Nikolaevich," Iukhorev magisterially cut me off, "I'm speakin' now… For us, Zemlianskii ain't a commander, but almost, it may said, our brother! We dunno as much as you, but we're completely satisfied with this medic."

"For us prisoners he's a good soul!" Shmatov buzzed.

"That's talkin'!" underscored Bykov.

"Are you not going to say anything bad about this medic?" I asked, gazing around the circle and feeling deeply indignant once more, and noticed certain prisoners squinting their eyes to avoid my look.

"We got various claims 'gainst you by the medic," Iukhorev again began speaking, "'bout this 'n' ever'thin'. You dunno our prisoners' ways. Howe'er, I ain't talkin' 'bout that. It's very nice to hear, o' course, that you didn't inform Six-Eyes 'bout my drinkin', but ne'ertheless I ain't guilty o' slander. At your invitation, a clerk suddenly 'pears in prison, 'n' after first questionin' you he begins askin' ever'one 'bout the alcohol. The case is clear, 'n' anyone would know what to think! 'N' what would the boys say if I explained it any other way. Here's Ivan Nikolaevich, they'd say, who's so indignant at me talkin' 'bout his sneakiness, 'n' he spreads the *bumó* round prison that when Iukhorev goes to the com'dant with a request he tells him things 'bout the prisoners."

"Iukhorev, are you crazy?!"

"Don't get upset. You told Ogurtsov that I asked the com'dant to kick him outta the kitchen 'cause he's lazy 'n' opposes me."

At that moment I felt stunned, deflated. I vaguely recalled that something of the sort had actually happened! Less than six months ago, during one of our conversations in his office, Luchezarov had said:

"Now there are only two real heroes left in the prison—Iukhorev and Ogurtsov. Strictly speaking, they should be assigned to the mine, but they're very necessary in their positions. But, apropos this, what's your opinion of them?"

"Nothing, they seem like nice fellows," I evasively answered.

"I'll tell you candidly, I simply love Iukhorev: what a fine young man to look at! And the rogue's smart. But he's always complaining about Ogurtsov—that he's very lazy and burns things in the kitchen."

I confess that at that time these words did not strike me pleasantly: and up until now, I hadn't imagined that Iukhorev was in a struggle with enemies and not averse to resorting to denunciation. That very same day, Ogurtsov came to me and began complaining that, lately, Six-Eyes was nagging and upbraiding him for laziness and threatening solitary confinement. The chap seemed so deeply distressed and bewildered that I felt my former predisposition toward him and for some reason said:

"I could tell you who's putting you down, but I'm afraid you'll give me away…"

Ogurtsov crossed himself with both hands and swore to God that he'd be as quiet as a grave.

What notion, what intention was communicated to him about my conversation with Luchezarov? Needless to say, it was stupid in the extreme, but sometimes there are insane moments in life, and I told Ogurtsov that it was Iukhorev. I had told him—and now

I understood what unpardonable tactlessness I'd committed, but it was impossible to take back what was said. I had tried to mitigate Iukhorev's guilt, to make it seem like a joke, even saying the brave captain was lying—but Ogurtsov simply repeated:

"No, it ain't no lie… So that's where that bitch has been showin' hisself! I thought so, y'know… Well, I'll be watchin' that crap, 'n' I won't forgive 'im!"

It was left for me to make Ogurtsov once more raise his eyes toward heaven and confirm his solemn oath to be silent and never invoke my name in his arguments with Iukhorev, and I left, still cursing my soul for my outspokenness. So, half a year went by, and I completely forgot about this incident, considering it forever buried.

"Ogurtsov, Ogurtsov, come to this stand-off here!" Bykov, Shmatov, and Iukhorev's other well-wishers shouted at the top of their lungs in savage exultation. Meanwhile, people clambered into the ward in rows.

Someone ran to the kitchen for Ogurtsov. I devised a working plan. The matter was assuming a most hostile form. Of course, I could have said before the entire assembly that I'd never spoken to Ogurtsov, but certain considerations of what were said flashed into my mind with such lightening rapidity that I felt it better not to do so. Indeed, what proofs could I offer? Couldn't Iukhorev and his comrades tell me: "Ah, so you been talkin' to the com'dant 'bout the prisoners? After this, how could you *not* be a sneak?" And what would Luchezarov himself say, if at any time I should tell the mare the words he'd told me in confidence? I therefore awaited Ogurtsov's arrival with understandable apprehension. He did not respond to the summons quickly. Reluctantly, with an unsteady gait, phlegmatic, bloated with fat, in a white kitchen apron and with sleeves rolled up, he entered the ward.

"Ogurtsov, did Ivan Nikolaevich tell you 'bout Iukhorev, that he tattled on you to the com'dant?"

The moment of silence following this question from Bykov seemed to me eternal.

"But why should Ivan Nikolaevich tell me, when I myself know this very well?" Ogurtsov finally sluggishly boomed, eyeing his enemy from head to toe with a hateful gaze.

A weight lifted from my heart: Ogurtsov hadn't given me away!…

"What do *you* know, wolf-face?" Iukhorev came running at him with clenched fists.

"Bitch-face!" responded the young Hercules, for his part getting into his opponent's face. "Don't you know I also got a meaty fist? I'll stick one straight in your belly."

"But didn't you tell Mishka Birkin 'bout Ivan Nikolaevich?" Iukhorev, immediately lowering his tone, backed off to a more comfortable position.

"I said nuthin'."

"Mishka! Hey, Postal Hound!" Iukhorev shouted, looking in all directions like an enraged tiger who's lost its catch.

"Eh-hey!" replied the young man Mishka, already making for the door.

"What'd Ogurtsov tell you?"

"Jus' what you said… that you asked the com'dant for another baker in his place."

"You ain't bein' asked 'bout that, you bastard! That's what I told Ogurtsov to his face… But what'd Nikolaich tell 'im?"

"Maybe you was star-gazin' when I told you 'bout this?" Ogurtsov asked, also approaching Mishka. "Or maybe you wants me to tickle your rib?"

The wretched Astrologer was dangling between two fires; it was clear to me that Ogurtsov had not confided my secret to Birkin but had indeed blathered something to him and that he was now prepared, however, to let loose his terrible fists if only to prove something to my eyes, and that his simpleminded confidant was smiling little at the prospect of those significant fists.

"So'd he tell you 'bout Mikolaich or not?" the no less terrible Iukhorev raged at Birkin.

"Well, you, 'twas a long time ago, Iukhorev… I've forgotten!" and the cowardly Mishka, red as a crab, shut up.

In the blink of an eye Iukhorev's steel hand grabbed him by the scruff of the neck, lifted and shook him a couple times, and tossed him out the door. The mare started laughing, but Iukhorev was swearing furiously. With rapid steps he then came up to me and, extending his hand, said:

"Well, you've reconciled yourself in this case, Nikolaevich. I trusted that bastard, Postal Hound, who jus' has to play decent people off 'gainst one another. I now believe you completely 'n' beg your forgiveness for my slander."

VII. HEROES OF THE NEW GROUP; PRONIA'S DISCOVERY

For a long time after the abovementioned incident I was disturbed by mixed emotions. There was the extremely annoying recognition of the pathetic role that had befallen me, and a no less bitter sense of outrage of unappreciated love for the unfortunate, beaten-down mare, of my sincere readiness to always and in all things fight for its interests. Indeed, it was not easy to reconcile myself to the idea that *I* had had a confrontation with some Ogurtsov or Mishka-the-Astrologer at a capricious moment during which a single word might have put me in an ignoble position! On one side of the scale there was my human dignity, on the other Iukhorev's authority, which I had been forced to await with sinking heart, and which of these two sides would draw the gazes of judging witnesses who would pass upon one of us a sentence of guilty or innocent! In summoning the meeting, I had in my soul's depths evidently calculated that the mare, as one man, would come to my defense and deliver Iukhorev a sharp reprimand for leveling an accusation against me. Nothing like that happened, however. Not a single voice rose on my behalf; out of what I'd expected the sole thing was this—that Ogurtsov decided not to openly betray me. But then, I was rescued by his vengeful hatred toward Iukhorev: yet, were there not that, would this pureblooded representative of the herd, had he considered it necessary to please the chief headman, really have acted so nobly were Iukhorev not there? Who knows?...

That same day, Chirok, who'd not been at the meeting, conspiratorially said to me in the bathhouse where he was washing linen and where I'd happened to wander:

"Mikolaich, we well know that Iukhorev's a throat. 'N' we knows ever'thin', absolutely ever'thin', that he does in the prison 'n' tells to Six-Eyes. But it's jus' absolutely impossible for us to stand up for you."

"Why not?"

"Ech, you're really like a little child! You really dunno prisoners' ways? Y'know we won't survive under the Ivans, 'cause they'll say, 'You was bought with *makhorka* 'n' meat, you mercenary creatures!'..."

I'd been secretly told the same expression by other prisoners from both the old and the new group. Several men from the latter had even attended the meeting. The newcomers, still full of horrible impressions from the march route and also having heard about the sickening food regimes at other mines, were evidently completely bewildered: how was such callous disregard possible toward people the prison was so obligated to?

"Mercy, but you must always pray to God for such peoples, 'n' not for nuthin'... Without a bit o' tobacky they'd go 'bout like dogs from the scurvy alone... But, you show a little help, 'n' our protectors are in a real calamity! E'en on the road we heard enough o' the rumors that've been goin' through here: they ain't people, but *angles* straight outta Heaven! So, don't pity us, sir. Our group's gonna make ever'thin' like new. We'll be your throats, your other Iukhorevs, 'n' we'll barely chirp… You've spoilt 'em too much."

Thus initially spoke the ingratiating tongues of the majority of new arrivals. For a long time I'd not heard such language from the old group's usual types. Shelai's old prisoners, whether "spoiled" by our delicate treatment or "educated" by Six-Eyes's stern regime, carried themselves more proudly and independently, were ambitious in the extreme and prickly about their human dignity in relations with us. Therefore, as soon as the new group, having been distributed among all nine wards, mixed with the old, this independent spirit was communicated to most of the new arrivals…

Six newcomers found themselves among us in the new ward to which Shteinhart and I were transferred. One, the son of some petty official who went by the surname Gribskii, had at one time been a student and came to *katorga* because of false banknotes. In dealing with us he tried, as if from high society, to flash bookish turns of speech, grimaces, and mannerisms, but his extreme boorishness and petty little soul tarnished his superficial polish. The most cherished of this man's notions revolved around the cultivation of his own vulgarity and primitiveness, and among even prisoners he soon earned the cynical nickname "The Amateur." Gribskii so quickly introduced to the ward such a loathsome atmosphere of verbal dissoluteness that, time and again, Shteinhart and I shuddered upon hearing his endless, scabrous anecdotes, his filthy and perverted wittiness. Upon "The Amateur's" first appearance in our ward an assortment of the offended came into existence. One evening, when the population, finding itself under lock and key from evening to morning roll call, was in an extremely placid mood, Shteinhart thought to suggest that it not utter a single swear word. "And whoever commits an offense gets a whacking!" I jokingly added… Contrary to all hopes, the ward enthusiastically accepted the proposal… It must be said that there had been great restraint in language without this, and to the credit of most residents, cynical slurs were resorted to in only the rarest instances. The suggestion was therefore directed primarily at Chirok. He immediately began scratching every inch of his body, since he was always very agitated, and complained:

"Boys, I see how clever you is! Y'know very well I can't live without that word… It's easy for you to give up, but as for me, don't this mean I'll be gettin' a whackin' ev'ry day? No, I don't agree!"

And a forbidden expression immediately let loose from his tongue… Then Elk, Lunkov, Nogaitsev, Iron Cat, Bear's Ears, and others attacked him in a horde and meted out such healthy "whacks" that the ill-fated Chirok bawled in a voice not his own, crossed himself, and swore that he'd be cautious in the future… And, indeed, although he would receive still more whacks, he was from then on as "cautious" as he could be, and our ward became a model of linguistic restraint. On occasion, zealous adherents of morality happened to whack even residents from other wards who came to visit us…

Upon the appearance of the six newcomers, who lacked any kinds of ideas, qualities, or internal motives not entirely familiar to anyone, all this restraint went to ruin. The prison's aboriginals, having not yet been able to get to know their new comrades, not only did not restrain them, but themselves began little by little to be infected anew by their different example: once again, a round of abusive vulgarity dinned, and once again, the moral atmosphere was made stuffy by the unbearable stench. With regard to "The Amateur" Gribskii, he didn't notice that Shteinhart and I were repelled by his company, and time and again he continued to engage us in conversation and, moreover, regarded himself in a most gallant and, in his view, refinedly magisterial fashion. But, one evening, when, having just loudly told one of his innumerable salacious anecdotes, he approached our platform with the most carefree look and posed Shteinhart some question, the latter rose, quivering all over from indignation, and shouted:

"Get away from me… Dare never to speak to me again!"

Not having anticipated such a rebuff, Gribskii backed away. Terribly blanched and shrunken, he suddenly took on a most pathetic appearance.

"Dmitrii Petrovich, just what did I do?" he muttered.

Shteinhart turned his back on him. "Tell you what, Gribskii," Chirok then said, "Mitrii Petrovich 'n' Ivan Mikolaich don't like them strong words. Souls can't bear 'em! But you're so low, brother, that what you like covers my Permian talk in shame, 'n' I'll tell you, you're gettin' dreary at times…"

"You're such an idiot," Elk cut in, neither that seriously nor as ironical as usual. "You need to unnerstand what sort o' prison you've ended up in 'n' what sort o' people you're dealin' with now. You was thinkin' 'this is *katorga*,' but in fact this here's an *inaversity*, 'n' as a student you need to mind yourself, 'n' that's that!"

"Each o' you who bad-mouths your mother gets whacked," Lunkov added with gusto.

"But, fellas, this is a most unpleasin' matter, y'know!" a broad-shouldered peasant, wearing a gloomy expression on a pimply face red as a carrot and with ginger mustaches, who went by the surname Karasev, suddenly jumped from the platform. "I meself don't like the demise of our silly habit… Boys, let's agree on this. Whack the sonofabitch who e'en once invokes his mother or father with a bad word!"

And after this energetic shout he forcefully shot a fist into the air.

"What kasha 'ave you cooked, brother Gribskii?" laughed another prisoner, peacefully lounging on the platform.

He had for a long time been making an extremely unpleasant impression on me, what with his insolent, bright gray eyes, teeth constantly bared like a wolf's and white as elephant tusk, and his entire face dazzlingly white and perfectly plump. Alongside this antipathetic free-and-easy blond, whose surname was Tropin, there was a lean brunet with long mustaches and a sharp, straight nose who ranked fourth among the newcomers; his deep-set dark eyes gazed with a direct and nearly savage look. He was called Shooter; he had till now not uttered a single word.

Gribskii walked over and stood next to our platform, hanging his head and wearing a most guilty look.

"I am… I, like ever'one, gentlemen," he continued to try to expiate himself, "I will never go against the community. I'll even be glad… O' course, our silly habit is a reason for ever'one… Moreover, other true gentlemen are also most very opposed to the strong word… I seen decent society, too… But, if your character is of another sort, please be so kind as to forgive me, I didn't know, y'see …"

The wretched "Amateur" had a very comical, pathetically confused, look.

"This means you won't do it anymore?" Shteinhart sternly asked him.

"I'll let you cut off my tongue!" Gribskii rejoiced. "I'll take a knife, put it in your hand, 'n': 'Cut, Dmitrii Petrovich, I deserve it!'"

"Well, this means we gotta 'ply for a dif'rent ward, 'cause we ain't livin' like sheep!" the lean, gloomy brunet, having arisen from the platform, suddenly angrily said. And, stamping his feet and loudly clanking his shackles, he began pacing back and forth through the ward, twirling one mustache and glowering in our direction with malicious, penetrating looks.

"Ha-ha-ha! Ho-ho-ho! Young man Shooter, splendidly rebuffed, brother!" Tropin spilled over with joyous laughter, wagging his head from side to side and flashing his sharp white teeth.

"You ignorant ducks, wooden ducks!" Karasev—that peasant with a pimply red face who'd earlier proposed an "agreement"—venomously shot at both of them.

For a long time now, I'd noticed that inside this man—whether he was working, relaxing, or talking with someone—there always seemed to be boiling and bubbling a secret dissatisfaction, a hatred toward someone or a grudge against something. He was always grousing at something, cursing the administration, prisoners, even himself. When there were no grounds for carping at something he was stubbornly quiet for whole hours, having morosely knitted his brows, his bloodshot eyes without eyelashes suspiciously casting sideways looks, as if vigilantly anticipating and spotting where to detect even a shadow of an insult or offense against him. Evidently, here was a man from the ranks of those who devour themselves—the dull-witted, pointlessly cruel and peevish who manage to make themselves and all people around them miserable. When Karasev did happen to receive breaks of kindheartedness, there was something unnatural and saccharine in them, and, of course, these breaks were always extremely fleeting and ended by a twofold abusing of cohabitants… Hence, without rhyme or reason, he stood up in defense of decency at that actual moment and angrily turned upon two comrades he declared his opponents.

"What, are you educated?" Tropin laughed even more, placing his impudent face on his elbow. "I'm extremely lit'rate, but until today you've suggested only bitin' into a book what's covered wid tea 'n' sugar! Ain't for nuthin' you're named Karasev: boys, y'knows carp[41] is the dumbest of fish."

Karasev's face turned red.

"But how 'bout your name?" he asked, comically stepping toward his antagonist's platform, quivering with rage and racking his brains for a shattering response. "'Tropin'? What's yours mean?"

"Well, 'Tropin.' But certainly not what 'Karasev' means. Tomorrow, if'n I want, I'll be 'Goodriddance,' but certainly not 'Karasev'!"

Karasev was obviously completely stupefied by his failure to understand this wittiness, and stood for several moments as if out of his head, not knowing what to say. Yet, suddenly, after he gave it some thought, there rolled out such a choice, three-story curse word as rarely came to even the best prison virtuosos! The mare started roaring with laughter as one man; even the gloomy Shooter, who'd been pacing about the ward the whole time, couldn't hold back.

"Ouch, it's the monk! The monk jus' plucked up his courage… Well, one good turn deserves another! Well done!"

Karasev absolutely lost himself.

"But what garbage is he tellin' me?" he said in a hoarse voice, as if trying to vindicate himself. "I can lay down some garbage myself…"

In such way the squabbling between the newcomers went on for a long time, until everyone finally lay down to sleep. I cannot now remember in what connection, but late in the evening Shooter was telling Tropin, lying beside him on the platform, a certain terrible story from his distant past. At first, I couldn't hear this story: it seemed Shooter was telling about his bandits' actions somewhere in southern Russia. Their gang had been captured, and evil peasant-bumpkins had put the three ringleaders including Shooter inside a cold cellar.

"So we're sittin' there, 'member, we're jus' in our blouses, with our hands 'n' feets tied! We look round—darkness, ice. Terrible cold. 'Well, boys, seems we're gonna die,' I says to ever'one. You gonna die—so die! We're huggin' each other, tryin' to sleep; teeth's chatt'rin'. Suddenly, there's fires in the night. We hear lots o' folks runnin'. 'Beat the scoundrels!' Well, 'twas bad. The crowd jumped on us. I'm tellin' you, they thrashed us so's we was barely left alive. But they didn't beat us to death. But whaddya think they did? Tied our hands behind our backs, hung us from a beam, poured a bucket o' water o'er each of us, 'n' left. We was covered in ice…So there we is, like icicles hangin' from the roof in winter… We're hangin' there, my brother, 'n' a day or two slowly passes: they pour water on us then go away. I 'member whole days passed that way…"

"But how was it you didn't die? Brother, you musta caught such a chill?"

"Chill didn't get me there. Three of us lost our voices, 'n' one died soon o' fever. One comrade lost his voice for the rest of his life, but mine came back later."

"So how long did they keep you in that cellar?"

"Just 'bout six weeks."

"You lyin'?"

"Ain't lyin' 'bout nuthin'. Brother, you jus' dunno them bumpkins: no such other barbarians in the world."

But in getting indignant over the barbaric bumpkin-executioners, his listeners apparently never thought to contemplate the storyteller's own barbarisms that had earned him that vicious punishment. I'd long ago become accustomed to such one-sided humanitarianism among my cohabitants; nonetheless, hearing a story in which truth could be sensed drew my attention to Shooter: this man had graduated from a school such as I didn't want to imagine, and inside his soul considerable darkness and hatred and probably an unbendingly strong quality had built up…

With regard to Gribskii, the aforementioned incident for some reason turned out in a most salutary way for him: he not only stopped swearing but somehow generally faded into the ward's background. His earlier role was assumed by Tropin, who was clearly pleased to present Shteinhart and me with possibly greater discomfort. Gribskii had, as it were, merely told filthy anecdotes, but now he tried to amplify them, to adorn, variegate, and savor each one. To snub such a man in the same way Shteinhart had snubbed Gribskii was unthinkable: for this would mean occasioning a huge scandal in which

Tropin's malevolent comrade Shooter would undoubtedly involve himself. Moreover, from their very first days, both cemented a friendship with Iukhorev, and they all spent their free time together inseparably strolling through the prison yard.

On the very day I had reconciled with Iukhorev, the latter rushed in and grandly announced:

"Ivan Nikolaevich! My comrades 'n' I'll take the tobacco 'n' make use o' the meat right now. This is jus' like a pact, 'n' this means the pact's solid."

This was said in an overjoyed tone that communicated to me perfectly that I was being done a great favor... However, at the time I felt that this pact was quite insincere and flimsy, since in a major way it necessitated that Iukhorev mix in a rather skillful maneuver to escape the uneasy, ambiguous situation he'd found himself in during the meeting. The whole clique did indeed immediately start taking our *makhorka* and eating our modest food on fast-days, but the feeling of strain and tension in relations with us didn't end.

There immediately appeared elements among the new group who quickly sniffed it out and concluded a defensive and offensive alliance: their ringleaders were Tropin and Shooter.

The former of this worthy pair deserves to be dwelled upon a bit more. Like Sokoltsev Tropin was a sophist by nature, but a sophist of an entirely different breed, a sophist-tormentor who found the greatest pleasure in the opportunity (if not having the chance to physically torture someone) to shred someone's soul, to strip away someone's nerve-fibers, and, finally, to blaspheme and scoff at everything acknowledged as sacred. A desperate chatterer, he orated for whole evenings on, for example, the theme that honor is nonsense and utter hypocrisy, that all who promote it are, if not obtuse fools like peasants, then first-rate scoundrels and good-for-nothings in the depths of their souls, or rich people living off others, off others' sweat and labor. Having read some novel somewhere on the life of the Jesuits, Tropin now proselytized erecting such a monastic order, which would spread its web all over Russia and become invincibly strong. The muddle of ideas in these wild dreams was extreme!

Entering into some argument with Tropin was absolutely pointless, since everything said by him was said intemperately, out of a desire to tease Shteinhart and me out of ourselves. Shteinhart was actually sometimes patient and grappled with and tried to shame and reason with him. But this only further inflamed the shameless man, and in opposing him I preferred to use murderous contempt.

But what—the reader may ask—strictly speaking, was the reason for his hatred toward us, toward people from whom he enjoyed material benefits and before whom, it should seem, his worthless, petty nature ought to have cringed and ingratiated itself? I think there was only one reason—among those prisoners of the "enlightenment" a consuming boredom, a terrible irritation toward the model *katorga* prison, had for a long time now been popular. Almost every day he pestered—not less than Shteinhart and me—the brave captain to transfer him to another mine. Also, he lodged these requests in the most carefree and even brazen way, assuming, however, an appearance half nitwit and half youngster and, as such, leaving himself a loophole from punishment for cheekiness.

"Mister Com'dant," he began one such routine, "my nose is disappearin'."

"What?" the magnificent captain lowered his head in surprise.

"I got syph'lis, y'know, 'n' it's a very strong syph'lis: I might infect all the prisoners here, prob'ly e'en the guards. Ever'day a pustule breaks out in one or another spot."

"So apply to the medic for hospital!"

"Medic says he don't got beds for such patients. But I'm tellin' you the truth, Mister Com'dant, my nose is gonna disappear soon…"

"What the hell, lad! Am I to put another nose on you? Why are you poking your nose at me?"

And, wrinkling his own olfactory organ in disgust, Luchezarov flew like a bomb out of the ward and into the corridor. Tropin, flashing his teeth impudently, approached our platform and, paying no attention to what we had one time told him about not wanting any dealings with him, began to inform my comrade about his illness. Despite all his enmity for us, he did not stop being formally courteous and did not address us otherwise than with the formal "you" and such formulas as "Ivan Nikolaevich, "Dmitrii Petrovich," and "Mister Shtengor."

"Mister Shtengor, I read somewhere—I dunno if it's true or not—that at the present time two-thirds o' the human race is infected with syph'lis, 'n' it'd be best if the remaining third can get infected soon. Then the illness would end itself. I ain't only suggestin' there's nuthin' to be ashamed of 'bout this illness, but that we should be proud of it."

The previous life of Tropin, a twenty-year-old penal laborer (a recidivist and, it seems, officially recognized under that pseudonym[42]), was in prisoners' terms not serious. He began his prison career in the capacity of a most average petty thief from among those young "toughs" as are especially known in the city of Nikolaev,[43] his birthplace. I don't know where he learned to read or where he came by those bookish summits, by the knowledge of which he undoubtedly surpassed the majority of Shelai's residents. If among us there were people who'd read no less than he and had even completed grammar and high school, then Tropin, being inferior to them in purely superficial polish and by his rudeness sooner resembling a boorish commoner, was nonetheless above them all in a versatile, cynically resourceful native intelligence that was steeped in all sorts of sophisticated venom. Of all the various riff-raff I saw in the outcasts' world he was perhaps the sterling example, concerning which I'd be hard-pressed to say: did he have in the innermost depths of his soul, in those depths hardly known to the possessor himself, something nonetheless cherished and sacred? Semënov, for example, had a most highly developed sense of some particular, gloomy, and probably even terrible human dignity, a sense of the peculiar prisoners' honor and comradeship; something of the sort was undoubtedly in Iukhorev, Sokoltsev, and other major representatives of *katorga*'s world; but it seems to me that Tropin possessed nothing save naked, openly cynical egoism, for whose satisfaction he would probably have not forsaken any foulness or evil deed. All the same, it should be added that in spite of all his ease and cheekiness, he made the impression of being a terrible coward capable of whining and crying because of a cut finger. I have already recalled how, conducting himself cheekily and sometimes outright impudently with the guards and Six-Eyes himself, and often even landing in a dark isolator, he nevertheless never crossed the boundary to commit what would have been an obvious crime. He likely curbed those very policies at will so that he didn't proceed, like other prisoners, heedless of consequences, but accomplished secret tricks out of sight or through petty accomplices, always leaving himself a catch-release to safety. Not hiding from comrades, Tropin himself loudly told us with cynical sarcasm that what he feared most of all in the world was the noose!... At the height of my war with Iukhorev, I could be intrigued and even carried away by this man, such was his power; but not once during all of our acquaintanceship, nor even during a single brief moment, did Tropin manage to inspire in me the smallest feeling of sympathy or accord, and I fear that in painting my portrait of this youth I've layered on some rather dark colors... Who knows, maybe I'm to blame for a lack of insight and consideration on my part? Maybe another, more indulgent and impartial, observer would have been able to discover in Tropin the holy spark without which it is somehow difficult to imagine an intelligent being—a human... But I'm simply writing what I myself saw and felt.

Mishka-the-Astrologer did not give up, and after the above-related incident he cringed before me. One of his weaknesses, among others, was learning odd foreign words that he could flaunt before the herd, and time and again he'd approach Shteinhart or me with questions.

"Well, now, Ivan Nikolaevich, I already know that I'm a *gallant* 'n' *intelligent* man, an *individual*, a *liberal*, a *cosmopolitan*, 'n' a *professional astronomer*... But explain to me: what is this 'inishtiv'?"

And, having barely satisfied his curiosity, he'd hurry off somewhere on a pressing errand.

"Oh, you Postal Hound!" prisoners would say after him.

But once, having in this manner circled several times around Shteinhart, who was strolling through the prison yard, he came up to us and asked with his usual carefree look:

"Please tell me, Dmitrii Petrovich, what's *morphine* for?"

Shteinhart explained. He then became curious to know what opium, atropine, and other variations of these poisons do to a person. Shteinhart immediately became guarded: all these poisons were in the prison pharmacy and, moreover, in posing these questions Mishka was, contrary to usual, acting very nervous. The young doctor suddenly had a disturbing suspicion and began sternly interrogating Birkin about the reasons for his curiosity. Birkin completely lost his wits and—to use a prisoners' expression—began wagging his tail in all directions. Shteinhart, for his part, adopted an even stricter tone and finally forced from Mishka the following confession:

"I'm 'fraid, Dmitrii Petrovich, that I couldn't keep outta trouble... I need to stop bein' a hospital attendant 'cause they're threatenin' to beat me."

"Who's threatening to beat you?"

"Our Ivans... They've forged a key to the pharmacy 'n' they want me to go there at night 'n' take these very poisons."

"Aha, that's it. Those scoundrels! Only, you know what, Birkin? If you don't fulfill their request they'll only beat you a little, and maybe not beat you at all. The prison here is not so... Well, but if you do fulfill it you won't escape the gallows or a new, stiffer *katorga* term, you know. Aren't you to be released to settlement in four months?"

Mishka paled.

"Please tell me, what do I do?"

"Tell them there's none of those poisons in the pharmacy."

"Impossible. Tropin himself saw a death's head in the cabinets. He goes to the medic almost ev'ry day for treatment."

"Here's what: I'll give you some magnesium or some other kind of rubbish, but you tell them it's the poison. Their tongues won't know the difference, those villains!"

Mishka was clearly overjoyed by this plan, and having thanked Shteinhart for his advice, he whirled quickly away.

But Shteinhart remained pensive. He talked for a long time with Bashurov and me, but we were unable to reach a life-saving decision. Informing Six-Eyes of the prisoners' stupid venture did not, of course, enter our heads; and it would have been foolish to recommend caution to Zemlianskii, who had so befriended Iukhorev that, when all was said and done, he would have personally given him anything he asked for, especially when drunk. I advised my comrade to check at the first convenient opportunity the number of poisons in the pharmacy and then watch not only Birkin but Zemlianskii. However, such an accounting could not be managed soon.

Almost the same day as our talk with Mishka-the-Astrologer Tropin approached Shteinhart in front of the entire ward and asked, with his usual carefree smile:

"Dmitrii Petrovich, tell me, please, is this atropine a joke? Is it true, what I read in some book, that such a poison exists?"

Shteinhart steadily looked him in the eye and measured out his words:

"Actually, it *is* a joke. The word's first letter, *a*, is a Greek particle designating negation: it's saying it's unnecessary… And it follows that *atropine* means 'that about which it's unnecessary for *Tropin* to know!' There you have it."

Tropin chuckled gleefully: he seemed terribly pleased by the witty joke.

"But why do these rascals need poison?" the put-out Shteinhart kept assaying me during those days.

"Well, I perfectly understand why," I explained, "I've happened to hear them talk in this regard many times. The poison is a refined, quality poison—the sort of alchemical philosopher's stone that these Tropins, Iukhorevs, and Sokoltsevs are always dreaming of. Possessing such a weapon, they believe they'll be able to murder and rob with complete impunity and without retribution."

"So, you think they want to get it now for exploits on the outside, but not in prison?"

"I almost believe this. They're stockpiling for a distant future. But, then again, why distant? Iukhorev is to be released to the free command in a few days."

During their long strolls through the prison yard together Iukhorev, Tropin, Shooter, and others had secret conversations daily. Sometimes included in this secret society was Shmatov-Buzzy. Iukhorev was indeed soon to leave for the free command, and as was necessary he hastened to give his students lessons from his lengthy swindling experience. One beautiful evening, his name was read from a list of those released to live outside the prison; he grabbed his things and instantly left through the gates. I confess I heaved an unconcealed sigh of relief, thinking that none of the other prisoners could so skillfully manage to lord it over the mare, finance officer, medic, and Six-Eyes himself.

It was already the middle of summer.

A pleasing quiet entered the prison, a relief after all the past excitement. All that time prisoners were making fun of Shmatov-Buzzy, who'd gotten it into his ear to fall in love with one of the female-convict sylphs and was constantly hovering around the gates in the secret hope of catching sight of his passion. The guards at first suspected Shmatov of some underhanded plans and intentions, but hearing the mare constantly laughing at Buzzy, they soon fell in with the general tone.

"Buzzy, oh Buzzy? Is she blowin' you off?" they'd say. "I say, the sands'll soon be fallin' from you…"

"Go shave yer beard, stupid—you'll look younger!"

"Well, whattabout our Buzzy, boys! A lover, in a word…"

Then, one beautiful morning, the whole prison was thus rolling with laughter: Buzzy had actually shaved his beard and, having twisted his long mustaches, was pacing back and forth through the yard so much like a youngster that it was as if he were no more than twenty years old… Every time, as soon as the gates opened and the domestic workers, fulfilling oxen's duties, went for barrels of water, Buzzy would voluntarily harness himself to the wagon with them so that, perchance encountering her somewhere beyond the fence, he might gaze upon his beauty with his own eyes. True, he himself said nothing about this, but his sickly plump face—with its bared rotten teeth and huge nose wheezing no less than a boiler-engine—smiled so blissfully in place of his cunning smile that prisoners split their sides in a fit of hilarity. From time to time Shmatov simply hummed:

"I s'pose yer envious, scoundrels?"

"But if'n she brings you a note, how you gonna read it, Buzzy?"

"I hope it'll get read out loud."

"Sonsabitches'll mess it up, y'know!"

For a long time not only his prisoner-comrades but the guards, having heard no less than they and also having found a pretext to scoff, did not as such give Shmatov a break. Only Pronia-the-Living-Dead, silent, pedantic, and mistrustful, who had been carrying out his prison duties just like a mannequin, doing everything "according to regulations," presented the only exclusion. He didn't laugh like the others at Shmatov, and more than once I noticed, going into the kitchen for hot water, how he, having settled himself on the prison's main porch, would watch from the side Buzzy strolling along the prison's facade and would, at that moment, somehow especially sharpen his lynx's ears and eyes regardless of the fact that Buzzy, for his part, was trying with all his might to ingratiate himself and constantly saying:

"Prokopii Filippovich, but certainly our com'dant'll soon become a lieutenant-colonel?"

Or:

"But, Prokopii Filippovich, shouldn't you be gettin' a raise? I heard you're fifty years old 'n' will be finishin' in a few days?"

But the exemplary guard's smooth-shaven, thinly pale face twitched not a muscle. He would answer monosyllabically with words of no significance, and continue his suspicious observations unnoticed by anyone. But here came Buzzy, having strolled back and forth several times with hands clasped behind his back, and with quick movements turning and disappearing behind a corner of the prison. What was special about this, it seems?

The man got bored going to the same spot, so he left. But the immobility of the commodore's statue instantly disappeared from Pronia and, as if shot from a bow, he flew to the opposite corner of the prison as if wanting to run in a circle for exercise.

This *katorga* Lecoq's[44] searches and surveillance did not prove fruitless, and during one deathly still post-lunch time when most prisoners, taking advantage of the short break, had fallen into a heroic sleep, Pronia-the-Living-Dead made an important discovery that fomented a terrible commotion in the prison. Having pulled up the boards on one side of the prison porch, he found beneath them an entire cache of things: a bunch of hospital linen, prisoners' footwear, blouses, mittens, etc. Moreover: upon his giving the signal immediately after this, and as a bunch of prisoners including Buzzy exited the prison gates to water cabbages in the garden, some of the same hospital linen was found in a bed, having evidently only just been buried there.

The brave captain himself immediately appeared in the prison, almost bursting from the irate flow of blood to his face, and, seeing the porch with its secret cache, ordered a general search of all the wards to be conducted in his presence. This search did not, however, yield any new discoveries.

"I know those who are most guilty!" shouted Six-Eyes, threatening to manacle and haul them before the court. "No, the court's not enough, I'll kill them and not answer for it!"

Yet he obviously did not in fact know who was responsible, and this time had learned from earlier unfortunate experiences to not be led by pure suspicion. This was why even Shmatov, whom Pronia saw running from the porch, was not arrested, and reprisals regarding the prison were limited to the duty officer again putting the wards under strict lock and key and allowing no one out except for extreme necessity. Concerning Pronia, instead of receiving the anticipated praise and incentives, he got a severe reprimand:

"Ah, you idiot! An ambush needed to be designed to catch these prisoners red-handed." And Luchezarov turned his back on the exemplary guard.

We even listened through the kitchen's open window to him threatening to drag the medic Zemlianskii to court. But nothing came of this threat, since the medic brought to his defense some fact casting blame on the finance officer, though the latter also somehow twisted things and so the case of the stolen linen finally died away.

The only clear fact of Pronia's discovery was that, on that same day, the hand of Buzzy's "love" was taken… He ceased wandering beneath the prison gates and voluntarily harnessing himself to the water-wagon, stopped dressing the fop and smugly flashing his teeth, by them giving one to understand how adroitly he'd been leading not just guards but his prisoner-cohabitants by the nose.

"Ay, that Buzz-man!" said the latter, sagely shaking their heads.

It was also said in secret (and, of course, not without foundation) that the cache of stolen things belonged, in essence, to Iukhorev, and that Shmatov had been no more than his subordinate agent. After the chief-of-comradeship's exit to the free command, Buzzy seems to have liquidated his items and was already managing to transport so many things beyond the prison gates that Pronia's discovery seized only some pitiful remains of greatness.

VIII. THE MISUNDERSTANDINGS CONTINUE; SIX-EYES'S INTERVENTION

Having ended up in the free command, Iukhorev immediately lost importance and charm and turned into a most average prisoner. He very soon squandered on *katorga* sweeties the money he'd made in prison, and now had to perform dirty work on the same level as all of the free command. Of course, he could have seen his brief term through and left for settlement had there not been a misfortune, had he not gotten "tangled up" with Mariushka, one of the housemaids of the brave captain. The mare said (it knew everything) that, for his part, he himself was not indifferent to the robust, rosy-cheeked convict, and dressed her up like a "lady"; that, apropos Mariushka, she was, needless to say, ready to accept clothes from anyone you like and not averse to devoting her attentions to anyone you like, though her female heart could not resist the dashingly twisted mustaches of such a young man as Iukhorev, regardless of his forty years; furthermore, he was "her brother," a prisoner. Iukhorev got into the habit of visiting Mariushka, and as soon as Luchezarov left for somewhere, he raised hell in the house with guitar playing, rollicking songs, and all other kinds of joys. Having several times caught Iukhorev in his kitchen, the brave captain discontentedly wrinkled his nose and sternly instructed his former favorite to busy himself in the barracks with his own affairs. Snapping to attention like a soldier, Iukhorev would answer: "I'm listenin'!" He'd go and, taking advantage of the commandant's next absence, turn up in his kitchen again. Finally, Six-Eyes banned him from showing up there by threatening to return him to the prison.

One night, Luchezarov returned unexpectedly from the works (from which he'd not been expected until the following evening), soundlessly approached his house, and, after dismissing the guards, went straight to his kitchen. As usual, bedlam was going on there. Hearing the familiar footsteps, Iukhorev tried to hide in the cellar, but was too late: the magnificent Luchezarov was already standing face-to-face before him with angrily flared cheeks and nostrils.

"Take this artist to the prison immediately!" he ordered, sententiously yet impressively, and as if from beneath the ground two hefty guards arose ready to execute his instructions.

"Whate'er for, Mister Com'dant?" beseeched Iukhorev.

"For many, many things you yourself know, boy-o."

"Seems I do mine 'n' e'en others' job, 'n' so what if I liven up my evenin's…"

"I'll liven you up! You've instituted a den of debauchery in my home… You're leading my servant astray… And I also know all about your tricks in the prison… But up to now I've covered for you, been predisposed toward you… Yet this is how you repay my kindness!

You're now going to rot in prison! No matter that your sentence ends in a few days—I can send you to *katorga* again."

As such, Iukhorev hadn't lasted a month in the free command. This time, he ended up in my ward. When, late at night, the lock growled and the door opened, I was imagining that someone was coming to summon Shteinhart to one of his many patients, and I could hardly believe my eyes upon seeing Iukhorev with his things. Many of the prisoners also awoke and stirred; questionings and stories began, with the usual curses against the law, faith, God, and Six-Eyes especially.

"Well, now he'll drive me off the rails 'membrin' Mariushka!" said Iukhorev, stretching out to sleep.

Indeed, Iukhorev was brought to the mine the next day because it so happened that Luchezarov had asked Monakhov and Petushkov to assign him the most difficult labor. But Six-Eyes was not master inside the mine, and they gave Iukhorev the very same as what the rest of the prisoners were doing. Given his iron muscles, it cost him no great difficulty to bore a full quota, and he warmed himself in the sunshine for a long time, lying on a slag-heap bantering with Cossack guards, nearly all of whom he'd enjoyed relations with during his brief sojourn in freedom.

His friendly walks and conversations in the prison yard with Tropin, Shooter, Bykov, and Shmatov resumed. Regardless of the fact that he was now lacking any official power or authority, his previous importance still told on everything in the prison. He gave the impression of a dethroned king who had descended into the mass of his former underlings, and they all continued to fear him and experience his former charm. When Iukhorev wanted, he really could be extremely charming. I vividly recall one scene. It was an ugly, cold morning. Having summoned prisoners for roll call in the corridor, one of the most unpopular guards, the one they called Snake Head, strode back and forth in front of the rows without hurrying to count us, cheerfully gossiping with another orderly about something.

"We gonna be standin' here long?" Iukhorev's courageous voice at last broke from the silent mare's ranks.

"But, howe'er long we want," Snake Head rudely responded. "Who's flappin' his lips there?"

"Though he's a convict, it's a *man* who's flappin' his lips!" Iukhorev fired back with the same authoritative voice. "'N' allow me to note, Vasilii Andreevich, that you can't make us stand here accordin' to your wishes if they ain't legal but is simply capricious."

"You've taken it into your head to spar with me?"

"I taken it 'n' am *still* takin' it."

"I'll send you to the isolator."

"Send me. You don't frighten me with your isolator, but, afterwards, the prisoners'll know for sure what you is!"

A profound silence permeated the corridor; everyone expected that immediately after this, Iukhorev would be hauled into seclusion. Snake Head's face changed several times from white to red, a series of tics spread here and there, he jangled his keys and suddenly called in a shrill voice for prayers. During this entire scene I unwillingly fell in love with Iukhorev, who'd stood immobile as a statue, face expressing neither fear nor anger nor the satisfaction of his victory. Roll call ended and he went with the same external indifference to the ward, saying not a word to anyone, and threw himself on his bedding intending to sleep a bit more. And within a minute he was indeed sleeping and snoring like a lord.

Absolutely no relations whatsoever had existed between Iukhorev and me since his return to prison. Although we'd parted on superficially friendly terms before he left for the free command, now, by some silent consent, it was established that we did not acknowledge each other's presence in the ward. But from time to time it seemed to me that he, who despite sometimes not being averse to rich expressions had not loved cynicism just for cynicism's sake, was now occasionally reciting filthy couplets and songs with intent. Yet he also sometimes sang marvelous, intimate tunes (a native of Saratov, he knew the old Russian songs better than anyone in the prison), and I, hearing these heartfelt sounds, wanted at the time to go to him and, taking his hand, say in a voice moved by emotion:

"Iukhorev, why do you put on an act? Don't you know you're not as bad a man as you want to appear? We should sincerely reconcile for good!"

But just as the final chord died away—voicing a heartfelt poetic complaint that fate and cruel people had destroyed the life of a kind young man and severed him from his homeland and a young woman's sweet heart—than an exceedingly obscene, shamelessly lewd, refrain—forbidden fruit from the latest common culture fantasy—came spewing out of Iukhorev's mouth… The charm fluttered off: and, once again, I saw before me a bitter, narcissistic, depraved man for whom no object, no home, no *foi*, no *loi* was sacred.

One Sunday, I was standing with my two comrades in a side corridor of the prison, talking about something in an undertone. Our conversation was brief, and when it ended Shteinhart and I left for the hospital, but Bashurov opened the door to the main corridor. In doing so, he noticed someone quickly jump back from the door and hurry away; yet Valerian had recognized Karasev, that mistrusting self-devourer who lived in my ward. Perhaps he was not trying to eavesdrop at all but had found himself near the door by accident, yet, Bashurov being for his part mistrusting, reproachfully called to him:

"Karasev, this isn't good, you know!"

"What ain't good?" asked Karasev, blushing red.

"Putting your ear to the door."

It is difficult to describe what happened after these words. Returning from the hospital to our ward, Shteinhart and I happened upon the following scene in the corridor: a whole crowd of prisoners had surrounded Bashurov and Karasev and the latter, with foam at the mouth, bloodshot eyes, and spasmodically clenching fists, had backed into a corner a stunned and confused Valerian who did not know what to do or say.

"What right you got to tell me what's right?" shouted Karasev. "I'm a passin' bitch to you? But mebbe I'm e'en better'n you? Mebbe I should show yer fibbin' 'bout me? Yer sayin': 'that ain't right'? I go past the door, so this means I don't dare go past you? You all accused Iukhorev of havin' great power o'er the prison. But who's put 'im in prison now? We know very well who. You yerselves wanna take power!"

This disconnectedly absurd litany of accusations met with a profoundly approving grumble from the pressing crowd. Iukhorev himself was standing off to the side with an alarmed look; in front of him, Shmatov-Buzzy was pathetically wringing his hands and loudly buzzing about something. Bykov, having emerged from the crowd with his white skeleton's face, was also telling some story in his snarling bass.

"He reproached me with his bread… We was borin' in the gal'ry… He got his auger stuck 'n' calls me to pull it out 'n' fix it. I coulda told him—why don't *you* pull it out? But I weren't wishin' 'im any ill, 'n' I just say: 'Whoa! I still ain't finished my quota…' But he suddenly blurts out: 'You're forgettin' our bread 'n' salt!' So, that's how they is, boys!"

As the last words of this Bykovian story reached my ears, I suddenly realized that his speech was about no one else but *me*. But how this vain and stubborn man was distorting and altering what was in fact the case! Here is what had happened. Bykov and I were boring in the gallery and, seeing that I was sitting down, resting and not doing anything, he asked me to fetch some new candles from the watch house. I gladly carried out this request. When, after several minutes, I in my turn appealed to him for a favor, he gave me his phrase "I still ain't finished my quota" and I, in response, jokingly said: "Aha! Is the old man forgetting his bread 'n' salt?"—by which I meant the bread 'n' salt simply to be, of course, my going for the candles… At that time, it never entered my head that my comment might somehow have offended Bykov; I hadn't even noticed he was sulking… But it now turned out I'd caused the man grave injury, and the innocent occurrence was taking on the quality of one of my many crimes against the suspicious mare's pride…

However, I limited myself to a rebuttal for now:

"You so misunderstood me, Bykov!"—and I hurried over to Karasev. Up to now, I had still been on sufficiently friendly terms with the latter. Having quickly sized up this mistrusting, sickeningly ambitious character, I had during our arguments overcome his reserve and intractability and he clearly regarded me with respect. Having just seen him lay hands on my comrade, I sympathetically began asking Karasev what happened. Before me, he once more spilled out his whole litany of accusations and reproaches. I tried to calm him, explaining Valerian's words as being a simple misunderstanding for which, of course, he would not hesitate to apologize. For a long time still, Karasev continued spitting, repeating himself, and shouting, but he had already clearly relaxed; the appearance of the guard occasioned a joke, and little by little the mare broke up.

Nevertheless, the episode proved far from over, such that the electricity in the air was enough for the leaders to try to discharge it. And, indeed, toward evening a huge assembly formed in the kitchen. We, of course, could not attend it, but our secret friends like Ogurtsov and the "educated gallant" and spy-by-profession Mishka Birkin, soon passed on all the details to us. Iukhorev suggested informing Six-Eyes that the prison did not want to eat the food forbidden during fasts; he was supported by Bykov, Shmatov, Tropin, Shooter, and others. Elk—whom I would have degraded by telling anyone that, if he wanted to, he could lead him, Elk, with a rope—unexpectedly sided with us completely. With his bloodshot eyes, Karasev appeared again, shouting out once more all the details of his squabble with Bashurov. Such long-forgotten, precise, and nearly imperceptible insults swam to the surface that, in another time and according to different values, one might have heartily laughed having heard them. But there was no laughter now. Now, this absurd incident filled all three of us with bitterness and profound irritation. Akh, you nitwits, you nitwits! You are thirty- and forty-year-old brutish children, misunderstanding who your true friends and enemies are, and ready to tear to pieces those who sincerely wish you well and to embrace those who in actual fact can betray and destroy you!

The assembly, however, did not take up the heroic resolution Iukhorev put before his comrades. Even many of the ringleaders were more willing to shout and wave their arms than to make complaints in their own interest; energetically joining in the indignant noise and uproar, the majority followed the leaders when they tried to formulate their complaints. But this was insufficient. A man from whom it seemed heroism could be expected least of all, but who was nevertheless openly and loudly standing up against everyone, found himself comically declaiming with inimitable sincerity:

"I disagree! You're makin' up 'n' writin' a protocol: 'n' I disagree!"

This was none other than Lunkov. Weak and puny beneath the threats that were threatening him, he did not stop shouting:

"You don't got my agreement! The ol' men wanna catch you out! Ain't nuthin' for them, these throats 'n' snorters, to refuse meat 'n' tobacco, 'cause they'll find ever'thin', but we'll be left stupidly starvin'... 'n' I don't see any fault in Ivan Nikolaich, 'Mitre Petrovich, 'n' Valerian Mikhalych, 'cept for one fault, that they spend too much attention on us: 'Eat, dearies, drink!' I fault Ivan Nikolaich for this. If'n I were in their place..."

Lunkov was grabbed by the throat and tossed out the kitchen door; but the prisoners' Sejm[45] had been spoiled nonetheless. Lunkov's speech made such an impression among most of the mare—perhaps because it simply was tired from the fruitless shouting and uproar—that the kitchen quickly emptied and a significant portion of the loudmouths dispersed among the wards. Afterward, when Iukhorev and Tropin began to tot up and gather those who agreed to tell Six-Eyes about the food, they counted all of eight men... Of course, it was impossible to stand before the entire prison with this number, and the gang simply decided to cook fasting food for themselves in a separate cauldron. Our friend Karpushka Lipatov had in some way wormed his way into the protestors' group. During all the next day, a day off from work, having rakishly cocked his cap and somehow thrusting forward his knees especially heroically, he paced the prison yard, but when he encountered any one of us three, he shot us murderous looks and sardonic laughs. But when yet another day passed (the first fast day since the meeting) and we'd not paid him the slightest attention, he approached and said:

"So, what'll it be, gentlemen... Karpushka Lipatov's goin' 'bout with an empty stomach 'n' you don't give a damn! Wouldn't it be better for youse to take me into your gang again? Gimme another pound o' tobacky, 'n' I'll prob'ly be ready to eat some more o' yer vittles... I don't hold a grudge, y'know... But, y'know, I'm hurt, gentlemen, so hurt that you won't e'en talk to me!"

"In what is your grievance, Karpushka?"

"In the gentlemen dokhtur, in 'Mitre Petrovich, that's where! I'm askin' 'im for real *khananiia*, 'cause they're stuffin' my trap with more 'n' more *kalidat.* They're sayin' it ain't *kalidat.* But I knows full well the medic Zemlianskii's feedin' it to me—ya can't fool Karpushka, brother, so don't e'en try!"

"Well, good health to you, and see you later."

"No, stop, gentlemen... I came to make peace with you. I wanna eat that meat o' yours again..."

"You'll be in terrible debt to us for it!"

"Yes, I'll be in debt! 'Cause the meat's very useful for my sickness. It'll prob'ly be better'n any *khananiia*!"

That same day, Karpushka explained to everyone that he was ending his protest. As for the other seven men, they were preparing fasting food, they told Lunkov, only for show; separated from it, they ate meat in enormous quantities, drank milk, and, as if celebrating some victory, even acquired vodka from God knows where… Bashurov proposed to temporarily eliminate, at one's volition, any emoluments to the community pot, and to watch what the mare would do if, to show our complete indifference to its stupid capriciousness, we stopped "spoiling" it; but Shteinhart energetically opposed this plan, and we decided that if we did not at all change any of our behavior and each maintained our earlier approach, then this more than anything would demonstrate our indifference. All the same, when Saturday came and I distributed, as usual, the *makhorka* among the wards, we were all extremely surprised that not just the prison "Ivans" but a total of forty men, that is, nearly a third of the prison, did not accept their portions… What explained this strange occurrence? How had our number of malcontents grown so quickly? Did the tobacco simply offend the eye, or were there critical obstacles to accepting better food? Except for the initial group of disgruntled ringleaders, among those refusing the *makhorka* were those like Sokoltsev, Iron Cat, Zvonarenko, Mishka Birkin, the Tatar Ravilov, and many others who, until now, had been amicable toward us. With each day the obscure fermentation in the prison did not end, but clearly strengthened and grew. Several times a day, guards were dispersing groups of prisoners that gathered here and there. Vague rumors came to us from friends about what was being said in the gatherings, that, in general, powerful motions on our behalf were being noticed. Certain leaders were apparently now tired of the disturbances and others had fallen out with each other. Behind the alliances inconceivable intrigues, gossip, and conspiracies were somehow taking place: today, Iukhorev was being cursed and blamed for everything, tomorrow, by contrast, it was being asserted that Iukhorev had long ago washed his hands of everything and that only Tropin, who wanted to rule the prison, was messing things up. Dull-witted Zhebreek, adopting a heroic pose in the middle of the ward and openly referring to Shteinhart, prophesized that all the world's evil came from "dokhturniks," and if they were all burned at once many of the world's poor people would breathe easier… Karasev was at the same time shouting that he could slander Elk, who had somehow offended him… In a word, nothing that was going on in this circle or what these people ultimately wanted was making sense!

Meanwhile, another two fast days passed and the prison, as if it were nothing, continued to eat the tasty forbidden skilly; we guiltlessly decided not to approach the fasting clique of protestors, whose own means were moreover being exhausted. Then came ingratiating overtures towards us on the part of those same persons who had initiated the unrest. Tropin first of all began cheerfully flashing his teeth and speaking amicably, first with me and then with Shteinhart; Karasev and Bykov suddenly became astonishingly affectionate and pliable; Elk tried several times to engage me in friendly conversation:

"What'd I do? I ain't done nuthin'… all them others was the malcontents…"

"But, Petin, why did you torment Shteinhart with the augers? Was it necessary on those days to keep sending him to the smithy out of anger?"

Petin blushed and protested.

Regarding Iukhorev, during these latter days he actually had the appearance of a man fatigued and interested by nothing of prison life.

All this confusion would probably have lasted much longer and produced no definite results whatsoever, had the strong arm of Six-Eyes not finally interfered in the matter. By some path, he'd received information about the disorder in the prison, and he immediately summoned the collective's new headman, a secretive yokel and true politician, who as such had at some point during recitation of Pushkin's *Boris Godunov* received from the mare the nickname Godunov.[46] The latter was trying to plead ignorance. Then the brave captain shouted at him:

"Don't you dare evade me! I've heard there's some mess going on with the rations?"

Godunov cowered.

"Yes, that's right, Mister Com'dant… On Wednesdays 'n' Fridays the noodles is bein' made with meat… So it don't taste good to many…"

"The noodle soup's not tasty? Have you lost your mind? No, you're confusing, hiding, something, boy."

Suddenly an explanation dawned in Luchezarov's head:

"Aha, I understand! It's likely that religious sentiments are being offended… Yes, yes, this is very possible! Why didn't I think of this before! In such a case there will be a strict prohibition on emoluments during fast days."

Godunov did not personally belong to the protestors, and therefore began passionately refuting the commandant's assumption. For a long time, the latter meditatively nodded his head.

"So, here's what, boy," he finally decided, "go to the prison right now, and I'll give you my answer at evening roll call: if even just five men can be found who want to observe the fasts, I'll immediately cancel any emoluments."

With this sensational news Godunov, profoundly agitated, ran to the prison and instantly called a meeting in the kitchen.

"See what your capers have got to!" the mare shouted, falling on the Ivans.

"Whose capers? Ever'one was in support, y'know, weren't jus' us…"

There began, as always, a fruitless to-and-fro in which Tropin heaped blame on Karasev, Karasev on Iukhorev, and so on without end. They finally decided to invite me to the meeting as the "headman" of our little group. I set out, having decided beforehand to keep myself politely, but coldly, from either entering into or carrying on any unnecessary arguments. I found a crowd of people in the kitchen. Deathly silence greeted me.

"What do you need from me, gentlemen?" I asked.

"Why're youse bein' quiet? Speak up!" someone's mocking voice burst out. "At one point they wouldn't shut up, but now they're bitin' their tongues…"

The voice, evidently, was in my favor.

"Here's what, Ivan Nikolaevich," the headman Godunov stepped from the crowd. His eyes were diplomatically lowered, his right hand placed behind the bosom of his shirt in an appearance of virtue. He measured precisely and weighed painstakingly each word before pronouncing it.

"You can see that we, the mare, live 'cordin' to our silly rules 'n' conventions. Please don't misunnerstand us. 'Mong other things, many been offended by your actions 'n' manners… So's we'd like to sort into final form which of us, for certain, is right 'n' who's wrong."

"Well, please allow me," I quietly said, "to know what your grievances are."

Red-haired Zhebreek elbowed his way out of the crowd to be closest of all to me. He stood grandly with stubby legs apart and, after scrunching up his mug with a murderously scornful laugh, hoarsely said:

"Grievances? But what if I got a sickiness in my stomach? I'm tellin' you, there's a serious sickiness in my gut, 'n' it's your lousy dokhturnik…"

"Can't you speak without insults?"

"He's talkin' like he ain't heard there's a kinda sickiness in me. Cups his ear 'n' talks, don't lissen. Don't you recognize 'n' lissen to who's nearest you? What if I myself feel there's a real serious sickiness in my stomach?"

"Well, you suf'rin' Zhebrei! You gab 'bout the problem, but don't regret it," someone shouted at the half-witted old man, whose stories about his "serious sickiness" had long ago gotten on the entire prison's nerves.

"You with the pointy nose, am I gonna do what you say?"

"You're a cur."

"Snake!"

"Froggy!"

Everyone burst out laughing at these well aimed verbal insults. A dozen pairs of hands grabbed Zhebreik and dragged him out the kitchen door as he elbowed, shouted, and swore.

Then the Moldavan Strizhevskii stepped forward, an old man with a beautiful gray beard and extremely handsome face. Quiet and shy, this man had always stood somehow to the side, and talking with him was nearly impossible. Having now come forward with a "grievance," he expressed in a very delicate form his dissatisfaction that Shteinhart had recommended to the medic that he be released from hospital, even though he'd not fully recovered. Not speaking Russian completely fluently, he nonetheless used an almost literary language.

"Can you verify, Strizhevskii," I, for my part, softly asked, "who told you this?"

"Told me no one, but myself I heard Dmitrii Petrovich to the medic say behind the door: 'that's enough!'"

"Dmitrii Petrovich said his words were, in all likelihood, about some medicines, but not about you at all. You believe that Zemlianskii signed you in himself, without a recommendation from anywhere. How can you suspect Shteinhart, who devotes all his strength and health to sick prisoners, doesn't sleep at night, and skips dinner so he can run at first call to a patient?"

"There's really no problem, ol' man," sympathetic voices rang out, "you're wrong 'bout this, Dmitrii Petrovich ain't such a man!"

Strizhevskii became embarrassed and blushed.

"I can't confirm it's true," he said in a trembling voice, "these just my suspicions, of course… But prisoners being offended… They're people, too, despite being beaten by

God… Youse don't want to understand us… don't want to acknowledge that we, like youse, have heart and soul…"

"For God's sake, Strizhevskii, where did you get *this* from?"

"Dmitrii Petrovich once said to me: 'How do *you* do, old man.' But I'd never insulted him once and always used the formal *youse* with him."

Such a delicacy of feelings, I confess, I had never anticipated encountering in one of the *katorga* mare's representatives… Reserved, always terribly quiet and controlled, this marvelous old man, with facial features of aristocratic precision and a physique composed almost completely of sinew, had always seemed to me, it's true, an enigma and an exception. I hastened to console him that if Shteinhart had actually referred to him with the informal "you" then, of course, he meant no offense, but, on the contrary, had done so out of a warm feeling toward him as a sick old man.

"Well, this is certainly makin' more sense!" good humored voices, among which was Bykov's voice, calmingly resounded once again. I needed to strike while the iron was hot, and I went quickly to the point.

"Fellows, we're not going to get into this business and flog a dead horse in vain. From time to time disputes emerge between us, but in the end they've always turned out to be trivialities. We should stop with this. Either trust that we're your friends and comrades in misfortune and then we can live in peace, or we'll break with each for good and have nothing in common. Here we've given you *makhorka*, added to the common pot, and done all this with the friendliest feelings. We're living in the same prison, suffering the same misfortune; we have means that you do not—well, we wanted to help you, I repeat, as comrades in misfortune! But many of you are dissatisfied with this. That's your business, of course. Now Six-Eyes is mixed up in this: with a single word, he can tell you you can never accept from anyone any *makhorka* or any meat on fast days! And we and you will go hungry at the same time. There's nothing more for me to say. You decide as you know best."

With these words, I left the kitchen. I heard from behind the door an unusual noise and racket suddenly begin. Several dozen voices were speaking at once.

The meeting reached a completely unanticipated result. Now, almost without exception, the former trouble-making ringleaders insisted on making peace and that it was unnecessary to punish a future generation of Shelai prisoners by refusing the assistance of "friendly people"; but the typically voiceless majority, which itself had had nothing against us, suddenly grew restive… Even such of my devoted friends and well-wishers as Chirok, Lunkov, and Nogaitsev were shouting:

"Now it's impossible to make peace, absolutely impossible!…"

I was utterly perplexed. But before the very next roll call, Shooter (who had not long before transferred, upon his own request, to Bashurov's ward) came into our ward and, with extreme indignation, began speaking in front of Shteinhart and me about how the Ivans had somehow been fishing in troubled waters and plunged the "simple" mare into a sort of tizzy (evidently, Shooter included himself in this simple mare!).

"They ain't gonna lissen no more to their father 'n' mother if'n they said: 'Shooter, express your dissatisfaction, be the Ivans' voice!' From this day on, I spit on all their laws!"

Having listened to this speech, I still couldn't understand what the problem was. Iron Cat hotly took up his words:

"I already spit on 'em a long time ago. That's why we's always left with the idiots… Well, with what eyes could I look at Ivan Mikolaevich if, after all that's happened, after all our boastin', I went to 'im 'n' said: 'Gimme some more tobacco. I wanna eat some more vittles!' No, in my opinion, 'tis much better to make peace with hunger than to burn with shame!"

"Sure is better!" gloomily underscored Shooter.

"Up to now, I was takin' the tobacco 'n' eatin' the food, but I'm layin' off ever'thin' now, ever'thin'!" the poet Vladimirov suddenly added, bounding off the sleeping platform with unaccustomed alacrity.

"Yes, we's refusin' ever'thin' now, ever'thin'!" Lunkov supported him. "Maybe they got no shame 'cause they's monsters, but we's humans."

"What's your problem, Lunkov?" I finally lost patience, rising from my spot as well.

The whole time, the company had obviously seen me and was talking purposely loudly in order to drag me into the conversation.

"Point is," Lunkov, Chirok, and Iron Cat kept shouting, "we can't make peace with you *now*, Mikolaich! 'Cause with what eyes is we gonna make peace with you? Our eyes're shameful, 'n' we can't give such advice. As it goes, ain't no way we can make peace with you."

Shteinhart and I unwillingly broke out laughing.

"Well, come-come, peace is always possible… If you don't now recognize that you've been arguing with us over a trifle and that the Ivans have simply been egging you on, won't there be more trouble? We ourselves would be deeply happy to end this silly episode."

"Oi? Jus' like that, boys? Should we make peace? Take the tobacco?"

"Take it!"

"Make peace!!!" frenzied voices roared out… Chirok, Vodianin, Shooter, Lunkov, and others flew on their heels into the corridor to propagate the new decision. No more than five minutes remained until roll call, at which time the headman was to give Six-Eyes one or the other answer.

"Make peace!"

"Ta-a-ake it!" riotous voices carried in from the corridor. Shteinhart looked at me with a smile.

"Well, how can one be cross at these grown-up boys? Really, they're just true children."

IX. A STORY OUT OF *ROCAMBOLE*[47]

We could not finalize the abovementioned disturbances with a brilliant peace accord because, one evening soon after roll call, a huge event occurred, and inside a day the normally quiet flow of life was again turned upside-down. Loud noise, pounding on the door, and prisoners' shouts at the door's viewing window were suddenly heard from one of the far wards. Everyone in our ward sprang to his feet.

"Where's that? Somethin's 'appened… Sound the alarm bell, boys—oh, our alarm ain't workin', o' course…"

"Shout louder for the guard! Oh, what the hell's happened to 'im, where's 'e gone off to?"

"Went outside the gate to drink tea, o' course…"

At last the orderly flung himself headlong down the corridor. One, two, three… The key growled… One of the wards was unlocked and, with the help of prisoners, guards dragged past us down the corridor three men resembling corpses. A group of people pushed together at our door's window, continually jostling with all their might to see through it.

"What's that there?"

"Dead bodies…"

"From which ward?"

"The sixth. Bykov, get the hell outta the way…"

This was the ward where Valerian lived. Shteinhart and I were terribly worried… However, in less than ten minutes there was a banging at our door as well, and a guard summoned Shteinhart to hospital. Everyone began throwing out questions.

"Seems they was gonna make peace, but somethin' stupid's happened with Shooter, Lipatov, 'n' Chinaman, somethin' real stupid."

"Well, the scoundrels musta been slurpin' up the skilly," the mare decided, soon calming down. "Y'see, they stuff their traps each time like they ain't had a crumb in two years!…"

But in the meantime the issue was incomparably more serious. Shteinhart stayed in hospital all night. The next morning, just as roll call came, a rumor passed through the prison that Lipatov, Chinaman, and Shooter had been poisoned and the poison was put in their tea.

"W-well?… Who did it? How? Why?"

"They dead or alive?"

"Alive. Mitrii Petrovich saved 'em."

"What rubbish folks is dreamin' up! Where'd they get poison from in prison?" Iukhorev scornfully muttered. "They weren't showin' their tongues earlier, but now they're hangin' a millstone round their neck."

"It's a story straight outta *Rocambole*!" Tropin sympathetically supported him, flashing his teeth.

Our ward's other residents looked confused and didn't know what to think, say, or do. I inquired of Bashurov, and this is what he told me:

"Last night before roll call, I came into the kitchen to brew tea. Lately, Aziadinov has really been trying to make up with me and paying me false compliments. 'Don't you want s'more spoonfuls o' milk, Valerian Mikhalych,' he was asking, 'from what's left o' my hospital rations?' He practically forced his kettle on me—and in the bottom of it were two spoonfuls of milk; after those episodes, I confess I didn't want to refuse… Suddenly, Karpushka Lipatov rushes in: 'Sir, y'know ya don't want them two spoonfuls o' milk, but the little bone in my back might grow from drinkin' it.' I started laughing, and for good luck gave it to him for his malady. After roll call, Karpushka pulled the kettle out from under his cassock and grandly proclaimed: 'Who'll bow down to Karpushka 'n' drink some milky tea today?' Shooter and Chinaman were right there: 'We don't bow e'en to God, but if'n you wanna be our comrade, pour us a cupful.' And they started drinking the tea. Half an hour later, all three were suffering. Karpushka, naturally, had drunk the most—he collapsed as if dead, his eyes were even rolled back. Chinaman kept groaning and grabbing his stomach. It was really weird to see such a strapping man whining like a peasant woman: 'Oh, boys, my death's a-comin'! Oh, the barbarians o'erfed me!' Shooter was conscious the whole time, but even though he was in no less torment he didn't lose courage. He just threatened to break Aziadinov's and Iukhorev's necks after he recovered."

"Iukhorev? What's this about Iukhorev?"

"But who is he if not a bastard?" the entire ward piped up, having heard Bashurov's story. "He, that snake, didn't share that poison with anyone else in our prison! It was jus' their gang: Iukhorev, Zemlianskii, 'n' Aziadinov!"

"If'n I stood up for 'em, does it mean I know anythin' 'bout this?" growled Bykov, extremely flustered and rising from the platform to address me. "I'm jus' standin' up for the truth, 'cause I'se insulted…"

"But all the same, boys, the past o' this matter's gotta be investigated," said Palchikov, my mining boss and also a secret admirer of Iukhorev. "Might be others turn out guilty, curse 'em with the fallin' sickness! How can we blame a man off the cuff? Let the actual physicians investigate 'n' show us; maybe it weren't e'en poison at all, but an ulcer that did it!"

"That's it in itself," Bykov snatched this up, "'n' mebbe an innocent man's bein' blamed for hardly no reason… You can't jus' suddenly say: 'Iukhorev, Iukhorev'… Maybe it's someone else."

I was in full agreement with these views, and went straight to the infirmary to learn the patients' condition and ask Shteinhart about everything. The latter hadn't closed his eyes all night and could barely stand on his feet from fatigue. The following had happened in the hospital that night. Arriving to see the patients, he found a clearly manifested portrait of illness: vomiting, convulsions, dilated pupils, burning in the throat, agonizing thirst… Of course, had there not been the earlier discussions about poison, about the prisoners' dream of robbing the hospital's pharmacy, Shteinhart, regardless of all evident signs, would have been in the dark, but a terrible suspicion now entered his head. He immediately sent for Luchezarov. The latter appeared instantly, very anxious and nervous.

"What's going on here? Could we have been infected by an Asiatic host? There hasn't yet been a cholera case in Transbaikal District, you know."

"This isn't cholera, but it's no better than cholera," replied Shteinhart, "this is a poisoning…"

The brave captain nearly suffered an apoplectic attack.

"Impossible… In my prison? You're mistaken."

"See for yourself."

And Shteinhart showed him a medical textbook describing the same symptoms as a poisoning by atropine.

"Where did the scoundrels get the poison?"

"Please dwell on this later. For now, if you want to save those who've been poisoned, you'll have to accept the responsibility for their method of treatment. Heroic means should be employed: another poison—morphine."

"But is their condition already so bad?"

Shteinhart brought him to the patients' room. Karpushka had already begun wheezing; Shooter barely turned his head; and Chinaman was groaning beseechingly:

"Com'dant Little Father… Save me… Be my own father!…"

"Do anything you want, just save them!" a greatly upset Luchezarov turned toward Shteinhart.

The latter immediately set to work. Zemlianskii was gone—having been given three days leave by Luchezarov, he'd left for the factory town a day earlier.

The brave captain gazed at everyone with a horribly distressed look and continually peppered Shteinhart with questions:

"But what do you think? How will this turn out?… Whom are you worried about?"

Shteinhart merely shrugged his shoulders.

"My job will be to ascertain the facts, but now's the time to care for the sick. You're in charge of everything. Simply permit me to recommend you collect the patients' vomit and seal it in a container."

"Absolutely right! Without fail! Birkin, Birkin! You know what to do: I order you right now to fetch the kettle that tea was in, maybe there's a little bit of it left still…"

But this idea came to the brave captain too late: the kettle turned out to have been cleanly washed and thoroughly dried by someone. Because Shteinhart had not concealed from prisoners the nature and name of the illness, within half an hour everyone knew everything in the hospital. Squatting indulgently on a bunk, Luchezarov himself, as soon as the afflicted showed signs of recovery, said to them:

"Name these scurrilous poisoners immediately! I'll hang them from the first aspen tree… Just get well, friends, get well!"

Chinaman, Karpushka, and even the gloomy Shooter were drawn to the aggrieved commandant's tender expression of affection for them; deeply moved, they kissed his hands and, had they been able to stand up, would have bowed as model prisoners do. Chinaman continued groaning and complaining, though he now seemed not to be experiencing especial agonies; all Shooter's hatred was now directed at Iukhorev, and he said that he would disembowel him, that "corruptor of men." He appealed to Shteinhart with sincere affection, and met each of his acts of heroic succor with a big, gentle smile. As for Karpushka Lipatov, he actually seemed to be delirious.

"Mister Dokhtur, I feel this awful poison's gotten the best o' me," he explained to Shteinhart, "'cause it's pushin' the blood outta my bones. If you'd gimme some more o' that *khananiia* you poured in my mouth last night, then I know I'd be a real man! That'd really hit my pain on the spot. But you're stingy, Mister Dokhtur… you just dabbed my teeth, 'n' so it's clear you don't wanna straighten Karpushka's back for good… But I'm tellin' you, that very spot is up for treatment, 'cause this poison… it's drivin' the blood outta my bones."

In a word, by morning the whole prison was talking about "the poison," and everyone unanimously blamed Iukhorev behind his back, blamed him with the deepest hatred, and openly asserted that Aziadinov and Iukhorev had wanted to poison Bashurov, Shteinhart, and me, but that fate decreed otherwise and the unfortunate Karpushka and a pair from Iukhorev's gang swallowed the bait… Even the guards were pointing to Iukhorev. However, Six-Eyes, for whom fairness was "superior to everything on earth," decided at that time to arrest only Aziadinov, since he'd disingenuously offered Valerian Bashurov the milk from which the poisoning occurred. The Tatar baker was immediately put in a dark isolator cell, forbidden cooked food, and shackled in manacles. The commandant himself visited him during each evening roll call and tried to scare him into confessing and naming his accomplices. But Aziadinov stubbornly insisted:

"I'm suf'rin' innocently, Mister Com'dant! I know absolutely nuthin', 'n' I didn't do nuthin'."

Touring the wards during roll calls, Six-Eyes shot Iukhorev a penetrating look each time, but he stood stiffly at attention as always, looking cold and impassive and not moving a muscle. By the same token, regardless of this icy mask, careful observation nevertheless revealed that he was worried and at times feeling a certain terror. One morning, word went round the prison that Aziadinov had decided to give some sort of honest testimony; and during the evening of that same day, just before roll call, the mare was rocked as if one man by sensational news: Iukhorev had been caught red-handed…

"Who caught 'im? Doin' what?"

"Ogurtsov… Iukhorev jumped onto the isolator's window ledge, 'n' after lookin' round, started shoutin' to Aziadinov to shut up right now 'bout ever'thin', 'n' was promisin' to give 'im twenty rubles…"

Entering the yard, I'd actually seen Ogurtsov at the gates speaking in great agitation to the guards about something; he asked them to immediately inform the commandant that he needed to communicate an urgent matter to him. Having noticed me, Ogurtsov gleefully shouted:

"I caught 'im, Ivan Nikolaevich, I really caught that bitch!… Y'know I told you I wouldn't be Ogurtsov if I didn't pay 'im back sooner or later. I nailed 'im on the spot! Day 'n' night I was followin' 'im, the bastard!"

Ogurtsov's pale, puffy, and typically apathetic face glowed with joyous vivacity; his large black eyes sparkled vengefully, his fists clenched spasmodically… I thought: not long ago, was this not a naïve, simple youth who would have been called nothing other than "dummy"? Here's what this abnormal, accursed prison existence has made of his life!

I was unable, however, to give Ogurtsov any response, since the bell sounded for roll call and prisoners began forming ranks in the middle of the yard. This time, Six-Eyes did not make us wait long, and his figure appeared beneath the gates.

First of all, he summoned Ogurtsov to the guardhouse and discussed something with him for a long time. Then roll call began with the usual ceremonial arrangements. We expected that something would be said or explained following the reading of orders, but the brave captain maintained the same awesome silence, and there was only heard the curt:

"Distribute prisoners to their wards!"

Everyone separated in considerable bewilderment, as disappointed as they were secretly alarmed. The two sides once again formed themselves in the wards, but neither the usual jokes nor banter was heard. I unwillingly cast a sidelong look in Iukhorev's direction. Having sat himself on the platform's edge in anticipation of roll call, he was nervously drumming his fingers and his face seemed unusually dark and rather pinched… None of this comrades looked at him, and he, too, was not speaking with anyone. So heavy was the silence that everyone turned at the same time when the full-throated order burst out: "Attention!"—and Luchczarov did not walk but ran in, with quick, unnerving steps. Looking at no one, he performed the usual ceremony, walked around the ward, and glanced behind the partition and sniffed the air there. He began exiting with quiet, measured steps… Only upon reaching the door did he suddenly turn and say in a loud, authoritative voice:

"Iukhorev, I am arresting and bringing you to court. Guards, take him outside the gates to the soldiers' isolator."

Iukhorev had anticipated this very order for a long time and said not a word: he silently got up from the platform, grabbed his cap from it, and walked with even, manly steps toward the exit. But on the threshold he suddenly turned and said in a rather shaky tone:

"Please, boys, don't 'member me badly… I'm simply bein' unjustly blamed in this business!"

The door closed, the key clicked in the lock. And suddenly everyone in the ward started making noise and talking at once…

"They finally got the bastard!" declared Elk, who'd leaned toward Iukhorev prior to the poisoning incident but had since turned decisively away from him.

"It still ain't gonna stop someone else! There's still enough o' that sort left," Lunkov said, tossing Tropin an ill-intentioned look.

"That Iukhorev's quite accustomed to playin' the hero," Karasev poisonously added. "Since we wasn't here, we can't know what to think: he's either a prisoner like us, or he's a sekletary or e'en a senator!… Here we been waitin' for the senator hisself, like expectin' a chicken from an egg. Thank God all us yellow-nosed *cheldony* ain't been o'erfed."

"But why're you hittin' us on the nose with 'im? *Your* Iukhorev, *yours* indeed." Chirok added for the honor of the original group. "Well, ain't he one of us? You ain't sayin' your group was closer to 'im?"

"'N' who're you sayin' was closer?" the touchy Karasev's blood was rising. "Me? No, you're lyin'! I still ain't bent to no one in my life! Maybe you ain't an independent man, but me… I'm a demon-devil, 'n' I won't please some Iukhorev. I, brother, don't take not-a-nuthin'!…"

"You had a few friends round you! Tropin o'er there…"

"Don't bother Tropin!" Tropin—who immediately after roll call had laid down to sleep and covered his head with his cassock—quickly shot back from the sleeping platform. "I don't bother no one, brother; but whoe'er bothers me, I'll crack his skull."

For some reason, Chirok did not think fit to argue with him, and shut up.

"But, boys, y'know what it means for people to live their life here with a bit o' honesty," his opponent then added, "yet, believe me, at night I still dream o' women!"

And Tropin, chuckling merrily, turned on his other side and soon began demonstratively snoring.

During the first days after Iukhorev's arrest the overwhelming majority of the prison was clearly against him; even those like Bykov or Palchikov, who at first tentatively tried to defend him from blame in the poisoning, were now silent since he'd been removed from the prison and come to represent an irrevocable fall from grace, and they no longer protested against the vicious and cutting slander. Amid the upsurge of candor and trustfulness, Elk told Shteinhart that Iukhorev had dipped his hand into some kind of powder in a little paper and said: "I say, pour a tiny bit into the tea in Shtengor's kettle or into the skilly in his cistern." Needless to say, he, Elk, had luckily rebuffed this proposal… During this time, smart-alecks like Tropin constrained themselves, insofar as they didn't say out loud what they were for or what they were against, and were sufficiently ambiguously ironical toward the general consensus… The leaders disappeared somewhere, as if they'd fallen through the ground, and the typically characterless and voiceless herd, with its banal opinions and no less banal emotions, reigned unbridled. Before my comrades and me, and especially before Shteinhart, everyone deferentially made way, greeting us with the most affable smiles, speaking ingratiatingly… In general, this was the most vulgar, the most shameless and unconcealed reversal I'd ever encountered in my life!

But such an attitude among the multitude did not last two weeks. A reversal in favor of Iukhorev began to emerge once more. Rumors began percolating into prison that Iukhorev, chained in manacles and leg-irons and lolling on the earthen floor of the dark soldiers' isolator (outside the prison gates), was being treated extremely severely and inhumanely, and was starving and thirsty. A cleaner, who every day under close watch entered his tiny space, saw him wasting away from scurvy and fever…

"Tell it in the prison, ol' man, that I ain't leavin' here alive, that I'm bein' destroyed here!" Iukhorev had managed to whisper to him.

The mare's heart-strings were plucked… They recalled how Iukhorev, leaving for seclusion, had said:

"I'm bein' unjustly blamed in this business."

"But what, boys, in pointy fact, was it he directly did, 'n' what 'n' such is the evidence? Maybe it was just Aziadinov? Could turn out that Ogurtsov tried killin' 'im outta spite, y'know… His fat snout's been threatenin' Iukhorev for a long time…," voices said, at first timidly, but then more and more boldly.

But the change that astounded me most of all was Shooter's fading recovery. Not long earlier, he'd called Shteinhart his savior and vowed to disembowel Iukhorev, but now, for no apparent reason, he was again staring at all of us with savage, hostile looks and, strolling through the prison yard in his yellow baker's cassock, was consorting primarily with Tropin, Bykov, Shmatov, and other members of the depraved gang that had been. This man, with a gloomy temper and intransigently careless manner of speaking to the fact, evidently possessed a flaccid and inconsistent will and a rickety and perhaps dissolute life filled with all sorts of nightmares.

It soon became apparent that this new change was decorative: Tropin spread through the prison the new *bumó* that the poison was dropped into the kettle by none other than Valerian Bashurov and had been obtained by, needless to say, Shteinhart, who was welcome in the pharmacy. All this had been done to destroy Iukhorev and increase the renown of that very same Shteinhart in his capacity as savior of the poisoned men… However scandalous this vile fabrication, refuting it was impossible, since it spread on the quiet, and upon encountering us Tropin merely flashed his sharp teeth brazenly and looked us straight in the face with his shameless blue-as-water eyes.

X. FAREWELLS

Two months passed. The poisoning episode dragged on for a long time. An investigator came, and one night he interrogated Aziadinov, Iukhorev, and Ogurtsov face-to-face, summoned certain other prisoners including Bashurov, but reached no definite conclusion whatsoever. It turned out there was too little evidence for formal charges. It was said that in conversations with the investigator, Luchezarov himself was now joking about the prisoners' insistence on poison as if it were a boyish invention: where did they get the poison in prison, and in such a *strict* prison? "Of course, Shteinhart's a fine young man, imbued with the best intentions and feelings and serving in place of the physician who so rarely comes to Shelai Prison, but… don't forget that he's no more than a student, hasn't finished his studies, and doesn't have a lot of experience"… Needless to say, no one, for example Shteinhart or me or Mishka Birkin or his comrades, could tell the investigator what he knew, and it was no surprise that, in taking the matter higher, he was washing his hands of it. Regarding the medical analysis of the sealed vomit, the results remained unknown to us.

Much later, I learned the truth that two full jars of poison had actually turned up in the prisoners' hands. One of them, it was said, was taken outside the gates and lost somewhere, but the other had for a long time been hidden from the administration's watchful eyes and roamed the prison, being passed from hand to hand. It finally got to the point that prisoners began betting it against one another at cards. Only after a year, when I was no longer in Shelai Prison, was Shteinhart able to track down this dangerous weapon, *purchase* it, and throw it in the oven…

Upon the conclusion of the investigation, Iukhorev and Aziadinov were released from the isolators and once again installed in the prison. This situation was at first terribly embarrassing for those prisoners who'd openly declared themselves their enemies. In talks among themselves they expressed genuine fear that Iukhorev would now poison them all wholesale… At one of the roll calls Ogurtsov opined this to Luchezarov himself.

"Yes, yes, this isn't entirely convenient, not entirely, I understand," Luchezarov worriedly agreed with him, "but nothing can be done about it now. I don't have the authority to have him removed. I'll do what I can, but be patient and careful for now."

Regarding Iukhorev himself, he however now kept himself proudly aloof and completely separate from general prison affairs, and not only did he not get mixed up in them, he didn't even listen in on any of the prisoners' talk about the collective. For whole days his voice went unheard in the prison; he worked, slept without stirring, and even rarely strolled with his old friends. Obviously, he was deeply grieving… Life and an ebullient thirst for freedom still raged within this man's powerful constitution; no more than four months remained before he'd be released to settlement, yet, for some reason, he was convinced that Luchezarov would slap several more years' *katorga* on him… Sometimes, lying on the sleeping platform after evening roll call, he hummed to himself some lovely melody from his rich repertoire of folksongs, but would then suddenly stop, jump up, and pound his fists on the platform in despair, muttering a strong word:

"Ekh, it's gone, the hell with it, life's gone for neither this nor that!…"

Thanks only to the poisoning episode did Luchezarov finally remove the medic Zemlianskii and put in his place a young medic who'd just barely completed his training, a mustache-less youth, shy as a young woman, soft and kindhearted. Upon my first request, he assigned me to the hospital and put me in a small private room, the same one where Marazgali had at some point died and to which, after each day's labor in the mines, Bashurov and Shteinhart came to chat and relax away from the prison's hurly-burly. On holidays our little group, having settled itself on the edge of my bunk, would not separate from between the morning to the evening roll call, and what did we not discuss, what did we not argue about!

The summer's events had a terrible impact on Valerian. He sharply changed his initial view of the prisoners as having accidently splintered off from the world of the commonfolk and, in essence, as being indistinguishable from this world. Now, by contrast, he called *katorga*'s inhabitants the people's "refuse," and saw in most an inveterate people and deliberate criminals whom nothing could rehabilitate. With the same passionate certainty, the same youthful aplomb as of his former views, he now defended the new as if they comprised a cherished conviction achieved after long years of hard experience and difficult struggle, and not all of a few months of comparatively petty disappointments and grievances. If earlier I'd tried to cool my comrade's optimistic fervor and show him the other side, "the refuse from the world of the commonfolk," I now attempted only to protect and defend his wretched cohabitants against excessive attacks, against being utterly dragged through the muck. As for Shteinhart, he was obviously little interested in our disputes and maintained a gloomy neutrality; it was evident that some deep personal grief was again torturing and making him gloomy and unsociable. His eternal busying over patients, outside and inside prison walls, his work in the pharmacy, days, evenings, and sometimes even at night, left him too little free time for the heartfelt conversations of old with me, and now it even seemed he was beginning to deliberately avoid them, that between us of late an estrangement was once again occurring. This much distressed me, though I did not want an outpouring of friendliness, especially as I couldn't admit to the change in his attitude toward me and ascribed the cause of his alienation to some new complications within his bitter romance… Shteinhart rushed to my cell quite often, but each time not for long, and listened absent-mindedly to my conversations with Valerian.

"Well, but all the same," Bashurov was indefatigably shouting, "you are however not denying that people like Tropin and his comrades are hopelessly injurious members of society, and that nothing—no schools or books whatsoever—can correct them now? Can all the recent events really not have convinced you of this?"

"Bashurov, you've been living among these people less than a year, you know, and are incapable of knowing them well!"

Bashurov then flashed like gunpowder, and pride spoke up in him.

"First, don't forget that I was on the road with them, and before I arrived at Shelai mine I certainly wasn't wholly ignorant, and second—and this is the main thing—before us, during the two and a half years with which you're pluming yourself, how were you living?"

"Pluming myself?!"

"Yes, that's no great sin… According to your own story, you were getting by peacefully, quietly, as if in the clover… No, stop, don't get angry! I know you want to object, but we're not talking about that now. The stormy life inside the prison began only with us, and your experience has been literally the same as mine in this regard."

Often, after such "trifling" conversations, we would separate with feelings of wounded pride and irritation against each other, yet meet again that same day as if nothing happened. Bashurov would approach me, smiling broadly and amicably extending his hand. And not ten minutes would pass before we were once again grappling for some reason.

"A couple words about recent events, Valerian Mikhailovich," I said one day, "do you know my opinion of them?"

"Well, I'd be very curious to know."

"I think a bright side might be found to these bitter events. These God-beaten people, criminal and ignorant, are all reasonable creatures, you know, to whom a sense of self-respect is not alien. Usually, in their humdrum life, so to speak, this feeling, it's true, flickers in their soul like a spark beneath the ashes and cannot be appreciated by them. But then we call them worthless and are exasperated by their baseness, servility, and venality… But for a certain moment in their lives, a holiday from life, these wretches would be standing on their feet like other people, would be of a higher sort and feel that they, too, are people, and not cattle. And when their 'betters' repeatedly deal tactlessly with them, that once smoldering spark suddenly flames up and their sense of dignity awakens… But here we become indignant again—this time that the habitual lackeys have dared display the ticklishness of Spanish grandees! And the forms of this explosion, its immediate consequences for us and everything about it, seem to us foolish, absurd, wild… It's simply that the gust of wind that blew the spark into flame is more reasonable!"

"Ivan Nikolaevich, forgive me, but this is just some decadent theory… No, you're finding meaning, depth, and practically even beauty where there is decidedly nothing except senselessness and ugliness."

"But, you, Dmitrii Petrovich, what's your opinion of the mare?" I turned to Shteinhart, reclining silently on my bunk and nervously chewing his beard.

"Ah, it's all a bore!" he answered, frowning still more. "People are the same everywhere, whether they're highly or lowly developed and educated."

And with this enigmatic declaration he jumped up and left to do his business.

In the final days of October that same year, at one of the evening roll calls, on a Saturday as snow fell onto our heads from the sky, an order was read transferring to other mines for bad behavior Iukhorev, Shmatov, Aziadinov, and Tropin, and sending Shooter, because he was sick, to the Zerentui infirmary (following the poisoning, he came down with some kind of weird nervous paroxysms, stomach pains, and body cramps; many suspected he was simply faking). A significant portion of prisoners listened to this order with deeply hidden envy and amazement: it was as if, with all this, the leadership were once more emphasizing that in order to break from the claws of Shelai's stifling regime you had to keep causing trouble and concocting any sort of scandal, and neither stop at nor fear anything. However, the faces of Iukhorev, Shmatov, and Tropin were not radiating triumph but, on the contrary, were very serious: they were evidently worried by a secret fear that only part of the written order had been read out for now, and that upon arriving in a new place they would immediately be subjected to birch rods or even lashes and then have their *katorga* terms extended.

The five friends' removal took place the following morning, when the whole prison was in, because it happened to be a Sunday. I was strolling through the hospital corridor when the door suddenly opened and Shmatov-Buzzy entered the hospital, loudly clanking the irons in which he'd only just been shackled. Not glancing at me, he went into the large chamber to tell his comrades goodbye.

"Farewell, boys, they's haulin' me away!" his droning voice could be solemnly heard from there. "They's haulin' me away… What'll be t'ain't known… it turns out that others 'ave been ruined like us!"

With curiosity, I settled onto a bench, waiting to see if he'd give me any kind of farewell. His chains falling loudly, Shmatov entered the corridor and, doffing his cap, he gave me a low, theatrical bow.

"'N' a farewell to you, Mikolaich," he droned, sarcastically baring his rotten teeth, "farewell! Thanks for puttin' me in chains… I'm 'bliged to ya!"

I confess, I hadn't expected such a rude, fundamentally malicious slander being flung straight in my face, even from Shmatov. Yet, before I—beside myself with surprise—could utter a word in response, Buzzy had already marched solemnly off with measured steps, hands folded behind his back.

After this, Tropin poked his head through the door. For him, there would clearly be no leave-takings with anyone; he'd showed up merely to shout at the top of his lungs at Shooter:

"You wastin' time o'er there? Hurry up, you slacker!"

He cast a hurried, disinterested look at me and, having vouchsafed me not a word, disappeared. And what was there for him to say? He'd gotten his way, yet this man, who had absolutely nothing for a soul, had not the slightest regard for anyone else in the world, for truths or lies…

Shooter came out of the chamber and, also having given me nothing of a farewell, hurried toward the gates. I looked out the window. Standing there beneath the rain in anticipation were Aziadinov, Tropin, and Shmatov. With a quick, easy gait, prisoner's cap cocked rakishly askew, a sack of things slung across his shoulder, Iukhorev exited the prison and approached them. The lock growled, the gates opened wide, took into their jaws the five friends, and loudly closed once more. On to a new life! Would these people ever pity Shelai Prison, ever recall with sympathy those they were now leaving behind and trying to spit and sling mud upon?…

Bashurov and Shteinhart came to me with the prison news.

"Well, Ivan Nikolaevich, did they tell you goodbye?"

I told them about the scene Buzzy had staged for me.

"Well, you know, that's word for word the song we heard," Shteinhart bitterly laughed. "Shmatov and Iukhorev came up to us together. The former droned something not entirely intelligible, accused somebody of something, and bid farewell to someone, time and again interrupting Iukhorev, who as usual finally shouted: 'Shut up, Buzzy, don't be stupid!' He carried himself with his usual dignity, and made clear from the first that he harbors no animus against us two and considers Ivan Nikolaevich alone to be his enemy. 'Aren't you ashamed to say such things?' I exclaimed. 'Ivan Nikolaevich has lived for years in this prison, and everyone's met only kindness from him.' 'Maybe others, but not me at all! He's my enemy, 'n' I'll pay him back at some point!' 'He put us in chains!' Buzzy droned again. I turned to Iukhorev: 'You really believe such slander? Shmatov's simply idiotic, but you?…' He made a decisive gesture with his hand: 'Don't argue with me, Dmitrii Petrovich; ev'ry man has his views… 'n' so, gentlemen, farewell, 'n' thanks for your bread 'n' salt. Valerian, don't 'member me badly!' But we refused to shake his hand: 'If you're thinking so foolishly about our comrade, whom we respect, then we cannot part with you as friends.' Then Iukhorev proudly straightened up, thought a bit, and, after a slight bow, hurried off. His veritable henchman scurried behind him, continually droning about something."

"Wherefrom such pride, such language from, in essence, a thoroughbred herd!" Valerian erupted. "Here, Ivan Nikolaevich, is the fruit of your many years' spoiling them."

But Shteinhart harshly cut him off:

"Remember, Valerian, you were hail-fellow-well-met with Iukhorev…"

Bashurov blushed bright red and, having fallen quiet for a certain time, sulked as usual.

Left alone when my comrades went to the prison, I was seized by a tragic mood. I mentally fingered my prison memories, year after year and month after month, trying to discern what had been my errors, blunders, offenses against my associates whom fate had dispatched, so as to find the key to a proper understanding of their simple yet at the same time enigmatic psychology in whose soil first our misunderstanding, then enmity, had been created. I'm thinking now… The story of these petty prison tempests has led to a notion of broader analogies and scenes: are such conflicts (albeit incomparably more distressing due to their enormous scale and important consequences) unavoidable between the educated people and the dark common masses in general?…

It was a gloomy, autumnal morning, just before winter's onset. Now and again, cold gusts of wind blew enormous raindrops against the window. A lowering dark sky hung unpleasantly over the unpleasant, wet prison building, rendering it gloomier than ever and the existence beneath its roof even more terrible and suffocating. Now came the sharp, actually cutting, sounds of the dinner bell; hunched over due to the cold, bending from their loads, the wards' headmen brought cisterns of skilly from the kitchen. Bustling behind them were several useless figures who'd been banished from lolling about in the kitchen. The prison day was following its usual rut…

XI. ANXIETIES OF A DIFFERENT SORT

I have described in previous chapters events of an unhappy nature. And if these events had been the finale in the complicated story of relations between the dark *katorga* mare and the small group of educated prisoners, had they turned out to be something like the last word in this story, the fateful and irretrievable word, then the reader, perhaps, would have reached an even sadder conclusion than that to which I myself came in a moment of despondency and spiritual weakness. And he would, perhaps, be right… But, fortunately, reality as a whole was not so dark. In essence, my abovementioned misunderstandings and arguments were no more than a passing moment from out of our many years' combined existence with *katorga*, a moment that surfaced completely unforeseen from the most quiet and kindly peacefulness, that burst forth alongside tempestuous conflicts of a more or less tragicomic nature and then, following the prison chieftains' removal, yielded to the former friendly relations, such that the years once more began dragging on. Nonetheless, this comparatively brief period did not seem bereft of meaning and character; it has occurred to me that my limiting of the picture, in the early chapters, of interactions with prisoners to being something atypical and fleeting is an insincerity of its own type, such that a sickly sweet sentimentalism could be flowing at important stages from my notes, as from everything that is incomplete and not fully stated.

Apropos this, it merely remains for me to say that the anxieties survived were not without aftereffects for either anyone on the opposing side or for *katorga* or for my comrades and me. Regarding the first, I candidly admit that their behavior never surprised me in the least. Of course, it could not be supposed that they would quickly or completely forget that summer's events; on the contrary, per the general mood it was often felt that prisoners never forgot a thing… However, in our presence none (even the most mentally and morally dissolute) ever spoke about the past events. There was in fact a sort of silent, albeit solid, compact formed between us and them on this account: to be quiet, to never bring up what had happened. Was delicacy, in its own way, being expressed here? Did that circumstance—to take a firm stand to show indifference to their fate, and that in the end was a policy we mastered—play a certain role? How was it, I repeat, that I never again saw on the part of our cohabitants the slightest intention to renew the argument?

The bitterness of the insult that once enraged and pushed Bashurov to thoughtless words and deeds quickly subsided as well: he was by nature kind and not vengeful. Over time, his extreme opinions about prisoners, so incompatibly opposed to each other and rapidly changing, softened and evened out; in the end, our views grew close and were reconciled. But, moreover, the unpleasant experiences taught all three of us to be more restrained, to take each step more vigilantly with a circumstantial regard for *katorga* and its interests. If, owing to this, our behavior might have lost some of its earlier naturalness and spontaneity, then, by the same token, it guaranteed against new big mistakes, and this was of course the main thing.

In the meantime, autumn's arrival prepared experiences and anxieties for us of an entirely different sort—a unique nightmare that could only occur in prison and only for educated people.

More than six months before the newcomers' arrival at Shelai, I had a conversation with the brave captain that, at the time, I did not count as being especially significant but rather as one of the captain's innumerable passing fancies that in most instances were never realized.

"I'm rather dissatisfied with the state of the prison," he said in connection with something else, furrowing his brows, though in an almost amicably confidential tone. "Not so long ago, I sometimes dreamt about what tempted me to accept the position of commandant."

I became curious to know what, strictly speaking, was causing him dissatisfaction.

"Yes, if you will, everything, absolutely everything! The initial plan, in the composition of which I took part, was to build at Shelai mine a model prison distinguishable from all other *katorga* prisons. Strictness, an unwavering, utterly martial strictness throughout the regime—that was the basic principle I had in view. I then composed, you understand, a report in which I laid all this out. I know these artists very well, know what's needed to control them!… The then governor agreed with me about everything. But… you know our Russian procedures? Bureaucratic tyranny, red tape… Every reasonable project is looked into by dozens of persons of power, each of whom has his own fantasies! Everything new and original goes unacknowledged… According to my plan, the commandant of Shelai Prison would have had to depend only on God and the governor or, to speak more honestly, ultimately only on the established regulations. Nerchinsk's *katorga* director would have had nothing to do with this prison: he might be informed—but nothing more… Such was my ideal. But, you see what's happened in reality! As always, there've been only half-measures! The prison was constructed as a model, but at the same time—everything's remained as in the past. The chief problem is the traditional way of managing *katorga* and the institution is—I'll candidly tell you—antediluvian, saturated throughout with bureaucratic formalism and negligence! So, what's become of all my initiatives? Absolutely nothing. I have absolutely no freedom of action, my hands are completely tied… My monetary expenditures are limited, I'm forced to waste time on trivialities. I'll give you a little example: according to staffing regulations, I'm supposed to have an assistant whose responsibility it is to carry out certain dirty jobs—conduct prisoner roll calls, inspect the orderliness of the prison, of the guards… Well, of course, this is imperative for a certain prestige of the commandant's authority… But, what do you know? Did they give me an assistant, or did they give me someone else? I requested an officer, an energetic, decisive man, sufficiently capable of replacing me in necessary instances, but they assigned… some retired chancery clerk, a drunkard and veal-calf I'm afraid even to let into the prison, who's capable only of sitting in the office and scribbling on paper…"

I recall vividly the physique of this "veal-calf and drunkard"—pitiful, hunchbacked, with shaking hands and head, in some sort of long woman's housecoat with brown buttons meant to resemble a clerk's greatcoat. He very rarely appeared in the prison, we almost never heard his voice, and none of the prisoners even knew about his official title of "assistant" and so everyone called him "the letter manager."

"Under such conditions the prison cannot be exemplary!" Luchezarov was passionately continuing. "Essentially, absolutely nothing distinguishes it from the other *katorga* prisons."

"However, judging from prisoners' stories, there's incomparably more freedom in the other prisons…"

"That is, you mean to say—dissoluteness? But do you know why this is? Only because *I'm* here… Appoint a typical warden in my place—and tomorrow you won't be able to tell Shelai Prison from Zerentui, Algacha, or any other!"

The brave captain's smug, roseate face took on a dreamy sadness: he ardently twirled his mustaches and, waving his hand, quickly went to the window.

"However," he'd suddenly got the better of his anxiety and once again began speaking in an irrefutable, powerful tone, "I'm still not losing hope… No! I'm nourishing hope! I almost believe… The new governor *will* approve my plans… Moreover, I have sympathizers in Petersburg… friends… My report is currently being distributed, and it's entirely possible that in the near future you'll become familiar with it in practice."

His eyes suddenly blazed with playful fire… However, he could not read in my face the strong desire to sooner know "in practice" his bellicose plans, because he hurriedly changed the conversation to another topic and the audience soon ended.

I repeat, I did not at that time give great significance to this conversation, and excluded it from my mind almost that very day. But, following the newcomers' arrival to the prison, I more than once had a vague premonition of some impending, severe new arrangements. Even the guards were talking about this, although it must be said that most sided openly with the prisoners and were unabashedly easygoing; several even ventured that "in case of this" they would retire… Only Pronia-the-Living-Dead turned out to be even more insufferable than before, and fastened everyone's buttons tighter and tighter. For a long time now, he had been Luchezarov's favorite and right hand.

Eventually, a new rumor troubled our imaginations every other day, but quickly slipped out of mind: monotonous, destructive reality did not grant us very long to dwell on either good or bad rumors. Contrarily, amid every kind of grievance and dissatisfaction that fate gave us, the hapless and deprived of rights, there was someone whose honest devotion supported us in moments of dejection more than once and who later rendered us a priceless service more than once. This someone was—a woman… Shteinhart initially benefited only from an acquaintance, but later from a friendship, with the wife of the commander of the Cossack squadron stationed at Shelai—with the "kind mother-officer," as the ingenuous mare called her. It so happened that soon after his arrival to Shelai mine, she fell seriously ill with pneumonia and, by universal recognition, was spared death thanks only to Shteinhart. In order to understand and fully appreciate the feeling that suffused the recovered patient's soul, it is somewhat necessary to introduce this kind and profoundly unfortunate woman's situation and moral constitution.

Young, beautiful, and, to tell the truth, poorly educated, albeit with a kind and responsive heart and humanitarian inclinations, she had married a middle-aged officer she barely knew, as is done—that is, simplemindedly and without thought—by most young women in out-of-the-way, remote provinces. Life in all its severe unsightliness was revealed to her startled eyes the very day after her wedding. Her husband was not an evil man by nature, but he was obtuse and close to a vulgarian, whose opinions of people and social activities she, who was herself fumblingly and instinctively tracking down the truths and falsehoods of life, had not the power to change. Anna Arkadevna wandered with her husband among Transbaikal District's various remote corners for a long time, and finally ended up in the gloomy hole that was our *katorga* township, in the taiga amid cheerless hills. Here, not just a backward and colorless society greeted her—no, here was a real serfdom environment, cruel, soulless, and with the most anti-humanitarian notions worthy of primeval savages; it was like a piece of the Middle Ages, defensively preserved and legally thriving within a civilized country during enlightened times… The most barbaric crudeness and nakedly bestial immorality reigned everywhere, and there were no lofty interests whatsoever. Guards' wives proved to be the Shelai *beau monde*'s top ladies, given that Luchezarov, Monakhov, and the young Cossack cornet were bachelors; squabbling among themselves, these ladies openly called each other "scoundrels" and "strumpets"…

Anna Arkadevna was herself fated to replicate the usual grim story in Rus of sufferings unknown to anyone, of the same drowning of the sensitive but weak female soul… Correspondence with her unsophisticated girlfriends, in the absence of shared interests, gradually became boring and slackened off; she had no children; no books to read; and tears were not withheld… How would this pathetic tale end? Of course, it was most likely of all that Anna Arkadevna, like hundreds and thousands of her predecessors, would eventually give in to the world-weary slime's sucking strength; several more years would pass and she, like everyone, would lose her human form and became the same as everyone… But at that very moment, when it was still not too late, salvation arrived. Before her—sick, weak, overwhelmed by burning fever and excitation, calling for death at the same time as agonizingly wanting to live—suddenly appeared a young, energetic, and not at all bad-looking physician outfitted with the most unusual accouterments—a soldier's bayonet behind his back, rumbling chains on his ankles, and a shaved head. A soft light burned in his eyes, encouragement and hope resounded in his every word… Anna Arkadevna's imagination was aroused, her desire won over from the very first; meanwhile, each new visit by Shteinhart, with its accompanying mysteriousness and oddness, only heightened this fascination, revealing in the young convict-physician ever new and unsuspected characteristics and virtues; by the time the patient found her life completely out of danger, they had established between them a close, deep friendship. It was completely natural that the young woman's selfless, touchingly faithful devotion soon carried over to her savior's comrades, whom she'd never seen in her life, though Shteinhart, returning from their meetings, invariably communicated his patient's greetings and regards to Bashurov and me, and then, when the personal meetings came to an end, all three of us began receiving perfumed notes rapturously addressed : "My Dears!" with the signature: "Your faithful and loving friend." As I said above, this love and faith was later manifested more than once, but if you still exist anywhere, dear, selfless soul, loving so much yet so little compensated for this love, accept my gratitude, however belated but nonetheless passionate and sincere!…

Having recovered, Anna Arkadevna understandably tried to find all possible pretexts to again meet Shteinhart from time to time: first she'd have some new ailment, then a medical consultation was needed to eliminate traces of the difficult illness suffered during the spring… At this time she became extremely interested in getting to know the magnificent Luchezarov, the sight of whom she'd previously not been able to stand and toward whom she'd always expressed every sort of obvious ill will. The beautiful young woman now began smiling at him not without coquetry and speaking with him amicably, and the brave captain, never having been insensitive to a woman's charms, each time melted like beeswax and, upon the charming Cossack officer's wife's slightest indisposition, would have agreed to become a shade so as to save her from that world of all famous physicians of ages past; he became all the more disposed to allow Shteinhart to respond upon the Cossack officer's first call…

It was from this source that Shteinhart one day delivered incontestable information about the new displeasures threatening us, and about which various dark rumors had now been circulating for a long time. Before then, he'd not seen Anna Arkadevna for around three weeks, and only once during all that time was a brief note received from her: "Every instant I'm seeking to summon an opportunity, but nothing at all can be managed. I'm afraid that L. suspects something. There is important news." She'd finally managed to arrange a meeting.

"Just imagine, gentlemen," said Shteinhart, having returned to the prison, "I've fallen into disfavor!"

"Six-Eyes's?"

"Well, needless to say. Let's assume that for a long time he has clearly been looking at me sideways. Lately, I've been summoned to patients outside prison gates very rarely, and not long ago, they say, a Cossack rode in from afar and tearfully pleaded for me to be allowed to examine him, but permission wasn't granted… However, I've explained all this in offhand moments."

"But what happened just now?"

"It turns out he does not view me with indifference. Yesterday, when Anna Arkadevna pressed him to summon me, he burst like gunpowder and exploded with a long monologue in which he frankly declared: 'Shteinhart is a little boy who's completely spoilt owing to my soft treatment of him! He's utterly forgotten that he's a penal laborer, that he's supposed to work in the mine, and he fancies himself somehow akin to the leadership and supposes we owe him something.' 'Forgive me,' interrupted Anna Arkadevna, 'but don't we indeed owe him a lot?' Then Luchezarov was definitely 'jumpin' outta himself,' as the prisoners say, and began to disclaim all my knowledge and ability: 'If there were certain successful outcomes in his practice, then this is simply fortunate happenstance, nothing more. I don't recognize a physician in this arrogant… half-educated person!…' Anna Arkadevna nearly wept at these words, but Luchezarov continued with his candor: 'Even if you got some use out of him, this axiom would be even further confirmed. Shteinhart is a penal laborer, and his business is that of a penal laborer, not a physician. But any day now there begins…' 'What exactly begins?' 'A new regime in general. I finally received long awaited instructions to organize the prison according to my visions and convictions. And I will build a truly model prison, and not some hotel, as it's been up to now.'

The captain gradually told everything: printed rules (at this word 'printed' he positively choked up with delight!) will be hung on the wards' walls, and not following them will occasion the most serious punishments... Moreover, any day he'll have a real assistant such as he's always wished for, a man courageous and efficient and not as gentle as he is. Ah, Luchezarov... Anna Arkadevna sighed when she recognized this new assistant's name: she personally knows Second Lieutenant Lomov well and has heard much about him in her time. 'He's a blockhead, you know,' she cried, 'there's nothing human in him at all!' 'From a certain point-of-view,' the captain replied, 'in any case, the second lieutenant has many incontestable virtues. First of all, he is honest and incorruptible, but mainly—he's assiduous. And, in *our* business, this is an invaluable quality! Obedience, assiduousness, energy...' Anna Arkadevna had to summon up an heroic effort of will to restrain her indignation, and this all managed to come out thanks only to her outward calm. 'Tell your comrades,' she told me in conclusion, 'that I'm now very frightened for you all! I might still have had influence over Luchezarov alone, and my husband is also not an evil man and could as well be restrained a bit by me. But it will be impossible to reach an understanding with Lomov: he doesn't have a head, but a wooden block... In all probability our meetings will now end completely and we'll be limited to written messages, though we'll have to write very, very carefully. If you're doing too poorly, let me know. I'll write to Chita—I have old contacts there, friends, and I may be able to subdue these Luchezarovian escapades...'

"Well, that's my news for today," Shteinhart concluded his story. "Not very pleasant, is it?"

"Before deciding anything, we'll await developments," we decided, dispersing to our locations. I was still in hospital; Bashurov and Shteinhart were now in the same ward.

Developments did not keep us waiting. One morning, the "lisping devil," the senior guard himself, brought to the prison a bunch of printed "Rules of Shelai *Katorga* Prison," beneath which Captain Luchezarov's signature had been significantly emblazoned, and he solemnly began nailing them onto the front wall of each of the nine wards. The literate among the mare took to reading them with curiosity. Strictly speaking, there was nothing new or unexpected in these rules, but everything previously required of prisoners was now emphasized and empowered by a quite definite threat, by recourse to that or another stern legal statute. The words "birch rods," "lashes," "court," "manacles," "shackles," "isolation cell," "corporal punishment," "disfranchisement from the free command" so struck the eye, so gripped the heart, it was like fingernails on a chalkboard. On the other hand, this declaration made not the slightest impression on most prisoners.

"Oh, them all!... I reckoned it was sumpin' of a manifesto, but we knows what this means without their paper," they said, still not having reached the end of the rules and stalking off without a care.

"What'd they hang that rag up there for?" asked those returning from work and who'd still not heard anything.

"It's 'bout trousers, brother. Com'dant noticed ours was all wrinkled, so here he's promisin' to iron 'em."

The joke met with universal laughter and the questioner lost interest in the poster's contents.

But, contrarily for us, these contents were of extreme importance, since we distinctly understood that their calculated impact was mainly aimed at us. "At exactly 9 o'clock in the evening," we read, "at the first drumbeat, prisoners in the wards are required to immediately lie down to sleep. Disobedience and infringements of this rule detected by the guards will the first time incur a punishment of isolation, the second time—birch rods." This rule, minus the recent threat, had been known earlier; during Shelai Prison's first year of existence not observing it had led to verbal clashes with guards; prisoners had even been removed to the isolator two or three times, but all this was forgotten ages earlier, especially as the prisoners, fatigued by the day's labors, were asleep no later than nine o'clock. It concerned my comrades and me that we often did not lie down for another hour and a half or two hours. The guards distinctly paid no attention to this, and Luchezarov himself, carrying out an evening inspection of the prison, sometimes saw but said nothing to any of us. Now, an imposing and very significant threat had been printed regarding this… "For refusing to work under the pretext of illness unconfirmed by a physician or medic [!], and, likewise, for not completing an assignment without sufficient [!] causes," the same punishment was designated: the isolator at first, then the birch rods…

"For not doffing one's cap to an official," "for sharply answering the guards," "for ignoring the alarm and whistle," and for many other things of the same sort there was the ancient rod, it seemed, whistling through the air, terrorizing irregardless of an oppressive and sickly construction of the imagination. Further on, it was precisely dictated which of the administration's figures had to be called "Your Excellency" and "Your Worship," and in what instances "to your health" or "very good, sir" had to be said;[48] and at the end of everything, there was a quite curious point: "Guards shall not use the formal *you* with any of the prisoners, but will address all of them invariably with the informal *you*"… In the series of prisoners' rules this article, which had been directed with a reprimand at guards, stood out as particularly odd and obviously unnecessary. This obvious lack of necessity betrayed the regulations' composer: it was clear he'd given this special significance, that a bureaucrat's quill had at this precise point squeaked into the paper with extraordinary vehemence…

Be that as it may, the posting of the printed rules made a sickeningly depressing impact on three of the 150 prisoners. It's true we were silent, even between ourselves, and held no councils whatsoever and made no sort of peremptory decisions, but each of our hearts clenched agonizingly and dark presentiments occluded our souls in a cold fog… The prospect of a new battle, a battle for human dignity, at the very time our weary souls thirsted for peace and quiet, even if this peace was the regular hard regime of *katorga* life—this prospect frightened and depressed us… For whom and why was it necessary? What did they want from us?

The "new order" began insofar as the senior guard, having nailed the rules on the walls, approached Shteinhart and Bashurov and, smirking shamelessly and whimsically, demanded—lisping as usual—their personal bed sheets, which we'd been using since time immemorial. With great pleasure the brave captain, always having favored and encouraged cleanliness and tidiness, had in his time permitted me to use sheets; this precedent had already been long established by the time the newcomers arrived.

"According to what article are you taking the sheets?" Shteinhart asked in astonishment.

"What article! Saysth in the rulesth that bedding, clothesth, and all other thingsth should only be gov'ment issthue."

"Don't you know the bedding is inconceivably filthy?"

"The pristhnersth destherve filth," the guard tried to joke, "but on th'other hand, com'dant sthaysth that if all the pristhnersth get sheetsth, then it'sth allowed."

But all the prisoners, of course, could not "get" sheets, and henceforth we, too, had to sleep on just the filthy bedding. However Six-Eyes loved cleanliness and tidiness, for him, the principle was more important! The assault was obviously deliberate and completely planned…

The author himself appeared that very evening at roll call, resplendent and terrible, surrounded by all of Shelai's guards. From a window in the hospital corridor, I observed the ceremony with curiosity and a certain trepidation; every booming exclamation came through the little open window distinctly. I saw Bashurov and Shteinhart, contrary to waiting for the permission that usually came immediately to put caps back on (and, not out of any sort of protest, as they later explained, but simply mechanically, by force of habit), put theirs on without waiting for the order. The brave captain noticed this and, turning purple, screamed at the top of his voice:

"Never put on your caps until I say so!"

A long and awkward silence ensued. The offenders continued standing there in their caps. Another instant, and the more zealous among the guards would have hurled shouts and threats at them, but Luchezarov menacingly ordered:

"Caps on… Just so!" he continued, still raising his voice. "Some of you are wearing your trousers over your boots. Form demands that trousers be tucked inside… Besides, it looks so bad—only *Yids* wear 'em like that."

And, having blurted out this surprising moniker, he fell gloomily silent. This speech made an even greater impression on me because I knew against whom it was directed; out of everyone in the prison, Bashurov alone wore his trousers against regulations…

This, however, did not end the problems. When the guards ordered prisoners to disperse among the wards, Luchezarov's rage burst forth again; a shrill cry such as I'd not yet heard resounded through the yard:

"They're not walking in step! Who dares to leave out of order? Who…"

But the column at which this cry was directed and in which my two comrades were had already managed to enter the prison doors and hide from sight. Luchezarov for some reason did not recall it, though he kept screaming in the yard for a long time—indeed, so that I couldn't keep listening. I walked away from the window with heaviness and gloom in my heart.

As it happened, Luchezarov delivered brief, albeit oppressive, speeches in many wards that evening, and, of course, he could not imagine that we would not learn their substance.

"There will be certain restrictions introduced in the prison," he informed prisoners, "but you shouldn't fear them. Those who are meek and obedient will encounter nothing bad from me.

"But among you are men that are arrogant… obstinate… You must help me to curb them. I've heard they're not to your fancy—all the better!"

I confess I'd not at all anticipated that the brave captain, amid all the changes of his morals and "principles," would ever descend to such humiliating and unsightly methods of combat. But he was too late: the "alarm" was given only in the aftermath, when any discord between us and the mare was no longer being mentioned… On the other hand, I believe he could have achieved nothing on this basis any earlier; unlike the administration, even the prison ringleaders who'd opposed us hardly wanted an alliance in this matter… At that present moment, Luchezarov achieved results utterly contrary to those he wished for: it must be said to the mare's credit that not one man among them could be found who would go along (at the very least out loud) with the commandant's blunt speech; on this and the following days the entire prison treated us with exaggerated attention and respect; they hastily parted before us, smiled at us amicably, and spoke to us with a clear wish to encourage and relax… And during the entire subsequent difficult time we lived through, the mare conducted itself with positive nobility, deeply touching to us at times.

Several days later, the anticipated "assistant" arrived. From break of dawn that day, guards sped through the prison, everywhere establishing with especial diligence cleanliness, quiet, and order, as if expecting some high-ranking general. Two or three prisoners ended up in the isolators for bad manners. Everyone awaited evening roll call with intense curiosity. The bell rang somehow completely unexpectedly, and prisoners began rummaging about just like an annoyed swarm of bees in a hive.

"Hurry, get your kettles, you devils, you demons!" shouts burst all around, and the ward headmen who'd been lagging ran as fast as they could to the kitchen for tea. The orderly was straining himself to the limit, urging them on with his "barks." The convict-poet Vladimirov, by this time one of the wards' former headmen, stumbled on the main porch's steps and stretched too far to hand a container of tea to us. Broad streams of brown-colored liquid splashed onto the porch. There was inconceivable embarrassment: with rabid curses the chortling mare laughed at the guard, and bakers and cooks ran out of the kitchen with rags to hurriedly wipe up, to hide, the traces of this "disgrace"; but Bear's Ears, the very instigator of all the craziness, hobbling on his bruised feet and with dangling head humbly lowered, smiled embarrassedly and hurried to take his place in the ranks now forming and where prisoners cheerfully ribbed him.

"Hey, uncle! How many whacks should you get now that you lost the wards' tea?"

Everyone formed proper ranks with difficulty. Barely had ranks formed than was heard: "They're comin'! They're comin'!—and everyone quieted down. The gates opened wide and, in the company of a group of guards, there entered Six-Eyes and beside him his new assistant, Second Lieutenant Lomov. All eyes fixed on this new figure, whose appearance had been preceded by so much gossip and so many rumors. The figure was unusually imposing: although not as tall as Luchezarov, his shoulders were much broader, and Lomov produced the impression of an awkward, pigeon-toed bear that had been put on a torture rack. To complete the similarity, he was evidently unable to hold his head straight on his shoulders but rather aslant and he gazed from beneath his brows with gray, unpleasant eyes. Indeed, his entire face was shaped like a bear's, with hair of a somewhat earthy gray color and features that are difficult to describe or remember.

"In a word, boys—he's a Lomov!" Thus the mare later summed up its impression.[49] However, what had become of the brave captain? For he did not resemble the thundering

Jupiter, the Prometheus, that had been showing up in the prison for the past several days! On the contrary, he now gave off brightness and goodwill and gazed upon the subdued mare like a kind and equitable father would his own beloved children; entering the gateway, he'd even smiled at everyone in passing… He ordered caps on at almost the very same moment the guard gave the order to remove them. Upon listening to the orderly's report on the prison's favorable status, he charitably appealed to the prisoners with a salutation, and moreover did not even say "*Hullo*, boys!", but rather "*Greetings*, old chaps"… And when the "old chaps" responded to this with the deafening roar: "To your health, Mister Com'dant!"—he gazed upon them still more solicitously and, pointing to Lomov, said:

"Here, old chaps… I ask you to love and favor my new assistant!"

What he said probably seemed rather odd to the brave captain himself: he seemed to get embarrassed and fell silent. By the same token, his good nature did not abandon him. In the meantime, Lomov was standing as before, enormous and gray, immovable, an absolute statue of a commander, his oblique head tilting toward the ground somewhat, and only during the commandant's unexpected speech did it move rather nervously, like a draught-horse's nose when a fly touches on it.[50]

The prison choir sang the established hymns. With utter sanctimony, Luchezarov set out for the back rows of prisoners, where he moved during the singing (probably so it didn't seem the prisoners were praying to him!).

"Here's what I'll tell you, Petin," he loudly began speaking to him, putting his papakha on at the end of the hymn and striding toward the front again, "it seems you're a bass, but your head's probably as hollow as an empty bucket. You don't know a note and you drone where it's absolutely unnecessary!"

This comment was made, however, in such a friendly tone, that here and there within the prisoners' ranks there escaped the words "empty bucket" and even a quiet laugh—the most the mare risked. This was quite enough to forestall the commandant being carried further away by his joy, and he suddenly adopted a controlled, stern visage. The mare happily dispersed among the wards. From my observation post I observed how, afterward, Six-Eyes for a long time continued standing in the middle of the yard and good-naturedly discoursed about something to his gray and silent assistant. The conversation was apparently completely casual—nonetheless, Lomov saluted the commandant now and then. The guards kept themselves at a respectful distance. Finally, the entire suite went to the prison and remained there over an hour. My nerves were shattered and my head ached due to the long wait, and I'd already concluded that this protracted ceremony would never end. But at last here came the procession and it went straight toward the kitchen: marching briskly in front, the skirts of his greatcoat flapping, was Six-Eyes; some distance behind, head cocked to the side, Lomov grimly strode, and bringing up the rear in pairs that stolidly proceeded exactly 28 inches at a time, were six or seven guards. From the kitchen the procession went… to the cesspit. There, the brave captain, gesticulating colorfully, explained something to the gloomy second lieutenant for a long time; and only after a thorough examination of the cesspit did he finally set off for the hospital. Only then did I abandon my post and hurry into the ward.

Lately, I hadn't been the only one in it, but had as a cohabitant the old Ukrainian yokel, Tkachenko.

The vestibule's doors thundered open, and dozens of boots pounded along the corridor floor. As he approached my room, Luchezarov could be heard saying something under his breath to Lomov. And then all the empty space before Tkachenko and me quickly filled with the greatcoat of the brave captain, who nearly pinned me to the small table in-between the pair of beds. Entering prison wards, the captain never removed his hat, yet, by contrast, he always bared his head when he appeared in patients' rooms; the guards who entered did just the same. Now, at the edge of my cell, he removed his papakha with a gracious sweep of his arm, not forgetting to immediately blow the dust from it. Lomov had stopped at the threshold, and the guards were clustered in the corridor. I wasn't looking at the threshold, but I felt as if something huge, burdensome, and dark was there…

Luchezarov slowly removed his kid gloves from his hands and filled the room with the scent of his spicy cologne, toward which I'd always been drawn. With neither whimsical nor favorable eyes he gazed down at me from above for several moments.

"Well, then, how are we doing?"

I silently shrugged my shoulders.

"Are we improving?"

"A little."

The conversation did not go at all well, and the brave captain hastily turned to Tkachenko.

"Well, but you, old-timer, what are you doing?"

"Chewin' bread, Mister Com'dant, 'n' prayin' to God," the prisoner tried to joke, seeing the commandant's kind mien. But this answer clearly did not please Luchezarov.

"Aha," he frowned, "you're chewing bread? I can do that, old chap… The infirmary's not for chewing bread, but for lying down from illness."

"I got a good nuff excuse, Mister Com'dant! Thousands o' ailments, simply beyond count… 'ow me back alone aches!"

"He's lived energetically!" Luchezarov, slightly cocking his head, meaningfully blurted at me, and suddenly rushed out of the chamber.

The corridor once again thundered from the clatter of a multitude of footsteps.

"What does it mean: ''e's lived energetically'?" Tkachenko unwontedly addressed me.

Laughing, I explained it to him. The old man's cunning, slanted eyes angrily flitted here and there; his gray side-whiskers and thick mustaches bristled amusingly. He either did not really understand or did not want to understand my explanation.

"Energetically?…," he exclaimed with comical indignation. "No, you're naughty, brother! No, I ain't been livin' foolishly e'en at all. Not foolishly, for sure! Foolishly ended up 'ere in prison—that's true, quite true."

Lomov appeared by himself at the following day's evening roll call. He didn't utter a single word during the entire ceremony. Now and then the orderly came galloping up with questions: "As you like, Mister Assistant?"—and he simply glumly nodded his head at everything. Of itself, it goes without saying that he did not order caps on, and so the prisoners, with the exclusion of Shteinhart and Bashurov, stood from the beginning to the end of roll call in the bitter December frost with heads uncovered. Having slightly inclined his neck to the side, Lomov seemed not to notice anything and to be thinking about completely extraneous things. The prisoners dispersed among the wards, still not having gotten to the core of the new assistant's character: someone compared him to a sheep, but someone else to a wolf at bay; yet, in general, the interest raised was extremely weak.

Another day passed, and there came a second roll call that Lomov again attended, and once more I watched the proceedings with curiosity and suppressed alarm. Hardly had the prayer concluded than he pulled from his pocket what at first seemed a pack of cards and began distributing them to the prisoners, loudly announcing each by his surname. His voice turned out to be thunderous, albeit with a kind of irritable, bilious peal in the concluding words.

"Milo-serdov! Grib-skii! Vla-a-dimirov!"

Those named humbly removed their caps, stepped from the ranks, and, approaching Lomov, took the cards from his hand. He looked steadily at each, as if wanting to memorize his physiognomy. The patients avidly watching with me sensed what these cards were.

"Tickets! He's givin' out tickets, boys… He's goin' along 'cordin' to the rows… Is there any he won't get?"

"Chi-rok! Ishni-iazov! Ogur-tsov!" Lomov continued shouting.

My heart pounded in anticipation of the inevitable event.

"Shara-fetdinov! No-gaitsev! Ba-a-shurov!"

The little Tatar Sharafetdinov and the fat Nogaitsev, having quickly tucked their caps in their armpits, ran to get their tickets. Bashurov took a slow path behind them, and on his head was stuck his ill-starred cap. Lomov, thrusting the piece of paper toward him, raised his eyes.

"You forgot to remove your cap… What's your name?"

The cap was not removed.

"Cap off!!" the assistant practically screamed, and advanced on Bashurov. "Disorder!!"

The response was the previous silence.

"What's his name?"

A guard flew over like an arrow and, saluting, announced his name.

"Take him to the isolator!" Lomov screamed still louder. Bashurov was brought to the isolator. Along the way, he looked into the hospital window and, with a joyous smile, nodded at me… In the meantime, Lomov, until the guards returned from the isolator compound, paced in front of the prisoners' ranks in obvious agitation; Tkachenko even believed he saw his entire face twist…

"Well, there's evil in 'im! 'E'll be e'en worse'n Six-Eyes. A real wolf! I said a wolf's a-comin'—now it's come, in my view… E'en though its head's bent sideways, as ever'one sees!"

Upon the guards' return, the shouting continued as if nothing had happened. I waited with a sinking heart for Shteinhart to be called… However, by some miracle his ticket did not turn up, and the rest of roll call passed uneventfully.

The following morning, I abandoned the infirmary and returned to the prison: now that the battle was beginning, I wanted to be with my comrades. By order of the guard,

I ended up in a ward other than Shteinhart's. The latter insisted that I immediately ask to see Luchezarov for negotiations. This was not an onerous responsibility, and no other option presented itself because it was known that Shteinhart had taken advantage of the captain's favorable disposition, so I announced to the orderly my desire to meet with the prison commandant on an urgent matter. I wasn't assigned to work that day, in view of the fact that I'd just been released from hospital, and I spent the entire day wandering the prison yard, nervous and impatiently expecting I would suddenly be called to the office. During the more than three years of my stay in Shelai Luchezarov had rather spoiled me in this regard: each time I reported a need to meet, he summoned me immediately. But today something strange was happening: hour followed hour, but no decision was made to call for me. Finally, the mine laborers returned.

"Well? What happened?" Shteinhart rushed toward me.

"Nothing."

"They still haven't called you at all?"

"No."

"What does this mean?"

"I really don't know. We'll wait a bit longer…"

"Well, but what about Valerian?"

I shared what details I'd managed to get about our arrested comrade.

Lomov appeared again at that evening's roll call. Shteinhart and I stood the entire time in our caps, but he evidently failed to notice the "disorder" and everything went smoothly. Luchezarov showed no signs of life for another two days, and it's no joke we began to get irritated… However, in conversations with Shteinhart I regarded it as my duty to dampen as possible his indignation, and even tried to endow the episode with a comical aspect. This angered Shteinhart.

"I don't understand what you see funny here!" he said with ardor. "And are you and I doing anything?"

"Of course I'm doing something, but this doesn't mean I can't have a laugh to myself. Just think: we're enduring *katorga*, enduring a soldier's regime, enduring God knows what, yet suddenly we're up in arms over some wretched caps!"

"Ivan Nikolaevich, a single extra drop can overflow a cup of patience, you know…"

"But this doesn't eliminate the possibility of judging logically. In the final analysis, removing caps is a formality like everything else. It goes without saying I'll never renounce comradeship; if I were living here alone without you, I'd act just as I now am with you. But, on the other hand, as I'm advising you, if comrades decided to spit on this matter, I wouldn't dig in my heels…"

Shteinhart hotly protested against such a view.

"I don't see it this way… In my opinion, even corporal punishment does not so humiliate a man! What can a man with bound hands do against brute physical force? Does this really *humiliate* him? Yet, in your view, this question about having to remove your cap is comparatively small and ridiculous—oh, it's a completely different matter! For I'm not passively, but *actively*, debasing myself, and out of a selfish fear I myself, with my own hand, do what is most extremely unpleasant to me…"

"Well then, Dmitrii Petrovich… Forgive my asking, but do you remember the decision you took the first evening you arrived here: 'I'll suffer everything, but not an offense against the fundamentals of my dignity'? There had been a request, about which… But do you really think this is one of the fundamentals being offended?"

Shteinhart flared then paled again.

"Of course I remember," he said, lowering his voice and letting his head sadly drop, "but, in the first place, such decisions are taken in a moment of despondency or, contrarily, of a joyous upsurge of feelings. And, in the second place, how exactly can you tell where any fundamental ends and where it begins? You don't decide that with logic at all, it's an area of moral sensibility…"

But it was the "logic" in me that had been silent for so long, having been replaced by a discord of various thoughts and emotions. More than anything I, like Shteinhart, feared that the issue of caps I insisted held no essential significance for me might be only the first step along a path of systematic outrage against our dignity. That Six-Eyes had concocted a systematic plan, I had no great doubt. Within this plan, Lomov appeared to be merely an obedient and capable instrument. Something had evidently happened in the brave captain that, given all the cruelty of his character, prevented him from personally addressing this issue; his obtuse and straightforwardly rude assistant stepped into this thankless role in the best possible way. And the thought that we now found ourselves under the limitless control of two such men and that above our heads were hanging, just like a Damoclean sword, "instructions" designating the ever so slight gradations in their system of punishments—this thought chilled and anesthetized the soul.

Bashurov had now spent three full days in a dark isolator.

In the evening, we attended roll call in a deep spiritual depression. The gates opened, and a riotous gang of just guards came through, talking freely and joyfully. The mare happily roused itself as well.

"Well then, what the hell can happen today!"

Before leaving our ward, I met with Shteinhart once more.

"What do we do now? Isn't it obvious they don't want to talk with us at all?"

Shteinhart's face became severe.

"We won't go to tomorrow's roll call—end of matter! Let them make us, if they want!"

However, less than a half hour after roll call the key growled throughout my ward again, and a guard summoned me to the prison commandant. The brave captain was awaiting me in the little orderly's room adjoining one of the prison corridors. His greatcoat was casually flung across his powerful shoulders, his papakha courteously removed from his head. As usual, there was a strong smell of eau-de-cologne in the room and, as always, Luchezarov's face and entire physique emanated vigor and satisfaction.

"What's going on?" he quickly said, nearly startling me. "All these days I was terribly busy, and was not at all able…" He turned to the guard: "Give us a minute."

The latter respectfully jingled his keys and disappeared like an apparition.

"What is going on?" repeated the brave captain, as though he really did not suspect the reason for my call.

"You know perfectly well what," I answered, controlling my agitation with difficulty, "it's now been four days you're holding our comrade under arrest."

"I? Bashurov? You're mistaken… He was arrested by my assistant."

"And is your assistant the master of the prison?"

"I, needless to say, am master, but… my assistant also has his own responsibilities and rights. I cannot infringe on them. I've been given a report about what happened, and I must take account of the facts."

"In a word, you want to wash your hands of it? What happens if someone else instigates the prisoners against us?"

"Instigates the prisoners? What nonsense! On the contrary, they always complain to me…"

The brave captain got tangled up and turned crimson to the roots of his hair.

"What is it you want from me? The regulations, which I'm obliged to follow, are stated unequivocally."

"The regulations, which you yourself composed and obtained after so many years? We want very little, so, to all appearances, legal…"

"Namely?"

"That your subordinate at the very least address us no worse than he does you… Suggesting this to him depends entirely upon you. You yourself know: not once have you had any kind of incident with us in the four years you've been in charge of the prison. Why is this? Because, of course, you have as possible curbed the severity of the dead letter of the regulations…"

I clearly saw that my words hit the captain's soft spot: his round face took on a sudden sheen, and a rush of righteous pride made his head rise higher than usual.

"Yes, yes," he hastened to agree, "this is my quality, I really am a very moderate man… Truth is, there are minutes when I lose my self-control with these artists [he waved his hand in the direction of the wards], but with those who are deserving… with refined people… I can't be just a commandant, but a human being!"

"So, why now, after three years' peace and quiet, have clashes and incidents suddenly become necessary?"

"Tell me, how did the business with this prisoner happen?"

I told him, possibly dwelling more on the psychology of the educated man and emphasizing that he, Luchezarov, had up to now always considered that circumstance. The brave captain, as if agreeing with me, nodded his head the whole time.

"Well, I suggest no further incidents occur," he said at last, and after some thought suddenly added: "I trust that you, for example, will conduct yourself more prudently than Bashurov. The law requires what should be!"

I confess such a conclusion was for me completely unexpected. It had at first seemed that my skilful diplomacy was carrying the day and that Six-Eyes was ready to concede—now here we were at the stove again, as they say!

"You're mistaken, you're terribly mistaken!" I ardently shouted. "My conduct will never be different from my comrades' conduct. I'd just as soon rot in the isolator if you don't quickly forbid your assistant from carrying out the regulations too punctiliously! And after that, what should be will be!"

Luchezarov, somewhat taken aback, frowned.

"I'll give it some thought," he said, making a sign toward the door that the audience was over, "in any case, I'll speak with my assistant… I'll try to convince him, since I don't have the right to order him."

"But when will Bashurov be released?"

"His term ends tomorrow evening… Or rather, possibly even today… Yes, yes, I'll order him released right now!"

"In that case, allow me to wait for him."

A guard flew like an arrow to the isolator. Luchezarov, securely wrapped in his greatcoat, began magisterially pacing the corridor. I stood in silent anticipation. After several minutes, hurried steps sounded on the porch, an audacious hand flung open the door, and I saw Valerian, full of life and carefree as ever. Standing face-to-face with me, he broke into cheerful laughter and noisily locked me in an embrace.

"Aha, it's you? You rescued me? But I'd just lain down to sleep… Here I was, relaxing splendidly! Well then, you've been fighting with Six-Eyes? But where's Dmitrii?"

Only then did he notice in the corridor's opposite corner Six-Eyes's grand figure… In obvious embarrassment, the latter opened the door and noiselessly slipped behind it. Bashurov once again spilled over with booming laughter.

XII. TRIUMPH OF A LADY POLITICIAN

The incidents, however, did not end. The only visible result of my conversation with Luchezarov was that for several days afterward, Lomov did not show up at evening roll calls, though, on the other hand, as if wishing to reward himself for this absence, he held the prison in a state of siege at all other hours of the day. Time and again the guard's shrill whistle notifying prisoners of the leadership's arrival was heard in the prison's yard and corridors: it was Lomov coming to inspect his domains… It seemed an enormous delight for him to contemplate as being everywhere images of his glowering gray figure of fear and veneration. As soon as he appeared at the prison gates, everyone who merely had the misfortune of coming that moment into his field of vision was immediately paralyzed into stony poses on the very spots they'd been caught by the whistle, and, after doffing their caps and straightening their arms at their sides, they stood motionless until the gloomy second lieutenant disappeared from sight. Regarding this, I don't recall the living statues receiving permission to cover their bared heads (whatever the weather in the yard), though, at the same time, there often erupted from Lomov's mouth the sharp and typically nervous pealing cry:

"Hul-lo-o!"

But this cry did not at all reveal any kind of goodwill toward the mare—no, it was manufactured in the interests of that very subordination, since everyone was required to give the response:

"Wish-ing your health, Mister Assistant!"

And were this answer not forthcoming, the disorder would be immediately crushed and the doors of the isolator would swing…

Lomov toured the prison corridors several times a day, looking into the wards themselves, the kitchen, tradesmen's area, and hospital, and upon his appearance anywhere prisoners had to jump up, stand at attention, and shout: "Wishing your health!" The guard's whistle would hardly reach our ears and the three of us would instinctively hurry to wherever Lomov typically did not look: encountering him could not be especially nice for us… However, this need to be always vigilant, to constantly run and hide, was also not very nice. Nerves very soon frayed, and every minute free from work was utterly poisoned. More than once, Shteinhart spoke of preferring to sit in the isolator rather than play the role of a rabbit fleeing the hunter… However, things were speeding toward their denouement.

One clear Sunday morning, Shteinhart was unhurriedly returning to his ward with a kettle of tea when, completely unexpectedly, he was caught unawares by urgent deafening whistles in the middle of the yard; the gates growled, and a guard bellowed the usual: "Attention, caps off!" At that instant, everyone in the yard turned on the spot and bared his head. Quickening his step, Shteinhart alone continued walking with cap on head. He'd just reached the prison porch when, from behind, came the insanely shrill cry:

"Sto-op! Sto-op! Disorder!"

He automatically stopped and awaited Lomov.

"Who are you?"

Shteinhart identified himself.

"Ca-ap off!…"

"You take it off."

"To the isolator!! The i-so-la-tor!!"

Lomov's scream ascended in hysterics to the high notes. Completely calmly, Shteinhart began following the arriving guard to the isolator, and the assistant went back outside the prison gates to compose a report to the commandant.

This arrest created a great sensation among the guards and outside the prison in general. No one yet knew about Shteinhart's falling out of favor and that Six-Eyes had firmly decided to limit his medical practice to within prison walls; everyone continued treating him with great love and respect. By contrast, Lomov had everywhere managed to win enmity and even hatred. It was said that someone even decided to say to him about this arrest:

"Whatcha done, Mister Assistant? You've arrested a *gentleman doctor*, y'know."

Lomov, of course, only widened his eyes in surprise. But when someone else mentioned to him that influenza was raging throughout Shelai's environs and Shteinhart might be needed at any moment by the commandant himself, who had fallen ill, he gave this truly noteworthy answer:

"Well, so what! If he's needed—we'll bring him."

"From the isolator?"

"Why not?"

"And then put him in the isolator again?"

"If he hasn't completed his sentence, he goes back again."

This answer passed from mouth to mouth, and all of Shelai "society" was openly indignant toward Lomov.

As for Bashurov and me, our comrade's arrest made a terrible impression on us. We spent the whole day wandering the yard, impatiently watching the gates and burning with a desire to land in the isolator ourselves. But our desire was not realized: Lomov did not show up anymore that day, and even roll call went by with just the guards. Early next morning, before going to the mine, I once more informed the orderly of my desire to see the commandant regarding a most pressing matter… That day in the mine dragged on unusually slowly, in excruciating languor. But upon returning to the prison, we heard more unpleasant news from the collective's headman: the prisoner was refusing to take any food, and had sent back not only bread but water, having ordered that Six-Eyes be told he'd rather die than submit to Lomov. The matter had taken a serious turn… With the assistance of Lunkov, Chirok, and other prisoner-friends who stood watch nearby, Valerian and I climbed onto the isolator's window-ledge to speak to Shteinhart. Through the tightly latched shutter the sound of his voice, deep and strange, reached us as if from far away… We first of all asked him the reasons for his hunger strike.

"I'm sorry I began this without telling you ahead of time," Shteinhart began, "but it somehow began on its own. I wasn't given any food at all yesterday evening… And, today, when the guard put some bread in my door-window, I was just about to take it when I suddenly heard familiar steps in the corridor and saw a familiar figure…"

"Lomov? Had he really brought you the bread?"

"Yes, himself… Well, right then a terrible rage overtook me, and I threw the bread away and said… What I said I can't now remember exactly. On the other hand, I'm not complaining: perhaps this is really the best way to force Luchezarov and Lomov to be more careful in the future."

Needless to say, Shteinhart's hope was in absolute vain with regard to Lomov. Having heard out his declaration, he set off for the kitchen and told the bakers and headman there he would "thrash" them if he learned they secretly gave the prisoner bread or meat.

"And don't dare give him water, either! We'll see if he maintains his brazenness!"

With these words, Lomov departed. He really had not the ability to halt before a tragic denouement, yet Six-Eyes evidently saw the matter otherwise: following his assistant's categorical prohibition, guards received from him an order to bring an entire cistern of clean water and a large chunk of fresh-baked bread to the isolator. The next morning, however, all this proved to have gone untouched.

Hard days dragged on, one gloomier and more depressing than the next. Six-Eyes was in no hurry to summon me for talks. Valerian and I devised a multitude of plans, but under close inspection not one of them withstood scrutiny. It was out of the question, for example, for us to go on a hunger strike: neither Lomov nor Six-Eyes himself, of course, would for a moment doubt that we, given our personal contact with the prisoners, would continue to accept food in secret while merely appearing to starve. Therefore, there was only one thing left: to do what we could to be sent to the isolator; but how to accomplish this? Lomov, expressly on purpose, showed up in the prison only during those hours we were in the mine and similarly didn't appear at roll calls. The fiery Bashurov proposed a very simple and elegant choice, however.

"Let's smash the windows!" he said in a most serious tone. "Then they'll likely put us in the isolator."

But I did not agree to "smash the windows." In the end, in all likelihood, we would have refused to go to the mine, had not an unforeseen situation prevented us. With an entirely conspiratorial look, the headman Godunov called me to the side and gave me a note (I never learned how he acquired it). Opening it, I instantly discerned a familiar female hand. "Be calm, don't lose spirit. But mainly—don't do anything obviously illegal, and don't extend the caps issue to any other demands. God keep you from refusing to work. I implore you, otherwise, everything will fail. Remember, your friends are being active and vigilant. For now, I will say one thing—there is hope, good news is coming. Be patient a bit longer. Your friend."

Although the "friend"'s solecisms were as unsubstantiated as they were naïve, and it was presumably obvious that a weak woman lacking any power whatsoever could do nothing for our current condition, they nevertheless cheered Valerian and me: it's well known a utopian will clutch at straw… We hurried to share our happiness with Shteinhart. But he listened to it impassively and, as such, rather dampened our ardor.

Moreover, in general he now came to the isolator's vent reluctantly and responded to our endless questions sluggishly. It was possible that, starving for four days now, he felt weak, though he insisted he was not enduring any particular agonies.

"Strictly speaking, only during the second day was there the urge to eat. That's when there really were some unpleasant moments. But, after that, my appetite completely disappeared. Only, for some reason, my legs ache, so it's hard even to fall asleep."

"Well, but the thirst?"

"For the first three days I wasn't thirsty at all. As you know, I generally drink very little. But today I've become thirsty, and it's torturous at times… Last night, I dreamt of such magical oases in a desert! I now understand well the feeling of a caravan passing through Arabia… Well, but I need a little nap, gentlemen, so please leave…"

We left with heavy weights on our hearts.

I felt like some moral stupor was gradually gaining possession of me. The guard, the prisoners, existence, and all things surrounding me were indeed falling into a dark, bottomless void, and a world of shadows and morbid reveries, a stained and funereal color, was replacing them. I mechanically performed all that necessity demanded of me: I ate, lay down to sleep, worked, answered all question posed me. Given these most terrible moments of existence, was it so long ago I'd been able to see the bright and even funny side of things? Was it not long ago I'd considered myself a Stoic philosopher, and recommended my comrades console themselves with philosophical meditations? This whole self-deception evaporated in a moment. Every day, a greater and greater pessimism penetrated my soul. By something clear and logically inevitable it occurred to me that the "cap issue" had brought with it a whole range of complications that must end for us either in utter disgrace or complete defeat: there could be no other outcome. To perish… Standing at that time face to face with destruction, when life promised so much light and joy still ahead, I—as I remember—did not blanch or tremble before a fatal conclusion, especially now that life's best enticements had been irrevocably taken away and the present was so dark and depressing and the future so full of such cold unknowns, now… akh, why hide? Thinking about dying in *katorga* tormented me, and the thirst for life, the thirst for freedom, parched me into unbearable pain and suffering!

Legions of gloomy visions passed before my eyes in a slow, funereal procession; and, at night, my disordered imagination summoned dreams still darker. I saw the people dearest me suffering from something so horrifying and unnamable that they laid hands on themselves and lay motionless, with eyes closed and a terrible half-dead wheezing in their throats. I myself, like Cato the Younger,[51] opened my veins, my friends' crestfallen faces surrounding me… Deep mineshafts, dark precipices, dangerous escapes, somber executions—such now were my nightly visions' inescapable themes, and more than once, sweating icy rivulets and shivering head to toe, I tipped over into horror and felt my eyes stinging with tears… Sudden joy spread warmth throughout my body, but was just as suddenly replaced by a feeling of deep melancholy and disappointment: I was reminded of the full horror of reality, that it was no easier than my nightmares…

On the sixth day, morning roll call having just ended, we ran as fast as we could to the isolator, forgetting even to post a lookout.

For a long time, Shteinhart did not answer our calls. Bashurov began pounding with all his might on the wall:

"Dmitrii! Dmitrii!"

"What?" a weak voice finally responded.

"You really scared us! We thought… Well, so? How are you feeling?"

"Nothing. Damned hallucinations won't give me peace… There she is, there, there!"

"Who? Who do you see there?"

"Water, so she can…"

"Gentlemen, away from the window! We're very strictly forbidden!" the approaching guard's voice pleadingly, almost pityingly, said.

But paying him no attention, we continued talking several more minutes; jangling his keys and shivering from the cold, he stood quietly in front of the isolator, not knowing what to do.

We finally bounded off the window ledge. Valerian was pale and tears were streaming from his eyes. He gripped my arm tightly.

"Ivan Nikolaevich, what are we waiting for, are we statues? We can't wait any longer, you know; he could die!…"

I, too, was overcome with horror and indignation at myself. So! A comrade was perishing before my eyes, dwindling toward a terrible, slow death for a cause that closely affected us all at the same time—and I was not lifting a finger to save him, but if he could not be saved, then would I share his fate? I only futilely whined, giving myself over, both awake and in my dreams, to morbid reveries, gloomy nightmares, and the doing of nothing, nothing… Whereas it is known that a week without water is quite enough for a human organism to perish, why had I disregarded so much precious time, six days already, while a vivacious, healthy man neither ate nor drank? Yes, this too was some sort of dream, some sort of wild nightmare that I was living, mute to all that I was seeing, placidly awaiting a fateful and unavoidable outcome! These notions flashed into my brain like lightening; I shuddered all over and shook off entirely the hypnosis's oppressive charms… Act! Save him, now and not later! Perish myself, but fulfill the duties of honor and comradeship!

Trembling, nervous, we ran to the prison gates with decisiveness in our souls, though without any preconceived plan in our heads…

"This way to the commandant, please!" the orderly shouted, opening the gates before us.

"Aha, just the right moment! Both of us?"

"No, only you this way, please."

The invitation applied to me. Recently, all the guards had been treating us with a sort of exaggerated, even unprecedented, graciousness and favorability… A Cossack with a rifle immediately led me to the office. In an instant, I crossed the threshold of the very familiar room—where behind the writing table Luchezarov alone was sitting (the clerks were in other rooms)—as the brave captain jerked himself to his feet. That day he looked unusually pale to me; irritation evidently boiled inside him, and his eyes cast a lightening gaze.

"Just what is it you want, sir?" he nearly screamed, throwing some papers down on the desk. "You're committing a whole series of… indiscretions! You're organizing protests!

Hunger strikes! What do you expect? You're only hurting yourselves by this, all the more so anyone who now believes in starving!"

"What do you mean by 'now'?"

"Well, after what this doctor what's-his-name—Tanner, that's it… The man starved forty days—and he nevertheless remained alive!"

"It seems strange to me that such audacious conclusions are made on the basis of newspaper stories. That's in the first place. In the second, concerning what happened, Tanner, I recall, always had water at his post."

"Yes? Well, but Shteinhart… is he, seriously? I've ordered water brought to him every day, you know."

"So you're actually being told he's drinking this water? That's a lie. He's not touching it!"

"So what are you telling me to do, for God's sake? What can I do?"

"First of all, release Shteinhart immediately, and then…"

"Release him! But don't you know"—Luchezarov suddenly came right up to me and said in a near whisper—"don't you know that without this there's already been a denunciation sent on me?"

"By whom? What denunciation?"

"Well, this I can't tell you—by whom, though of course I know by whom… But the fact is, it's already been sent. I released Bashurov from the isolator after three days, when he'd been given five…"

"You yourself sentenced him!"

"Lately, I've done you enormous favors, which you've been unable, needless to say, to notice…"

"And what were these favors?"

"My assistant doesn't go to evening roll calls anymore, even though this is his express duty."

"That is not his express duty, as demonstrated by the example of his predecessor of three years ago, who sat in the office and never even looked at the prison. Everything was fine and quiet then."

"Akh, you're irritating my sore spot!" Luchezarov walked to his desk and wrathfully tossed aside a paper lying on it. "My previous assistant was not the type to be sent to the prison because he'd lower the administration's prestige, but he was extremely knowledgeable about office business. The current… What complete irony that the courts are investigating me! It's absolutely impossible for him to seriously deal with a document, you know, he instantly makes a mess of everything! He cannot compose the simplest report of ten lines without twenty grammatical errors. As you can see, all the work's now weighing on me alone! I'm completely exhausted, and I'll soon have to take to my bed… I'm not accustomed to hunching over a writing desk!"

Fury once again overtook the brave captain, his round cheeks twitched nervously, and it once more seemed he was paler and sicker than usual.

"Is it our fault you've been given an unsuitable assistant?" I said, taking advantage of the propitious moment. "It seems to me there's one way out of this situation: dismiss Second Lieutenant Lomov as soon as possible… This will in all respects be healthy for you *and* the prison."

"Yes, as if such things depended on us…"

Luchezarov frowned and drummed a kind of march on his desk.

"In any case," he decided, "one must endure. We'll bear our cross and await better times."

"Unfortunately," I rejoined, laughing bitterly, "our crosses are unequally heavy, and so it's impossible for us to wait. Now that it's been thought over, there should be no dilemma. Otherwise, Shteinhart will die in the isolator today, and tomorrow I will…"

"Well, I shouldn't want that!"

"However, that will be unavoidable!"

A heated argument erupted between us again. We skipped from precise facts to theories and principles, from theories to actual facts once more. Luchezarov appealed to my sensibility and customary restraint, on which he heaped praise; I, by contrast, appealed to his humanity. My interlocutor then hinted very unambiguously at the possibility of most severe repercussions we could bring upon ourselves, and the notion set him, the captain, to trembling nervously… I responded that I was not closing my eyes to the future, but I nonetheless was insisting that he alone, as prison commandant, was responsible for everyone and everything, and near the end of the talk—Olympian gods, forgive this possibly inappropriate spilling of sacerdotal pearls—I reminded the brave captain about the judgment of posterity and what twentieth-century issues of *Russian Olden Times* would say…[52] Six-Eyes was visibly subdued by the onslaught of my unforeseen oratory. He was struck by the notion that he would in his own way be a man of history—he crimsoned and puffed out his chest like a turkey-cock.

"I think… I shall release Shteinhart today… We'll look into it."

"No, he should be released now, this minute, otherwise it will be too late. He's already having hallucinations… We won't go to work until he's released!"

"I'll release him the instant you leave for work. That's the condition."

"Do you give your word?"

"Yes. But you have to go to work."

The closer I got to the prison, the darker and colder my joy became. And when the familiar trellised gates swung open I once again saw before me the gloomy building and no less gloomy yard, having for so many years now been witness to all sorts of offenses and humiliations, this huge yard through which sullen, wasted figures—contorted by the cold—scurried here and there; once more, the future stood before me so bitterly and terribly. What did all these ephemeral and flimsy oratorical victories mean when a whole series of long, horrible years still remained ahead? Would strength be found to endure them? Would we ever be ordained to see once more the "clean, free world," where people proudly hold their heads high and live knowing neither humiliation nor fear?

That day, Valerian and I didn't manage to return from the mine because a guard, after pulling some prisoners out of the convoy and grinning pleasantly at us, explained:

"Mister Shtengor's jus' been released!"

"Yes? Where is he?"

"In hospital… Very weak, 'tis said…"

We immediately went to the hospital and did indeed find Shteinhart: pale, emaciated, he joyfully smiled at us and squeezed our hands.

"There's good news," he said.

"What is it?"

"One of the guards secretly told me that Six-Eyes has completely forbidden Lomov to visit the prison."

We loudly exulted. I began detailing my morning's battle.

"Yes, our friend, for his part, is probably being watchful."

"He should be! It may be necessary to send him a little note."

We dove into our everyday worries and concerns. Regardless of categorical news that Lomov had been "restricted" from the prison (the mare knew and was jabbering about this), we still did not have definitive verification and awaited evening roll call with the usual trepidation. Then the alarm sounded and the orderly called from the guardhouse to the inside guard: "Confirm. There won't be anyone!" After this, the gates opened and a throng of other guards spilled through them with noise and commotion. They were evidently enjoying the freedom as well.

"Order the prayer!" one of those entering shouted, and the mare, not waiting for the orderly's command, began singing sloppily, so to speak, hurrying and worrying little about the accuracy of the melody.

Suddenly, everyone flinched and pulled himself up at once; for a few moments the singers seemed to be choking, but then began singing the song as they should. Unanticipated by everyone, Lomov's gloomy figure had appeared behind the gates… Valerian and I exchanged looks: "What's this mean?"

Having stepped slowly and taken his hat off during the singing of the prayer, he'd entered the orderly's office. We were then all watching him through the window that opened onto the prison yard—he was greedily pressing his face against the pane and seemed to be all concentration… Not daring to disobey Six-Eyes's direct order forbidding him to enter the prison, he nonetheless wanted to sweeten his heart with the spectacle of prisoners' subordination from afar…

From that time on we were all day-to-day witnesses of the same pathetic spectacle: during every evening roll call Lomov would come to the orderly's office behind the prison gates and, having positioned himself behind the window, make himself out to be a criminal spirit banished from paradise. He also did not appear in the prison during daytime, but conducted all his duties in the free command, where he discovered all kinds of "disorders" and disciplinary infractions. Six-Eyes had granted his zealous assistant complete freedom of action there, and the gloomy second lieutenant exercised his power to the broadest extent, even resorting to the assistance of the birch rod. Rumors of corporal punishment now occasionally reached our ears, and were no less sickening to the nerves than when I was still alone in Shelai and Luchezarov had been beset by a streak of wild tyranny. It was exceedingly characteristic of Lomov that he personally attended each corporal execution and accounted for each falling blow.

"Attention!" came the guard's order when he approached the execution spot behind his apartment. "Cap off!"

And the prisoner sentenced to the rods, having submissively removed his cap, silently waited out the long-winded orders.

"Strip!..." Lomov ordered, and the wretch, trembling all over, removed his clothes. Two sturdy Cossacks performed the job of carrying out the execution, for Lomov was always screaming:

"For real!... As it should be!... Without craftiness!..."

The "job" complete, he left for home with his sense of duty honorably fulfilled.

It was said, among other things, that he deeply regretted that Shelai did not have its own executioner, and that for punishment by the lash the court ordered prisoners sent to Algacha. Lately, of course, the mare had been extremely lucky, since a similar enthusiast for legality would probably have used the lash to send more than one condemned man to his grave: it was well known that a single blow of the lash "for real" was enough to make a man give up the ghost...

In any case, inside the prison a satisfying peacefulness reigned. We rather simplemindedly began imagining that the gloomy period we'd just lived through had passed into the realm of legend, never to return again... Our sudden rude awakening from this reverie was therefore all the more unpleasant. One morning, Bashurov and I were getting ready to go to work in the mine (Shteinhart was still lying in hospital, slowly recovering from his nervous derangement), when suddenly a guard, extremely anxious, tore into the corridor shouting:

"Mine laborers, form ranks! Hurry up! The assistant'll be here soon..."

The mare hurriedly lined up in the yard according to work groups. At a loss, the two of us took our places. The bolt snapped startlingly, the gates opened menacingly—and with heavy, ceremoniously pounding steps, Lomov came straight toward us.

"At-ten-tion! Caps o-off!" ordered the guard. In an instant, all heads were bared.

Bashurov and I lifted our caps, then put them on again moments later. This was all Lomov needed.

"Dis-or-der!" a screeching shout was suddenly heard. "Who's that? Who's in caps?"

He brought himself close to Bashurov.

"I bowed to you," explained the latter, "didn't you see?"

And, removing his cap again, he lowered it and then put it on once more. This was such an unheard-of disorder that for several seconds Lomov appeared to have lost both his tongue and all his wits. At last he came to himself:

"We are not comrades... Here, there's no familiarity, only subordination. Guard, take him to the isolator!"

"Arrest me as well, I'm in a cap, too." I stepped forward, suspecting that Lomov wanted to satisfy himself with Bashurov only.

"Well, then take him!" Lomov, having turned on his heel, screamed out as if pitying me, and walked toward the gates.

In such way he came that morning into the prison, and we never learned whether he had received permission from Six-Eyes or decided on his own volition to penetrate his lost Eden; but be that as it may, Lomov had achieved his goal, and was probably completely satisfied with himself. It cannot be said, however, that I didn't feel a certain moral satisfaction. It was as though a mountain fell off my shoulders when the lock on the isolator door closed and I found myself in a low, dark closet, only weakly illuminated by the light falling through the door's window. Opening onto the prison yard, the window was always tightly shuttered. I was unable to gather my thoughts and emotions, since from the other end of the corridor came the sound of Valerian's laughter:

"Ivan Nikolaevich, how're you doing? What do you think you'll order this morning—beefsteak or roast beef?"

"Ah, joking aside, how can you think about food?"

"To tell the truth, I don't especially like sitting here on an empty stomach..."

"That is so, but, you know, after what Shteinhart..."

"I'm thinking exactly the same. We'll give it a try, for pots won't scald the gods, you know!"

Thus we called to each other for a rather long time.

Finally, I heard Shteinhart's voice beneath my window. He'd come from hospital to ask us about that morning. After him, someone else knocked on the shutter:

"Mikolaich, friend!"

I recognized Chirok's voice.

"Want some meat? Ogurtsov 'n' Lunkov are on the lookout, I'll give ya some quick."

With difficulty I convinced my friend to abandon his intention.

"You ain't decided to be like Shtengor, have ya?"

"How so?"

"Jus' so, not eatin'... You nut, you'll die, y'know! Who's that gonna help?"

But, not waiting for an answer to his own question, the good man suddenly jumped down from the window-ledge, and I heard his awkward, hobbling gait making off as fast as it could; it was probably a sign of impending danger...

Agonizingly, hour dragged on after hour. There was the bell for dinner. The cheerful talk of returning prisoner-tradesmen, hurrying into their wards to eat and to relax, drifted through the yard. I clearly discerned certain of their voices; everyone was talking about extraneous things. Evidently, most were not particularly interested in our case; few understood and so few felt any sympathy.

"Stepsha! Gimme yer meat, I really need to wolf somethin' down today."

"But he's tellin' me: 'You,' he says..."

"I'm gonna drive a pick in yer side if I hears another word like that!"

With such talk group after group of prisoners passed beneath our windows, until finally all became quiet. Dinner began, and then relaxation. The collective headman accompanied by the orderly brought us bread and water.

"Don't get mad, Ivan Nikolaevich, you ain't gettin' hot food today, but we'll gives you breakfast first thing tomorrow," Godunov, sticking his red face in my door's window, tenderly, almost ingratiatingly, said.

I responded that it didn't matter and that I wouldn't be eating anything.

"That's a mistake, really, a mistake!" the headman and guard commented with one voice. The window-latch snapped shut and their footsteps faded away.

After a while, I broke off conversing with Valerian—I was sick to death of having to shout so loud. I tried to lie down on the short, sharp bench securely fastened to the wall, but lying there was too uncomfortable and sleep wouldn't come. My head was swimming and aching from all the nervous excitement; ideas, one more disconnected and absurd than the next, swarmed through my brain. I stood up, trying to walk back and forth in the isolator, but my walk brought not the slightest pleasure, since I was free only to go all of two steps.

Once again there sounded the bell for work, and once again there was the noise of groups of prisoners passing beneath my window. After an hour, I heard the mine workers returning. Then everything was silent as a grave again and there was only the loud pumping of blood in my temples: "Tuk-tuk-tuk! Tuk-tuk-tuk!" Shteinhart ran to my window several times during the day, but he had neither information nor relief for us. There was absolutely nothing to tell each other.

In the meantime, I began to feel a torturous hunger: as ill luck would have it, in the mornings I left for work touching neither bread nor tea. On the other hand, I still did not have an especial urge to drink. By contrast, Bashurov had for a long time been complaining about a powerful thirst, which the proximity of a heated stove made still greater. Shteinhart tried to persuade us both not to imitate him, and to at least drink water—but we stuck to our decision. At last, the little bell rang for evening roll call. At that moment, someone hurriedly shouted from the window ledge.

"Gentlemen!"

"Is that you, Dmitrii Petrovich?"

"Now hear this news: seems there's been a decision to divide us among different prisons. However, this is a rumor being spread by the mare—but perhaps they believe it. But a letter's been promised this morning—from a friend, probably—and then we'll know everything."

Shteinhart hastily left, and after this I heard the command to pray: this meant that, once again, just the guards were at roll call.

I spent the night without sleep, in burdensome languor and brooding meditations. My bunk was so short that my aching feet couldn't be rested on it, and there was absolutely nothing to place beneath my head. In contrast to Bashurov, terribly warmed by his neighboring iron stove, I was cold. The isolator constituted its own little mouse-trap in which it was impossible to lie down or walk. The starving worm paused to suck in the pit of my stomach, and my head simply ached more unendurably than before, as if getting ready to explode into pieces…

"This is all so stupid, so annoyingly stupid! What an ignoble situation!" a cry now and then burst from my chest, and in impotent rage I tried to complete two abbreviated paces inside my coop. My comrade's ward was quiet. "Lucky man," I thought with envy, "must be asleep without thoughts!" Just before morning, having been reduced to submission, half lying, half sitting, I lost myself at a certain point in vacant, leaden dreams; but this sleep seemed to last all of one second. I awoke, shivering all over and chattering my teeth from the unbearable cold, and some kind of metallic echo still buzzing in my ears. "Aha! That must be the summons to roll call." There was still not a ray of light from the corridor: it was dark in the yard. But here came the sounds of voices and footsteps and the jangling of chains and keys. Bashurov was calling loudly from the end of the corridor. Inside me, the starving worm began to play around once more.

"How do you feel, Ivan Nikolaevich? Just imagine what I endured all night: a magnificent breakfast! Game hens, cold veal, wine, but mainly—water… Akh, it was the water!

Clear, pure, aromatic… I swear to you, I'd never drunk anything like it! But what did you dream about?"

"Pretty much the same thing."

"Ha-ha-ha! However, what's going on, hasn't it been a long time since Dmitrii showed up? What, is he sleeping? Anyway, they should soon be splitting us up among the prisons! But you could sell out here from the boredom."

We really did have to wait a long time for Shteinhart. It was already broad daylight and prisoners were dispersing to their jobs when his feverishly hurried footsteps were heard at last. Having not even managed to climb onto the ledge, he loudly shouted:

"Hur-ray, gentlemen! Be joyful: vic-to-ry!"

"What happened? What's going on?"

"Lomov's leaving… Completely! You're going to be released immediately…"

"But, you're lying?"

"So as to wait for the genuine news, I didn't come straight over earlier. My friend reports that a new telegram arrived today, ordering Lomov to leave Shelai within twenty-four hours and go to a new place. Some sort of police duty…"

"Well, I'll be! This really is victory!"

"So this is what 'friends are acting' meant…"

"Well, that Anna Arkadevna's a fine woman! You know what, Shteinhart? As soon as you see her, give her a kiss from me… Alright?"

"But, Dmitrii Petrovich, is there any doubt about all this?"

"Ah! Ivan Nikolaevich, you haven't lost your usual skepticism here? I heard from the guards that Lomov's leaving today. Early this morning, Lomov ordered a chest made for his things…"

"But maybe he wants to die from grief—and so it's a coffin for him?" joked Valerian.

"I really don't know. By the same token, it hardly… He doesn't seem the kind to lose spirit."

Talk was cut short by the rumbling of the lock in the isolator's corridor. Shteinhart proved to be correct, and the orderly, a pleased smirk across his face, showed up to release us, and so afterward Shteinhart was calling to us from outside the gates. He only came back from there an hour and a half later.

"What, did Luchezarov summon you?" we ran up to him while he was still in the middle of the yard.

"You guessed wrong: I went to see a patient."

"How so? Does this mean you're no longer out of favor?"

"Completely, without anything left over. Do you know whom I visited? Our friend."

"Well, tell everything from the beginning!"

"It turns out that three days ago, Anna Arkadevna received a telegram of allegorical content, from which she concluded she'd won us some time and that Lomov's prison career was over. However, she ascribes her success not just to her efforts alone; sufficiently complicated machinations were effected… The point is that Six-Eyes himself has lately been deluging the leadership with denunciations of Lomov: he was referring to them as counter-denunciations, since he suspected that Lomov had been dispatching denunciations of *him*… I personally gather that that business would not have occurred without the most sweet Anna Arkadevna."

"In what way?"

"It seems she managed to instill in the brave captain such suspicions regarding Lomov, when in actual fact he was probably more innocent than a nursing baby… On the other hand, I'm not insisting that I'm correct. In any case, without knowing it, Six-Eyes played into our hands. Anna Arkadevna has shown enormous political skill."

"Gentlemen, we must send her a thank you note."

"Well, Dmitrii Petrovich, go on!"

"An official telegram about Lomov's retirement arrived yesterday at midnight, and Luchezarov brought it first thing to Anna Arkadevna. Over the past few days, they've once again become generally very good friends… He was beaming as if he'd won the greatest victory of his life and as if Lomov were nothing but a child in his hands! However, when Anna Arkadevna suggested he immediately grant you freedom, he deflected this proposal: 'Let them sit out the night, they'll be even happier then.' She reasoned, of course, that it was best not to insist on this. But then, towards the end of their meeting, she acted foolishly and began moaning and complaining about a sudden fit of heart palpitations. Her old husband became alarmed, and Luchezarov became even more so, and called for me to come… But at that point, Anna Arkadevna displayed ingenious tact. She did not at all want to see me in the presence of the brave captain, and declared last night that it was not really necessary to see me, that she would get better, and that if she felt worse again in the morning, then… Well, needless to say, she felt worse this morning, and so I found myself there outside the gates."

"But how's Lomov dealing with his sudden retirement? Uncertainty?"

"What uncertainty! Anna Arkadevna's husband saw him and felt compelled to offer condolences."

"So what about *him*?"

"'It's the will of the leadership,' he says, 'and ours is not to question but to obey.'"

"What a numbskull!"

"No, Valerian, in my opinion he's a fine man. He's staying true to himself to the end. But I still haven't told you everything, gentlemen. Just imagine: I'm about to leave, when all of a sudden in flies… the magnificent Luchezarov himself! Cheerful, rosy… Well, he's dressed himself without too much haste, but there's so much eau-de-cologne flooding the room… Straight out, he says to me: 'Good health to you! How do you find our patient? Is she not well enough to take a stroll today? Well, but how's your health? I hope you won't be getting sick anymore now?' He said this last phrase with a most pleasant smile but a look that was playful. I, of course, also responded with an expression of hope that *now* everything would be like new, would be better, and we parted from each other with friendly bows… However, I noticed him furrowing his brow when Anna Arkadevna later grabbed me by the hand, squeezed it hard several times, and expressed out loud a series of the kindest wishes for my comrades and me. On top of all this, her Cossack officer had suddenly returned from somewhere and without a moment's hesitation offered me his hand as well. Six-Eyes was utterly crushed!

"But, now, gentlemen," concluded Shteinhart, "you must come to my little room and we'll celebrate our fortuitous deliverance from the destruction of the three Biblical lads thrown into a roaring furnace[53] (Valerian, without joking, weren't you really baking yesterday?). I have milk and brewed black tea, and we can put our feet up!"

This proposal met with universal acclaim, and with merry laughter and loud talk we repaired to the hospital.[54]

XIII. LIFE RETURNS TO ITS USUAL RUT

Such a mild regime as that which followed Lomov's dismissal had not been seen at Shelai for a long time. For the most part, evening roll calls began to be conducted in the presence of just the guards; wards were left unlocked morning to evening; the isolator was empty; Six-Eyes stopped showing up in the prison completely—evidently, after such an unsuccessful effort to establish an ideal exemplary structure, it oppressed him. The notorious printed rules were now hanging on the wards' walls in utter contempt and oblivion; first, dirty, greasy smudges appeared on them from somewhere, then the paper began splitting and tearing, and, finally, all that remained of the big red lists were pathetic, unprepossessing scraps.

Contrarily, it must be said that all these new trends' happy outcomes were felt principally by my two comrades and me, and were comparatively hardly noticed by the mass of prisoners complaining first and foremost about the difficulties of life in Shelai and dreaming of other prisons. Primarily, what always distinguished Shelai from the latter, and nurtured an irreconcilable hatred in the mare, was the prohibition against improving the official rations: this prohibition had been in full force up to now. The wealthiest prisoners had to content themselves with what was put in the communal pot, and were separately able to order only tea, tobacco, and sugar, and then only within prescribed maximums. Money earned in prison or received from home never made its way into prisoners' hands, and this all made it impossible for either a *maidan* or remunerative card games to exist in the prison. By nature, prisoners are generally great individualists, but even those for whom there would seem to have been no reason to use money freely—the paupers and all sorts of wretches, the bad craftsmen and the still worse gamblers—even they did not always respond to the hexadocular "prigime" with anything other than the most extreme irritation.

"Where would you get money from in a different prison?" we asked some of these wretches. "It's said you're always gambling at cards, but can't win anything…"

"Ekh, gentlemen, gentlemen," came the usual response, "I been in prison six years already, y'know. So, in so many years I never coulda once gotten a kopek?"

"Well, what would you do with this kopek?"

"Do? Gosh me, do!… I'll tell you straight, I'd buy two or three pounds o' meat 'n' cook meself me own cabbage soup in me own pot! You can be sure I'd eat what was mine down to the bottom."

So reasoned the mare. But for us three, of course, it was comparatively easier to live and breathe than before. Shteinhart resumed his general practice outside prison walls and often even brought newspaper reports back from somewhere, each time generating a huge sensation within our little circle… There was only one thing we could not obtain, despite all the laxness of the period that had begun—this was the return of the dear books seized earlier. Six-Eyes, when we directly questioned him regarding this, did not, it's true, respond with a categorical refusal; by the same token, by not giving us his bird-in-hand he promised us two in the bush.

"Long ago, I sent a formal request regarding the reading of secular books by prisoners, and day by day I've been awaiting a response. I believe the answer will be favorable… I'll tell you even more: you can expect a pleasant surprise! In all likelihood, an official library is to be built in the prison (using prisoners' means, of course), and I will appoint one of you to direct it."

"But while waiting for such a surprise," we proposed, "you could on your own authority quickly decide to make use of the books you already have. Weren't you able to do so before?"

"That was because I was not then dealing with it as a formal request. I'm now obligated to follow the letter of the law."

Thus spoke our brave captain; but at the very same time, he responded in an entirely different spirit to questions from other prisoners who also sometimes begged for the "little bookies":

"I'll show you bookies! Nonsense, nonsense! The Gospels and the Bible should be all a prisoner needs for spiritual sustenance."

In a word, Luchezarov hadn't changed, and during this peaceful time continued to be the same magnificent Luchezarov. It therefore wouldn't do to dream about the books much.

On the other hand, at a certain point, nearly the entire prison to a man was once again being carried away by learning how to read and write. The most popular representative of us three proved at that time to be Shteinhart, who was found to have great talent for teaching and even great tact in dealing with students. He was surprisingly somehow able to avoid all those Scyllas and Charybdises—like favoring or hating certain students above others—that undercut my strengths so many times. A single word from him proved completely sufficient to stop a quarrel or one prisoner's charges against another (in some sort of "academic" dispute), so that, as they say, Dmitrii Petrovich spoke and all argument was usually ended. In Shteinhart's dealings with prisoners there was never any hint of a desire to conform to their views or understandings; in general, he soon distinguished himself by silence and was incomparably more willing to answer than to ask questions; gentle and patient toward human deficiencies, he never took on the role of moralist or preacher; however, everyone distinctly knew that a boundary existed beyond which this patience ended, and Shteinhart could rise to the surface and let loose a heap of the most cutting things. It was above all surprising to me that no one was ever offended by my comrade's sharp outbursts; and that, on the contrary, they only seemed to strengthen the mare's esteem for him. That same Gribskii he'd so rudely snubbed for his cynicism positively revered Shteinhart, and he implored me with tear-filled eyes to do something to save him during his six-day hunger strike… I was extremely concerned with this issue: did Shteinhart's Jewish origins stay secret from the prisoners, or did it somehow influence their attitude toward him? It seems to me the prison knew perfectly well he was Jewish—knew this from the guards and Shteinhart himself—but, nonetheless, only the lunatic Zhebreek, who had taken the doctor's medicine, alone among the prisoners sometimes dragged some rubbish about Yids into his philippics, yet got no response, even during our well-known conflict with the mare. In general, I think that in the mind of a commoner, the word "Jew" or "Yid" doesn't correspond with the notion of an educated person who speaks Russian better than he does. For this reason, the information about Shteinhart's Jewishness somehow went in one ear and out the other and bypassed the mare's comprehension, and I recall more than once fielding the question:

"But whaddya s'pose Mister Shteingor's father is, Ivan Nikolaevich, a big landowner as well?"

Others identified him as the son of a general, of a senator, etc.

It is significant that, at one point, there was among Shteinhart's students a Jew we came to know, a man who in prison took advantage of his very stupid infamy; and whom the mare often cursed as "the Yid." Shteinhart, like Bashurov and I, would take this wretched youth under our protection, and then prisoners would say to him:

"Dmitrii Petrovich, why're you stickin' up for such a bastard? One word—he's a Yid."

"I'm Jewish myself," interjected Shteinhart, "but is this some kind of sin?"

Prisoners would then abashedly scratch the backs of their heads and not know what to say.

"Ekh, Mitrii Petrovich, who you're comparin' yerself with. You or that prison bastard be damned!"

I believe that, in general, it would have been a thankless task to search out even among the dregs of our simple people any sort of antisemitic tendencies such as those found in our various homespun Drumontchiks and Rochefortchiks.[55] The latters' antisemitism and judeophobia are purely cultural phenomena constructed by educated and bookish propaganda of a well-known type. Russian *katorga* absolutely shuns religious, and even more so racist, intolerance. Here you have the commonfolk, about whom it may actually be said that for them, neither a Hellene nor a Jew exists, and who know only two races of people—the oppressors and the oppressed. True, at every step you may hear from their mouths such vulgarisms as "Gypsy scum," "Ukrainian mug," "damn Finn" or "Polack," etc., but all these are merely the result of the typical Russian's passion for a strong word and do not evince any sort of serious notion behind them. Even less so, fortunately, has there emerged among our simple people a jingoistic patriotism, as demonstrated, for example, by the curious fact that in many of Russia's backwaters the very word "Russian" is completely unknown or understood quite vaguely, and often some twenty-year-old chap, in response to a question about what language he speaks, naïvely answers you: "the right one"… I recall a great many prisoners saying:

"Today there was five of us *Russians* workin' in the upper shaft."

It would turn out that among these "Russians" were a Pole, a Gypsy, a Mordvin, a Ukrainian, and only two Great Russians, but by the same token, neither myself nor Bashurov nor Shteinhart was there, and this is precisely the point this given prisoner wished to make. Obviously, in the minds of these people, "Russian" pertains for the most part to simple, uneducated people—and nothing more.

I return, however, to my reminiscences of the softer period that began after Second Lieutenant Lomov's dismissal. Appearing most often to me is a certain holiday from work. All the wards have been left wide open, the orderly has gone missing somewhere. No one is sleeping, since it's close to lunch hour. You look into a ward and it's completely empty, with only two or three fellows in some corner reclining on the sleeping platform, drinking their tea and talking quietly. These are somewhat solid friends of phlegmatic temperament, little interested by the noisy social life and preferring their intimate conversation about olden days and various events from their lives on the outside. You proceed to a second, a third, ward—and they're completely empty, as if everyone's died. Yet, by contrast, lively words and noise are issuing from the next ward. There's a whole crowd of folks here, and it's hard pushing through. What is this spectacle that has brought nearly the entire prison together?

Two wards, mine and Shteinhart's, have today arranged a contest between us, an "exam": whose students are more knowledgeable? Of course, only just the "students" are competing with each other, but their lively participation has attracted their illiterate cohabitants to the event. I'm dictating a poem (Maikov's "The Swallow"[56]) to Shteinhart's students, and he's reading the same poem to mine. A large stone table has been moved into the center of the room, and everything that might hinder the exam has been thrown off it: cups, spoons, *bachki*,[57] bread. Individuals are writing seriously and studiously; some are obviously nervous, others have a dark look, but all maintain a strict silence and only enigmatically move their lips, repeating each word of the dictation to themselves. The illiterate spectators, by contrast, bustle noisily around the table, shouting, shoving, gesticulating, and even cursing their opponents; wanting in any way to encourage their side, they only distract it with their shouting and misplaced instructions.

"See ya don't shame our ward or make us look stupid," one shouts, "or I'll give ya such a whackin'!..."

"You, Egorka, know what-a letter to choose, but here-a comes another argument: yer sayin' '*o*,' but Mitrii Petrovich's sayin' '*a*'... That's-a what'd be if'n you weren't confusticated!"

"No, that's it!" announces a third. "By me own whackin'—no joke. An if'n yer students is weaker'n ours prove ta be, then we ain't gonna let you outta our ward: we're gonna whack all you sonsabitches with spoons: the students 'n' the not-students! Don't go to an exam 'n' brag!"

The others met this proposal with laughter.

"Well, ya really do got some belly. Still ain't known who's gonna get the spoons..."

"I ain't agreein' to the whackin's, boys—me devoted student Lunkov's jus' broken off from his notebook—but take Elk... He's a big dummy, writes worse, but I should answer fer 'im? I'll answer fer meself, ol' men, not fer anyone more..."

"Akh, you bullshitter!" Elk snaps at him, "we'll soon see who's makin' the bigger mistakes!"

Shteinhart sternly interrupts the argument:

"Gentlemen, I repeat for the fortieth time, write:

"By habit I gaze beneath the roof—
The empty nest beneath the window."

Among other things, I see that Elk's work is poor; he's looking around side to side like a hunted wolf and staring at his neighbors' notebooks; confusing him most of all, evidently, is the phrase "by habit," of which he cannot make any sense at all. At the same time, Shteinhart's students, to whom I'm dictating, have already managed to reach the line: "So joyful, so deft, was our labor."

"Nogaitsev, why ain't you writin'?" someone asks the third of my former students.

Nogaitsev's lying in a corner of the ward, covered up in his sheepskin jacket and not at all participating in the exam.

"Stomach hurts," he answers in a weak, sickly voice.

"Better tell me, Little Miss Screw, you 'fraid of a whackin'?"

"Nah, I'm really sick..."

But the dictation has finally ended. The teachers are giving their students one more chance to go over what they've written.

"Look here, it's finished!" Lunkov boastfully exclaims, and gives me his notebook, but many others, including Elk, continue for a long time to sit at the table, absorbed in their writing and maintaining a grim silence. Elk has gone completely silent and now and then shoots me a puzzled look, as if seeking aid and support. This does not escape people's notice, of course, and earns him a series of malicious comments. Finally, Petin angrily rolls up his notebook and, having shown someone his fist, hands in his work. Shteinhart and I proceed to examine the dictations, and an unusual anxiety and terrible crowding starts up in the ward; students and observers are literally climbing on each others' backs and shoulders, each wanting to see with his own eyes what the teachers will do. Even we ourselves are infected by the general excitement... I cannot without envy note the huge success of Shteinhart's students. Some have in the briefest time begun distinguishing between prepositions preceding nouns and prepositions preceding verbs, and they always write the first separately and the second as part of the verb (this has always presented a major stumbling block for my students). One of Shteinhart's five students who showed up for the exam has managed not to commit a single flagrant error, even with commas (we had earlier established most precisely and emphasized what exactly is considered a flagrant error). This student was, however, literate even in freedom, and so I'd proposed he not be allowed to take the exam, but my students had, out of pride, not wanted to "reject" him and boastfully declared that in "dictin' we ain't 'fraid o' no one." Now they've had to reap the harvest of this boast. Three of the other students on the opposing side turn out to have each committed ten to twenty flagrant errors; the fifth has made all of seven errors.

"Not fair!" Elk has suddenly shouted, all this time menacingly flashing his calf-eyes and attentively following as we underline his errors. "It's clearly a fix!"

"Where? How?"

"But there, what'd Miloserdov write? Nuthin's wrong? That should be underlined! Ivan Nikolaevich is lettin' Shteingor off the hook!"

"How's there an error, where do you see an error?"

Elk silently points to the phrase "by habit."

Shteinhart and I laugh merrily, and all the students after us, and then all the observers (the illiterate and even more so the literate) erupt into huge guffaws. Elk is at first stupefied, then becomes confused: he makes an effort to grab his notebook from the table because he's clearly written "by a bit," but the crowd won't let him do so.

"Don't try it, boy! You're pointin' to the others' mistakes—'n' they're gonna pay for their wits."

Elk is trying to twist hands, snarls and waves his fists and causes an unusual uproar, a fight; with difficulty, the previous calm succeeds the insurrection. My students' efforts turn out to have been hopelessly played out, and all thanks to Elk: he alone has managed to commit fifty-two flagrant errors in his dictation (though at another time and in another setting he could have done twice or even three times better).

"Whackin's, dispense the whackin's!" erupts a savage howling, and in the chaos that follows it's actually hard to tell who's giving whom the whackings. My comrades and I have already managed to find ourselves at the ward's door—we were pushed away from the table in an instant, and none of our protests or reproaches are now making any impact whatsoever, since no one is listening and no one can hear us. We're left to mournfully watch the ongoing mêlée.

"Whack Elk!" they shout in unison.

"Ever'one. The whole ward!" others furiously scream.

Little Lunkov is already lying in the middle of the floor, red, sweaty, kicking and biting, and being sat on by several men. Suddenly, a gang of other warriors flies into this group: these are ten prisoners who've grabbed the giant Petin from all sides and are trying to knock him off his feet. Stumbling over the prostrate Lunkov, this whole gang falls over in an instant on top of his executioners; some of them sprawl their entire length, others somersault into the corner. Freed at this moment by the fall, Elk quickly springs to his feet, shoots past us like a bullet, and flies through the ward door…

"Get 'im! Catch 'im!" twenty voices rabidly howl, and several men run after him.

In the meantime, the mêlée in the ward goes on. To my surprise, I notice that among those whacking Lunkov with "the spoons" is his ward-mate and comrade-in-studies Nogaitsev, who earlier had "a stomach ache"…

Shteinhart is angry.

"I'm never giving another exam. It always ends in total chaos… And today they gave me their word that everything would be fine!"

But here's the lunch bell, and the headman appears from the kitchen with the skilly in his hands.

Everyone instantly quiets down.

After lunch, all to a man sleep like the dead for an hour and a half or even two hours. A prisoner occasionally slips down the corridor on the way to the kitchen or hospital. By contrast, by late afternoon everyone is lively once again. Everywhere, they're drinking tea, carrying on animated conversations, and singing songs together. The guard appears every now and then and asks them to "bawl a little quieter."

But what's this unusual sound coming from the fourth ward? The entire prison runs over there, as to an intriguing spectacle, but upon leaving from there the mare bursts into merry laughter. The sound of a balalaika and some strange unfamiliar tune comes from the ward. Where in the prison could one have gotten a violin or balalaika?

"What's going on there?" I ask the first prisoner I encounter who's been there.

"It's Chashchin"—thus he was named—"gettin' under Mikhailo Ivanych's skin!"

Mikhailo Ivanych is my friend Nogaitsev—and with curiosity I go to the ward. Chashchin is a prisoner I generally acknowledge as not "worthless," indeed, in my view this man is exceptional in strength and mind. He's a recidivist, sentenced for eternity, and a Siberian of the same well-known type of adventurers as hail from Eniseisk Province and wherefrom came Semënov, Goncharov, Rakitin, and a great number of other Shelai residents. He's a bit taller than average, thin, sinewy, as if molded completely out of steel, and is reputedly the strongest man in prison; solidity is always stamped across his barren, hollow face, though a bemused irony glitters in his intelligent gray eyes; Chashchin's never at a loss for words, and extreme maliciousness distinguishes his barbs. In general, I'm not at all certain about his character.

It turns out that the balalaika sounds have been coming from a simple comb and Chashchin's own skilled lips. Gradually and grandiloquently, without a shade of a smile on his lips, he dances heavily in front of "Mikhailo Ivanych" without ceasing to play his strange—now cheerful, now particularly heart-rending—tune.

"You're a fool, my fo-o-ol!…" the wheezy, rather nasal sounds now and then rip from out of his chest, and elicit an interruption of cheerful laughter from spectators.

Fat man Nogaitsev is sitting in a hat and sheepskin on the platform's edge, puffing silently and flaring his nostrils and, clearly, growing more and more infuriated by the minute. But he's still restraining himself and wants to appear extremely disinterested toward what is at times a quite forced mockery and unnatural laughter.

"There's the fool! There's the numbskull!" he scornfully retorts and, hearing this, the mare grows all the merrier.

"You're a fo-o-o-o-o-ol…" once more issues the lips of Chashchin, hilariously stamping in time and staring at his victim; and Nogaitsev swells up even more, reddens, puffs, and finally blurts out:

"Need to go to the kitchen for a good fire-log!…"

Homeric guffaws drown out these indignant words. Chashchin, of course, does not stop.

"Gentlemen, what's going on between you?" I approach my friend, wishing to support him.

"Jus' look, Mikolaich, at the fool," he appeals to me animatedly, "look what birch-baskets grow on our backs in Siberia!" And he points to Chashchin.

"But here's what's goin' on, Ivan Nikolaevich," Chashchin himself explains to me, "I'm singin' him a homespun song, you see… 'cause our *cheldon*, our beloved little Siberian, is layin' in a fool's throat when the *pelmeni*[58] burst open, and y'know he's singin': 'Fo-o-o-ol…'"

"Phooey, you swine!" and, having lost restraint, a boiling Nogaitsev spits straight at his face. A new thunderclap of furious laughter greets his expectoration. But the forward-looking Chashchin has managed to discern Mikhailo Ivanych's intention: he turns away so as to receive only a few drops of saliva, and all the spit goes into the very mouth of the Tatar Zulkarnaev, who's been standing behind him and shouting wide-throated. The latter spits and curses in his guttural dialect, but Chashchin's already jumped past him and is again strumming his comb and drawling from out of his upper chest the endlessly monotonous tune that's been eating at the *cheldon*. A "*cheldon*" himself, he portrays splendidly and exaggerates comically a Siberian's mannerisms and intonations.

"Mikhailo Ivanych," having vented his mounting fury, is once again sitting on the sleeping platform in forced imperturbability, awaiting the next declaration. I get ready to leave, recognizing I'm not needed here. Suddenly, the door opens, and on the threshold stands Shteinhart.

He's already heard what's been going on here, of course, but gives a look as if he knows nothing, and shouts without entering the ward:

"Nogaitsev, don't you want to take a stroll with me? It's almost roll call, y'know."

Nogaitsev is extremely gladdened by this unforeseen deliverance. Beaming all over, he immediately gets up from the platform and waddles over to the door, paying no mind to the mare's laughter and jabs. Only at the threshold does he pause for a moment and, having glared at Chashchin, says in friendly reproach:

"Well, whaddya s'pose, dummy? Whaddya s'pose?"

For the last time the mare erupts in thunderous guffaws, but Chashchin strums on his makeshift balalaika a parting chord:

"Fo-o-o-…"

Shteinhart silently distracts Nogaitsev, who, wrapping himself more tightly in his sheepskin and comically swaying his clumsy body from side to side, hurriedly follows him into the prison yard. Spectacle over, the mare joyfully disperses among their spots. There's still nearly an hour before roll call, and half the prison spills into the yard to breathe the fresh air and stretch their stiff legs. During this time most prisoners stroll in pairs; each of these strollers has once-and-for-all confirmed an irreplaceable comrade. Especial friendship is not evident among the others—they live in different wards, work separate jobs, and—you can see—simply meet up when they go for the evening stroll. They walk and walk without stopping, circling prison buildings or the hospital in deep silence or exchanging meaningless phrases. Thus Chirok usually strolls with Stepka Cheldonchik, Elk with collective headman Godunov (with whom he's constantly arguing and bickering at other times), Lunkov with Mishka-the-Astrologer, and so on, and so on. To everyone's surprise, Nogaitsev has lately made great friends with Shteinhart, and strays not a foot from him… And Shteinhart has evidently taken to heart the society of the estimable Mikhailo Ivanych, since he rarely goes during walk time with me or Bashurov, a circumstance that has distressed the latter not a little, and Valerian even often converses with me on this topic.

"How strange Dmitrii's gotten lately! He seems to be avoiding you and me, and this friendship he's got with Nogaitsev is positively disgraceful…"

"He's got every right," I try to defend Shteinhart, "to live as he wants during peaceful times and according to his inner life."

"So it may be," protests Bashurov, "but why are you and I drawn to each other, and not, say, to Karpushka Lipatov?"

On the other hand, Valerian essentially distinctly believes that all the "strangeness" lately noticeable in Shteinhart—his silence, unsociability toward comrades, and gloomy, depressed mien—has in all likelihood a single primary cause: it's now been around six months since he's had any news about his beloved… This long, seemingly inexplicable absence of letters occasionally troubles us as well, and we secretly construct all kinds of gloomy scenarios, though don't share them with each other. The silence of a man deprived of freedom, deprived of everything in the world that is good for him, and likewise suffering far from home, from the people closest to him, is hardly susceptible to explanation by some normal, natural causes: he's always dreaming of sickness, death, oblivion… There, beyond gloomy prison walls, life drags on in its usual insipid rut: rivers overflow, delaying the post for a long time; letters, as if out of spite, disappear without any apparent reasons or, more simply, are penned later than usual; but the poor outcast knows nothing of this and goes about dark as night, death in his soul…

How great was Shteinhart's joy when his sufferings finally proved idle and he suddenly received a whole series of glorious, life-affirming letters filled with hope. All his alienation once again disappeared in a minute, and one day, when I was working alongside him in the upper shaft and the other prisoners had surfaced to drink tea, he sat himself next to me and, like that memorable first night of our acquaintance, passionately and for a long time with an open soul told me about his recent mental state.

"You really don't know why I avoided you and Valerian? I saw in your eyes the constant questions: 'What's with you? Can't we help you?' And this was difficult, so unbearably difficult… When you're ready to run and hide from yourself, then the company of those like you may even be less satisfying. Well, so there's a Nogaitsev… Akh, that's a completely different matter! Believe me, Ivan Nikolaevich, I've only just begun learning to appreciate as I should this simple soul, alien to any sort of conniving enterprise. If you could know what affectionate tenderness I've discovered in the heart of this half-beast, this triple-murderer! One evening—as I now recall, it was before roll call—I'm sitting on the bench beneath the kitchen windows, away from everybody, and I see he's toddling straight toward me, grinning: 'Why're you sad, little friend? Have all good ways been lost?' I can't tell you how simply, how sincerely and simply he said this!… Those words so warmly encouraged me, and suddenly everything brightened in my eyes… Indeed, I thought, had all good ways been lost for me? Can a man, deserving of the name, satisfy by himself all his interests and feelings? Even were all my personal attachments and joys destroyed, would a star not continue to illuminate the ideal to which I've dedicated my life and freedom? Toward that, in any case, good ways had not been lost!…

"So you see," concluded Shteinhart with a joyous smile, "what complex notions and feelings were aroused in me by the simplest and easiest question from our funny fat bumpkin Mikhailo Ivanych… And our affectionate friendship began from that day!"

XIV. "ATAMAN STORM" AND THE BEGINNING OF HIS CAREER

In one of the new parties that arrived at Shelai there was a young Jewish boy named Shuster. According to him, he was twenty-three years old, but he looked considerably younger. Short, fresh, and always clean and glowing, with large gray eyes unusually lively and bright, he was distinguished by his discriminatingly courteous manners, and when exchanging bows with me he always bowed gracefully; his speech, slightly burring, also identified a man who had received a certain gloss of education and, indeed, under questioning the youth proved to have placed somewhere in the second rank of high school and, what's more, to have read a little something; he was in general no fool, was intellectually mature, wrote almost completely grammatically, and one necessarily concluded there was no connection between this fellow and the prison masses, other than the gray prisoner's jacket and some happenstance misfortune that had tossed him into the midst of these criminal and dissolute people. Shuster bore little in his features that was specifically Jewish, and at first I was extremely surprised that the prisoners nonetheless almost always called him a Yid and said this with a distinct unfriendliness, almost with contempt. It happened there were in our prison other Jews, incomparably more typical, and they were also cursed as Yids, but in this curse, as I've already said above, there wasn't any hatred; for the meantime, Shuster constituted a rather strange exception in this regard. The mare undoubtedly disliked him, and for a long time I explained this by believing that he, as they say, was distant from and did not join others. Actually, even the gray prisoner's trousers and jacket, with its pair of black aces on the back, rested on his lithe frame somehow more fittingly—I almost said "more elegantly"—than on other penal laborers; with everyone, he was affectionate and apparently unctuously polite, and when he walked, as it were, down the corridor or through the ward in a quick, graceful way, glowing, smoothly combed, casting bright, shy, tender glances about, I was each time reminded of a kitten wanting to be fondled at any encounter… Yet Shuster was not fondled, but, on the contrary, slapped at every step with an angry exclamation:

"Akh, you mangy Jewess!"

Against him handcarts were tipped over, all possible smears were made, and whackings administered. Shuster never defended himself in such instances, and didn't even curse or shout, but merely persisted with an ingratiating voice to induce or implore his persecutor not to bother or torture him… At the same time, he obviously tried to ingratiate himself with the prison's strongmen and big-wheels, and in their presence was, as prisoners say, a tail, joking, posturing, and sometimes managing to achieve his goal: some Chashchin or Bykov would be walking about the yard with him, conversing amicably and hugging him familiarly. But several minutes later that same Chashchin would give him a healthy kick and violently shout:

"Get away from me, you sheep-skinned wolf!..."

At the time, I happened to sincerely pity this downtrodden, universally loathed Jewish boy. But the prisoners, when I asked about the reasons for their universal contempt, dissimulated with the usual jokes or vague phrases.

Yet, one beautiful day, our ward learned that someone in the first ward, where up till then Shuster had been living, beat him so badly that he was being transferred to us. This news was greeted with unanimous grumbling.

"Ya hear they's transferrin' a Yid to us?"

"Is it Kitty-Cat?"

"Well, they's condemned her to hell!... Alëshka won't be able to keep her—that slime—from gettin' finished off!"

"Brothers, I ain't lyin' beside her for nuthin'; Six-Eyes better stick her in the 'slator, 'cause I ain't lyin' next to her!"

"Me too. Let her lie on the floor!"

It was then that my eyes were opened; my cohabitants had this time spoken too unambiguously to leave any room for doubt... And though doubt continued to stir in me (prisoners cast so few aspersions at each other!), I confess to a feeling of disgust toward this youth, whom I had until then regarded so well.

The door opened, and into the ward with his things came Shuster, timid, confused, and encountering a deathly silence, as if the prisoners hadn't noticed him. But, running behind him was Petin-the-Elk, who had been absent during the preceding discussion, and he joyously shouted:

"Here, Shustry, lie down next to me, we'll be comrades!"

These words produced a universal snigger, but Elk paid it no attention. He was a man of caprice and moods: today, as if on purpose, he'd go against prevailing opinion, but tomorrow he'd be an obedient slave. All this was well known, and no one was therefore surprised by his decision to pair with Shuster. The latter, of course, gladly accepted Elk's invitation and, having instantly placed his bedding down beside him in a corner of the ward, openly tended to his powerful protector the whole day, running to the kitchen to brew his tea, gazing into his eyes like a dog, anticipating his merest whim... The rest of the prisoners acted as if they didn't notice the presence of a new cohabitant in the ward. As for me, I chose to remain neutral and to observe; however, as I've already said, a feeling of disgust stirred in me at Shuster and Elk carrying on, befriending each other so suspiciously: against my wishes, I began to maintain a dry and exaggerated coldness toward both of them... But after several days, my suspicions were completely disabused. Relations between Shuster and Elk were evidently completely innocent, and Shuster himself continued to produce the impression of an intimidated boy with very sympathetic, delicate sensibilities and an intelligent mentality; he attended with much attentiveness, much avarice, any conversation I participated in and from which he hoped to extract anything interesting or instructive. And it occurred to me: even if this boy carried the shameful stigma the mare had recently accused him of, it could perhaps be explained by the dissolute atmosphere governing most *katorga* prisons; *here*, given the better conditions, under my and my comrades' attention, this young, able soul could still awaken and revivify, and become horrified at his earlier degradation… His transfer to our ward seemed in all respects salutary for Shuster. He conducted himself quietly and meekly, and so ready was he to serve each man that soon the entire ward was reconciled to his presence, and I began noticing that those very prisoners who had not long before agreed it was better to go to another ward than to lie beside a "filthy Yid-girl," now enthusiastically drank tea and strolled through the yard with him. One evening, Shuster actually appeared the hero, attracting universal attention and sympathy. Everyone had already lain down to sleep, when suddenly, from out of the corner where Elk and his new friend were located, came the following speech:

"I am Ataman Storm! Who wants to measure himself against my courage and strength? Thunder and lightning! Who dares take my beloved damsel away? In the ocean's depths I will find her, from the wastes of Hell I will fetch her, from the talons of a thousand demons I will wrest her! Hi-o, my senior Cossack captain has answered his ataman's call!"

"I'm here, valiant ataman. What pleases your grace?"

"Where are my fine fellows?"

"Not far, in the ravine behind the wood…"

"All should be ready at exactly twelve o'clock midnight! There will be a bloody wedding feast for us… We shall awaken our swords, gladden our fine fellows' daring!"

"Listen, brave ataman. We will all gladly lay down our lives for you. Yet our enemy will not meet with sweetness! We will swoop down like kite-birds, we will cut off every rebel head, we will capture every fair maiden!"

Etc., etc.

As one man, the prisoners hopped off the platforms and rushed over to the scene. It was Shuster delivering Elk a free performance. He began quietly, voice hardly audible, but, having noticed the impression he was making, he gathered himself up and began booming so that it was like he was indeed imagining himself to be Ataman Storm… I, too, was listening curiously. His song's content was utterly ridiculous, in that same pseudo-romantic style from beginning to end, but it brought the mare to frenzied delight. It turned out that in Algacha, where Shuster had lived about a year earlier, there was a certain prisoner who'd learned by heart all of "King Maximilien" and other similarly anonymously authored songs enormously popular in our prisons and among soldiers to this day. Shuster adapted several scenes from it that particularly captured his imagination. Prisoners made him repeat the presentation many evenings in succession and, by day, they pursued this same goal in the other wards, and so he performed his roles with great pleasure and willingness, letting himself go further and further and shouting Ataman Storm's monolog in such a laceratingly shrill voice that guards came to the door's little window intending to calm him. Shuster suddenly became one of the most popular persons in prison; upon meeting him, everyone smiled and said:

"Ah, Ataman Storm! How's it goin'? Where're yer fine courageous fellows right now?"

"Thunder and lightning!" the newly revealed ataman typically responded. "Evil enemies have locked me in an iron cage, clipped the falcon's powerful wings…

But my beauteous day I foresee, and I will break free to liberty—and terrible will be my vengeance upon those who betrayed and undid me!"

A group of the curious would immediately gather round him. Shuster's previous timidity and broken-heartedness disappeared: he became garrulous, lively, sociable, and more than once I saw him sitting on top of someone and whacking him…

The mare, it seemed, completely forgot about the rumors it had previously energetically slandered him with.

With me, he maintained his original deference, almost reverence, and since I'd only just begun dealing with my students, he quietly sat himself down at the table and listened attentively, posing me questions from time to time. Upon its conclusion, I invited him into my class (several days earlier, he'd been studying with Shteinhart). Needless to say, he proved to have forgotten much that he'd learned in high school somewhere; however, he managed to solve several mathematical problems and to take down some dictations, and soon everything that had been forgotten was retrieved from his memory: in a letter, he began to correctly use not only the letter *iat*,[59] but even punctuation marks. Shuster showed great readiness to enter into conversation on various topics, regardless of their relevance to the lesson, and I was each time struck by the profound sincerity conveyed by his rationales about the need to survive through honest labor, about the terrible misfortune of wasting one's youth in *katorga*, and so on. One day, I brought up the latter with him, and asked what brought him to prison.

"Ekh, Ivan Nikolaevich, it would take a long time to tell!" sighed Shuster. "It began thirteen years ago with me… I've terribly wanted to tell you, as if confessing to a priest."

"Why have you so wanted to?"

"A lot has already built up on my soul, Ivan Nikolaevich, all kinds of injuries, humiliations… What have I not gone through these ten years! I won't hide from you that I've committed many dirty deeds in my time… I can't call myself a good man, and that's why I'm a hypocrite! But I just fully hope that I'm still not a completely ruined man, and have fallen into good company and will still be able to shed my foolish habits. Well, that's everything I should've told you… Perhaps you could give me some kind advice."

"Is that all? You've only just begun, and I'm ready to listen to you with pleasure."

"No, Ivan Nikolaevich. There's much that would certainly be shameful for me to explain to you in words, and I might exaggerate… But it's occurred to me to write you a letter about my life."

"That would be even better"—I jumped at this curious proposal—"only, will you be able to do so?"

"I think so. I'll just need a lot of paper."

However, paper needed to be found—I agreed to get it in sufficient quantity, and the job commenced. I was left simply astonished by how quickly Shuster filled notebook after notebook and handed them to me. I'd barely obtained paper and pencils. The contents of this autobiography that I have are rather interesting, and, as possible, I want to relate it here in the original expressions. I will allow myself only to abridge and to correct merely formulistic mistakes, of which there are not very many. What is most surprising in Shuster's work are the foreign words to be encountered in abundance, always deployed by him correctly and completely appropriately.

My father was an old-style fanatic and, regardless of this, lived many years in Petersburg among civilized Jews and didn't wrangle with them over the Talmudic superstitions he regarded as law. He knew ancient Hebrew, the Pentateuch, the Talmud, and the Hemorah perfectly, and, occupying himself with teaching Jewish children all this wisdom, he lived not only not poorly but even in a certain comfort. By contrast, he considered all science to be nonsense and contrary to the Talmud and couldn't even write his name in Russian. My mother, who was a woman of the current generation, had more than a little difficulty persuading my father to let me go to Aleksandrovsk High School. But fate pursued me out of childhood, and so, as soon as I turned thirteen—a year in which every Jew attains his majority—father pulled me out of the second class under the pretext that, in high school, they were making me write on Saturdays and this was contrary to the Talmud; he feared that, because of this, I'd become utterly depraved and refuse to perform religious rituals. The loss of studying among educated people was bitter for me, but there was nothing that could be done; I left high school with the barest education. Father stuck me in his own hosiery shop. I must say that he himself did not understand a thing about this business, but put together a hosiery workshop primarily so as to have the right to live in Petersburg, and he initially spent a lot of money to buy a master's certificate in one of Vilno's Jewish community associations and then, not having in actual fact any knowledge whatsoever, he took the Saint Petersburg's Craftsmen's Board's verification exam. After this, he bought ten shops for 400 to 500 rubles each and hired craftsmen to work in them. As you can see, my father had money…

And so, after a year, I was the top boss in this workshop. But I felt no sort of inclination toward commerce and, annoyed at father for the harm he'd caused me, I treated the business extremely carelessly: I began swiping a bit of money from the shop and getting to know streetwalkers… Father soon noticed this and began ferociously punishing me, beating, tormenting, and giving me nothing to eat for two or three days. Of course, all these measures only embittered me still more; out of terror, I disappeared from home for several days and was discovered, and then came a new, even more severe punishment… Having beaten me in like manner for three or four months, father one fine day handed me over to study under a jeweler he knew, on the condition that if he could teach me the jeweler's art within two years, he would pay him 200 rubles. I took the new work to heart and began to settle down. My boss was very good, since he didn't make me do any dirty domestic chores, as is often with young apprentices. From the first day, he began teaching me to solder, burnish, polish, make a chain, etc. I worked diligently. The boss himself happened to work poorly, and loved instead to dress foppishly and go strolling, and he almost never appeared in his own shop; however, he had an assistant craftsman who knew his business very well, but who bore a singular sin—a love of vodka and cards. On the other hand, Bogdanov was an honest youth, and the boss loved him.

Every day, since father didn't want me to eat the boss's non-kosher food, I had lunch and spent the night at home. So went half a year. Once, it happened that a drunken Bogdanov was forging a bracelet of twenty-three ounces of gold and hit it so hard with the hammer that the gold shot out of his hand and landed somewhere on the floor. This was in the evening and the boss wasn't home. Bogdanov and I began searching but couldn't find anything and he told me to go home, saying it would turn up the next day. I went home, but Bogdanov went to a tavern. At home, I told father about the incident, and father immediately concluded from my account that I'd stolen the gold, even though I said nothing like this to him. Next morning, having had my tea, I went as always to the shop. Bogdanov had still not returned from his night's festivities, and the boss began asking me what happened to the gold the previous night. Suddenly, my father entered. Having greeted my boss, he immediately called him aside and asked if the gold had been found. My boss replied that it had not. Father then informed him of all my earlier sins and declared that I must have stolen the gold and should be punished. How could he not believe my own father? The jeweler, promising not to punish or to get rid of me, told me to plead guilty and immediately return the stolen item. But how could I plead guilty? I wept, swore, promised—nothing helped; suddenly, they laid me out and gave me fifty birch strokes, after which my boss told me not to come back until I gave him the gold. Leading me home, father beat me again in the same vicious way. My Lord! I simply couldn't endure such torments, and had mother not summoned the neighbors and they not taken me away, I probably would have died at my father's hands; thus my cushy little job was lost…

Four days later, my boss came to our house, apologized, and told my father that while cleaning the shop floor that morning the gold was found under a mat. But father answered that this still didn't prove my innocence: I must have taken the gold and hidden it there, and therefore it was no shame they had punished me; it served me a good lesson for the future… My boss nonetheless ordered me to dress and go with him to the shop. There he treated me kindly, and everything proceeded as of old.

Then one Christmas Eve a certain gentleman brought a silver purse and asked to have it gilded. We had a great many jobs and the boss, after laying the purse on the bench, said it would be finished after the holidays. The holidays went by. I spent New Year's Day itself at home and never went out. The following day, my boss told me to polish and clean the purse. I looked on the bench—it wasn't there; I searched through the cabinet—it wasn't there; I looked through all the containers, asked Bogdanov and, finally, the boss himself. The latter turned over the whole shop and found nothing as well. Then he summoned me and asked if I'd taken it. He would forgive me if I returned it to him immediately, and neither my father nor anyone else would ever know a thing. I, of course, swore and protested that I hadn't taken it. The boss then told Bogdanov not to let me out of the room. In the evening, the jailhouse warden visited him (he'd probably been called on purpose). The pair sat together in his office and discussed something for a long time, then called me in. My boss told me that if I didn't confess, the warden would immediately arrest and take me to prison. The warden then added: "I'll shackle your hands and legs and starve you. It'd be better, lad, to confess and show where you hid the purse." I got scared… At that time, I didn't even know they had no right to arrest me when there wasn't a shred of evidence, and so I believed their threat. So as to somehow avoid prison and postpone punishment, I explained with tears in my eyes that I had actually stolen the purse and hidden it in the snow in the yard. Then the warden burst into laughter, and with the words: "That's much better!" he excused himself and went home. But the boss fired up a lantern and ordered me to the place I'd named. We dug for a long time without any results, but I continued to assure the boss that I was not mistaken and had hidden it in that very spot. He finally called off the search and ordered me to spend the night at his place. This didn't exactly please me, but of course there was nothing I could do. It turned out that my hat and coat had already been hidden, and I was being watched closely. In the morning, just after dawn, the boss sent a servant for my father, and only then did I understand that I'd made a stupid confession the night before. Seizing a propitious moment, I jumped out and as such got onto the street and ran to where I was looking down Ekaterinhof Prospect. Running to the Garden, I stopped. The morning was cold, the January frost crackling, and I was without a hat and in just a worker's smock. Tears began falling from my eyes due to the cold, my injuries, and my grief: there wasn't a kopek in my pocket, I had no friends… But I decided not to go back home. Circling round to Malkov Lane, I found myself near a Jewish synagogue. Fortunately, the service had already ended and there was only a lone, blind old man. Passing him unnoticed, I crawled beneath the *bimah*; so called is the platform that stands like a pulpit in the middle of a synagogue and under which a small larder is built for holding various beat-up books and papers (the *Shema*[60]). According to Jewish law, it's forbidden to throw them away, and they must be collected and brought at a specific time of the year to a cemetery and buried in the ground. So it was that I crawled in there and closed the door behind me.

Father, having learned about everything from my boss, ran out of the shop, grabbed a cabby, and went looking for me all over the city. Some friend told him he'd seen me turn onto Malkov Lane. Having reasoned there was nowhere else I could have disappeared to, father went straight to the synagogue; but the synagogue turned out to be closed. Father then told the watchman everything and asked him to open the synagogue. My Lord! My heart died when I heard father's footsteps and voice and realized he was rummaging through the cabinet and looking under the benches… I was thinking that he'd find me right then, and I buried myself all the deeper into the beat-up papers and books. But in time the threat passed, and I heard father order the watchman to let him know if I turned up. The watchman locked the door and I breathed freely once again. But I soon felt a terrible hunger which, needless to say, could not at all be satisfied, and for several hours I slept fitfully. I remember that this was on a Friday. I was awoken by loud noise inside the synagogue: it was Jews gathering for evening prayer (*maariv*). It ended quickly, however, and the watchman summoned the yard-keeper to extinguish the candles (Jews are forbidden to extinguish fires on Saturdays), and all that was left burning was a single large candle memorializing someone who had died (a *Yahrzeit* candle is not to be extinguished).[61] Having taken care of everything as needed, the watchman left and locked the door once again. However, I knew very well that this lock was only for show, and with one shove it would fall into dust. I listened intently for some time—everything was quiet, and I decided to crawl out from under the *bimen* and look around. From behind a wall came the clatter of plates and people talking: the guard who lived there was eating supper with his family. I realized how terribly hungry I was; I had to get out of the synagogue and go somewhere. But I had neither warm clothes nor money. Then I saw on the wall three circular tins in which the donations were kept, and decided right away that I would get by with this money. The Jewish belief that the dead come to the synagogue to pray between Friday and Saturday is well known, and knowing for certain that not a single fanatic would enter at this time, I wasn't going to wait until everyone in the guard's place was sleeping: I quickly grabbed the tins and stuffed into my pockets all the silver and copper there was (it later turned out I had around twelve rubles); then I grabbed a bench and smashed it with all my might into the door. The hasp that poorly held it flew off, the door swung wide open, and I dashed into the corridor... But then something I had not foreseen happened. There was at that moment a young Jew visiting the watchman, and when he heard a noise in the synagogue that scared the watchman and his family to death, this young man didn't cower but, regardless of the Sabbath, picked up a candle, ran into the corridor, and grabbed a passing dead man by the collar. Nothing could be said about any resistance on my part—I was unarmed, and I was guilty. The young man brought me to the watchman, but it took at least half an hour for the watchman to recover himself and trust that I was me and not an evil spirit that had assumed my form...Having collected himself, he dressed and went to tell my boss what had happened, knowing full well that he'd fall into the soup for this. Meanwhile, the young Jew who'd apprehended me was guarding me vigilantly and even wanted to give me something to eat; but the watchman's wife objected, saying I was a dangerous criminal and that feeding me would be sinful.

Finally, my boss appeared. Hailing a cabby, he took me to his place and kept telling me along the way to say where I'd put the purse (it had proven not to be under the snow anywhere), for he promised not only to defend me against my father's wrath but even to reward me. But I refuted my previous testimony, saying I'd lied earlier out of fear of the prison warden and had in fact taken nothing and knew nothing. Having arrived at the shop, the boss sent for my father. Father appeared and, learning I had once again denied everything, demanded that my boss allow me to be brought home, where he would soon get the truth out of me. I knew very well the means by which he'd get the truth out of me and began beseeching my boss not to release me. "I don't have the right to hold you," answered my boss, "since I don't have a shred of evidence against you. If you confess right now, it's a different matter, and then I can hold you." Once again, I decided it was better to calumniate myself than fall into my father's hands. Opposite our shop lived a German bookbinder with a boy apprentice. Remembering him, I told my boss that I'd stolen the purse and secretly given it to this boy. The boss was overjoyed at my confession, praised me, and even asked if I'd eaten that day. I was dying from hunger. He gave me a wineglass of vodka to drink and part of a sandwich to eat, but then, having locked me in the storeroom, he went with my father to see the German bookbinder; this was already at twelve o'clock at night. Having heard their story, the bookbinder invited them to search through the boy's things, and when nothing was found he woke the boy, who'd been asleep for a while already, and began interrogating him. The boy vowed and swore he'd taken nothing from me, that he hadn't even seen me on New Year's Eve. So, having accomplished nothing, my boss and father returned to the shop. Father again demanded to take me home, but my boss, in view of my confession, summoned a policeman. In reply to the policeman's query as to whether I'd actually stolen the purse, I gave an affirmative answer, and after this nothing remained for my father but to go home alone, and I was brought to the police station. The first thing they did in the station was to take my coat and hat and search me, and so they found the money I'd stolen from the synagogue. They entered this in a log; then they opened a door, shoved me inside, and locked it. Inside my new space, I was suddenly overcome by the terribly stuffy air and a filthy stench from uncovered waste pails. A lantern without a glass smoked and barely illuminated the huge room. A group of human bodies was lying disorderedly on sleeping platforms and strewn across a naked floor, in filth, in ragged blouses and down-at-heel shoes on bare feet. I nearly lost my wits and began loudly pounding the door and demanding cold water. Then one of the prisoners who'd been woken jumped onto his feet and shouted: "What're you snortin' for? People's sleepin', it's three o'clock at night, 'n' you've decided to make some noise? If you dare make a peep we'll take care o' you our way." Naturally, I didn't pound anymore, but went into a corner and stood in one spot until morning, since there was absolutely nowhere to sit or lie down. In the morning, I ended up spending a long time in the superintendent's room in the chancery until my turn came. There I saw for the first time how the superintendent used his own fists to mete out punishment to those imprisoned for drunkenness. When he finally got to me, I explained I hadn't stolen the purse, but had taken this crime on myself only so as not fall into my father's hands and be beaten by him. Hearing this, the superintendent became enraged, stamped his feet at me, and began shouting and cursing unprintable words and striking me in the face so hard that a fountain of blood shot out of my nose. He even wanted to send me back to the station house, but then my father showed up; I don't know what he spoke about with the superintendent, since I was in the anteroom—but several minutes later, the superintendent shouted to me, and when I came he said: "I'm releasing you into your father's hands, but you're to be here next Saturday, when I'll draw up charges against you." My heart sank when I saw my father assuredly standing there: I knew he was going to do something terrible to me… Having brought me home, father first of all bound my hands and tethered me to the wall, saying he'd have a talk with me after lunch, and because this was happening on a Saturday, he then washed his hands, drank some vodka, and sat down to eat *cholent* (food cooked the evening before, since Jews are forbidden to boil or cook on Saturday). He ate all the while placidly, as if nothing had happened. Mother, looking at me the whole time with tears in her eyes, wanted to give me something to eat, but father grabbed a knife from the table and threatened to murder her and me if she even tried to move. Having properly eaten, he stood and approached me. "Well, now I'm going to talk to you. Tell me, dear, where you put the purse." I began swearing that I hadn't taken it, but he didn't want to listen to me. "You can tell these stories to the superintendent and your boss, but you can't dupe me. I won't believe you. You'd better tell me, where did you hide it?" With these words, he threw me on the floor and began striking me wherever his boots landed—my ribs, my chest, my head. I instantly reasoned that I had to somehow cleverly distract him, so as to gain time and get away. I began begging him to stop the beating, assuring him I would then tell the whole truth. Father stopped, and with a bloodied face I raised myself up from the floor. "Actually, I did steal the purse," I said, "and sold it to a certain Christianized Jew." Father immediately dressed and ordered me to take him to this Jew. I washed (because I was covered in blood) and, summoning my final reserves, started off, not at all knowing what might come of this. I was simply lucky that my horrible torment had been postponed for an hour.

In Aleksandrovsk market there was a certain Christianized Jew who dealt in used things; there was also a rumor he accepted stolen goods. We got there and I pointed him out, though I barely knew his face. We went straight up to his bench. Having noticed us, the dealer obviously got frightened, since he knew very well what a fanatical Jew my father was and that he'd not come to buy on a Saturday. "Well, tell this swindler straight to his face," father turned to me. I was insufferably ashamed to slander a completely unknown person, but it was too late to turn back now. Gathering all the insolence I was capable of at the time and without batting an eye, I said: "Give us the purse I sold you for three rubles. My father will return your money, because I stole this thing from my boss, and now that I've confessed this thing has to be returned." The dealer widened his eyes in unfeigned amazement: "Mercy, you're mistaken… First I've ever seen of you!" But to this I said: "Have you really forgotten the beautiful silver purse I brought you before New Year's? I know it'll be a pity for you to part with it, since it's worth ten times more." And seeing that he was silent, continuing to be astonished, I added: "Instead of shamming, it'd be better for you to give it back and take our money. Otherwise, we'll call the police right now and they'll arrest you." I spoke so sincerely and veritably that father completely believed my assertion and, for his part, turned toward the trader initially with gentle persuasion but then with rage. But nothing at all came of this, naturally. Having awoken from his momentary stupor brought on by utter astonishment, the trader began shouting and driving us away, threatening for his part to have us arrested. It was already dusk and father, afraid of missing service, took me away with him to the synagogue. Along the way, he once again began to doubt me, and said: "It's impossible to believe anything from you! You've been questioned ten times already, but each time something new comes out. Can you not live without adventure? What aren't you capable of, bad boy? Who did you learn to steal from? There are no thieves in our family. I've tried to raise you as I should, taught you the Pentateuch, the Talmud, the Hemorah, and have never begrudged you money, and this is how you repay me! This is all because of your greater carrying-on with Russians and not following our sacred law." I was so shamed by all his talk that I nearly fell to my knees and confessed to everything: but I restrained myself, having reasoned that this would lead to nothing since there was nothing for me to confess to. Thus we reached the synagogue. A crowd of fellows surrounded us there and father, having well and truly condemned me to punishment, handed me over to them. They swarmed over me like bees and began cruelly poking fun at me, so that I fell through the earth out of shame and impotent fury: there were several dozen of them, but I was alone. In the meantime, an entire horde of Jews also accosted my father as he went into the synagogue: they pestered and breathlessly told him that during the night, I'd broken into the tins and stolen the communion money. My father hadn't expected such a shock! He immediately summoned and asked me about everything and whether this new charge was true. My legs quivered from terror and my tongue stuck to the roof of my mouth, but I couldn't deny the obvious fact, and I confessed… Father then flew into such a fury that he grabbed a bench and wanted to finish me off right there, but was refrained from doing so. Having asked the *gabbai*[62] how much communion money was stolen and learning it was around fifteen rubles, he said he'd pay a quarter-note[63] on my behalf. After this, the service began. Upon conclusion, father led me home, tightly gripping my arm all the way…

At home, he stripped me naked and tied me by the hands and feet to a pillar, so that I couldn't budge; then he took a cane and began beating me, saying: "I don't believe you at all now, and so don't think I'll forgive you as soon as you confess. It's all the same whether you stole the purse or not, for it's enough that you disgraced me in synagogue before the entire community. This means you can be silent. Tonight I'm going to beat you until you die at my hands. I will most assuredly know that I myself have killed you and that you will no longer steal or disgrace me." He set a decanter of vodka next to him, and with great enjoyment on his face continued to torment me. Unable to endure, I began screaming; then he coolly took his handkerchief and stuffed it so far into my mouth that not only could I not scream but it became difficult to breathe, and he resumed his work as before, gulping vodka from a tea glass from time to time. And, of course, he would have kept his word—he would have killed me, had my mother not unexpectedly returned from a visit to see what was happening: father, already very intoxicated, lying on his back in just a shirt and trousers, calmly, methodically working his cane, and me, bound to a pillar and with a stopped-up mouth, hanging there without the slightest movement, emitting not even a groan… Clasping her hands in horror, she rushed into the yard, screamed for the attendant and neighbors, and, with their help, managed with great difficulty to untie me and get me away from the hands of my father. I was carried senseless into another room and laid on a divan. Mother sent for a doctor, and he spent a long time over me returning me to life. I was given food, but although I'd already gone entire days without, I could keep almost nothing in my mouth. I was ill, of course, and could feel nothing, but my entire body was welted and hacked to pieces; my bloodied flesh hung in tatters…

Please allow me to stop here until tomorrow. I cannot write about this without shuddering, without damning my own father! That night, I was overwhelmed by delirium. The doctor, having examined me a second time, announced that I was beginning a fever… I can't remember the following two weeks, and when I later regained consciousness, I felt so terribly weak that I spent a month and a half in bed. Father began treating me with greater tenderness, and when I'd sufficiently recovered so that I could speak, explained to me that the purse had been found. I was curious to know how, and he told me the following. The purse's cover had been inscribed with its owner's name, and it somehow happened that while I was lying in delirium a gentleman visited a watchmaker—a good friend of my former boss—to buy a silver chain, and, while paying for it, took from his pocket a purse: the watchmaker immediately noticed on it the name my boss had told him. Without letting the buyer know he suspected him, the watchmaker engaged him in a long conversation, but at the same time sent someone to the police station and also to my boss. The police appeared and began to interrogate the anonymous gentleman about how and from whom he'd gotten the purse: he was a bit confused, but nevertheless explained that he'd bought it somewhere. During this, my former boss arrived. He instantly recognized not only the purse but the gentleman himself, who on New Year's Eve, that is, the day it was lost, called upon him in the shop and traded in some cuff-links but did not buy anything with them. At the police station, he was immediately identified as a well-known swindler who went around to stores and exchanged various things yet never bought anything, and only used the opportunity to pinch something. He soon confessed to stealing the purse that had played such a doleful role in my life. "Yes, in this instance you've suffered unfairly," father concluded his account, "that is true. But you stole money in synagogue, and you probably tried to steal the gold from your boss… And you were associated with these sins earlier… In a word, you can't imagine that you're as pure as a dove. You're infamous, and all who know you are pointing at you. You should think long and hard about this. Under me, you were living submissively and honorably and no one knew you, but now everyone calls you a thief and even the police know you. But I'll tell you quite a tale right now. In the old days there lived a certain pauper. And by the time he'd reached his ninetieth year he was very crippled and weak. The pauper thought: 'Clearly, it's time for me to die… But as soon as I've reached my ninetieth year I should up and die? No one in the world will ever know I was alive. That's a real pity!' The pauper gathered together his last coppers, hobbled to a store, and bought a large antique sword. With this sword he snuck into the garden of a rich and famous grandee in that country. And when the grandee came into the garden for a stroll, the old man ambushed him and threatened him with the sword… Needless to say, his retinue seized the criminal and disarmed him. Then the grandee ordered the old man brought before him, stared at him angrily, and asked: 'Why do you want to kill me? Have I done you any harm?' 'No,' answered the pauper, 'you've done me no harm, but I'm getting ready to die and I wanted to leave behind a kind of fame concerning me, so that folks would say that there lived such-and-such a famous grandee and that such-and-such a pauper tried to kill him.' Then the grandee burst out laughing and allowed the pauper to go home without any punishment: 'Go home, old fool, it truly is clearly time for you to die!' Well, young fool you, isn't it clear you've wanted fame like this pauper? Except, I'll tell you that you're far dumber than the pauper, because no scam artists in your position would have stolen, but since you did steal something, you should bear the utmost responsibility." Such was my father's parable to me, and, I confess, it lies deep in my soul…

Having recovered from my illness, I stopped going to my jeweler boss: after two misfortunes in a very short time he was now ashamed to accept me for a third try, so I stayed home. Father accepted my word that I'd never steal again, and assigned me to a desk in his shop, to receive and ship goods—in short, he made me top boss. But I must confess to you that, although I held out for a long time, I couldn't keep my word. I happened to get to know salesmen and various young merchants and began to feel the need for spending money, because I wanted to attend the theater and zoological garden and to host comrades, but, to compensate his honor, father was being extremely tight-fisted and I saw not a kopek from him. And so I began to steal, but so cleverly that I always made everything tally up and was never caught. Thus passed an entire year.

Trade was brisk, we had a lot of hawkers, and our goods earned a high profit. I especially became friends with one of our hawkers, a young man of twenty-two, a townsman from Staraia Russa named Ivan Brusnitsyn. He was a rather dull-witted and, when sober, remarkably submissive chap, still not completely dissolute, so that friendship with him apparently promised me no foolishness. But, in fact, this was not to be. Ivan Brusnitsyn had an elder brother who was a senior servant of the Pole Krasinski, acting state councilor in charge of the Izmailovskii Regiment's Second Company. This Krasinski was a terribly rich man who owned his own house, but was an incomparable cheap-skate and lived in two rooms on the third floor while letting out the rest as apartments. The old man was a bachelor, but living with him was a beautiful young woman simultaneously playing the role of stewardess, cook, housemaid, and, it was even said, mistress. Young Brusnitsyn often visited his brother in the Izmailovskii Regiment and there became acquainted with Lizaveta (as this woman was called).

One day in early May—I'd just locked the store for the evening—Brusnitsyn, sad and pensive, came to me and said: "Let's go to a pub, you know, I wanna tell you a little something." There were absolutely no secrets between us. Arriving at the pub, we ordered four bottles of beer, poured them in our glasses, and Ivan began his story. "Mishka, I daresay you know you're as dear to me as Lizaveta is… Well, quite often I go to her when the general's not at home. So, today she told me they're leaving in a few days to take the mineral waters at Staraia Russa. And the general, among other things, is bringing twenty-five thousand rubles with him… He's then leaving for three days in Moscow and she'll be left by herself to guard the money… Well, brother, what do you suppose she, Lizaveta, was thinking? She's suggesting I go to Staraia Russa as well, and when the general's gone in Moscow, I come and take the money from her and she'll take responsibility for it. It's so spotless, she says, and everything will be arranged so that no suspicion falls on me. She's asking me to think hard about all this and give my answer tomorrow. I stupidly told her I'll think about it, but now all this is making me hot and cold, and God knows what if this fails!" When he said these words I myself went hot and cold, only not from cowardice, of course. I was thinking: twenty-five thousand! Much might be risked for so much… Father's parable had obviously landed in fertile soil… Having finished a friendly fourth bottle of beer, I invited him to dinner at a restaurant and there undertook to prove to him all the benefits of the enterprise, calling into view that with such money he could go from being a simple hawker to a merchant of the first guild, and that only one in a million persons gets such a stroke of luck; I asked him to take me on as his partner and promised to do everything necessary. After a lot of persuading, he agreed. We arranged that, next day, he would tell his brother he was going home for a while, but on 15 May he would be ready and waiting for me at the Nikolaevsk railroad station. I myself decided to deceive my father in the following way. He had several debtors in Staraia Russa who hadn't paid their bills for a long time; he'd been ready to go there several times, but never managed to do so. The following day, I had a conversation with him and spoke with deliberate irritation about these faulty debtors; I knew in advance that he would once again mention his lack of time, sickness, etc. And so, hardly had he said this than I offered myself in his service: if he would allow, I would go to Staraia Russa and pressure the debtors, and incidentally, I would look into the benefit of trading at the forthcoming fair there. Father heartily agreed to my suggestion, assigned me thirty rubles for traveling, and released me for two weeks. On the appointed day, I bade my parents farewell, hired a cabby, and left for the station.

XV. A STEEP FALL

Brusnitsyn was already waiting for me.

En route, I did not speak about the matter with him, since I saw he was in low spirits, was frowning and nervous, and so, to cheer him, I told various amusing stories and jokes. At almost every station we drank tea and I treated him to wines and appetizers. We entered Staraia Russa at seven o'clock in the morning. Brusnitsyn asked me which of the two hotels we were staying in—the London or the Petersburg. All this time, my imagination had been working feverishly; an unusual matter-of-factness and shrewdness had awoken in me; in good time, I decided to provide for and secure myself from all sides; never in my life had I seen Staraia Russa, but from certain conversations with comrades I already knew it like the back of my hand, and, after quickly deciding, I announced that we should stay in the Petersburg: I calculated that this hotel, standing on the riverbank opposite the cathedral, was situated in a quiet place where there were few people… In the Petersburg, I got two rooms with separate entrances for two rubles a day, and told Ivan he should tell his brother that he'd come there with his boss's son on business. After this, we separated. I didn't get any money from father's debtors that day—all protested poor sales and promised to pay soon. All the next day, Brusnitsyn and I wandered aimlessly through the city, looking at the market square and the bazaar. In the bazaar, we encountered a policeman who immediately saw from my face that I was a visitor.[64] He approached and asked who I was, where I was from, and if I had my passport. My passport turned out to be in order and, after inspecting it, he simply ordered me to send it to the station for a registration stamp. That day, I got 340 rubles from Jewish debtors and immediately mailed them to father, keeping not a kopek for myself, despite the fact that my own money was already running out: I wanted father to be completely relaxed regarding me and to allow me to stay there as long as necessary. I reasoned thus: if I take and spend some of father's money, won't our scheme quickly collapse, and there'll be nothing for us to replace what gets squandered? Then, because of some trifles, I would always be without father's trust, which I very much needed. And so I began devising how to get money from a different source.

In the evening, I went to the park where there was a theater, but one and the same idea was gnawing at me the whole time there. Upon leaving the park, I went into Popov's store to buy cigarettes, and while there an idea at first glance crazy but instead brilliant popped into my head—to rob this wealthy store. But how to realize such a plan? I little knew the city; I didn't have the partner for such a job because Brusnitsyn, of course, wouldn't have done it for however many millions, and even talking to him about this undertaking was out of the question; to top it off, I still had not once in my life tested all my strength in such a major and audacious theft. But something persistently told me: "All the same, I'll do it, I'll do it!"—and the whole night, I couldn't sleep, running over in my head hundreds of possible schemes, criticizing them and tossing out one after another. By morning, I already knew what had to be done.

After these two days I'd managed to notice that in the evening, after work, most of Staraia Russa's cityfolk carried in their carts small, special kegs of twelve or fifteen gallons for their water, and I decided to acquire for myself such a keg and a cart. That morning, Ivan called on me to take a walk with his friends, but I protested a headache and he went off by himself the whole day, but I went to the bazaar, bought there a cart and a keg for two rubles and sixty-five kopeks, and told the seller to deliver them to me at my quarters. The purchase was delivered on time; I then lowered one of the keg's hoops and knocked the bottom off one side before replacing the hoop. Why did I do this? Here's why. I calculated that were I to be successful getting into the store, it would be impossible to haul a bundle of goods down the city's main streets at night—I'd probably be arrested. It would be possible to put what I wanted into the keg and then go back and forth three times without arousing the slightest suspicion. That evening, I again went to the theater and upon my return entered Popov's store once more and bought cigarettes, nuts, candies, and a couple of oranges. I didn't so much need these purchases as I wanted to inspect the whole layout, and I purposely tarried buying these items. After leaving the store, I strolled along the opposite side of the pavement for a long time, hoping to see how the store was locked. Indeed, the shopkeepers soon locked it and went home; I then approached and saw two simple padlocks, which when the opportunity arose would be easy to break, though to risk breaking them at that point would have been an inexcusable mistake: almost opposite, at the entrance to the park, there always stood a guard, and the slightest alarming sound would have ruined me. I therefore took from my pocket a piece of beeswax that I'd prepared earlier and made a mold of the keyhole. It was already one o'clock at night and, extremely satisfied with my observations, I went home. At home, I found a slightly drunk Brusnitsyn. I told him I'd received a telegram from my father ordering me to leave the following day and spend two days in Novgorod, and I therefore advised him that instead of paying for the room, I was going to spend these two days with relatives. He agreed, and on this basis instantly began snoring. As soon as I left him that morning for my relatives, having said that I would depart in an hour, my soul lightened and I now felt neither afraid nor ashamed. I went straight to ironworkers' row to have a key made according to the mold I'd taken. But in this I was extremely cunning and careful; I made it appear that I was simply trying to find more secure locks and, needless to say, did not show the shopkeeper the waxen imprint. Similar locks were soon found, and I, without haggling, paid what was owed. The rest of the day, sitting in my room and thinking over all the details of my future crime, I didn't show my nose anywhere, and moreover fortified my spirit with beer and cognac. However, toward evening, something like pangs of conscience awoke in me; I asked myself: Am I undertaking a good venture? Do I have the right to take money that's probably been earned through the blood of several generations? Would it please me if I was the one robbed? My head was spinning from these untimely and importune questions and, so as to avoid them, I dressed myself with a quick hand, exited, locked my quarters, and went upstairs to listen to the hotel's organ. There, I ordered half a bottle of cognac and some appetizers. After that, I was however unable to relax and drank a small glass of vodka for courage, and then went to the theater. As I now recall, *Poverty is not a Vice*[65] was playing in the theater, and I very much liked this piece, so that I stayed till the show was over and was thoroughly cheered up. At the stroke of one, I took my cart, put the keg on it, grabbed a stearine candle, matches, and the keys from the locks I'd bought that morning, and went to Ilinskii Street. Immediately, I encountered a night-watchman standing near the store with his rattle; I went past him, turned a corner, and, having parked the cart, walked toward the store. It was dead quiet, and only the knocking sound of a paddlewheel somewhere could be heard. Taking my keys, I opened the locks and quietly opened the door; behind it was a glass door, and had this also been locked I would then have had either to force out a pane, that is, make a noise, or to abandon my enterprise completely. But, to my fortune or misfortune, it wasn't locked. Looking around once more, I walked back to the cart, brought it up to the store, pulled the doors wide open, pushed it through, then closed them tightly behind me. My heart was pounding—I sensed that half the business was done, that I was now utter master of the store. Relaxing, I lit a candle and immediately turned my attention to the office where the earnings were kept. In a little chest, I found fifty paper, nineteen silver, and nine copper rubles. Having taken and counted the money, I was rather disappointed… I then began looking over the goods: there were whole heads of sugar and bags of sugar cubes, candies, spice cakes, chocolate, expensive wheat flour, but most of all there was the Popov firm's own tea, and I decided to take only the tea, since this was the most valuable commodity. I stuffed my keg full of five-ruble and three-ruble tea—in pounds, half-pounds, quarter-pounds, and eighth-pounds. Having put the bottom on the keg and resituating the hoop, I extinguished the candle and listened; opening the door slightly, I looked around, and with no one on the street and convinced the coast was clear, I quietly opened the door, pushed my cart out of the store, closed and locked the door again, and went home with the booty. At home, I dumped everything out and divided it into new portions. To speak succinctly, I repeated this operation three times. The final time I took, in addition to tea, three hundred cigars (at ten rubles per one hundred) and a fifty-pound tin of fruit drops. During these three trips I encountered cabbies, night-watchmen, late-night strollers, and policemen and no one, absolutely no one, thought to stop me. The point is that at night, it was possible to encounter several dozen people going about with such barrels for water: some never did so until nightfall because for some it was embarrassing to be carrying their water, and so they got it only when everyone was sleeping, and if they nevertheless bumped into an acquaintance, then, having turned aside, they tried to make such a sour face that it cancelled the desire of any friend or acquaintance to greet them.

Having ended the drive, I put all the tea in a corner of my room, laid out my sheets, and slept soundly, since it was already light. At seven in the morning, I went to the bazaar and bought three wooden boxes and several bast mats. I then realized the whole city was, like a disturbed ant-hill, in an uproar over my nighttime heist… Popov had gotten all the police on their feet; they had arrested most of the suspicious folks. In the end, they decided that no one believed in the audacious heist save the old salesman, because the locks were intact and he had the keys… In a word, I was beyond suspicion. Burning all the tea wrappers, I poured all my tea into boxes (lowest quality first, then the best on top), nailed the boxes shut, sheathed them with the bast matting, and brought them to the station, where I put them on the goods train and also bought myself a ticket to Novgorod. In Novgorod, I sold the tea to a certain Jew for eighty rubles per pood, and having received 800 rubles from him, I went back the next evening to Staraia Russa. Brusnitsyn met me at the station, very angry that instead of two days I'd been gone three: according to him, the general and Lizaveta had arrived just the day before, and if he, Ivan, hadn't finally met me that day, he would have spit on it all and left for Petersburg. After getting to the hotel, I tried to mollify Ivan and invited him to a bottle of Madera. He then explained to me that he had an appointment to meet Lizaveta in the morning in the bazaar. Indeed, next day, after drinking our morning coffee, we went to the bazaar and met Lizaveta. She hesitated and, engaging Brusnitsyn in conversation, asked who I was. He responded: "This is my good comrade. I invited him on purpose from Petersburg, so don't be shy in front of him. So, tell me, how long are you staying here?" She laughed: "See how impatient you are! Take comfort. My skinflint's leaving for Moscow in the morning, and in the evening, we'll invite my sweetheart to a cup of tea." At this, we separated, and I went strolling with Ivan. I didn't need more money, and will tell you in short that during these two days, he and I blew 440 rubles. Brusnitsyn kept asking where I'd gotten so much money, but I deflected him with jokes and said: "Now's the time to drink, eat, and play! Who knows, these may be our last good times." I didn't know this joke was prophetic…

At the designated time of twelve midnight, we showed up at General Krasinski's. He had indeed left that day for Moscow aboard the evening train, and Lizaveta was awaiting us impatiently. She immediately placed appetizers and a bottle of champagne on the table; however, Brusnitsyn was already so drunk he could hardly stand, but I, knowing what a task was before us, was just a little tipsy. Having seated us, Lizaveta began: "I think I've put a good plan together. The money's in his office, in the writing desk. We'll bust open the door, and when the general returns, I'll tell him that while he was gone some people broke in and, after putting a knife to my throat, threatened to kill me if I so much as screamed during the robbery. I'll tell him I fainted and don't know what happened afterward, but when I came to, I found the apartment in disorder, all the locks broken, and even the front door open. If you, gentlemen, like my plan, then you can undertake this business right away." I confess that as for me, I didn't take this plan to heart: something in her voice sounded false, and her eyes were guilty, since they seemed to be looking off to the side. At that moment, a horrifying plan suddenly popped into my head: take the money and murder this young woman so there'd be no witness. But after glancing at Ivan, I instantly banished all such thoughts from my head: he melted in front of Lizaveta, and shouted in his drunken voice: "Agreed!... Outstanding!..." Following this, he grabbed an axe lying in the kitchen and smashed the lock with all his might. I went into the apartment and searched the office and bedroom and rummaged through everything—but there wasn't a single kopek anywhere. All this time, Lizaveta was managing to get Brusnitsyn thoroughly drunk, and when I returned to the kitchen he was already sleeping like a dead man. Hearing from me that there was no money, Lizaveta feigned utter astonishment and surprise and went to the office with me to make another search. She threw everything from place to place, rifled through the desk's drawers and papers (in the meantime, I stood at the door watching her every move), and finally turned to me with rage and said: "Well, I made a blunder! He must've taken the money with him... And I, a fool, could think that such a skinflint would leave such a lot of money here!..." I then hurried over to Ivan, shook him and whispered in his ear that we'd been ruined, that Lizaveta had undercut us and that only one thing remained to save ourselves—to kill her. Ivan nearly killed me for these words, but I made a joke out of them. Then, so as not to begrudge a gift and leave the apartment empty-handed, I took for myself a silver table service, a gold watch, and some knick-knacks and also, for whatever case, elicited from Lizaveta a promise that she would not reveal our names (though in my heart this promise meant very little). After we returned to the hotel, Ivan fell on the floor and slept as if murdered, but I hailed a cabby and went to see a certain sharp Jew who accepted stolen goods. It was good that I did, because the very next day around noon—Brusnitsyn and I still hadn't been able to open our eyes—an entire contingent of police visited us. A rumor about the commission of a burglary at General Krasinski's was going around the whole city, and in the doorway a bunch of extraneous folk had gathered alongside the policemen: among the curiosity-seekers I noticed my burglarized merchant Popov... "Are your papers in order?" the superintendent turned to me. I pulled my papers from my pocket and gave them to him. Having looked at them, he told Brusnitsyn and me: "I arrest you in the name of the law!" and ordered a quartet of policemen to search our place. Nothing suspicious was found. Suddenly, Popov told the superintendent that he recognized his tin of fruit drops, which was sitting on my table: this, he said, was the same tin stolen from his store a couple days earlier. The tin was opened, but inside there turned out to be not fruit drops but coffee. "By what marks do you recognize this?" the superintendent asked. Popov replied that as far as he knew, there were no other stores in the city except his with this make of candy, and moreover, this was the same five-pound tin he'd been missing. I took exception at this, laughing: "Perhaps you're right that you had such a tin, but I bought this in Petersburg, and Petersburg is not Staraia Russa—there you can get whatever you need at any little stand. So your charge is not true." As such, Popov was made to look a fool. Nonetheless, the four policemen accompanied us to the station. A door to a neighboring room unexpectedly opened, and in came our friend Lizaveta. I quickly guessed what was going on and made a look as if I'd never seen her in my life. "Were these gentlemen your guests last night?" the superintendent turned to her. "Yes, these are the very ones," she firmly answered, gazing at us with impudence. Brusnitsyn and I, for our part, denied this, and were then taken to the lock-up.

That same day, I sent father a telegram about my arrest, asking him to come quickly. It was impossible for me not to do so because, during the search, 1,200 rubles had been seized from me, of which 900 was father's, and were I to be prosecuted, this money could be lost or even used as evidence against me. Besides this, my father would know everything sooner or later. The next day, summoned by a telegram from Lizaveta, General Krasinski arrived in Staraia Russa aboard the morning train. As soon as he looked in his office and saw his writing table in shambles, he sighed: his 25,000 rubles were gone!... After this, Ivan and I were confronted by a new, far more serious charge: breaking and entering and the theft of not only the silverware (for which we'd been charged the day before on Lizaveta's words), but the 25,000 rubles as well. There was now no longer any doubt that this money had actually existed, but that it was taken by Lizaveta herself and that we'd been invited by her only as a blind. In a word, we'd been made fools of, as if we were the lowest schoolboys! After the charges were read against us, our interrogation formally began, and Brusnitsyn and I protested with one voice that we didn't know and hadn't done anything.

My father arrived toward evening. He was immediately permitted to see me, and I assured him that I did not at all understand why I'd been arrested and that the 1,200 rubles taken from me were his, was his blood money. The next day, I was taken to prison and the matter took a turn. I found myself for the first time in my life in a prisoner's blouse, cassock, and tattered cats:[66] my physical characteristics were noted down and I was put into the defendants' division. I won't undertake to describe the beginning of my prison career, but will merely note its principal features and most salient events. From the first, prisoners greeted me with jibes and even hostility; the prison Ivans assailed me with demands "behind the privy," threatening even to beat me if I didn't pay them ten or at least five rubles. But their attitudes toward me soon took on a strange, startling turn. Prisoners avoided me, and began gathering in clusters and whispering about something to each other; then some of the Ivans again approached me, albeit now with ingratiating talk and various offers of service. They put my things on the sleeping platform, gave me a straw-filled mattress and the same kind of pillow. It turned out that the reason for this sudden turn was that a guard had told them I'd stolen 25,000, and that this money wasn't found when my place was searched. "He hid it splendidly," the guard praised me, "no shame goin' to prison o'er such a sum." This inspired esteem for me among certain prisoners, while others hoped to snatch a little from me by winning at cards or through other means. There were suddenly several disputes regarding me and my crime, and I soon became familiar with several phrases from criminal speech: "Where can you go to unnerstand me?" one prisoner shouted at another. "I know *you* very well. *You're* just a little organ-grinder, all you know is how to nab tobacco pouches from drunks! You ain't stole nuthin' more in your day. But ever'one knows me! I done full-ons, I done good-mornin's, 'n', as it turns out, I done zips."[67]

As a result, there were even certain characters who found themselves beginning to believe they knew me, my father, and my brothers, of whom, by the way, I have none. A samovar with tea and French bread and a bottle of spirits soon appeared. I, however, refused the vodka point-blank, suspecting some trap. Suddenly, I found myself next to a rug that had been spread out and several fellows who'd settled down to play cards. The same thing began in another and in a third place, and here was a game of *shtos*, of smacker, of seducer, of preference, of kick-the-bucket. I was offered a card, but I didn't join in the game, saying I did not know how to play at all, didn't want to, didn't have any money with me—there was nothing for it. Some of them came running over offering to lend me as much as I needed, others insisted that not only was there nothing underhanded about the game but even nothing difficult, that my card was worth a try—and consequently, if I played, it would only be a matter of luck. In the end, I borrowed ten rubles and, for sure, lost that in about ten minutes, honestly speaking. I was at that time quite a horrible card-player and therefore didn't agree to continue playing, but, having drunk my tea, fell into a deep sleep. In the middle of the night, I was suddenly awakened by a terrible pain in my feet, and I jumped from my spot with a loud cry. Around me it was deathly quiet; the prisoners, heads wrapped in their cassocks and sheepskins, were lying on the platforms. Coming to my senses, I began examining my toes and saw that my skin had been burned; this indicated to me, as a novice, a blister beetle… Here's what happened. They soak strips of paper in kerosene and wrap them around a sleeper's toes and light them. When I jumped to my feet in fright, the paper flew away. In the morning, I realized whose escapade this was and decided to pay him back… Barely had he fallen asleep the next night than I took a handkerchief, tore it into thin strips, soaked them in kerosene, and, having tied the strips with thread to the sleeper's toes, lighted them. When the flames erupted he gave a savage roar and began picking at the imaginary paper on his feet, but this proved not so easy to do. In the morning, the poor man was taken to a hospital and remained there three months, but I had instantly dissuaded the prisoners from messing with me. True, a council formed that day to judge me, but I greased certain Ivans' palms and they vouched for me. Thus was accomplished my prison baptism…

I was held for an entire year pending trial, and only in May of '87 was I finally sentenced to sixteen months in a workhouse, but this was changed to solitary confinement; my comrade Brusnitsyn, since he was of age, was sentenced to four years in a penal battalion and exiled to Arkhangel Province. I served time in Staraia Russa's new prison, only just completed on the model of Petersburg's House of Detention. Prisoners received the usual discounts against their sentences, and solitary confinement was not strictly enforced. Nonetheless, my soul does not pine for my old prison, since prisoners there were forbidden private foodstuffs, even tea and sugar, to say nothing of tobacco; for a single bad word you got threatened with a week in the isolator… In a word, the regime was very strict, and the prisoners themselves, my cohabitants in the old prison who, it turned out, were not the Devil's brothers, conducted themselves more quietly than water beneath reeds, doffed their caps before every guard, and were positively ready to lick the warden's hand. But, as is with many youngsters still not tired by steep mountains, I began my prison career not with quiet and timid behavior but, on the contrary, my audacity shocked not only comrades but the leadership itself. I cursed so many times around the warden that he put me in the isolator. But I dreamed up something else. One day, a rumor went round the prison that one of the grand princes was coming to visit us. It's even funny to say that chaos arose because the warden and guards got cold feet. I was immediately transferred to the general ward, where there were also five underage peasants who'd been arrested for tree-felling—a couple had gotten two weeks, the others a month. At eleven o'clock in the morning, five troikas pulled up, and from them exited the grand prince and all the city's military and civilian officialdom. Our ward was nearest the entry and we were visited first of all. Walking around, the grand prince greeted everyone courteously, but no one save me knew at all what to call him, and so only I responded to him. Having looked at our records, he asked if we had any complaints. It was then I stepped forward. I showed him the bread they fed us and which was filled with sand; identified our communal cistern in which supper was kept and which was used for holding drinking water night and day, so that it was impossible to drink from because of the lingering stench of spoiled cabbage; complained that prisoners were not given boiled water; and said in conclusion: "Pay no attention, Your Highness, to what they'll offer you today in the kitchen as a tasty sample of the supper. This is for today only, and tomorrow they'll once more feed us spoiled cabbage and rotten meat." Having listened to my story with curiosity, the grand prince turned to the warden and asked whether all this was true, but in fright he could only respond: "Your Excellency!" and, thoroughly nonplussed, fell silent. The provincial prosecutor said something on his behalf, but the grand prince left in a rage.

Suddenly, everything changed. A new warden was appointed, prisoners began to be better fed, and they even began allowing in everything from the outside... But, not satisfied with this, I also removed the senior guard Vasilii Aleksandrovich. Strictly speaking, he was a good fellow, but he was a drunkard and perpetrated great cruelties when drunk: for amusement, he beat prisoners with his key and moreover loved to arrange major whackings, that is, he'd grab a fistful of your hair in one hand and, holding it tightly, punch you with his other fist... This cruel torment was his favorite pastime, and for its sake he wouldn't allow prisoners to cut their hair. One day, goofing off with the prisoners, I lightly bloodied my head and then, taking advantage of the occurrence, said as soon as Vasilii Aleksandrovich entered my ward: "Let go of my hair, Mishka!"—and ran like a shot straight to the doctor and told him the senior guard hit me in the head with his key... The doctor got so indignant that, after bandaging my little wound, he immediately sent for the warden and swore out an affidavit in his presence. It was even said that the guard would be put on trial, but he wasn't, since he was a nobleman, though he was summarily dismissed that very day.

So, my term of rehabilitation (it would be truer to say dissolution) ended uneventfully, and in April '88 I got out of prison. My mother came and brought new clothes for me, since during the two years I'd fairly grown and my old ones no longer fit. That same day, we left for Petersburg. We found father still in bed. As I entered, he got up and greeted me affectionately—at the time, he still believed fully in my innocence.

He immediately offered to appoint me his chief trader, and I warmly accepted this offer. I should tell you that despite all my dissoluteness while in prison, I often pondered my past and future and came to the conviction that honest labor and a piece of bread earned with a clear conscience are better than anything in the world. And I think that had people been kinder and more mature, and regarded somewhat otherwise and with humanitarianism a person who made a mistake one day, then my decision to follow the good path would not have been a lost dream. But people were not so, and upon my first approaching them, I received a terrible moral shock such as I'd never experienced: not only did no one give me a hand or friendly advice so as to extract me from the past and its dirty dealings, but, on the contrary, it seemed each person pushed me to the very brink of criminality and depravity, so that I now could not rest and come to my senses… Forgive me for this philosophy, but at that time, I went through so much suffering that I'm now able to remember and talk about it calmly.

From the first days I got behind the counter I noticed that my relatives' and acquaintances' attitudes toward me were absolutely not what they had been. Their every word, every smile, communicated contempt for me, a desire to wound, to offend, me, and this desire seemed to me to be there even when it was probably not there at all. When anyone I knew visited the store I went hot and cold; at a single glance from these people, I was ready to fly into a rage at anything… This condition ultimately began to recur so often that, in order to avoid doing something crazy, I decided to explain it to father and beg him to release me for a time from trading. My decision greatly surprised him; he hadn't finished telling me, he said, as he should have earlier, two years ago, everything he thought about this, and that if I wasn't ashamed of going to prison I shouldn't feel ashamed before others. In a word, on my father's part, I saw a complete misunderstanding of my emotional confusion; nonetheless, I refused point-blank to continue going to the shop. Father flared up and wanted to raise his hand against me, but he saw something in my eyes that made him stop: before him no longer stood a beaten and broken-spirited boy, but a young man in whom a conscience and awareness of his own worth had awakened…

He waved his hand at me, and from that time on I stayed home without a break, bored, despairing, and mad at everyone. I despised all that was old, but had nothing new in my head. Yet, in the meantime, I was young and hot-blooded… I thirsted for society, activity, friends, heartfelt conversations… During this chaotic time I needed a person with understanding who could lead me away from error and show me the path I should follow. But such a person did not turn up. And, against my will, I unnoticeably came to make peace with my past, to forgive my conscience my foolish actions. To make peace with the past, this shameful past, which cost me so much tears, anguish, and despair! And now, when conscience has arisen in me, I have begun to suffer and to cry futilely once more, without any purpose, since it was my fate to be utterly and forever ruined…

At that time, my father had to find a new, more comfortable apartment, and after a lot of searches and difficulties he happened to find a suitable one owned by the Izmailovskii Regiment's Second Company. We moved there in the summer, and I was terribly shocked to realize that our home was next to General Krasinski's. I was still trying to recover from this initial surprise when, upon entering the yard and gazing upward in curiosity, I saw in a third-story window… Lizaveta Semënova, the same woman who had once ruined me! Hardly believing my own eyes, I stood stupefied in the same spot for a full hour, though no one remained in the window. I shook as if from a fever and was at that moment ready for whatever sort of crime! I was burning all over, felt I was suffocating; I walked out to the street like a drunk man and mechanically, without any destination, followed wherever my eyes led me. My mind was blank. Everything I'd suffered because of this woman, all my not-distant past, passed vividly before me… I wanted vengeance, a terrible vengeance against her, and began thinking how best to get this. At one point I even imagined breaking into the general's quarters in broad daylight and viciously cutting Lizaveta into little pieces… But I rebuked this idea: naturally, I did not pity Lizaveta at all, but I didn't want to put myself in danger again. By the same token, to speak with a clear conscience, I would have enjoyed executing my plan in a secluded spot somewhere far from public gaze.

Having returned home later that evening, I was convinced that unpleasantness was awaiting me there, that Lizaveta had recognized me, told the general everything, and that my father would instantly throw me out of the apartment. However, my apprehension proved unfounded: as it was, and so in the following days, everything at our place was peaceful, and father suspected nothing…

....

With these words, Shuster's manuscript unfortunately breaks off. Here's why.

During the distractions of the Lomov period, which lasted around two months, I naturally had no time for pupils with their autobiographies; they fully understood this, and study and writing temporarily came to an end. But when my personal distractions ended and I was ready to resume my usual lifestyle and occupations, I once again became interested in my involuntary cohabitants' society, their grievances and joys, and to my surprise I saw that Shuster had once more managed to turn prisoners' attitudes towards him decisively for the worse. Everyone was again shunning him, refusing to eat out of the same serving bowl with him, calling him a "filthy Yid," and generally treating him with the loftiest disdain.

As for Mishka Shuster, he himself once again had a cowed and somewhat perplexed appearance; he'd lie quietly in his corner on the sleeping platform, absorbed in writing or some other task, and seemed to take no notice of the ward's attitude toward him. But this inattentiveness was undoubtedly manufactured; every time he approached the table for his ration of food he guiltily hung his head and looked timidly side to side. It was clear that he was guilty of and had been caught doing something… I wondered. Then, one day when Shuster was gone, Elk, flustered but at the same time in a fury, raced into the ward.

"Get that damned stinker away from me!" he shouted, throwing his recent friend's bedding off the platform.

"What 'appened? Don't like Kitty-Cat no more?" someone from the mare ironically inquired.

"You bastard, d'you know 'bout her, the way she… is? Why didn't you say somethin' if'n you'd heard?"

"That'll do! As if you didn't know?"

Elk crossed himself with both hands:

"By the Cross 'n' the most sacred Mother o' God, I'm tellin' you I didn't know! I might e'en catch an infection from her, that carrion: they're sayin' she's goin' to the hospital ever'day, takin' medicine for the syphilis."

"Whatta joke! Only the whole prison knew, but our Elk alone was a stupid kid! Can you believe this, boys?"

They roared in laughter at Elk. Utterly abashed, he started cursing and roaring profanities and began stomping on Shuster's mattress lying on the floor.

The brave captain appeared at evening roll call after having not been there for a long time. To everyone's surprise, Shuster turned to him with a complaint:

"Mister Commandant, they won't let me sleep on the platforms."

"*Who* won't allow you?"

"The prisoners."

"Why?"

"I can't say, Mister Commandant."

Luchezarov pursed his lips.

"Foolish rumors have been reported to me about you," he suddenly raised his voice, "*very* foolish, lad! I didn't want to believe these stories, but I'm coming to believe them. Know this: I will not permit such filthiness to occur in my prison! I've taken your measure already."

With this enigmatic threat, he walked off. The ward's long pent-up avalanche of temper then burst: everyone was shouting and blathering everything at once at the wretched Shuster. Spit and the words "bastard," "squealer," "Jew-boy," and "dirty filth" flew at him from all directions. Exhausted, covered in spit, he stood with his back pressed to a corner and was silent, but there seemed to be a distinct change in the features of his pale face: the timidity and perplexity so recently evident in his eyes had suddenly disappeared and given way to a kind of shameless impudence; inside his large brilliant eyes, black as a pair of plums, there burned a glowing hatred in which could be seen murderous contempt…

"Gentlemen, stop it!" I hurriedly turned to the milling crowd. "Shuster, put your bedding beside mine."

In silence, he hastily took advantage of my offer, and although prisoners continued shouting at him for a long time, he paid them no attention—or at least he quickly gave the appearance of having fallen asleep.

The next day, I happened to be speaking about him to the collective headman Godunov, now living in my ward. I suggested that Shuster was perhaps not in the least guilty of what he'd been accused of. The cunning yokel simply laughed at this.

"Ya prob'ly believed Elk, that he didn't know nuthin'? Come on, Ivan Nikolaevich! We know ever'one of 'em what's used this bastard, 'n' consider this: where's he get his fine tobacco, sugar, 'n' tea from? Or take that last week, the tailor Tikhtenko sewed a collar on his prison jacket. He charged me fifty kopeks for the very same service… That's how much money you'd need."

"But why aren't you going after such gentlemen? In my opinion, aren't they guiltier by comparison?…"

Godunov shrugged his shoulders.

"Our mare's got its own unnerstandin' in this regard. It keeps to the rule: if there's an opportunity—seize it, if not—move along. 'N' how can you prosecute if a good half o' the prison is guilty? Well, first the prisoners fatten for slaughter them bastards like Kitty-Cat, then they pound their mugs in. On the other hand, jus' to speak, Ivan Nikolaevich: in a dif'rent prison we prob'ly wouldn't pay any attention to such a stinker, but, well, here it's another matter, *here* we can't put up with him."

"Why *here* precisely? Isn't it all the same?"

"There's a big dif'rence."

However, Godunov did not make this difference completely clear to me. A different prison… different people… everyone's visible… greater shame… It seems the presence of people like me and my comrades exerted no small influence over the behavior of the prison. Unfortunately, this influence—"shame," as Godunov put it—was rather too one-sided: they despised and were prepared to persecute and beat Shuster, yet "a good half of the prison," simultaneously and on the quiet, did not regard it as disgraceful to join in his ignominy.

However, Shuster's notes, inspired by such a profoundly sad vengeance, have at times stumped me and prevent me from definitely believing all that was said about him. I still don't trust anything until I've seen it with my own eyes…

………………………………………………………………………………

What, I have thought to myself, attracted the wretch to such filth? Had he been in another prison, he still probably would have sought refuge in dissolute activities, systematic hunger strikes, or various opportunities to earn money, as in Shelai Prison…

After this discovery, it was like my heart broke, and all my previous sympathy for this wretched youth was lost. Not only did I not insist that he continue his notes, but I felt unalloyed disgust at the notebooks he had composed. It was disgusting to touch these filthy, soiled pages and not at once consign them to the flames… But then I somehow forgot about them, and they were saved thanks only to this. Several years passed, and completely by chance I came across these half-filled notebooks while disposing of some rubbish and, after reading them, deeply regretted that they had ended at such an interesting point. Had their author continued writing with the same doubtless truthfulness and candor, then the psychology of this pathetic, irrevocably ruined man might, I believe, be in its own way especially interesting…

I know nothing more of his fate. After writing down his notes he was transferred to another mine, presumably at Six-Eyes's insistence. The prisoners rejoiced loudly.

XVI. SHELAI'S RENOWN; PASSION FOR A WRITER; CONVICT DREAMERS

Shelai's name was now renowned throughout *katorga*, being threatening for some and, for others, by contrast, a kind of terrestrial El Dorado, a kind of *katorga* university from which those who so desired emerged as not only literate, but practically educated, individuals. Hundred-mouthed rumor stoked to improbable degrees everything good that distinguished Shelai Prison: word went round, for example, that in the prison we had an enormous library on hand and had, with the leadership's permission, constructed a veritable, strictly organized school of the best pupils whose terms were shortened and who were released to the free command; the fervent imagination of storytellers (that is, those prisoners who had left Shelai for settlement) painted in the rosiest and most flattering hues the intellectual and moral qualities of the teachers themselves, and most surprising was that there often turned out to be characters among these selfless panegyrists whose prison lifestyle proved least deserving of sympathy. But the past always presents itself in an alluring light, and it's no wonder that the hearts of people who have at last forsaken the accursed *katorga* life and are on the outside should briefly soften and that fantasy commence its playful dance. It stands to reason that the panegyrizing storytellers did not forget to commemorate, in addition to all that was exaggerated, the material assistance we showed the mare.

As it turned out, there were some pathetic misunderstandings as a result of all this. While the majority of Shelai's residents burst day and night from the power of dreams of freeing their souls from the model prison, out in Sretensk, where parties are assigned to mines, some prisoners were beseeching the command to assign them to Shelai. These requests were sometimes fulfilled and then, upon the first days of their arrival to us, these ill-starred dreamers met with the bitterest disillusionment: everything about our prison that had been trumpeted and glorified as good appeared in actuality to be miniscule to the point of scantiness… Of course, my comrades and I had rather gratified the mare's occasionally touching aspirations towards the educated world, and in this sense we had done something, but, in the end, all this merely bore results that were insignificant to the point of annoyance.

On the other hand, it could not be said that everyone who was being spoiled in Shelai deserved sympathy and stood indubitably above the majority of *katorga* in terms of intellect and morality. Various characters were to be found among them. One day, there was brought to our mine one of those Ivan *Nepomniashchye* who are brought to all the prisons and shown to guards and other servitors on the chance that someone recognizes an escaped penal laborer. Shelai's guards did not recognize him as "theirs," and, in anticipation of his removal to another mine, the unique guest was as usual put in the isolator. Needless to say, the mare wasted not a moment in starting up a detailed correspondence with him, supplying tobacco, and receiving in exchange a variety of sensational news about life in the prison world: this one "got loose," that one was "squealed on," a third had been "gotten"… My comrades and I were, of course, little interested in those news items that so indescribably vexed the entire prison. But then the ward attendant Miloserdov came running to me with an exceedingly conspiratorial look and handed me a letter in a soiled gray envelope with a huge, garishly applied wax seal.

"What's this? Who's it from?" I asked with surprise.

"From the Aleksandrovsk almshouse, from one o' yours," whispered Miloserdov, looking around. "A bit significant this was passed on. It's said Pronia almost found it durin' the search, but the ol' rascal proved more cunnin' 'n' managed to hide it. Most of all, he says, take care so's the markin's don't wear off."

"What markings?"

"But what markin's! On the envelope, there, see, the numbers that's been added on…"

The envelope was indeed marked by various inscrutable hieroglyphs and numbers: 80—40—70—100—400—71—12—00—44, etc., after which appeared: "within them lies the number 666." Also, the Latin letters "*cum deo*" were inscribed around the wax seal and a surprising recipient was emblazoned on the opposite side: "To the Society of Russian Satsyal."[68] "What is this nonsense?" I objected, shrugging my shoulders and trying to hand back the letter, since it wasn't addressed to me by name, but the postman waved both hands and so earnestly cried "For you, for you!" that I tore open the paper and read in it what literally follows:

> Gentlemen, I humbly beseech you to extend a hand to me, as I am a ruined sheep of the Israelites, lost in the side-chapelses of the emperor's house and priestesses. I've taken measures to be transferred to You in Shelai, but am not anyway able to break free. The Warden holds me and warned his finance inspector and whole prison to be careful. He allows himself to starve Prisoners for severally days, it has been, gives no fat dinner, has hand-picked gang of prison Aventureurs who run everything and no one dares say a word! He occasions insupportable corporal punishment: Valentii Shchapp suffered a subgation of heart and lungs, and he quickly died because *Epoplecsia* afflicted him from the blows he suffered. On 14 July of this year I wrote a *Confession* to the name of the *Governor* of Transbaikalia in the theme of a Nihilist teks regarding my desire to repent for my whole life; but the finance officers made the Warden fear I could harm him, and he held me in manacles and leg-irons around a month in the Hellish dark, as the isolator is called. I'm taken out because of a kinda illness of the lungs and subgation of my heart from corporal punishment, and I was took like a dog to the office and was occasioned cruel wounds formally on the bench, and I having two formal doctoral watching.
>
> I don't have any possible means for life, and am missing my physical strength and my mental abilities are coruined as a Vonpir kind of man. With the Ivans' help I get dinner on Wednesday and Friday, and they cook a paltry bit of kasha once a day.

I cannot be silent forever of the truth, I am pulling life out of death. I don't know how many birch lashes I got, because a split second after number three I lost feeling and consciousness; but when I came to, then I said to the Warden, You'll never get any kind of use out of me, and I beg you to direct my Confession to the proper quarters and transfer me to Shelai. He refused me this. I beg the generous hand of help from Your surpluses, please, be fortuous. I remain Lavrentii Pomiakshev. I request an answer. All my writingship accessories have been seized.

I, of course, was unable to offer any kind of response to this strange epistle; but a question involuntarily stirred in my soul: what if such a character got his wish and were transferred to Shelai? Would we welcome such a friend and admirer?… True, I'd earlier heard something about Aleksandrovsk Prison's warden, and so perhaps there was a shred of truth in Lavrentii Pomiakshev's denunciations, but at the same time, there was a sense that these denunciations had issued not from the pure soul of a man yearning for truth but from a sick passion for shared suffering, for information of any sort of intrigue, a passion practiced by those kinds of people who simultaneously hate their comrades as much as they do the authorities. Such a man takes any opportunity to regard with hostility the warden and to assume the guise of an innocent sufferer; but with no less ease can, in other circumstances, likely be one of this same warden's secret agents, placed among "Aventureurs" he'll now denounce. And a completely different plan then arises in his scandalmongering head: he writes to the governor a confession "in the theme of a Nihilistic teks," where he expresses a wish to undergo penance for his entire life and asks about a transfer to Shelai, perhaps promising in exchange to spy on his purported friends.[69] In the meantime, the example of Shuster, who had written his memoirs for me, was greatly influencing Shelai's residents, and so in quick order Shteinhart and Bashurov were literally bowled over by all sorts of manuscripts in verse and prose. The verses were hardly the best of all, and in these gentlemen's view, the poets sometimes proved so prosaic that they simply tore them up. Fortunately or unfortunately, most of these poems have perished, and I now only vaguely recall that they were of a denunciatory-descriptive character; the lyrics by Bear's Ears being a favorable exception. On the other hand, Bear's Ears had for a long time now not written poetry, indeed, surprisingly he now did not generally express the slightest desire to engage in any sort of writing. I was assaulted most of all by Petin-the-Elk's poems, and—to give him his due—they had a certain undeniable quality: measure was always sustained, and rhymes were distinguished by sufficient sonority. Nonetheless, I more than once candidly advised Elk to give up writing poetry. Petin took offense:

"Why? Ain't my rhymes good?"

"No, it's nothing about your rhyming," I explained, "it's just that you have no talent."

"How not? Lemme write you what you want in verse—it'll be ready tomorrow!"

"I fully believe you. It's just that that is not a poetic, but rather a versifying, talent."

"What's this ersifyin'? Somethin' abusive?"

"No, it's not abusive."

I tried to explain the difference between poetry and versification to Elk; he listened quite distractedly and, upon leaving, announced:

"I'm such a joke to you now that you'll help only a prima donna! Later, you'll 'member whatta fellow Elk is!... Maybe better'n your Pushkin or Nekrasov!"

One day, he gave me a little scrap of paper with the following poem:

"The Fugitive's Song"[70] Glorious sea—holy Baikal,
Glorious vessel—cask for *omul*![71] Well, the *barguzin*,[72] the toppling swell,
Does not wash a young man far.
A long time I dragged heavy chains,
A long time I wandered Akatui's mountain chains—
A good comrade helped me escape;
I've lived, sensing freedom.
And now Nerchinsk and the Shilka[73] do not terrify!
The mine police didn't capture me,
The wilds were disturbed by no voracious beast,
The rifleman's bullet passed me by.
I went about at night, about in broad daylight,
Outside the cities I looked keenly around:
Peasants fed me bread,
Chaps supplied me *makhorka*.
Glorious sea—holy Baikal,
Glorious sail—caftan of holes...
Well, the *barguzin*, the toppling swell,
The rolling storms do resound!

I confess I liked these verses very much.

"You are a poet indeed, Petin!" I exclaimed in surprise, gazing at Elk standing near me, curious of my face's expression while I read. He blushed deeply, chuckled in embarrassment, and left, grumbling:

"But what was ya thinkin'? Gimme more time 'n' I weren't gonna write anymore."

"Well-well, well-well, what's he written there? Forgive the eavesdroppin', Ivan Nikolaevich," headman Godunov, having heard my praise, came over. As with Lunkov, he was always sparring with Elk; one was continually accusing the other of some fraud or error. This Godunov, about whom I've more than once had occasion to recall in passing, thought of himself as a man able to avoid any (even the most educated) society's dirty laundry, but he always dealt with Elk ironically, as if he were a greenhorn and had never seen anything or possessed any significant information whatsoever. Actually, he had some reasons to be haughty about his "education": somewhere he'd read all twenty-nine volumes of Solovëv's history and all of Schlosser's world history,[74] and if much of what he read he understood in an extremely original way, then he distinctly remembered all the main facts, as I more than once had occasion to confirm; moreover, for some purpose unknown, Godunov studied German grammar under me, and I have ever since preserved for posterity in my papers his handwritten German vocabulary and declension of the demonstrative pronoun *dieser, diese, dieses*. True, amidst all this he wrote Russian so ungrammatically that it gave Elk abundant fodder for all kinds of wisecracks; but, as a man of a practical mold, Godunov did not regard knowledge of orthography to be a sign of true sophistication; accused of being guilty as a companion to incorrect spelling, he accordingly began rationalizing with the pretense characteristic of him:

"Well, I'm all o' forty-five years old, but you're twenty-eight, brother, 'n' this letter *iat* is to you as to an eight-year ol' boy. The letter *iat* don't encompass the mind of a man. What you got is an empty noggin, but what I got lyin' in here is what comes from seein' the world 'n' people, 'n' I know life—'n' this, I trust, is fully unnerstood 'n' valued by people, brother, who's better 'n' smarter'n you!"

Now and then the expressive gaze—fully of dignity—cast in my direction during these words put me in the most ticklish position, and if it did not make me directly accept Godunov's view, it pushed me into a silence of varied significance.

When at his request I read "The Fugitive's Song" aloud, Godunov clapped his hands.

"'N' you believed Elk wrote them verses? That gut-head?"

"Well, but what, did *you* write 'em?" growled Elk, calf-eyes glistening.

"You're such a blockhead, why don't you blush? Aha, but you *did* blush! Yes, Ivan Nikolaevich, this song's been round at least thirty years. Your Elk was still runnin' round without breeches when I first came to Siberia, 'n' it was then I heard this song; when ol' Akatui roared 'n' Kara weren't in such glory, as 'tis said 'bout them days."

With one word, Elk had been convicted of literary plagiarism and utterly humiliated; after grousing a while at Godunov, he, like a true sophist, decided to adopt a different position:

"Don't you know I told Ivan Nikolaevich that I collected them verses? Hardly said I wrote 'em."

But nothing could help now: Lunkov, Chirok, and the rest of the ward loudly expressed their pleasure at Elk's glaring flop, and Godunov walked around triumphantly, hands clasped behind his back, and didn't tire of moralizing. After such a poem, whatever Elk would bring, I would first of all ask: but did he really compose it?…

Among the innumerable prison versifiers there was even a Decadent. But perhaps he was a Symbolist[75]—it's not for me to decide so fine an issue; I only reliably know that this poet's verses positively stumped me every time, and I gazed in curiosity at the author's physiognomy, trying to tell if he was mocking me or not. But Kotikov (as this Shelai Péladan[76] was called) was obviously not joking and was most serious about his writing. Silent and unsociable, tall, lean, and bony, with a curved spine and frightened eyes running about inside a gaunt, consumptive face devoid of any hair, he was on the whole a strange man; comrades were even a little scared of him and reckoned he was mad. Kotikov would usually approach me in the prison yard when no other prisoners were near and speak almost in a whisper, always timidly looking off to the side. He'd complain about what the prison walls were doing to his brain and chest ailments (heart disease), and that the prison community, devoid of any spiritual concerns, was taking away his mind (Kotikov had evidently been a petty bureaucrat on the outside). In general, there was nothing straightforwardly crazy in his talk; with regard to his poetic exercises, he managed to make clear to me that rhymes gave him no rest—"the damned things are always buzzing in my ear"—and that in the moment of creation he sometimes felt his heart would burst into pieces and he'd die right there…

"Please read!" Kotikov concluded his declaration in a quiet voice, and having looked around preliminarily, he pulled from his pocket a tattered page densely inscribed in pencil and gave it to me, then immediately slipped off somewhere. He was soon released to the free command, so I was unable to ask him about his ideas and his poems' meanings. I have one of his pages, and reproduce it here exactly as written:

Dostoevskii wrote us
Dead House in prose,
And I complement him
In a poetic pose!
I present: the dead house
In the best taste.
Idea and rhyme, thunder and lightning,
In an exceptionally sensitive case!
A fantastic hero,
A gen'ral of art!
From the dead house a second
Genius of feeling's come out.
Big-shot over the hero!
Trampled to death, a shame to lose!
Composer: of the hymnal muses!
Fortepiano, of the muse!
A. Kotikov

Along with the poet-versifiers the prosaists did not tire of composing. However, not a single belletrist was among them and, like Shuster, all without exception engaged in writing autobiographies. The very same Petin-the-Elk presented me a total of eight notebooks, in which he however managed to describe his early childhood only. There was one thing common to all these autobiographies: their authors were concerned and tormented by one and the same question—why they'd been pushed onto the path of criminality and debauchery—and all simultaneously complained they were incapable of living honestly among non-dissolute, good people, or did not know how to do so, and—what was most important—their grief, these thoughts, always produced an indubitable, profound candor…

What made these people—the reader may ask—write about themselves so voluminously? I admit, this question greatly intrigued me. I initially had the fleeting suspicion they were seeking rehabilitation in my eyes, to show—though they could not prove—they'd been unfairly convicted and were suffering *katorga* innocently; but such a suspicion was mistaken. Not a single author made the slightest effort to mitigate his crime, to obscure any detail of his dark past, all the filth of which, by contrast, was dragged into the light with an almost mercilessly cynical frankness. Obviously, what was compelling these people to write was completely different and not especially difficult to ascertain, since it struck the eye and was quite blatantly revealed by these authors' memoirs; not only did these wretches seek to absolve their souls by confession to a man who, they hoped, understood everything, but they imagined he would tell the world of the errors, mistakes, experiences, and torments they'd lived through!…

I have several times now recalled in these notes that among prisoners there was some strange conviction that at some point I, having left prison, would immediately put into print everything I'd lived through in *katorga*, everything down to the smallest detail, and moreover would depict not only the prison administration but the mare. From this very conviction there originated, for example, the jokes regarding Chirok, who was tormented into thinking I would detail all the crimes they'd ever committed in freedom. True, I've also happened to recall somewhere that certain conspicuous prisoners, having read *Notes from a Dead House*, regarded its author with extreme disapproval and near hostility, supposing that he'd seriously harmed *katorga* by revealing its imaginary mysteries and secrets; however, these very same people regarded utterly favorably *my* supposed plan to write similar notes, evidently having been convinced that I would do so differently, that is, I would choose only *katorga*'s infamous tortures and expose its oppressors, and many of these people obviously had no objection to falling into the pages of a future publication… Naïve souls! Something should have told you, had you somehow or sometime realized, that I would indeed fulfill this mission you gave me, but fulfill it not so much as you wanted: I am in fact describing your great sorrows, but I have now and then told you the bitter truth…

Certain of my student friends not only "had no objection" but positively *burned with thirst* to end up in my future notes! I say this without a touch of exaggeration. I'm reminded especially often of a prisoner from among these glory-seeking dreamers named Penkin, a man who in all respects made a favorable and exceptionally sympathetic impression. Even his appearance was exceptional. He had long blond mustaches encircling red lips, in the corners of which was imprinted a continuously bitter irony that also shown in his intelligent blue eyes. Though Penkin was no more than forty years old, significant wrinkles already covered his lower cheeks; he had at some point evidently been a man of very cheerful disposition because he was still not averse to joking, clowning, or telling a cheeky anecdote, but his principal characteristic was now not cheerfulness but a dour sadness, a pensive seriousness. What tormented him? Penkin had already been in prison for exactly twenty-three years, and only once during all that time did he come briefly unhinged, because of which he was later secured more firmly "inside stone walls." I confess that a quivering horror gripped me each time I realized this man had not known freedom *since early 1870*, that is, since I'd barely begun a cognizant human existence as a young ten-year-old boy preparing to enter high school! Since then, I realized, an eternity had passed not only for specific individuals but for entire generations, entire peoples! But the man was alive, the man was able to suffer and feel, and all this time he'd persevered in the close, nightmarish atmosphere of *katorga* prisons! Yet Penkin's future circumstances appeared completely hopeless. For some reason, he'd reputedly been given a twenty-five year term after his second conviction for escape, and so the free command, according to the brave captain, was absolutely impossible for him.

To a man, the whole prison revered him, and during any prisoner conflict (in which he, however, did not like to participate) Penkin's word was considered especially weighty in their eyes; the administration itself valued him as a quiet, stolid prisoner, and a first-rate master carpenter as well.

Unfortunately, not once did I have the opportunity to live in the same ward with Penkin. Yet, prior to the mass enthusiasm for writing throughout the prison, he, pausing in private with me in the mining hut, spoke with me more than once:

"You should hear my life, Mikolaich! I don't think you'll be sorry. 'Cause not anyone can survive so much. What fates ain't I seen, ain't I experienced, on the outside 'n' inside prison… Ekh, this should all be written up! Only, no one's writin' it [Penkin himself was quasi-literate]… I'll die, 'n' so ever'thin'll disappear, like it ne'er happened."

This notion and this wish Penkin expressed many times, and it must be said that I would have been sincerely happy to hear the story of his life, all the more so as I learned from prisoners he was a peerless storyteller; but circumstances were somehow not especially propitious and for a long time the opportunity did not arise. Finally, a minor adjustment became necessary in our ward one day, and within the space of twenty-four hours the administration "drove" all its inhabitants including me to the same ward Penkin lived in. Needless to say, I hastened to take advantage of this situation and did not postpone asking Penkin to take up his story. He didn't make a face and, having settled himself beside me after evening roll call, began talking in his quiet, thoughtful, pleasingly melodious Saratovite's voice, telling not just his own life but also stories and ancient history he'd somewhere heard or read in books. Not several minutes passed before this story captured me, and I was no longer listening but literally burning, having utterly surrendered to the power of this strange man who continued to speak with measured peacefulness, albeit with a slightly melancholy voice. Not once did I stir—a deathly quiet descended in the ward and everyone was listening with rapt attention to Penkin, and when his story finally ended at two o'clock in the morning, I'd been shaken to the depths of my soul until my entire body was shivering… At that moment, I felt that no single book had ever in my life made such a powerful, such a visceral, impression; this story was reality itself, a horrible, completely other type of nightmare resembling a dark fable, seemingly vividly imprinted in the memory of the man who'd survived it and now rising anew before astonished listeners… It seemed to me that I should record word-for-word this story, this utterly, mercilessly, honest self-analysis—it would have been a remarkable literary production that could have made the same powerful impression on readers. But, unfortunately, I did not record it… Two or three weeks passed after that memorable night, and I was ready to commit to paper everything I'd heard—but I could not imbue it with any spirit at all; what came from my pencil was so pallid, so inert, that I was annoyed and ashamed… But Penkin several times appealed to me with the question:

"Well then, Mikolaich, still ain't written nuthin' down?"

And when I passionately undertook to assure him that I would soon fulfill his request directly, he'd reply, chuckling sadly:

"Well, it can't be writ! So ever'thin'll disappear, like it ne'er was…"

He turned out to be correct in his pessimism. Years passed, but I did not fulfill his heartfelt wish. With every passing month it became more and more difficult to fulfill because much was gradually and imperceptibly forgotten, but, time and again, memory bespeaks that or another important detail or feature, and at this present time, when I recall just the story's bare white skeleton, it sometimes makes such a profound impact on me that I cannot venture an attempt to inspire this skeleton with living breath to nourish a dead body with the beauty of life. And if Penkin never did manage to meet another educated person more fortunate than I, then his sad prophecy is being fulfilled in the most literal sense and his instructive life, rich in exterior and interior content, is vanishing without a trace as if it never happened…

Above all, that vice that destroys so many of the best, most talented people in Rus was this man's ruin and damnation: a passion for vodka ruled over him when still a boy. But to this was added a tempestuous obstinacy (that had been acquired under the influence of a vinous couple) whose proportions approached the baffling, unforgettable quality of our epic heroes—an obstinacy that, not for nothing, gave a lie to established morals and behavior; it's completely natural that, for its part, the humdrum, common, and petty present with its unpalatable home truths could not compete against this irrepressible phenom's rebellious outbursts. At every step, amid even the closest of people, ever new enemies arrayed themselves, and a tragic outcome seemed almost inevitable, like a Classical fate: an intoxicated Penkin stabbed his blood uncle and first cousin…

Penkin's subsequent fate turned out no less sad than all the rest of his life. By some miracle (everyone called it a miracle), Luchezarov allowed him into the free command, and there were no limits to Penkin's delight. Presumably, he sincerely dreamed of starting a new life… But then came from somewhere a rumor, perhaps false, that he'd fallen into a misunderstanding and would soon be put back in prison again. Then one stormy autumn evening the guards, having shown up at the free command barracks for roll call, didn't find Penkin there—he'd disappeared. I was no longer at Shelai mine when I learned he'd been captured near Verkhneudinsk and was sent into *katorga* again…

Godunov was distinguished by a no less terrible desire to inform the world about his bumptious past. That I was interested by the stories of such prison nonentities as Lunkov, for example, he regarded with profound contempt, and he said to him with his usual smugness:

"Were there a hunnerd, a thousernd, such stories collected 'bout your or some Elk's life, then all together they couldn't measure up to one page o' my life's biography. 'Cause I can honestly tell you that I've tasted sweet 'n' sour, clambered through copper 'n' iron pipes, so's a journal could not write 'bout me. Well, but what can you do with Elk? Seed for crows—nuthin' more."

Stung to the quick, Lunkov and Elk formed between them a defensive pact and hotly grappled with Godunov, but, a rhetorician by nature, he never once left a word in his pocket and during these disputes always grilled his opponents, as the prisoners put it, down to the smallest bubble… When Godunov finally also took to writing his memoirs he was obviously terribly nervous, and probably because the very act of writing was rather difficult for him and the words to express his ideas not easily found, he assigned an enormous value to his notebooks. By the same token, when his labor had come to the end of its tether and the notebooks I'd read were concealed among my things in the armory in anticipation of better times, Godunov beamed like never before and frequently orated to the ward:

"Jus' let Ivan Nikolaevich publish my notes anytime, then you'll see what comes o' this! You'll unnerstand what's the life of an exiled man! 'Cause right now, ya don't know nuthin'. You think we take up crime jus' for itself, with an easy spirit… Now you'll know that an exile's a man as well, that his heart bleeds any which time he lends another a helpin' hand! You'll know who's the real cause of all the evil!"

That these ideas and talk bore a sufficient relation to the "notes"' actual content is questionable, of course, but that Godunov dreamed of relating his history of errors and mishaps to society is significant…

More than once I came to define this man as a prison politician, a man mindful of himself but also quite boastful and smug. To describe these personal qualities in notes bereft of that most important and valuable virtue—honesty—would seem injudicious.

But what always struck me about less-cultivated people is that as soon as they take quill in hand, they become for the most part exceptionally honest and frank. Perhaps this stems from the fact that, having no understanding of the so called beauty of style, of artistic exposition, they encounter less temptation to avoid the truth, whereas educated writers often sacrifice it in pursuit of a witty phrase, circumlocution, and other literary appurtenances… Godunov's personality was, in truth, reflected in his work, albeit not only in an innocent but an almost comic form: his sense of self-importance so percolated his notes, regardless of their penitential tone, that it was made clear that he, Godunov, was loved and unquestioningly respected by anyone who merely bumped into him in life, not excluding police officials or barely even those who beat or birched him… On the whole, he loved himself terribly and poured into almost every page tears about his miserable luck, this one-dimensional sentiment that saturates what he wrote about how, one day, he happened to murder a man for the sake of a robbery and would have to make amends for it… only, alas, not for his victim but for himself!

Nonetheless, the factual side of the story made, I repeat, an impression of undoubted, profound truthfulness, all the more because the hero of the notes did not, on the whole, whitewash—but rather exposed and castigated—himself. I'll just note parenthetically: this self-castigating tone strongly reminded me of the wretched Shuster's notes; each author seemed to share many of the other's ideas and even expressions, though in fact these persons had never even spoken to each other. This phenomenon seems extremely characteristic to me.

Then again, in a different sense, Godunov's life reminds me of Penkin's life: some kind of fateful power that danced in the depths of their souls drew one, like the other, to *katorga*; for lack of a better word, I would call this power *melancholia*… Some innate irrepressibility and insatiability inciting him to struggle prevented either from reconciling himself with a peaceful and balanced existence… But the difference in natures was expressed in the divergent forms of this struggle. Penkin had a powerful nature, commanding but at the same time deeply honest. At a different moment in history and under different societal conditions, such a man could easily have turned himself into a social protestor or religious fanatic, but our dull reality made of him a simple drunk and brawler and then an unintentional killer. A softer and less refined nature pushed Godunov down the path of easy gain, having made of him a vagrant rogue and, ultimately, an acquisitive murderer.

Godunov was, it may be said, a man in the bloom of life. A brunet with a bushy beard and an intelligent, broad forehead, he wasn't bad-looking, was steady in his manners, words, and actions, and was a great phrase-monger and moralizer. He, as the reader can see, analyzed his past perfectly and knew he'd walked a foolish path. But will it be possible for him to find, upon conclusion of his *katorga* term and his release to settlement, another way—a way of honest labor and peaceful prosperity?

To be honest, dear reader, I don't think so… The dark path of his pathetic, indeed, *nightmarish*, life, punctuated by evil fate, is actually in its earliest years, and its final fatal point is probably not far off!…

Of course, I hope to God I'm mistaken.

XVII. NIGHTMARES

I spent all the last days of winter boring in the upper mine. During the just over three years of my sojourn at Shelai it had however deepened no more than seven feet. As a matter of fact, the boring was often halted for lack of convicts in the prison, and when working hands were again mustered, the shaft would prove to be so submerged in water that another two weeks were needed to pump it dry. Once again, a story about a white goby-fish began making the rounds. All the same, work in the mine proceeded incomparably better under Petushkov than under his predecessor. Not only did this man captivate the mare through his liberal improvements, but he ruled it with an iron rod and got from prisoners all he was supposed to take. Although it never happened in front of me, he'd dispatch a man to Six-Eyes "with a note," though this rather frightened him for some reason.

"Be better off fer me—confound his soul!—to be sittin' in the 'slator 'stead o' gettin' me nerves worn weak by his tongue!" those on whom his tenderly eloquent threats fell said regarding Petushkov. "Whate'er he's a-sayin', only his dog knows!… Scoundrel reckons he'll get tossed—Monakhov, he says, is gone– -'n' he reckons the mare's gettin' reported to Six-Eyes through our brother: when he hisself, he says, gets pushed out, ever'thin'll get worse for us. Such is the misery that worries his soul. No, it'd be better to bore through a foot 'n' a half o' the hardest rock than lissen to him complainin'!"

However, it cannot be said that Petushkov avoided direct threats. I myself saw how his consumptive eyes burned with a malicious flame when, with deliberate softness and brevity in his voice, he announced to those prisoners he considered to be loafing that he would no longer bring them to the mine. And for most prisoners this was a most impressive threat because the mine actually had many advantages over any other jobs. First of all, there you could forget for a brief while the yoke of the sexocular "prigime" that oppressed heart and mind and which you were made aware of by the second by the so called housework done not far outside prison walls; it was easier to breathe out in the open air, not to mention that the work itself, always on a quota basis, was incomparably easier. Needless to say, the monetary incentive that Monakhov, albeit rarely, had offered everyone played no small role in prisoners' predilection for the mine; the smith, joiner, and carpenters (mining timberers) received the most of all, but sometimes a little something fell to the simple laborers, borers, and even auger-haulers. Even I, last of the least laborers, received around six rubles during my several years in Shelai mine… The mining administration transferred money earned in this way to the prison's control office, and the very next evening at roll call Six-Eyes read aloud how much each had been designated. I well recall what a surprise I experienced when, for the first time in my life, I earned several rubles for *purely physical labor*…

In most of Shelai's mines the earth was unusually soft. But there were weeks and even entire months when the rock suddenly began—in the prisoners' expression—to misbehave: it turned so hard that the sharpest augers would flatten in just a minute; haulers couldn't get them to the smithy fast enough; and Palchikov couldn't find enough words in his forceful lexicon to express his indignation against the "law, religion, and life." On such unlucky days even strongmen like Bykov or Elk, almost never leaving the shaft for the entire day, bored no more than eleven inches whereas weaker and less skilled borers defeated fewer than seven inches. There's nothing to say about me: I recall instances when for two or three days I barely managed with the most diabolical labor to assiduously tap out two to three inches!… During this, my hands almost seemed to shake like those of an inveterate drunkard and my right shoulder ached as painfully as if it had been severely dislocated. In such hard strata even the signature prisoners' method—boring with the help of "a little bit o' vodka"—was impossible: this method proved only to make things worse. One day, I calculated that Bykov pounded his auger eight hundred times with all his might and without a breather and, having cleaned out the blasting hole afterward, Bykov announced with curses that almost no slag had been knocked out… On such days the mine generally ended up hearing for more than a week a sufficient quantity of the most convoluted, forceful expressions and friendly wishes!… Prisoners were gloomy, cross, and so terribly quiet that I feared even turning to them with any sort of question; everyone was in a distressed, depressed mood, as if in the presence of the deceased. At such time they forgot about singing, and only the hammers irritatingly and forcefully continued their uniform cracking. An insistent, angry "tick! tick! tick!" resounded without end and without interruption from beneath the true borers' capable blows. From me, however, came a despondent, minor-key "tick-da-tick! tick-da-tick!"—and from out of these minor tones the most melancholy song formed itself:

There, where the cold surrounds,
The hills tower round—
Dehumanized, shaven,
Enchained and under bayonets,
In a twilit, stuffy mine,
Arms working tirelessly,
We chisel out a breathless,
Monotonous "tick-da-tick!"
    Where the noble impulses,
Dreams of truth, of kindness?
You find yourself in a shallow grave,
A dark *katorga* hole.
Banner torn from your hands,
Good fortune's frauds are settled.
Wounds muffling the heart,
We simply knock: "tick-da-tick!"
    From the unpopulated East,
With the weeping of snowy weather,

This knocking carries far—
Falls into your country's heart
And turns hundreds of fresh hands
Toward more destructive business…
Pound, brothers, pound boldly
And tirelessly: "tick! tick! tick!"[77]

Once, I encountered such a hard spot that, having bored for three whole days without achieving more than two and a half inches, I found myself in despair. In the heat of the labor I forgot about the danger that forced almost all prisoners to put their sheepskins beneath them while boring, and worked on my knees on the bare ice-cold granite. Even though March had already begun, very cold temperatures persisted. From early in the morning the next day my head ached and there was some sort of pain throughout my body; by evening, a fever had arisen and Shteinhart quickly brought me to the infirmary.

Here once again, I cannot remember—I'm lying in my very familiar little closet, alone and day-dreaming, a peaceful silence fanning me from all directions. The hospital attendant asks me several times if I want hot tea, but I simply answer: "Akh, leave off for a bit… I'll let you know later." Sweet languor gradually spills through my body, and I so want to rest that hours, days, years don't budge. Indeed, have not entire years passed me by? What's this? Did I not somewhere already abandon prison walls, and wasn't I free, but in the meantime… is this really the prison again, *katorga* again?… Yes, they're here, the terribly familiar wards and corridors; only, the people are completely different… What dark, hostile faces… How unkindly they meet me, with such hateful distrust! Very well! By contrast, I carry the sun in my own heart; by contrast, a marvelously beautiful idea warms and lifts my spirit! This idea is a desire to regenerate them—the embittered and the wretched—with love and brotherhood through word and example. For the sake of this grand idea I have *voluntarily* returned behind the accursed walls where I suffered so, I have *voluntarily* put on myself the convict's marked jacket so that I may now find peace and happiness here. I dream that I have not come here alone with such a goal, that I have friends here, such selfless, rapturous dreamers; meeting furtively at times, we look timidly around (exactly as in a different dream) and whisper to one another: "Be careful! No one must know we're not really convicts… Only those out *there* know this." *There* means Russia, Petersburg…

And we're not too tired to experience all our sworn comrades' labors, deprivations, sufferings, to experience without rancor and complaint, without desiring to take a lighter burden upon ourselves, to hide from any kind of general misfortune or injury; but to each free moment we devote homilies. And how passionately, with what prophetic power and cogency, do we know how to speak, how our words touch the darkest reaches of coarsened hearts, how these hearts gradually soften and the malicious, dark eyes brighten and the angry fists unclench and hands reach for a fraternal handshake! Yet, what a strange style of speech—are these verses, actual sonorous verses, with meters and rhymes? However, astonishment flickers but briefly inside the mind. Evidently, one is supposed to talk that way here, and, passionate, lucid, and sure of myself, poetic improvisation continues to spill freely from my lips, and a happiness that cannot disappear continues to fill my soul…

"Ivan Nikolaevich, quiet down," a penal laborer quietly says, bending toward me, a tall brunet with red eyes and a pale face. He's probably afraid that my speech will be heard by a guard and will turn out badly for me; I well and truly understand it might do me wrong, since the local command considers me an actual convict, but what do threats and danger matter when my speech's topic is something so beautiful, at which my own heart stirs and listeners' eyes shed tears.

"You've been causing me trouble, Ivan Nikolaevich! I'd already seriously believed you'd decided to leave *ad patres*. Well, now I'll be sure not to let you out of my control!" said Shteinhart, affectionately bowing to me as he should have when, after four days, I finally came round. I could only smile in response and, weakly grasping my comrade's hand, fell into a deep sleep. But I'd now been rescued, and further sleep only fortified my strength.

"Darn you for kneeling on bare rock!" Shteinhart once again admonished me. "And in March? Well, you've contracted a severe case of rheumatism in your joints… You'll have to suffer this thing for a long time."[78] However, during my convalescence I suffered not so much from an awareness of possibly living with an unpleasant illness the rest of my life as from an unyielding, obsessive desire to remember something: either a wondrously beautiful dream or the discovery of my—if not all humanity's—limitless possibility. It seemed that having forgotten this I'd lost a precious treasure, possession of which would be great and fortunate, and then as now there has been a suitably pitiful and weak scorn… But, for a long time, I was unable to remember my strange dream.

Probably not many convalescing patients have experienced such a pleasant loss of mental control, when people, existence, and everything in the world seem so bright, so beautiful, and you feel in your heart only kindness and love and hope that with these you will be victorious over all evil and darkness in the universe. I had experienced just such a mental state; with a beatific smile I greeted even the guards coming in to me during roll call and, for their part, they also smiled broadly. I well remember how the first prisoner I saw after my delirium was the Polish cook Pendral, whose round, crafty, ingratiating face had earlier inspired very little sympathy in me, but now, when his faced appeared one morning at my door and his unctuously insinuating voice asked: "So, master wants diner—a lil' zup, a lil' broth?"—I nearly accosted the man with open arms, nearly kissed his cunning fat mug! It may be said that after this, I greeted with similar emotion those true friends like Kuzma Chirok who were trying to visit me.

"Well, how're you, Mikolaich?" he came toward me, grinning as joyfully as ever. "Thank God you've straightened yourself out. Mare's ter'bly sorry for you… As Mitrii Petrovich said, they was sayin' you was really poor, so I, believe me, shed another tear!"

Such regard from the prison touched me to the depths of my soul, and during those moments it seemed to me I began recalling that brightness and beauty I'd so vainly endeavored to remember for so long; when I recovered and returned to the prison, it seemed to me I'd become a completely different person—all, all our undivided love we will give to these thrice-unfortunate people of whom fate has made me a comrade. Having sat himself on the edge of my bed, Chirok told me in the meantime the prison news: Elk had had a fight with Miloserdov; Ogurtsov had been put in the isolator a day earlier; and the guard Snake Head had gotten married… Then he turned to his sore spot: his *katorga* sentence would end in November, but the mare was scaring him that it was being said that Six-Eyes would not release him because his term was to be extended for an escape attempt.

"They're sayin', 'You're here for life'… That's what the scoundrels're actually sayin': 'In November,' they're sayin', 'they'll send you to Verkhneudinsk Central for perm'nent individual isolation!'… What for? Did I kill my father or mother?"

"You're right, Chirok—what for!"

"But they're sayin', them scoundrels, damn their souls, they heard this from you, Mikolaich?…"

I hastened, of course, to assure Chirok that no one could have ever heard anything like that from me.

"Well, I says this: 'Mikolaich,' I says, 'is my friend, 'n' he ain't sayin' this!'… Indeed, what extra charge could there be, if'n I weren't in court 'n' no one gave me any extra charge at all."

"You weren't charged, you say?"

"By the Holy Cross, I weren't charged! I was given fifty… 'bout this, I won't argue—I was given it… Well, I was tried again in prison—'n' ever'one was there. 'N' my escape weren't reckoned an escape at all, jus' a simple absence."

In the end, Chirok went away from me beaming and consoled… Until, of course, the mare played its next favorite frights on him. The mine workers returned from the mine and, having hurriedly dined, Bashurov and Shteinhart visited me.

"Gentlemen," I turned to them one day, "please explain to me… Here I've just now remembered several lines that were evidently giving me no peace while I was sick…"

"That's true, in your delirium you were declaiming all kinds of verses," noted Shteinhart.

"The lines are very good in both sound and content, but I'll be beat as to whose they are or where they come from. It's as if they're something terribly familiar—but impossible to remember."

"But perhaps you're unconsciously creating a work of art? Well then, recite and we'll listen."

And I recited:

Only a God of the Russian heart
Can exhale deeply, freely,
To show Rus what is in its people,
What is in its coming days.

She does not know a middle way—
Do not stare at the blackness!
Yet I've not got to the heart
Of her disease…

"I don't remember anymore, but where do these lines come from?"

"They're from the poem 'The Unfortunates'… They're an excerpt from the homily by Krot, the poem's protagonist, upon whom it falls to regenerate the *katorga* cohabitants he's awakened to their best human feelings. I really loved this piece at one time, although it now occurs to me that there's more fantasy than reality or truth in it. So then, you've remembered?"

I really had remembered—the lines were from a Nekrasov poem, and the very subject of this poem had gripped me in a feverish delirium. The whole poem had suddenly unfolded before me in the minutest details… At one time, in the years of my rapturous youth, Nekrasov had been my favorite poet and I knew all his poems by heart, and now here in a delirium I'd happened to remember those long-forgotten verses: having identified myself with "the silent Krot," I'd taken on his role and recited to fellow prisoners his fiery tirade about the homeland, the great worker-tsar, those people "before whom blind folk sense rapture late and conscience sighs and medicates, having raised a splendid mausoleum."

The bell rang for roll call and my comrades went to the prison, leaving me alone. The form of Nekrasov's hero, so strangely yet at the same time so veritably modified by my sickened dream, continued to stand insistently before me. And I wondered: is this really a sickness-induced fantasy—just an empty and crazy delirium? Were such bright, such idealistically unselfish and self-sacrificing missionary apostles not possible in reality? There have been, and, it seems, even now *are*, preachers, religiously dutiful heroes, travelling in China, India, Abyssinia, devoting all their souls, all their lives to the various savages of Asia and Africa… Why go to enlighten other lands' savages, blissful in their barbarity, when among our own people, side-by-side all the gifts of culture and civilization, still live tens and hundreds of thousands of our *own homegrown* savages, not possessing, as the absolutely most recent of barbarians, the slightest comprehension of kindness, "of law, of God," dissolute, cruel, unthinking, and, primarily (and this is most primarily!), unfortunate, infinitely unfortunate, thanks namely to our own moral and intellectual savagery? Hundreds of thousands of people for whom a single road has been discovered—from prison to prison, and often to the gallows! Hundreds of thousands is easy to say—but this is not a fabrication, not a fairy tale. I read at some point in a Prison Department publication that every year, more than half a million people of both sexes and all ages pass through the school of prison in Russia, and that maintaining this enormous army costs the government fifteen million rubles a year, that is, exactly as much as the Ministry of Public Education spends to maintain all universities, high schools, grammar, and trade schools, all upper and middle education institutes…

What's to be done? Alas, what *is* to be done? How to eliminate this horror, this nightmare, this awesome darkness hanging over our future? At present, the times are not giving us answers to these questions and do not even want to acknowledge their seriousness. Instead of kind and loving prison missionaries, the prison knows for the time being only a cold and callous wardship of official formalism and all sorts of repression. Is this not strange, is it not savage? If in our times it is an immutable truth for each and every one that educational institutions' pedagogues and teachers must be humanitarian and cultivated people, then why are there not with even greater unanimity the same demands made for prison wardens and guards? No retired soldier or coarse officer should serve in these admittedly difficult capacities, as is now pretty often the practice, nor should the authority of the fist, the chain, or the stick be raised against prisons' and *katorga*'s unfortunate residents… As a matter of fact, isn't the stone wall surrounding a prison enough of a threat, and do the soldiers really have to be armed with rifles and bayonets? Should not a different, a higher, power and authority rule inside a prison—the power of love? Love is all-powerful, and were the unfortunate outcast to see with his own eyes that he's not being set upon with whip and rod but with words of kindness and trust, then—I'm convinced—there would be found in the dark depths of the most dissolute soul such light that it would blind many of those who now "enlighten" and "correct" *katorga*! This ill-starred *katorga* is itself wallowing in darkness, blood, and filth—itself does not know how many healthy, radiant seeds are hiding in its heart and how capable these seeds are of sprouting!

My brain is on fire, my soul aches, and once more I feel so powerless that I'm ready to weep. Yes, all these dreams are naïve, childishly impracticable!... Tens of thousands of young, strong, and talented people will as before perish without a trace or purpose for the homeland, and everything will proceed routinely from year to year, day to day, yet intelligent, educated people won't stop wracking their brains over refining methods of retribution, preventing escapes, improving the solitary confinement system! Peoples' souls, well known to be weak, will as before cast themselves into the outer darkness and exit by their own power toward the desired light! And this means Valerian Bashurov was right: Nekrasov, in creating his poem, was "fantasizing." Never will our "unfortunates" sing his song:

Yes! God sees us steeped
In the bloodied sweat of our guilt
And singing, not wrongly,
At work, our one song:
"Friends! There's shoveling to do,
Not for nothing were we brought here,
Not for nothing did God impregnate
Mother-Earth's womb with gold.
Work, hands must now serve,
Don't complain, don't loaf, don't cower.
Our grandchildren will thank us
When Rus grows rich.
Let us pine thirstily on the glacis,
Let us shiver in the cold winter—
Make use of each of her
Rocks we dig out!"

"Ivan Nikolaevich, heard the news?" collective headman Godunov, looking into my little room, asked me. "They say Iukhorev's been killed."

"What? By whom, what for?"

"He was escapin', didn't you hear?"

"I've heard nothing. Tell me, please."

"He was transferred from us to Algacha. Well, there, needless to say, he was released to the free command almost that same day, 'cause it turns out Six-Eyes had put him in prison on his own, without an order from the 'ministration. However, Iukhorev clearly unnerstood an order might not be long in comin', 'n' he decided it'd be better to take to his heels. He escaped, it might be said, with a noise 'n' a fuss that was heard for miles. He stole a troika o' three horses from a Cossack commander ridin' with a girl 'n' a comrade—'n' down the road he goes one fine night. Iukhorev can be judged variously: that he was a scoundrel of the first degree is, o' course, true, but he had quite a noggin! If, say, some Elk had made off in such a manner, then I'd call him a fool 'n' say he'd last two days. Well, but on account it was Iukhorev, when I heard, I jus' turned up my nose 'n' didn't say nuthin'... Indeed: the way he fled was jus' like sinkin' in water! That little Cossack woulda paid with his head, 'n' he wouldn't-a captured him 'live..."

"So, *who* killed him?"

"Some Tungus shot him, somewhere far off on the Onon or Chikoi river."

This news deeply upset me... With some difficulty, I convinced myself that Iukhorev had finally met an enemy who proved stronger than he, that this prison hero would no longer tread a heroic path, would not gaze with defiant eagle eyes, but was lying somewhere in the snow, a cold, motionless corpse... Godunov guffawed when I expressed this notion out loud.

"Ha-ha-ha! This little swinish business don't distinguish what's inside someone. There's no such heroes as your Iukhorev, fore'er in eternal rest!..."

I was seized with profound grief, and all the next night a heavy nightmare smothered me: Iukhorev in the most varied guises and situations appeared to me, first running at me menacingly, then tenderly and touchingly imploring me about something, calling to someone to save him, to escape somewhere with him... Then, next morning, just as I awoke, the infirmary attendant, sticking his head in the doorway, told me more sad news:

"Ivan Nikolaevich, they brought in Goldy 'n' Koliarov!"

These were two prisoners who'd escaped the previous summer from Shelai's free command, to which they'd only just been released from the prison. They were strange people—bosom buddies, but not the least bit like each other. Koliarov appeared to be a typical swindling speculator, and in his time had been banished to a Siberian settlement on suspicion of horse-stealing but then sent from his settlement to *katorga* thanks to new artistries. With his long, red shovel-beard, gray intelligent eyes, and a cap—which he didn't take off even for sleeping—pulled low over his eyes, he roamed incessantly throughout the ward from corner to corner, unhurriedly passing from one group of talkers to another, listening to prisoners' conversations and chuckling silently into his beard; but at the same time, it was evident that he wasn't at all seriously interested in these conversations, that his brief replications of laughter had a somewhat absent-minded, transient quality, and that his mind was preoccupied by his own, somewhat peculiar, obsession. As soon as the guard opened the ward, Koliarov would hurriedly slip into the yard and there walk with lowered head alongside the prison walls for hours, submerged in his own thoughts, inscrutable to anyone. On sunny days, idlers often and for a long time admired from the kitchen's window the lively character Koliarov, his own shadow cast against the white prison wall. At first, this shadow grew and grew; his long shovel-beard pointing menacingly forward; his figure quickly hobbling onward, waving an arm and resting on one knee, and suddenly rushing toward an invisible enemy who might be overcome by just a masterstroke… And suddenly, as if having suffered failure, the shadow began receding and receding; the beard narrowed, the hobbling walk became much smaller and funnier, and the figure finally disappeared entirely, but then a minute later a terrible assault began once more and the observers' Homeric laughter burst anew… What was Koliarov thinking during the hours of his singular stroll?… No one knew, since only the Ukrainian Zalata (christened "Goldy" by guards and prisoners[79]) was on occasion his sole travelling companion. He was, in all probability, the most quiet and inoffensive man in the entire prison. I personally never heard one untoward phrase of any kind from his mouth, despite living together for years: in response to all the jabbering and questions, Goldy managed only to wheeze significantly and smile equably; his smile really was priceless—gentle, prepossessing… He normally strolled with Koliarov while maintaining a profound silence, and it was difficult to understand what, strictly speaking, bound him to this man and what united them. Koliarov was a man still in the prime of life, full of energy and strength; at work, he had a reputation, it's true, as an inveterate idler, but when need be, of course, he could work extremely hard. Goldy was absolutely not so: he was by contrast an already middle-aged man with signs of gray at his temples and a dark beard that was thinning. His face was thin and haggard, he was sickly and weak, and at Shelai he'd served for years as a ward attendant.

So these strange friends fled the free command as soon as they were released there. Koliarov's escaping surprised absolutely no one—indeed, everyone would have been surprised had he not escaped: up to that point it was clear to everyone that escape was always his cherished dream.

"Well, but why'd the *old* devil hafta escape?" the mare wondered regarding Goldy. "Why that fellow? So—'like Volodia on account o' Kuzma.' Long time ago he was scatterin' 'bout like a grain seed, beggin' on his knees in an almshouse, but right then he decides to chase after Koliarov! What is this? He jus' better shave off his beard so no one in the world can spot 'im!"

All the same, both fugitives disappeared into the ground, and everyone had already decided they'd long ago safely made their way to Russia when it suddenly turned out they were being brought back to prison. Entering the hospital's corridor and looking out the window, I saw a crowd of prisoners at the prison gates curiously circling some fellow who amusingly sat himself down, energetically slapped his thigh, and thrust forward his little beard. This, apparently, was Koliarov, though it was not easy to identify him: his long, splendid beard had disappeared and been replaced by a short, thin scrap. But where was Goldy? The gates opened once more: the strongman Ogurtsov was carrying some small burden in his arms and taking it straight to the infirmary. "Can he have been wounded?" I apprehensively thought to myself. But Goldy was not wounded—he was simply ill. His thin physique with its emaciated and darkened face, on which hung his graying beard, was carried past me to one of the palettes.

"He 'scaped! Won't be 'scapin' again!" the fat and bloated Ogurtsov gruffly muttered, passing me by, and I looked with disgust at his thick oxen neck, the glossy white hide of his broad circular face, and his iron-muscled arms protruding from the rolled-up sleeves of his blouse.

The fugitives turned out to have actually been captured two months earlier and sent at first to Zerentui mine; but, having learned of this, Six-Eyes demanded they be returned to Shelai, and his wish was fulfilled. Along the way, Goldy caught a cold and almost died on the spot. It was possible at first glance to say with near certainty that the poor man was not long for this world. However, he died as quietly and uncomplainingly as he'd lived, and had there not been the horrifying cough occasionally welling up from his little chest and the strained nerves of everyone surrounding him, it would be easy to forget about the existence of this strange, silent man. He lay for days on his bed with unmoving, wide-open eyes and, it seemed, he was thinking… about his distant "Piltavshchina,"[80] where perhaps he had a wife, children, and "ox 'n' cows"? Or was he thinking something else? Was he carried away by the day-dream sound of his native poplars, the sweet scent of cherry orchards and steppe grass? Was it for this, his distant native land, that his Ukrainian soul yearned when he decided to escape *katorga*? Whom could this quiet, gentle man, seemingly unable to kill a fly, have ever harmed? Why had he ended up in *katorga*?

No one was ever interested in any of these questions, however. Once, when it seemed Goldy was feeling better than usual (not coughing, he'd propped himself up in his bed and was listening to some prisoners talk), I carefully approached and tried to strike up a conversation with him.

"Well, then, you're doing better, Goldy? It's springtime outside, the sunshine's warming things…"

The old man started with surprise, but, having appraised me with deep-set, gentle, seemingly faded gray eyes, he smiled tenderly.

"Were you arrested a long way from here, Goldy?"

I don't know how he would have answered my question (he was evidently getting ready to respond), for at that very moment one of the prison's garrulous sophists ran over and answered for the old man:

"Near or far, don't matter, you can't hide nowheres from yer fate! Indeed, it's always there, sittin' on our brother's shoulders!"

As he should have, Goldy tenderly smiled again in a sign of agreement, and suddenly began coughing violently…

The terrible illness slowly but surely ate away at his weak organism, and life disappeared with every day. Soon, the sick man could not even prop himself up in bed without another's help.

Once, on a clear April noon, the hospital's entryway door opened with a racket and Six-Eyes appeared with two guards in the corridor; a piece of paper was in his hands.

"Which ward is Zalata in?"

He was identified. Cracking open my door, I heard every word of the conversation that took place behind the wall.

"Don't trouble yourself, chap, lie down, lie down!" the brave captain began in an unusually tender tone (evidently, the patient had been struggling to stand at attention before the commandant, but was now unable to do so). "Eh, yes, I see you're doing poorly, and I was thinking you were better. You shouldn't have escaped at your age, chap, you should've peacefully awaited the end of your sentence, all the more because an amnesty might have been issued. Well, now you won't be doing anything! I've come to tell you… Lie down, I tell you—lie down! An order has come from the administration… On account of your escape with Koliarov… Of course, this could wait, but… better to carry out one's duty."

The brave captain had clearly been prepared to read the order; but he was somehow unusually pensive, as if he found himself in a quandary: perhaps he'd earlier really not known the extent of Goldy's illness and was now being affected by his deathly pallor… Having read a few lines, he suddenly stopped and put the paper down.

"I don't think it's necessary to read the whole thing," he said, "I'd better tell you in my own words… You can make of it what you will. You and Koliarov have been given another five years… Koliarov, of course, will be able to endure this punishment, but you… but as for you…"

The magnificent Luchezarov was at an absolute loss and nearly told the wretched man he'd be better off dying early; but he caught himself:

"But, old-timer, don't be dejected! I'll act on your behalf, and the punishment might be annulled! You've also been sentenced to forty-five lashes… For Koliarov, of course, the lashes will be counted out in full, but then he's earned them… He's an irresolute scoundrel, that Koliarov! Well, but you… you, I repeat, don't have to worry about the lashes at all. I'll act—and the doctor will give you a pass! Well, be well, get better, chap!"

And Luchezarov, red as a peony, hastily dashed from the ward. I barely managed to spring away from the door so as not to come face to face with him.

However, neither an attestation from the prison doctor nor the kind commandant's generous intercessions were soon necessary for Zalata: exactly two days later, he ceased to be. He died as quietly as he had lived; no one, neither a fellow prisoner nor a guard, witnessed his final moments. Patients awoke early in the morning and found his cold, stiff corpse in the neighboring bed. A gentle, content smile lay on the dead man's splinter-like, emaciated face, with its deeply-set eyelids tightly shut and its small, thinning, gray beard… The nightmare was over! Freedom!

XVIII. DAY-DREAM

Once more, summer began with all its irritating fascination. Needless to say, I could not foresee that this would be my last prison summer, and my soul was filled with the usual melancholy and grief. This summer was all the more difficult for me insofar as my March illness lingered on as a persistent pain in my arms and legs, though a physician who visited Shelai mine that spring had indefinitely released me from compulsory labor. My name stopped getting shouted at evening roll calls, and during those times I sat without leaving the prison walls, insufferably sad and bored. My favorite place, where I now spent whole hours growing accustomed to the chirruping of surrounding bee-eaters and prisoners' far-reaching voices, became one of what had been three sentry-boxes; this was the only place in the prison where it was possible to get away from human eyes for a minute. These sentry-boxes had the following origins. During the Shelai model prison's early existence, when the brave captain especially feared escapes, he insisted that Cossack guards be stationed not only outside the prison walls, as at all typical prisons, but inside them as well. Pursuant to this goal, four guard boxes were placed at various spots in our yard; around them Cossacks with rifles paced day and night. Prisoners' strolls through the yard were made difficult owing to this; now and then gruff shouts were heard: "Where ya goin'? Turn round!" Yet, of course it wasn't this situation that served as the immediate reason for the interior posts' abolition, but the sheer physical impossibility for an undermanned Cossack squadron to carry out all its designated functions. Mars's poor servants wore themselves out very quickly and, standing for hours, nearly fell off their feet from sleeplessness and fatigue; their commanding officer was forced to arrange to reduce the number of guard posts. The abolition of an interior guard was the result of his economizing. To the mutual delight of prisoners and Cossacks the latter were ordered to leave the prison, and from that day on the entire yard became accessible for our walks. The Cossacks dragged off one of their heavy guard boxes: the prisoners reckoned that the remaining three would be subjected to the same fate, but for some reason they were left "for the time being" in their old spots. Meanwhile, the time passed; the command predictably forgot all about the boxes' existence, and so they remained for good the property of the mare: one stood near the kitchen, another in a corner behind the hospital, and the third—the furthest of all from the noise and commotion—beneath the windows of one of the center wards. It was this last box that came to appeal to my day-dreaming: beneath its cozy roof I often wrote down from memory for myself my prison impressions. Having fallen into contemplation one day, I was so absorbed in my occupation that I didn't hear the orderly's piercing whistle forewarning prisoners of the commandant's inspection of the prison. I came to and started only when a familiar commanding voice sounded two paces from my retreat: it was Six-Eyes making his tour around the prison and talking about something with a guard, and I was barely able to pocket my pencil and paper when suddenly I met his eyes… In response to my bow the brave captain merely harrumphed significantly, but said nothing and continued on.

With the commencement of another spring the command began, as always, to sound the alarm and increase its watchfulness; but, one day, the brave captain (having soon anticipated, as we've said, some kind of promotion for service and therefore now especially fearful of escapes) actually decided, having departed from his usual measures, to influence his underlings' *reason*. Showing up at roll call with a sheet of paper in his hands, he turned to them with the following speech:

"I know that with the beginning of warm weather many of you have the foolish habit of contemplating the possibilities of escaping the prison. This, of course, is your business, just as it's *my* business not to allow escapes. Believe it, *I will not allow them*! Nonetheless, such simpletons who get carried away by a ridiculous dream or listening to ill-intentioned ringleaders are shameful to me. Therefore, I want them to use their brains… With this the goal, I've reviewed all the bulletins for Nerchinsk *katorga*… [and Luchezarov identified some very long period of time—I don't remember what exactly, but it was nearly the whole of the nineteenth century] and I've calculated how many escaped from *katorga* prisons during this period. And, what do you know? I was surprised by the results. It turns out that during this enormous period all of *seventy-nine men* attempted to flee from prison walls, and of them *only three*—note, *three*!—managed to disappear without a trace. Everyone else was either caught and killed at the very moment of escape or captured in the soonest time and returned to prison. So this is what the numbers say: they mean it's not so easy to escape!… Ponder this well, before you decide to carry out such stupidity!"

This speech was surely delivered for calculated effect, but it however made no effect at all. The brave captain's statistics seemed weakly improvised even to me, and after returning to the wards the prisoners laughed straight at them. In a moment, it was calculated that there had been about twenty escapes in the last few years, and of these nearly half seemed to have been successful… In this instance was the mare, always prone toward optimism, fantasizing? Or had the captain tendentiously made up his own curious calculation, had postulated, for example, the number 79 in place of 179, a simple 3 instead of 33? I have no data whatsoever to confirm this with certainty: it is even possible that Luchezarov was correct (if not absolutely, then approximately), but in such case, he would have had to establish more concretely his didactic numbers, to show prisoners their accuracy with documented information, to list all captured escapees by name. Only such complete, indisputable truthfulness could have been counted on to make some kind of impression on *katorga*.[81] For Luchezarov had now achieved goals directly contrary to those he'd attempted: having "used their brains," the simpletons criticized his speech up and down, had a laugh over it, and lay down to sleep more convinced than ever that for a "windy" fellow a successful escape was always possible from anywhere.

For his part, Six-Eyes evidently little believed in the power of his own words: he called upon the prison more usually than during the previous summer and had guards test the grilles on the windows. The latter was probably mostly to soothe his conscience, since everyone distinctly understood that if a prisoner decided to escape he'd choose a different route and leave the grilles at peace. At least those guards with whom I happened to talk about this believed not only that escape from the wards, but even from the prison yard, was a complete impossibility, and one of them (the same one prisoners called Pronia-the-Living-Dead) even told me one time:

"Mercy! What a day-dream it'd be if'n someone escaped from our prison… Inconceivable!"

These same prisoners, sometimes dreaming aloud of escape, almost never stopped imagining escaping through the prison garden or through a tunnel. The latter was really senseless, given the Shelai regime's strictures and the small number of prisoners; the same with regard to the garden, since escape through it would have been possible only during the day and hence in view of the watchmen; it therefore would have been incomparably easier to escape during work, within these same watchmen's view but somewhere nearer the woods and absent such a difficult barrier as a tall stone wall. As a matter of fact, prisoners' dreams of escape for the most part concerned the mine. Never having gotten ready to escape myself, even I could sometimes not shrug off the universal prisoner's inclination to dream of escaping. For example, it seemed to me that the best opportunity for it was presented by the mine watch house, around which always stood just a single watchman; the other convoy soldiers were always sitting in the little shack or sleeping in the open air, glancing to the side only vacantly and by chance. It seemed to me that, by taking advantage of an agreed upon signal from a comrade that the watchman would never decipher, and, hidden from his view by the shack itself, you could go to the mountain and hide in the woods. Accomplished as such early in the morning, the escape wouldn't be discovered any earlier than three o'clock in the afternoon, when prisoners usually returned to the prison—and what a distance a fugitive could cover in those seven or eight hours!… But what would happen next? I didn't dream about what would come next because, I repeat, I didn't seriously plan to escape and my fantasy concerned only the initial, most romantic, act of escaping. Indeed, because I couldn't fantasize about subsequent steps in my escape I was absolutely ignorant as to the terrain, people, and lifestyle in the Transbaikal region. I only knew from these same prisoners' stories that escape through Transbaikalia was incomparably more difficult than through any other part of Siberia, owing to the fact that it was inhabited by Cossacks, whose sons and brothers serve in the convoy and prison commands and must answer for each successful escape under their watch. Any unknown traveler therefore arouses suspicion among residents, and a known fugitive can expect no quarter.

That these and other prisoners were seriously dreaming of escape was no secret to either someone inside or even outside the prison; for example, the command was keeping constant account of Petin-the-Elk. A millstone of notorious renown had in the past too much encircled his name, though this renown had now faded and dimmed significantly, and though not only prisoners but guards had long been skeptical as to whether he would ever decide to escape from the "model" Shelai Prison—escape from which had been presented to them as "a day-dream"—they nevertheless looked for propriety's sake at him more than at anyone else. However, summer after summer passed, and Elk just sat and sat and sank lower and lower in the mocking mare's eyes. The previous summer a rumor had circulated that Elk was going to organize something; having abandoned his studies, he wandered through the prison sullen and angry, was being unmercifully lazy at work, and was clearly nervous, though this was still far from being serious preparations to escape. Moreover, that summer he'd suddenly snap at any prisoner who happened along and he remained completely isolated… The sole person with whom he was now friends in the prison was the young Tatar Kantaurov, called simply Malaika.[82] Thin and flighty as a gnat, beardless, Kantaurov was still utterly a boy, and his strange friendship with Elk evoked universal bewilderment and unambiguous insinuations occasionally.

"The devil's got hisself a baby!" the mare said about them, and if Elk was not the actual devil, then regarding his new friend it was said that he cried "Ma-ma!" in his sleep and smacked his lips just as if he were sucking a pacifier.[83] "Wanna go home, Malaika? *Iakshi*—'home,' *iaman*—'prison'?"

"*Iakshi* home, ooh, *iakshi*!" Malaika would answer, smiling broadly and screwing up his eyes, and even his long ears quivered with pleasure.

A strange circumstance brought this youth to *katorga*. His brothers were professional thieves. Kantaurov went with them on a robbery, not even fully understanding where and why they were going, but simply out of a childish, traditional sense of fraternal duty. All the robbers were soon found guilty, and though from the first it was clearly acknowledged that the youngest brother's participation in the crime was completely unpremeditated, he was in any case arrested and put in prison. Having sat, however, for two weeks under lock and key, Malaika became terribly sad. The prisoners who noticed began mocking him:

"Ain't ya gonna escape, Malaika? Ya ain't a-scared, are ya?"

Malaika's pride spoke up.

"Me want now to escape!"

"So you'd like, fool!"

But Malaika surprised the prison. One time, when a guard turned around to conduct prisoners with their water buckets, he ran as fast as he could out of the prison, kicked down a guard, and was already hiding in the surrounding bushes before the watchman was able to gather his wits and shoot.

"That's our dashin' fellow there!" said the amazed and enraptured herd, but this dash cost the dashing fellow himself dearly. When he was finally captured a month later, he could not shrug off the evidence as if he were an innocent child; in the view of the court, he'd revealed himself to be a cunning and audaciously daring criminal. And so my simple-minded hero was completely unable to understand why he ended up in Shelai. Apparently, the poor man was now wiser and the mare had no power at all to egg him on.

"No, me was stupid," he straightforwardly said, "and so I landed *katorga*… Four months imprisonment—let's go home. No, me didn't want… Well, so start *katorga*! Well, how not stupid? Now Malaika smart, will be sitting, to wait line. Line come—and commandant let me home!"

"You're a dummy, a dummy," prisoners chided him, "'cause where's yer home? In Kazan Province? Well, but after *katorga* you'll be settled in Transbaikalia or along the Iakutsk road. You won't be gettin' a whiff o' home! You can say goodbye to yer home for all eternity now!"

Malaika listened to such speeches not with mistrust but with growing alarm.

"Fool, it makes no dif'rence escapin' from a settlement, so it's better from prison," the mare laughingly continued egging him on.

"Me let's go home from settling!" Malaika joyfully took the bait and, muttering something incomprehensible in his own language, hurriedly ran off.

In recent times there had been especially many Tatars, Sarts, and Kirgiz gathered in Shelai Prison, but of all these none stood out as so foreign as the intrinsically unique Tatar from Orenburg Province Ibrahim Nureddin Sarafetdinov, rendered proverbial by his numerous escapes from under guard. His complicated name was difficult to pronounce for not only the prison but for guards, and so he was known to everyone under the brief sobriquet Dasher. Tall, of outstanding build with penetrating, slanted eyes in a handsome, lively face, Dasher produced the impression of being an extremely brave and fierce man. I never saw him in a relaxed state—either sitting or lying on the sleeping platforms; everything in this man was alive, seething and stirring; first he'd turn up in one ward, then a minute later you'd meet him in the yard at the opposite end of the prison. And always during this he was alone and gloomily silent. Dasher's walks through the yard were also of a strange character: he didn't take quiet or quick steps like all the other prisoners but made staccato dashes, bending his huge body forward and low, and frightening those he met with his fiery, slanted eyes glaring uncomprehendingly at anyone and anything, and in this way moving like a "well-ambling horse," as the mare put it, sometimes for a whole hour.

The Cossack convoy guards and prison administration always kept special watch over this man. Also held in suspicion of an impending escape were Sokoltsev, Chashchin, Karasev, and a number of others. However, the summer went well and the command breathed freely once again: as of late August, of course, no one was thinking of escaping. Moreover, the cold suddenly returned…

On one of the last days of August, toward evening, Bashurov and I were completely unexpectedly summoned to the control office. Looking at us, Six-Eyes was beaming like the sun.

"Well then, allow me to congratulate you, *gentlemen*," he said, rising magisterially from his spot, and this odd preamble made my heart jump not so much from joy as from a nauseous presentiment—"allow me to congratulate you on your freedom… I've only just now received the letter with the order. Here, read it. Pertaining to Valerian Bashurov is an amnesty by which he will immediately transfer to the exile-settler category… Well, with regards to you"—Luchezarov, smiling, turned to me—"you, of course, cannot go to settlement immediately, but you'll go to the free command."

Luchezarov gazed at me with a solemn look, as if seeking out an expression of joyful excitement in my face. Evidently, he didn't see much, hearing from my lips merely a single, cold question:

"I'm to go?… Where is it I'm to go to?"

"Yes, I was forgetting to tell you this," answered the captain, frowning a bit, "it's admittedly inconvenient to leave you in the free command at this prison… There have been various considerations, you know… So you'll be transferring to Kadaia mine."[84]

"How soon do we go?" Bashurov inquired.

"That'll depend on when the Sretensk convoy arrives. In any case, as of tomorrow you're released from *katorga* labor."

Having exchanged bows with the brave captain, we left for the prison. News of our freedom had been carried there quick as a flash, and prisoners with joyful smiles constantly approached us with congratulations and kind wishes.

However, we had to live through another whole month in Shelai Prison waiting for the Sretensk convoy's arrival, and during this month so many important events occurred that they would have required an entire year at any other time. It should be noted here that we were now observing our cohabitants with doubled curiosity, contemplating not without regret and sorrow what we were accomplishing within their society those final days, and so everything that happened was doubly impressed in our memory. There was a kind of unprecedented softness, almost a kind of loving, in the mare's treatment of Bashurov and me: upon their encountering us, there now appeared unfamiliarly bright smiles in the faces of the sternest, of the previously most uncommunicative, individuals, steps that slowed to meet our own, and language revealing an inclination toward expressing feelings… Our "students" especially profoundly regretted our departure, since the entire prison was now left with just Shteinhart as the solitary teacher; Lunkov would not stop showering me with all possible questions, striving over the remaining days to collect any bookish wisdom.

Among other things, there took place in the briefest time a visit by the governor, and everything in the prison was once again upset, moved, scraped, cleaned, and put in order. It was evening of the last day of August. After roll call, the usual row between Lunkov and Elk took place. The former wouldn't shut up, philosophizing on the theme that, on the outside, he'd now be literate had he not ended up in *katorga* "like them snorters 'n' throats." Elk was saying nothing, and now and then greeted his rival's boasting with a mocking snort. This finally annoyed Lunkov, and he turned to Elk:

"What're you snortin' for, you perm'nent prison resident?"

"What? *I'm* a perm'nent prison resident?" Elk rose from the sleeping platform.

"You, for sure! You're jus' sorry you can't live two or three lives in prison."

"Ass! If I want—I'll bid the prison g'bye *tomorrow*!"

"'N' there'll be a bit o' rain on Thursday, though tomorrow's only Saturday. Sometimes you bellow like Elk, but today you're bellowin' like my empty belly. Well, that's you, a perm'nent prison resident!"

"Repeat what you said, blatherer!"

"Here's what I said—you are a perm-a-nent pri-son res-i-dent, you kitchen bone-nibbler!"

Elk cast a silent, murderously contemptuous look at Lunkov and suddenly turned toward me:

"But do you, Ivan Nikolaevich, got the same view o' me as your *favorite* student?"

Having received my typically ambiguous reply in such instances, he laughed venomously and, falling silent, went off to sleep in his corner. With a victorious look, Lunkov orated for a long time still, but Elk was now paying no attention to his words. During this argument, the other prisoners maintained a silent neutrality, and only Godunov chuckled elliptically a couple times, obviously sympathizing with Lunkov. Soon, everyone lay down to sleep, and I dropped off as well.

When, next morning, it was still completely dark and the guard opened the ward and summoned prisoners into the corridor for roll call, I, having woken, was too lazy to go with everyone and, continuing to lie with eyes shut, heard only through a dream the lively shouting of the mare telling each other the sensational news: a deep snow had fallen overnight… No one could recall such a wild event, that snow had fallen on the first of September, and everyone interpreted it as either good or bad. Beneath this babble I slipped into a deep sleep once more.

I was suddenly awakened by an alarming noise, by shouting… Someone was touching me and shouting. I raised my heard—it was now completely light—and before me stood Bashurov and Shteinhart.

"Have you heard?"

"Snow? I heard…"

"What do you mean, snow! There was shooting, an escape!"

"An escape?"

"To the yard! Everyone to the yard!" someone rushing down the corridor roared in an inhuman voice. The mare had obviously been there for a long time, since the wards remained empty. Dressing quickly, I left with my comrades.

"Who escaped?" we asked excited prisoners we encountered along the way.

But no one knew anything.

"Chashchin escaped!" said someone, though not very persuasively.

"Devil, demons, but whereto 'n' what way?"

"Well, ask 'im yourself. A shame he didn't trust in youse!"

"He musta 'scaped this very minute, 'cause I saw him durin' roll call."

"We heard shootin' after less'n fifteen minutes. There, behind the hospital… Musta cut through the garden!"

"Sterlin'!…"

The prisoners' faces appeared unusually pale against the shining, milk-white snow that had fallen all over the yard; everyone was clearly excited; many were shaking as if in a fever.

Chashchin's name came up once again.

"Ah-oo! I'm-a here, so's why ya need to be thrashin' Chashchin, ya brainless sheep?"

"Akh, that damn clown, he *is* here! Who was blabbin' that Chashchin escaped?"

"Maybe no one escaped at all, but they're danglin' the noose for us," someone's skeptical voice put in.

"Indeed, the stupid mare…"

Meanwhile, guards were going all out, flying along the serried ranks and feverishly counting prisoners like madmen. But, in the end, their tabulation wasn't at all surprising: there seemed to be even more prisoners than they needed. Suddenly, the gates opened and through them did not walk but flew Luchezarov, red as a crab and having hastily donned some kind of faded Kirgiz housecoat that deprived him of his usual presence and magnificence. The startled duty officer even forgot to give the command: "Attention! Caps off!"—and the mare stood there in their caps, confused and out of sorts. But the brave captain did not at that moment care about superficial niceties; without paying any attention to standard protocol, he quickly approached the prisoners' ranks.

"Well then?" he asked the orderly on the double. "Who? How?"

"Dunno nuthin' right now, Mister Com'dant," one of the guards, saluting, reported.

"Idiots!" the captain snapped and began counting the ranks himself.

"Two are missing," he added at the top of his voice after casting an annihilating glance at the guards, and following this, he barked at the prisoners:

"To the wards! Get there in one minute!"

Everyone fled in disorder to their respective barracks. My eyes were suddenly struck by the absence of Elk among us.

"But, gentlemen, where's Petin?"

"Boys, where indeedy-do is Elk?" prisoners looked around at themselves. "He couldn't 'ave?…"

"Well, now, hold on!" Lunkov scornfully interrupted. "I just saw him. He's not escapin', it ain't so!"

"Where'd you see 'im? When?"

"Look, he was standin' beside me jus' now in roll call…"

"Well, that was at roll call, but jus' now was in the yard—you're a-lyin', he weren't there," Godunov noted thoughtfully.

"He weren't?!"

"Attention!…"

The door was unlocked—and into the ward came, irritated as before, Luchezarov with a group of pale, ashamed guards.

"One, two, three… Well, there it is: one's missing from here as well—now that means a third one!" he nearly screamed.

The guards were quiet, shaking, annihilated…

"Can you tell me who's missing? Answer, headman!"

We had both a headman of the ward and the collective headman, but both were hemming and hawing.

"There's no Petin, Mister Com'dant," Pronia's crushed voice finally blurted.

"Petin? Hm! Hm! So it would seem to be, of course."

And Six-Eyes hurried out. Following him from the ward, Pronia clapped a hand on his hip and said appropriately loudly:

"An absolute day-dream, and how!…"

"Yes, indeed, boys, who coulda thought it'd be Elk, huh?" Chirok observed, after we found ourselves under lock and key again.

"But whaddya suppose 'bout Elk? Brother, you ain't gonna catch 'im with your bare hands!" Godunov suddenly said: and these words quickly set the tone for the universal opinion. "I myself ne'er said he had a stupid noggin," continued Godunov, appealing for something on my part as if he was now being correct, "I e'en told him to his face, 'cause I like to speak the mother-truth. I'll speak the same now: seems he was a blockhead in certain of his notions… But which of us is either a saint or a sage, howe'er? Must be said of Elk that he ne'er told a lie to anyone, but if he did lie to someone, then it was to hisself. Well, but as regards bravery, what's called the prisoner's spirit, well, then, in this, Elk can always uphold his reputation!"

"That's sayin' it," agreed Chirok.

"I always knew," Godunov added, "that he couldn't stay in prison like any others! Well, he kept his patience, o' course, but now he's lost it."

"Wait a bit on yer fussin' o'er Elk," Lunkov tried to dampen the universal acclamation, "he's flown high, but we dunno where he's at."

But the entire ward rose as one man to defend Elk, and told him to shut up.

"Howe'er, *how* did he escape, boys? 'N' *who* was the other two? Well, the boys did good! Heck, they kept ever'thin' in the dark!"

"If there was an alarm, the bullets certainly missed. They 'scaped in true style!"

But how had the escapees managed to get over the high stone wall? One or another ridiculous conjecture was voiced concerning this. In the meantime, the command left the prison but decided not to open the wards.

"They ain't gonna open 'em now, yer waitin' in vain," Godunov, experienced in such matters, concluded, "'n' we ain't gonna be let out to work, not until the search is o'er. Ev'ry knoll 'n' bush is bein' searched now. We wish Petin the best: they ain't gonna file a tooth 'fore they bite."

Godunov turned out to be correct: four whole days passed under lock and key, and only headmen and ward attendants were let out, and with extreme caution. However, this didn't prevent the mare from definitively learning within several hours everything that was going on in the prison. Then Godunov, in his capacity as collective headman for receiving provisions, brought us the following news. Two other men had escaped with Elk: Dasher and Malaika Kantaurov.

"Has that Malaika gone bonkers? Didn't he know his term was gonna end soon?"

"You said it! Ain't for nuthin' what they was sayin' 'bout Elk, that the devil got tied up with a baby: he clearly managed to marry 'im!..."

"Well, but how'd they escape?"

"That, I tells you, is an absolute miracle in a sieve. The command itself put out a staircase for our prisoners."

"What're you sayin'?!"

"I'm speakin' honestly."

"Boys, 'member them soldiers' boxes?"

"Well?..."

"Well, so they dragged to the wall that one what was behind the hospital—'n' up they went. Watchman couldn't e'en get off a clean shot 'cause they ran straight for the guardhouse. 'N' as you know, taiga starts right behind that buildin'... At first, the little Cossack just fired 'n' shouted: 'Catch 'em! Grab 'em!' 'n' only then shootin' into the air as an alarm. Well, it was already too late... Now a cordon's been formed all round: they're sayin' they rounded up peasants from all the neighb'rin' villages 'n' dispatched the military command from the factory... 'n' y'know Six-Eyes is sittin' 'n' poundin' on that telegraph..."

Chirok scratched his belly nervously.

"But ain't this prob'ly bad for us? That snow—it was a big deal, there's gonna be clear signs..."

"Snow sure ain't gonna help 'em... Well, who coulda known that on this one night it'd fall knee-deep?"

"They shoulda postponed…"

"Postponed! That's you, brother, reasonin' with your calf's brains—well, but is Dasher such a fellow? Or is Elk? The boys, it must be said, is holy fire-boys… All the plans was made—'n' suddenly they're tossed? You think it's easy?"

In wishing that the fugitives not be captured the prisoners came together as one. But everyone was suddenly surprised by the strange discovery that Elk's, Dasher's, and Malaika's footwear were resting most peacefully beneath the sleeping platforms in their wards. The mare was thrown into astonishment: How was this? This was how they'd fled? They'd really gone barefoot? Through the snow?

"For lightfootedness, it means," certain individuals conjectured.

"If so," responded others, "then that's a lightfootedness you don't envy, brother… Don't seem nuthin' in the heat o' the moment, well, but after an hour you're lurchin' into a folk dance!"

"Nonsense," yet others said, "they prob'ly had 'rangements with someone who gave 'em freemen's clothes 'n' shoes for the taiga."

"Well, mebbe so."

Toward evening came consoling news: the fugitives had vanished without a trace. What especially perplexed the command was the complete lack of tracks in the snow's surface.

"It's like they flew off into thin air, the scoundrels!" said the guards.

Joyful feeling burst in the hearts of the prisoners; everyone breathed freely, everyone's voices proudly rose.

"I say, them's *ours*, y'know! That's the Shelai model prison for ya! That's Six-Ey-y-yes for ya!"

"They forgot one thing, fellas, that ev'ry prisoner's got three heads on his shoulders 'n' ev'ry one o' *them's* got three advisors: free will, Mother Taiga, 'n' Father Baikal… So there!"

During those days "they," that is, the guards, all the spooks, the entire command, were indeed gazing at the prisoners with an obviously sheepish and disgraced look.

Even something like self-esteem now emerged among what had just recently been the beaten, despised, but now more and more "nose-turning," herd…

"Elk won't get caught in this lifetime!" said the optimists. "All the evil misfortune got knocked from that chase the first day, they got some freemen's clothes, 'n' then it was good riddance all the way to Verkhneudinsk itself."

The pessimists were silent during those days. Only one piece of news, delivered by Godunov, made a not entirely pleasant impression: among others assigned to pursue the escapees was the Cossack Zausaev[85] who, mere days after joining the guards, received from prisoners the sobriquet "The Monk" for his gloomy and severe countenance. He had a reputation as a remarkably capable hunter, shot without missing, and had the keen eye of a hawk and the scent of a hound; he himself had begged Six-Eyes for the assignment, and with revolver in belt, and accompanied by that pair of ill-fated Cossacks near whose guard post the escape was successfully accomplished and who now faced a penal battalion, he took a direction all the other sleuth-hounds had completely ignored.

"This 'ere devil The Monk seems more terrible to me than all Shelai's Cossacks put together!" Godunov concluded his report.

This was the first evening after the escape, and the prison laid down to sleep fatigued by the day's excitement; and no one, absolutely no one in it, suspected that at that very moment the fugitives had, strictly speaking, *only just begun* their dangerous journey!

The matter unfolded this way.

Having clambered into the prison garden with the help of the sentry box and jumped from it nearly onto to the head of the watchman standing below, they carried themselves forward like the wind, unencumbered by either shackles—which, needless to say, had been sloughed off while still in the prison—or the awkward prison footwear. Instead of the latter they had put tall, fur-lined stockings on their feet. Such stockings were generally in vogue among Shelai's penal laborers; our tailors stitched them from the remains of regulation sheepskin jackets the finance officer issued as patching material and sold them at the dearest price. These stockings actually turned out to be outstandingly suitable footwear for escaping, but Elk and his colleagues failed to take account of their instability: after just a few hours all the stockings' seams split, so that they were going through the cold snow in bare feet…

Between the guardhouse and where a certain stretch of the taiga began there was a small hollow, covered by some bushes and piles of rocks. A small copse of trees had been somewhere in this spot, but with a view to hindering an escape behind the Shelai mine buildings that surrounded the whole prison, the trees had been felled, leaving a clear, openly viewable expanse. The other side of this hollow was darkened by true dense taiga, and it called to our escapees' eyes, promising them salvation. But only had they just reached the bottom of the depression when Elk's legs—because (as he later insisted) he'd bruised himself going over the high wall, or, as was all the more likely, because he was extremely nervous—suddenly became paralyzed: he instantly felt that he could not take one step more… and he laid down on the ground. In fear, Dasher, fleeing alongside, came to a halt and rapidly signaled his comrade to quickly get up and go on; but Elk point-blank refused to move and proposed hiding themselves somewhere there in the bushes. This suggestion seemed utterly insane since the hollow was completely exposed, the bushes in it small and sparse, and large rocks for hiding a grown man were similarly insufficient. Dasher stood there indecisively; he knew practically not one word of Russian, and his principal advantage was Elk, who, as a supposed master "*cheldon*," knew Siberia like he knew his five fingers and moreover enjoyed renown as an experienced runner. Yet, apart from these personal considerations, Dasher was distinguished by his chivalrous character: throwing a comrade to misfortune seemed an inconceivable crime to him. And so, having cursed Elk more than once as a dog and with every choice word he could summon from his Eastern lexicon, he bowed to fate with the fatalism of a true Asiatic and, having ended the argument, crawled into hiding among the bushes and rocks. Behind him followed Malaika, for whom, in essence, all methods of escape were indifferent, since he'd undertaken it more out of daring and comradeship than serious conviction. All three took on the appearance of sculptured stone and, with absolutely nothing concealed or defended, lay as such "in view of whole wide world," hardly believing in the possibility of their salvation. In the meantime, dawn had ended and it was completely light.

With rabid whoops and yells and rifles leveled, all the guards flew out of every side of the two-story guardhouse and, clattering weapons, stopped rooted to the ground down-slope from the hollow. Inside, it was completely empty; here and there were merely clumps of gray rocks powdered with snow and small crowns of dry bushes and hawthorn sticking up amidst them, and in the distance the dense taiga thickened… There could be no doubt: the prisoners had already managed to reach it and to hide. Without much deliberation the Cossacks set off in pursuit. Elk later said they flew by some twenty paces from him, that he distinctly heard not only the pounding of their feet but their quickened breathing (lying prone, burying his face in the snow, he could not of course see them), and considered himself truly forsaken. But the guards ran past as if insane, because "only a fool" would get the notion of searching so simply and close by… This amazing story unfolded more than once throughout the entire day the fugitives spent inside their absurd refuge: detachments of savage Cossacks ran one after the other a few paces from the half-frozen and fear-stiffened prisoners—and didn't notice them. Of course, were this not a completely verifiable fact, a fact insusceptible to the slightest doubt, then I would label this a poorly conceived story.

After the day-guards, first the entire Cossack squadron, then Shelai's guards and peasants, bounded into the chase. It was suggested that, as a feint, the fugitives had switched from their original, favorable direction; everyone therefore thoroughly searched the nearest surroundings where there were only tree and rock faces; the dare-devils had to be hiding in the most difficult spot, among the old constructions, the mines and shafts that had been slapped together long ago—but nowhere was there found any evidence of their escape.

This latter situation principally confused the investigators very much: where had the footprints in the snow disappeared to? However, from the very first, the dozens and hundreds of feet quickly tramping in all directions had made for chaos in the snow, so that distinguishing them became utterly impossible. Six-Eyes roared and raged in the literal sense of the word; he shouted at the guards that he would "kill them and not answer for it," dispatched in various directions couriers with detailed descriptions of the escapees, and finished by quarreling with the Cossack officer over the question as to whom the prison's guard boxes belonged and who'd been responsible for their disposal. As such, the brave captain's mood was more aggressive than it had been on the day he awaited the governor's visit.

Thus the searches proceeded by day and there befell the night, when the fugitives finally decided to abandon their ambush and slyly embark upon another path. Of course, they could have easily stumbled into the Cossack pickets still scattered throughout Shelai's environs, but the Cossacks themselves did not worry they could be stumbled upon: they were separated among various campfires and calling loudly to one another. Tired, annoyed by misfortune, they were continuing the search as a mere formality, convinced the fugitives were now long gone. Nothing therefore hindered the latter from stealing through the guards and leaving them behind at a completely safe distance. Only one thing was now tormenting them—growing hunger and the absence of shoes. Their improvised fur stockings had quickly torn on rocks and bushes, so that they ended up standing in cold snow in virtually bare feet scraped bloody.

Teeth chattering, the prisoners ran heedlessly ahead, hurrying to reach any sort of dwelling. At dawn, they finally reached a kind of winter encampment: there an old Tungus and his wife lived in a solitary wretched yurt. The homeowner was still sleeping peacefully when the uninvited guests burst in on him. They spent the whole day there, warming themselves with steaming tea, occupied in repairing their footwear, and greedily devouring the meager Tungus household's milk products. Unfortunately, they acquired no clothes because the Tungus himself was practically naked.

In the meantime, the snow had not considered stopping and winter seemed to have come into its own. It had turned colder. Having in due course slaughtered and roasted for themselves the homeowner's sole he-goat (the Tungus didn't dare make a sound and were glad they themselves were not cooked and eaten), our travelers finally left at dusk, after threatening the old man he would fare poorly if he jabbered about them. The second night of their escape went even better, since pursuers' shouts were now heard nowhere and no watchmen's fires were visible. The chase evidently remained far off. It was completely dawn when Dasher suddenly halted and stopped his comrades: he'd caught a whiff of smoke… Everyone instantly lay on their chests and crawled through the bushes like snakes. The reason for the alarm was soon apparent: at the edge of the forest, near the road itself, sitting at a campfire and boiling a kettle of tea, were three peasants, and rifles lay beside two of them; however, it became completely apparent they were not pursuers but merely hunters. One was a visibly frail old man who was mercilessly coughing and grumbling at his comrades the whole time for their unsuccessful hunt; the second was a broad-shouldered man with a red beard and kind gray eyes. He was constantly smiling into his beard and saying: "Well, alright, alright, there-there… What grumblin'!" The third of the hunters was a fifteen-year-old boy. Torn, worn-out garments hung on the shoulders of all three; but our wayfarers' attention focused entirely upon the hunters' feet, clad in beautiful, warm ichigo boots. They began whisperingly conferring with each other (Malaika served, as always, as interpreter between Elk and Dasher). Dasher proposed a simple but trustworthy method: rush the unsuspecting peasants and disarm and kill them… But Elk rejected this plan as too risky and suggested his own: jump out of the bushes and grab the rifles lying near the hunters, and deal with them peaceably. Thus it was done. Caught unawares, the hunters handled their misfortune sufficiently equably and even invited our fugitives to join them for tea. The latter did not refuse the tea, and then began to talk; Elk did not deny that he was escaping with comrades, and added only that he was fleeing the free command.

"Well, if'n it's from the free command then it's a triflin' matter!" said red beard, and patted Dasher's shoulder.

"Good chap, I wanna look-see at yer jacket," put in the old man, feeling the arm of Elk's sheepskin.

"Let's trade," Elk cunningly took him up, "besides, these clothes is nuthin' to us… Indeed, let's trade for them ichigos there!"

"You gots wondrous ichigos, brother, like I ain't ne'er seen in me life," the old man marveled, eyeing Elk's fur stockings.

"Such as you ne'er saw! Dontcha know yer lookin' at my Tratotonis?[86] These ichigos, brother, is Moscow-made, see whatta fine, soft product… Well, but the warmth, I'm tellin' ya—is terrible!"

The old man nodded his head not entirely convincingly but did not refuse to trade, probably knowing that the item's virtues were completely fictitious and that the prisoners would resort to force in case he refused. His comrades clearly thought the same thing. Therefore, wasting no time, they exchanged clothes. Elk was ecstatic and, to give expression to his feelings, even spat around the fire; Dasher and Malaika were also enlivened and joyfully mumbled something in Tatar. In the heat of their exultation the rifles they'd seized were laid on the ground once more… None of the fugitives noticed a sudden strange change in the hunters' faces: all three had immediately pricked up their ears and, continuing to smile somewhat unnaturally, seemed ready to rush their new friends.

"Don't move from that spot if you wanna live! You are un-der ar-rest!" a booming voice suddenly burst out.

Three paces from the fire, sitting on horseback as if having suddenly arisen from the earth, the gloomy Monk was aiming his revolver at Dasher, and behind him, also on horseback, sat the robust figures of two Cossacks armed with Berdans… At that very moment the hunters grabbed their rifles and pointed them at the fugitives from all sides. This all happened so quickly and unexpectedly that any resistance or escape or words were impossible. Even the desperate Dasher did not think of running, and stood in place as if stunned by a clap of thunder from a clear-blue sky. Knotted ropes appeared on the hands of all three young men. In the presence of this "little Cossack" they would, of course, have gladly responded to a capturing spook who gave them a good blow in the side, but their jokes with Zausaev were poor: he didn't "lay a finger" on the fugitives, having announced that "the guard would be sharpened now that *he* had captured them and was their *master*"…

[87]

"Well, boys, there'll be no laggin' on the road!" ordered the guard, and he even prevented the hunters from trading back their clothes with the prisoners. The unique procession set off. Ahead of everyone trudged Elk, Dasher, and Malaika Kantaurov, hanging their heads, hands bound behind them, and wearing "free" shoes, and from behind came six convoy guards, three of whom were in designated penal laborers' jackets.[88]

Here began the glorious and sensational escape's shameful epilogue, the circumstances of which I will not describe. I will merely report one extremely intriguing aspect. When the key growled in our ward's lock and Elk, dazed as if he'd just exited the bathhouse, appeared on the threshold in his torn stockings—over which tightly riveted fetters now clanged—I was for some reason convinced he would be met with laughter and mockery… Yet everyone treated Elk as if he'd just returned from work somewhere, as if not even noticing him, and in this was manifested, I think, their version of an eloquent delicacy… Only later that evening, lying on the sleeping platform, did Petin begin quietly telling one of his neighbors the story of their three-day adventure; the others acted as if they were asleep or simply not listening…

XIX. END OF THE SHELAI "MODEL PRISON"

The visit from the governor was fraught with all sorts of incidents and unforeseeables. Like a hurricane, he blew into the hitherto perfectly safe Shelai Prison, centrifugated toward himself what had seemed the most solid abutments and fundaments and spun them away like small blades of grass, and on one such blade of grass there was none other than the magisterial Captain Luchezarov himself. He, for so many years the terror of the entire *katorga* world, had become accustomed to thinking that God alone had barely more power and authority and, in moments of extreme rage at those who threatened him with insubordination, that he could kill them and not answer for it—in a single day, in a single hour, this grand and proud man fell from his pedestal to the ground and instantly became just a pitiful corpse!

Everything so came together in his misfortune that his fall was unforeseen, and neither earthly nor heavenly powers could have possibly prevented or even delayed it.

During construction of the Shelai "model prison" a strange vagueness and reticence had been allowed by the high command. First of all, no one even received a sufficiently intelligible point to the existence of this surprisingly unnecessary and at the same time excessively expensive institution, though all the administration's bureaucrats, in addition to those exclusive names, were nevertheless rewarded with salary raises. Even the limits and extents of the prison commandant's power were quite indeterminate: on the one hand, they were exactly like those of a warden and of the wardens of all the other *katorga* prisons, but on the other, they were not like those; his relationship to the *katorga* director seemed that of a merely business-like relation of one equal bureaucratic personage to another, though the relationship could also appear subordinate. *Katorga*'s director quite naturally aspired to supreme authority over Shelai Prison; Luchezarov, for his part, aspired to complete independence, acknowledging the director as only an intermediary between himself and the governor, a kind of transmissionary postal station; on this basis he sometimes decided to send his reports straight to the governor. Owing to what from the very beginning was a permissible, undefined audacity, no reprimands whatsoever were issued from the get-go, and then only feeble efforts were made to constrain the brave captain. His attitude toward the director took on an obviously hostile, almost combative, character. Furthermore, Luchezarov was unable to inspire either love or even basic sympathy in anyone. His animosity toward the military leadership, in the person of the Cossack commander, extended in the extreme to the governor. He was with no great exceptions hated by the guards, whom he slighted as if they were boys or lackeys, such that some even complained to prisoners on the quiet and enforced prison regulations most laxly. The story of the escape is bound up in all this. There seemed something ominous, wicked, in the very atmosphere…

However, I confess I wasn't personally convinced that the prisoners seriously complained one and all; indeed, in essence, what was there to complain about? The strictness of the regime, the prohibition against superior private rations? But this was all completely legal according to the written instructions of Shelai Prison's supreme authorities: Luchezarov sooner deserved praise for his vigilance… The one man in prison I'm convinced filed a complaint was a certain Dubasov, a prisoner who'd not be in Shelai long before managing to become extremely bitter toward prison regulations and, most of all, toward Six-Eyes himself. He was a family man of not few years, a cobbler by trade, staid and soft in appearance; at first, he expressed an unusual satisfaction that he'd ended up in Shelai, where there were no "Ivans" or typical prisoner "boors." The prisoners immediately concluded that this fellow would be one of those pious heathens and toadies of whom there were already plenty in the form of various Bulanovs and other of the guards' "boot-lickers." Dubasov's face, thin, pale, with hawk-like nose and hawk-like eyes, was also far from friendly. However, Dubasov managed not to become a boot-licker. He soon took note of the other side of the Shelai coin. One day, a guard found boot-trees in the repair shop where Dubasov worked.

"Whattabout these boot-trees? Whose is they?" he asked in surprise.

"Mine," Dubasov answered in a completely unconcerned tone.

"But where'd ya get 'em?"

"How 'where'? I asked Penkin—he carved 'em for me in the mine."

"In the mine? But who got 'em inside?"

A full investigation ensued. It turned out that none of the guards on duty at the gates had allowed a shoe-tree into the prison—consequently, Penkin had snuck them in. It also turned out that, inside prison, according to prison regulations, shoes—for which no trees were required—could only be mended, not stitched anew; if, contrary to expectation, there were some freely made commissions, then these were exclusively by permission of the authorities, which at that time would then allow the atypical shoe-trees. Penkin, only in light of his irreproachable reputation, which up to that point he still enjoyed, was not sent to the isolator, but Dubasov was given a stern reprimand and his shoe-trees taken away. Dubasov was at a complete loss: he could not at all comprehend what was the crime he'd committed; and so, having waited for one of Six-Eyes's evening roll calls, he turned to him with a question in which there resounded a profoundly offended dignity:

"Mister Commandant, permit me to ask you, what might be the harm in a shoe-tree? Among other things, you may know, a shoe is absolutely impossible without them!"

"Silence!" the captain menacingly shouted, obviously not pleased by the question's tone, and, adding not a word, he left.

The obstinate old man's self-esteem was even more deeply aggrieved, and now there were no limits to his indignation… Not a week passed before he endeavored by some means to get his shoe-trees out of the orderly's room where they'd been put. Once more, of course, the shoe-trees were seized, but this time Dubasov himself was put into a dark isolator. A long and stubborn battle then began between him and the authorities. Dubasov, by nature the most well-behaved of well-behaving prisoners, who probably never dreamed of ever opposing the authorities' will, suddenly rebelled. He refused to return to work in the shop. In response, Six-Eyes not only put him in the isolator again but prohibited meetings with his wife. This went on for more than a month; if Dubasov agreed to go to work, then, without fail, shoe-trees would turn up two or three days later: either someone from the mare would bring them to him from the mountain, or he himself would fashion them out of a simple log in the kitchen. Within the brave captain, for his part, self-esteem and obstinacy reared, and he threatened to let the ill-starred cobbler rot in the isolator. Just a few days before the governor's arrival, he was released from arrest.

"Aha? Given in? Lettin' me go?" bellowed Dubasov, thanks to which he wasn't "set free" during the governor's visit. With this his goal, he got into a noisy argument with the guards, and they willy-nilly responded to him as they would "in secret."

The governor, by all appearances already well-armed against Luchezarov, showed up in Shelai: his enemies were alert to and capable of putting on display—perhaps in an even exaggerated light—all the brave captain's failings and weaknesses. The latter was casting the general the exact same free-and-easy, independent look as he had several years earlier during the governor's first visit to Shelai, but from his very first words he made it impressively clear that he, the captain, should in the *katorga* director's presence speak second. Having exchanged significant looks with the director, Luchezarov instantly understood the matter: but he didn't want to surrender so early, and continued the fight.

Going into the prison and having received from the orderly the report on those arrested, the governor first of all expressed a desire to see the isolator. There, his gaze settled on a touching sight. Dubasov proved to be a man not devoid of acting talent and a certain inventiveness: having removed his top-clothes, he'd soiled his underwear with soot (he'd also rubbed a bit on his face) and torn the collar off his blouse, and in such a tattered and pitiful appearance was standing before the witnesses. Hanging his head low and with feet spread wide as if barely holding him up from exhaustion, he spoke in such a deep, frankly sepulchral, voice, that the governor started.

"Your Excellency!… I'm being underfed… Like a father, save me!"

"What's going on, chap? What is with you? Are you ill? What have you been confined here for?" the governor appealed with concern to the old man.

With the same slow and sickly short-windedness Dubasov responded that he'd been there for a month and a half, almost without a break in a darkened isolator, on bread and water and in filthy underwear, and forbidden contact with his wife, all on account of being a cobbler who used shoe-trees.

"He's lying, Your Excellency!" the brave captain suddenly interrupted. "He's lying about the underwear and the rations…"

"You will answer later," the governor stopped him, with a shallow look and murderous brevity in his voice.

"I don't understand what you're saying, chap," he continued, returning to Dubasov, "you're in the isolator because you were using some shoe-trees? You're a cobbler?…"

The prisoner told in detail the original story, adding that for even a good cobbler mending was impossible without a shoe-tree.

"But what was the harm from simple wooden shoe-trees?" The governor was at exactly the same loss as the prisoners themselves had been earlier. The *katorga* director to whom he querulously appealed merely shrugged his shoulders ironically.

"So release him from the isolator!" the governor shouted into the air, and quickly added: "And from now on, allow him to meet daily with his wife."

"According to prison regulations, Your Excellency, meetings are allowed only once a week," Luchezarov interrupted yet again.

Leaving the isolator the governor gave him no reply, and proceeded to the infirmary. By some unknown, almost miraculous, ways, the whole prison learned of the event within several minutes. The mare immediately cheered up, got excited, and caused a ruckus… All the dissatisfaction that had been accumulating in it for years, and would perhaps lurk in its soul's depths for entire years more (beginning with the most legitimate and measured and ending with the most foolish and ridiculous claims), all this exploded in a second like gunpowder from a lighted match and assumed the form of a terrible, uncontainable protest… No matter what ward the governor toured he everywhere encountered a raft of grumbles and complaints about Six-Eyes and appeals for salvation. However, he couldn't listen to all requests and, waving his arms, he simply said:

"I know, I know, all this will be investigated, calm down, chaps. I myself see there are all kinds of wrongs that have piled up here."

Having wished, among other things, to see the escapees, he looked for a long time at Elk and shook his head, either reproachfully or compassionately.

"How could you decide on such a course, dear?" the old general finally asked. "Don't you know you could've been killed, you little fool? And now it won't be so sweet: you do know I'll have to punish you? What do you have to say for yourself, my sweet?"

"Your Excellency," Elk answered with great feeling, "we fled from misfortune! From a sweet life, you yourself know, you don't run! Kantaurov had all of two months before release to settlement, but he ran away, too… Have mercy, Your Excellency, pray long and hard to God!"

The general silently shook his head once more.

"Yes, yes," he pensively said at last, "I'll take all this into account."

Upon leaving the prison, as the guards later reported, he loudly observed to the *katorga* director in the brave captain's presence:

"I don't understand, I'm un*able* to understand, what, in general, is the purpose of this model prison, an institution so foolishly established and at the same time so expensive to manage?"

This that had been buzzing in his ears from all sides during this whole time he expressed as if the very notion had resulted from an investigation. To Luchezarov's invitation to go to his quarters he said nothing, then answered politely but coldly and left to see the Cossack commander. At the latter's, the second act of this unfolding tragedy was played out: there, charges were made against Six-Eyes by the commander himself, Shelai's peasants, and a few of the guards… Six-Eyes had battled in vain: that same day he was given to understand unequivocally that it would be advisable for him to seek treatment for his nerves and, more or less, to provide a report about continuing his furlough…

It is easy, of course, to imagine what the brave captain must have gone through. At first, he was simply surprised, astonished, and stunned and time and again, as if this were all a dream, pinched himself to ascertain he wasn't sleeping; but then his sense of bewilderment turned into a deep hurt, a fiery indignation… What! He, who was not only the most honorable official in *katorga* but probably the entire Transbaikal administration; he, who was so fanatically devoted to the ideas of duty and lawfulness; he, finally, who over the course of four years had so zealously and selflessly tried to create a model *katorga* prison and make a little headway, dammit, in this direction—now appeared crushed, desecrated, degraded, and belittled before all of society, before his own subordinates!… Such was the disgrace suffered by this victim of intrigue, of the underhanded and dark power of bureaucratic formalities! Indeed, after this, what did it matter… if you couldn't do your duty to the utmost, why live?!

After that day, Luchezarov gave up on everything. While awaiting his substitute he sat at home without appearing anywhere, without even glancing into his office, degrading and cutting down with petty maliciousness those who came into his sights. But no one feared him now; there were even instances when his housekeeper openly disobeyed the sometimes menacing captain, when he couldn't summon up enough energy to show that he still held power. His spirit collapsed completely, and the mare gossiped that the governor had even forbid him to enter the prison.

The prison became more and more undisciplined each day. Guards looked through their fingers at card games that now went on in every corner, completely without the need for stirrups. In the meantime, the red-faced finance officer caused an actual revolution in the kitchen after announcing to prisoners that, henceforth, better, private, rations would be allowed and that tobacco, tea, and sugar could be bought from him in whatever quantities desired. Exulting and glowing like a buttered pancake, the "lisping devil" also opened a store in the kitchen. Normal prisoners' rations soon turned into slops you couldn't stick in your mouth; medical patients, not receiving any bread or milk, literally began starving. Hence the mare's festive mood very soon subsided and many, realizing they'd traded a hawk for a cuckoo, now began expressing regret for the old "prigime" and about Six-Eyes's departure. When a rumor came from somewhere that he was still not going to retire but would become Algacha's warden, some prisoners like Lunkov and Nogaitsev straightaway announced that *they* would request transfers there…

One evening during roll call, to everyone's surprise, there appeared at the doors the brave captain's familiar image. In a moment, the disorderly uproar ended and the mare formed ranks in some fear and bewilderment. There was none of the former pomp, however: the orderly delivered his orders rather sluggishly and uninspiredly, and Six-Eyes himself, sad and thoughtful and looking like a dethroned ruler, came in hanging his head. However, as always, he immediately allowed us to put our caps back on. Upon the conclusion of prayers he suddenly raised his head, and, with his former stateliness, cast his gaze over the prisoners' ranks, and announced:

"So that's it, old chaps! As you know, I'm leaving…"

His voice lightly quavered, but soon took on its usual hardness and sonority.

"Many of you have now been living with me here for exactly four years. Together, we began this journey, together—due to certain extreme measures—we are ending it.

The years have not been easy. You, old chaps, might think they were difficult only for you, that it was you who were enduring and suffering and that I was merely occupied deciding: Whom should be punished by sitting in the isolator? But those who bitterly think so are wrong. Each of us does what he is forced to by his one and chosen life's path. Your fate made you prisoners, but mine made me a prison commandant.... Hm! Hm!... Tell me honestly, was I the prison's enemy, did I wish it harm? I always acted according to the law... as I saw it, of course. I never deviated from the law, adhering to the rule: chosen to serve, I shall serve honorably! Well, and what did I get for my service? Am I leaving here with riches I've stolen from you? Am I being well treated by the leadership? Hm! Hm! Was I rewarded with your love? No, I know that you didn't love me!... This you have demonstrated... But I also know—yes, *this* I know!—that, after I go, you'll think kindly of me more than once... In any case, if I'm so hateful before you, if anyone... Well, in a word, remember me kindly!"

The brave captain's voice quavered again, and he quickly turned toward the gates. The bewildered mare maintained a deathlike silence. Suddenly, from out of its ranks, sobbing could be distinctly heard...

"Lit-tle fa-ther! Lit-tle fa-ther!" an old man's voice croaked.

Luchezarov instantly turned around, and a somehow heretofore unseen old man left the ranks and fell on his knees before him.

"Little Father Com'dant, not ever'one complained, not ever'one!... We're shamed by you... Now, it'll be much worse, much worse, for us, little father... We grumbled, little father, sure we's grumbled, but stupidly, y'know! Who in *katorga*, you says yourself, can be allowed to live like he was free? How can there be no strictness at all? But here's what you got for an answer, Little Father Com'dant: they's sayin' you're transferrin' to Algacha? Well, take me there with ya! Take me, my dear!"

And, once again, the old man flung himself at Luchezarov's feet, clutching at the skirts of his greatcoat and kissing them.

"Me, too, Mister Com'dant!"

"'N' me!"

"'N' me!" a dozen other crazed voices shouted from the ranks.

Luchezarov was stunned: he'd anticipated nothing like this. It was a true ovation, created impromptu without any preliminary agreements or preparations and emanating, apparently, from the sincere, unmediated emotion of simple Russian hearts... Tears glistened in his eyes; for several moments he couldn't make himself say a word.

"What! But you, Lunkov, are appealing to me? And you, Nogaitsev? And even you, Sokoltsev?"

"'N' us, 'n' us!"

"We don't wants to forsake you, Mister Com'dant," a still greater number of voices burst out.

"Then what to do, old chaps, what to do?" the deeply affected captain babbled. "Unfortunately, to my great regret, I, it turns out, cannot fulfill your request. I, it turns out, am indeed leaving... Yet, at the same time, I think I shall still give you an answer."

And, with head raised high, he hastened to escape behind the prison gates.

Everyone then began yelling again at the top of their lungs and making a row. Mocking exclamations were addressed to those who had made appeals.

"Ain't some of ya already been beaten into tinsel? Ya wants more?"

"Monsters! Lackeys!"

Sokoltsev passed by me.

"Ya don't unnerstand politics, fella," he was explaining to someone with his usual velvety laugh, "can it be said the prison here disgusts me? What if I don't see no grounds for a new order to take root in it? 'N' it seems to me that the captain, for example, has now lost his spirit!"

The day after this event a new party of forty men arrived in Shelai. The convoy leading it, after a full day's rest, was to take away with it the "returnees," that is, Bashurov and me and any other prisoners who'd completed their *katorga* terms. Only a certain Oska Nepomniashchii left the prison along with us; but another five or six men came out of the free command: Chinaman, who'd been poisoned the previous summer by Iukhorev's gang; the Tatar Ravilov, who'd been my student at one point; and one Pavel Nikolaev, a kindly old fellow who lived every summer in the mining hut in the capacity of watchman for the prisoners' gardens, and who served as the butt of constant jokes and jibes by not only the mare but Monakhov himself.

Thus commenced the last full day of my sojourn in Shelai Prison; this day came on a Sunday. The new party was ushered in with hardly a search, and that evening there began such desperate gambling as we had never had. It was said someone lost his regulation items… From early in the morning of the following day the prison was impossible to recognize: inside the wards, which were unimaginably filthy, there was a veritable Sodom, songs were being loudly sung, gutter talk was resounding; in places, drunks were appearing…

"Thus ended the 'model' Shelai Prison,' Shteinhart approached me with a smile in the corridor, "and now begins the reign of the herd… Let's go out to the yard, it's simply impossible to breathe in here. Isn't it odd, Ivan Nikolaevich, that this reversal has occurred just before you happen to be leaving? However, doesn't it make you especially glad you'll be free?"

In my soul, I was actually not so glad. As a storytelling convict accustomed to his chains, I was bitterly thinking I would be departing this prison where I'd lived and suffered for so long. It seemed to me that I was burying inside these walls my youth with its equally proud dreams, and also that the joy of freedom was coming to me too late, when fatigue and cracks had already appeared in my soul… Opposing this tardy—as it seemed to me—joyfulness was even an acknowledgement that I wanted to shun freedom and remain a comrade in prison!

I asked Shteinhart about his home, his mother, her age. He waved his hand hopelessly.

"She's already seventy-two, Ivan Nikolaevich, and evidently her powers have lately begun to quickly desert her. Do you know what strange fantasy popped into her head a little while ago? I fear that, to you, unfamiliar with Jewish religious thought, this fantasy may seem wild and probably even… *ugly*, but it's gone deep into my soul and causes me tears… So here it is… I somehow wrote to my old lady that from time to time prisoners receive money from the mining department for work in the mines. You remember you and I got some several times? I earned something around five rubles… Well, so in reference to this, she writes me: 'We can't manage to look after ourselves, and I know that I'm going to die soon; but when you earn fifteen rubles, get the money to me, so I can use it to buy my shroud. Then I won't be thinking that I'm anyone else's, and your hand will be closing my eyes…'"

Something caught in my throat; it felt like a current of cold air was running through my body…

Suddenly, from behind the hospital, there was a terrible din and uproar—it was either the simultaneous report of several rifle bullets or an earthquake. Having instinctively frozen, Shteinhart and I looked around in silence: "Can it be another escape?" With the same bewilderment and curiosity a crowd of prisoners ran through the yard to the spot in question. We hurried there as well, meeting up with Bashurov along the way.

The gates immediately opened, and through them, with rifles leveled, flew a dozen and a half Cossacks. A curious spectacle met our eyes: a corner where two of the garden's stone walls converged had, for some unknown reason, collapsed and a huge breach formed, through which you could not only see the expanse outside the prison but through which you could freely climb if you wished… Frightened Cossacks and guards appeared behind the wall as well. This was the same spot where Elk and his comrades had escaped not long earlier.

"Well, fellas, the much-vaunted Shelai Prison… They gonna make cow stocks now? Ha-ha-ha!" laughed prisoners for whom this was a real treat.

"But ain't ya heard? The guards' wives built that wall!"

"No, speak matter-a-factly, boys! A wall's a wall, but it up 'n' fell 'cause Elk 'n' Dasher landed on top of it. Them two stallions is gonna hafta support it!"

Meanwhile, beyond the wall, the Cossack commander was pacing back and forth and loudly shouting:

"For a thousand rubles this is what's called 'construction'?… It's an outrage!… Now what's to be done? Increase the guard till repairs are made?"

Six-Eyes was seen by no one. It was as if he was expressing by his absence utter contempt for anything that could still possibly happen.

"Official liquidation of the Six-Eyes *prigime*!" said Bashurov, summarizing the universal feeling. Chatting and laughing, we retired to the usual place for our strolls in front of the prison's façade.

Karpushka Lipatov appeared on the kitchen steps, cauldron in hand.

"Hur-rah, Ivan Mikolaich!" he shouted at the top of his lungs, noticing my comrades and me, "we're a-eatin' mutton!…"

He raised high his cauldron, from which a tempting steam poured forth in all directions. Cap jauntily cocked to the side, devilish smile all over his mug, red mustaches exultantly pointing skyward, feet comically widespread, Karpushka Lipatov, standing there in the bright sunlight, was at that moment picturesque! He seemed to us an embodied symbol of the new order rising on the shambles of the "model" Shelai Prison, and the cauldron of mutton in his hands seemed a victorious trophy for the herd, which had ascended to a sanctified place…

MARE ON THE ROAD[1]

In the twilight of a cold October day the Sretensk way-station opened its gates for the small returnee party marching to settlement from Nerchinsk's *katorga* mines. Such prisoners called themselves "freemen," and convoy guards did indeed treat them more leniently than penal laborers, not making them march in chains. Within the party there was, nonetheless, a chained man—a penal laborer who'd not yet completed his term and was transferring from one mine to another together with his family.

Admitting them with all their traveling baggage, knapsacks, bundles, and cauldrons into a dark narrow corridor of the prison where soggy kindling was weakly smoldering beneath a stove, the *gefreiter*[2] counted off the prisoners and silently pointed to a door to the right, behind which hid the ward assigned to us. By force of habit the prisoners immediately rushed in like madmen, jostling each other, shouting, cursing, and hurrying to occupy the best spots on the sleeping platforms, though such hastiness was not especially necessary since the place could have held twice as many people.

"Here, Oska Nepomniashchii, here!...," howled a stolid, red-bearded peasant, standing full height on a platform near a window and triumphantly waving his cap. "Here, comrades!"

A small, clumsy man, obviously a great phlegmatic by nature but at the same time also excited and exultant, hurried toward this summons with a heavy, hobbling gait. Another five young, strapping lads ran behind him to the window. All this group that obviously comprised a traveling fraternity and played a leading role in the party occupied several lengths of the best spots on the platforms. The worse places, farther away from the light, were occupied by the old men and families. The only shackled man in the party, a Jew of indeterminate age, thin, emaciated, with a wispy goatee and frightened, roving gray eyes, ended up being the nearest of all to the door. He was accompanied by his large family: his wife was a small, thin woman, completely sick and barely able to move her feet, though still bearing unmistakable signs of an original and attractive beauty. In his hands he held two little girls—one with curly hair red as fire, cheeks rosy from the frost, and cheerfully smiling in all directions, the other, by contrast, swarthy as a little Gypsy and looking around with large, dark, scared eyes apparently widened by her discoveries. Clutching her mother's skirts was a third little girl, older, with a serious, unchildlike, preoccupied little mask; a fourth was dragging a sack bigger than she. The father and a ten year-old boy who very much resembled him, with such a long, thin nose and gray eyes, were hauling the family's simple belongings.

"S'here, s'here, Enta!" the head of the family, piling their things on the empty platforms near the door, was saying in a characteristic lisp. "Abrashka, run quick to the door and see nothing's been forgotten."

Exhausted, Enta and the two girls settled on the platform. The redhead suddenly sprang up cheerfully and began helping her older sister arrange their things; the brunette, by contrast, continued to press herself against her mother.

"Well then, Entale? How're you feeling, my love?" the husband, gazing with tenderness and concern into his wife's eyes, asked in a hushed voice. The latter said nothing, and only nervously stroked the head of her favorite daughter pressing next to her.

"Now I'll make tea… It'll warm us up! Khasia, Brukhe, Surele! Help mother, I'm going to get water."

"Well, gentleman, but where'm I gonna settle in?" loudly boomed at that moment the last entry into the ward, an old man of handsome and honorable appearance with a rather witty expression in his intelligent, even cunning, gray eyes. "What, am I, an ol' man, to lie 'neath the platform?"

"Our complerments to Ol' Man Nikolaev! Please forgive us," the red-bearded peasant from the company of young Ivans at the window answered him.

"Come o'er to us, you ol' snake!" someone else shouted from there.

"Here you are already cussin'!… How's that, gentlemen? I'm bein' kindly, but you're diggin' deeper into such stupidities!"

"Well, don't come to *us* for a spot, Nikolaev," an unctuous voice could be heard from a different corner. This voice belonged to a middle-aged, stocky, pale peasant with an unpleasant expression in his oily eyes and a face that, despite constantly maintaining a sickly sweet smile, was entirely unkind.

"Over here, Pavel Nikolaevich, we're askin' you to come over with us, sweetie," insisted a woman sitting next to him, "you—you old men—it's quieter for you with a family."

"How true! Thank you for the invitation. We'll be neighbor-like."

"But the ol' devil's hustlin' up to a woman! The little idiot, she got no teeth!" red-beard called from the window. "Watch 'im there, Perminov. 'E's got sumpin' up his sleeve… We know these blessed old-timers… Seems like you can't be without a wife!"

During these words Perminov's whole face became cruelly distorted; he fell quiet, however, and merely threw a contemptuous look toward the window. Nikolaev, who'd already begun arranging his bags, also gave no reply to the ribbing; however, judging by the expression on his face, he was sooner flattered than stung by it.

The ward gradually began to take on a lived-in look. At Sretensk, returnee parties stayed no less than two weeks, and, frankly, everyone firmly and fundamentally settled in to live there for whole years. The most cherished bundles and bags were opened and their provisions poured out. At that time the ward was not even locked at night, and prisoners constantly scurried through the corridors and the station yard trying to better familiarize themselves with the place's rules and ways, and to get to know not just the other wards' prisoners but even more. It turned out that in the large neighboring barracks, locked during the arrival of the newcomers (who'd still not been officially admitted or searched), was a party of eighty men that arrived several days beforehand from Blagoveshchensk[3] and consisted of half penal laborers and half persons under investigation, who were to be tried in Irkutsk as part of a notorious case involving the robbery of gold from a caravan along the Amur. Standing at this ward's doors was a small group of the returnees who'd just arrived, speaking through the cracks with the locked-up "old men."

"Is the search strict?" inquired the jaded red-beard, whom comrades called "Chinaman."

"Might e'en say it's inhuman," the invisible voice of a man evidently no less jaded, worldly, and loquacious answered from behind the door. "Cap'm Petrovskii could easily pass for a gendarme. He'll e'en smack you on the cheek at the slightest prov'cation. But don't you worry, gentlemen. Near the stove, above our door, there's a hole stuffed with a rag. All of Adam or Eve's forbidden fruit you 'ave, pass it on to us to hold."

"But when'll they take us to be searched? T'day?"

"Not in any case. At Cap'm Petrovskii's, the rules 'ave been firmly 'stablished once 'n' for all. It'll be tomorrow at exactly eleven o'clock."

The invisible voice's offer was immediately taken into consideration, and Oska Nepomniashchii, who'd been sitting on the shoulders of the tall and sturdy Chinaman, lay on top of the stove to find the salutary hole. In his hands were several decks of cards and some other "forbidden fruit" that a prudent advisor had remembered.

"Soon as they search you tomorrow they'll unlock us. Then we'll get to know each other 'n', if'n you like, mix it up a little together!"

"It'd be our great pleasure. But does your party got cash?"

"It'll turn up. We're goin' to Irkutsk for that gold business, y'know. There's some rich Yids—we'll just hafta scratch 'em. Well, we'll see to it personally—this all can be decided 'n' arranged later. What was the route you yourselves was keepin' to?"

"We're from Shelai. Honestly, have you heard of it?"

"That's a warm spot, but nuthin's been heard. It's a grave, they say?"

"It's a damn holy cloister! Warden's the Father Superior, prisoners the monks. Ha-ha-ha!"

"So 'ave you got enough cash? You swindled a stack?"

"More or less, but we're bidin' our time," boasted Chinaman, winking at his comrades. "Howe'er, it's time to go home, boys. Seems they're gonna lock us in. Tomorrow then, lords!"

Indeed, walking down the corridor with his keys in the company of several soldiers was the *gefreiter*, and he ordered the waste tub dragged into the ward. The prisoners were counted and placed under lock and key.

"Mishter Efertor," the head of the Jewish family timidly appeared before him at this time, "your attention, please…"

"What is it?" the still beardless *gefreiter* haughtily asked, gazing somewhat aslant and looking him up and down.

"We have a woman… and many little girls… my daughters…"

"So what? No one's askin' 'bout 'em. Or is they askin' to go?"

"Regarding the waste tub, Mister Efertor, I ask for you to have Mister Okhficer not lock the ward, and put a bucket in the corridor."

"Ours is a submissive party, Mister Boss," someone from the corner interrupted the plea, "convoy guards was lenient with us ever'where."

"This is what's been heard 'bout 'em! Lock it, chaps! To your places, right now!" the *gefreiter* suddenly screamed.

The door banged shut, and the key growled in the lock.

"Whaddya want, Yid?" Chinaman grumbled. "Is it our brother's style to break up the manor-born on a whim? 'The woman, the woman'… Jus' what is she to ya—is she a little girl? I daresay she's bred enough little Yids, so's we ain't no worse'n you for all she knows."

And, as if to underscore these words, he suddenly went over to the waste tub…

Life followed its proper course. The ward's residents quickly separated into several groups. One consisted of the Jewish family; in another, Old Man Nikolaev was talking with the Perminov couple sheltering him; center and soul of a third, consisting of five or six young boys, was the garrulous Chinaman, a peasant no longer young, but now, upon the conclusion of his *katorga*, seemingly prepared to turn young and flourish once more. In the corner, on some opposite sleeping platforms, sat still another two men: one a tall and enfeebled old man, clearly bearing a brand on his forehead, a penal laborer of the Nicolaevan Era,[4] and only now having completed, after several escape attempts, his originally brief term of punishment. Largely deaf and having reached a condition of near infancy, he was irrepressible and always cheerful and was the party's universal favorite, a joker by profession. Not belonging to any one camp, he listened keenly to all conversations, regardless of his deafness, and occasionally added his comments. His name was Timofeev.

Alongside him, though having no connection to him, sat an unusually morose and quiet, shaggy peasant with a watery face and wild eyes gazing askance at everyone, constantly muttering something to himself. Prisoners called him "Bova"[5] and considered him insane.

Chinaman's group was especially cheery and boisterous. Chinaman chatted and boasted non-stop.

"He asks: 'How much cash ya got?' Well, you won't trick me, you ol' swindler! I daresay I know you, you family o' thieves. You're clever, but I'll wrap you Podolskians three times round my finger! I learnt under the Yids 'n' the Poles… I've known prison since sixty-seven. 'I got a fat pocket,' I answers, 'jus' see it don't burst.' Mark my word, boys, I ain't the Chinaman if'n tomorrow I don't strip naked this Rostov dandy 'n' all them Yids with 'im. Money! How could we have money if'n we're comin' from Shelai? Then again, we've noggins on our shoulders. Then again, our Father Superior learnt us!"

"Well, t'would indeed be a sin to beg o' you, Chinaman," he was suddenly addressed by Old Man Nikolaev, who, having listened from a distance to the interesting conversation, now moved from his spot over to the cheery group. In his white regulation blouse girdled with a thin belt beneath a round belly, with a wavy, graying beard like those that outline the faces of the saints, with rather curly hair carefully parted in the middle, with sly eyes and a bulbous nose on a handsome, wrinkled, but still rosy face, with arms gradually folding across his chest and a soft, melodious voice, he made at that moment the impression of a man utterly satisfied with the things of the world and with fate—that of his own and of people's—and also always ready to teach others and, moreover, to demonstrate his contentment and sagacious wisdom.

"T'would be a sin to beg o' you, Chinaman. But, I daresay you got a few rubles stashed away?"

"Akh, you ol' cur! 'N' 'ave you been feelin' for my stash?"

"You really don't think so? On what did you support Liubka at Shelai? Would such a dame 'ave really loved you without money?"

"'N' why wouldn't she? Ain't I got a mug? I'm forty-four, but if'n I find a calico shirt 'n' get an accordion in my hands it ain't just Liubka, brother, but another—I dunno who—what's might fall in love with me! Yer dumber'n dumb, you Novgorod tree stump! You can obverously judge for yerself, would a woman love *you* without money?"

"You stop with me. I've left them years ago. Nowadays, I pray to God."

"Pray to God?! No, you pray to the Devil, not to God. Jus' 'cause yer always readin' the Gospels 'n' singin' the Holy Psalms you decided I'm gonna scrape up some money for ya? Dearie, yer outstandin'!"

Chinaman's company began to guffaw ferociously. The old man, either from shame or self-satisfaction, screwed up his eyes and slightly grinned and shook his head reproachfully.

"He's talkin' nonsense… jus' nonsense… He's gone through such rubbish that his ears're stuffed up!"

"Rubbish? But tell us, didn't you rake in some money in the free command? I'll bet none of us 'ere has as much as you alone got squeezed inside yer fist. Yer jus' a snake. All us in our comp'ny pooled together ten rubles that we're allowin' ourselves to spend on vittles, 'n' you see we're eatin' mutton 'n' drinkin' fine black tea ever'day. But you—what'd you eat t'day? Tell us. Rusks with water? You didn't e'en drink hot tea?"

"Indeed, I find more taste in rusks than in your mutton. It only puts foolish notions in yer noggin."

"Ho-ho-ho! Foolish notions… Tut-tut, I daresay. Stay there, don't go, don't get mad. Here's what I'm gonna tell ya, Nikolaev, friendly-like. We ain't up to any overeatin'. We've spent a few years in more'n one prison. So here's some kindly advice for ya: set up a *maidan*! It's clear this party's sittin' on some wealth. You could make some good money out of 'em."

"Hm… You are a strange fellow, Chinaman! I got money? Where's my money?"

"Don't pretend, Nikolaev. Now, tell me honestly: how much ya got?"

"But, I dunno how much. There's the stipend I got yesserday… There's another twenty k'peks left o'er from my earlier stipends…"[6]

"Yer lyin'! There's more besides the stipend."

"Release me from you, Satan! Lord, forgive my trespasses…"

And Nikolaev, this time truly angry, walked away waving his hand to the accompaniment of the company's taunts and laughter. But Chinaman, donning after this a completely beneficent attitude and feeling himself the tsar of a small, albeit submissive, state, blew smugly on his saucer of tea and continued to hold forth:

"What, brother Oska Nepomniashchii? I daresay yer gonna split open clutchin' at yer sides like that: didja e'er dream of all this what's goin' on when you broke away from the Father Superior to go to settlement?"

"Better not to talk," the little man named Nepomniashchii wagged his beard.

"But I confess, brother, I thought this whole time you was comin' from Sakhalin. As ever'one knows, yer a dang'rous fellow, 'cause yer a *nepomniashchii*. Suddenly, there's an order fer ya—go settle in Kliuchevsk Canton!"

"They obverously forgot to look at yer paperwork," underscored the young, semi-Russified Tatar Ravilov, "but where could you go from Sakhalin? All the vagabonds'll be goin' there any day now."

"Tell us straight, lucky man! Kliuchevsk Canton! Are you really goin', Oska, to lend a hand to yer home village?"

"Quiet!" Nepomniashchii threateningly gestured, either seriously or jokingly.

"What! Still scared o' the Father Superior? You 'fraid o' bein' sent back? No, come off it, friend, you ain't goin' back now! Now, we're free as birds… Now, 'tween friends, you should explain yer history."

However, Nepomniashchii showed no intention of explaining his ancestry and maintained a stubborn silence.

"Keepin' a fat pocket, he's meanin', that's what!" Ravilov answered for him. "He's tough, the snake!"

"'N' yer nut's come loose in the last few months, oh, how loose!" continued Chinaman. "There he was, goin' round the prison yard, always think-thinkin' 'n' guessin': Sakhalin or *not* Sakhalin?…"

"I daresay you do think," Nepomniashchii curtly responded.

He was not talkative, and kept to himself, but his face nevertheless beamed rather joyfully during all this talk.

Fate had brought a dead man into God's world, and now fate had utterly buried the man! He remembered what a difficult, terrible nightmare the recent past had been. A quiet and humble little man, just married but unable, as he should have been, to enjoy family life, he ended up a soldier. An unwelcome hard existence in the ranks and barracks… Yearning for wife and home… A series of undeserved insults… Then this quiet, submissive soul suddenly erupted and earned itself a penal battalion. Rumors about the unbearably tough life in the battalion filled the young soldier's heart with mindless terror, and he made a daring escape from under strict guard with the danger of a watchman's bullet in his back, risking capture and return to a far more severe punishment than before. But, fortunately, fate protected him. He was arrested only after having gotten several hundred versts away from his place of escape: he called himself Osip Nepomniashchii and, having been taken for a fugitive laborer, was brought "down the street" past all of Nerchinsk *katorga*'s mines and was nowhere recognized and eventually sentenced, as a vagabond, to four years of provisional factory labor. All these four years he trembled day and night at the possibility of being removed to Sakhalin—when suddenly… instead of all this, as a place of settlement he was assigned to his own Palestinians! Now there were any possible terrible ends! If such a foe turned up as wanted to expose him, then the authorities would not take his time served into account: wouldn't anyone be in a fix if a fellow had several full years of bought-and-paid-for legitimate suffering under another name and status? In his own canton he would be able to get legal papers whenever he wanted, and with them travel to all four corners…

Yes, the terrible experience was over! His sleep might for the first time be as peaceful and serene as in the past. But, at times, newly troublesome thoughts darkened his soul: What of his wife? What would he learn about her? How would she perceive him? His heart clenched sweetly and at the same time moaned sickly from the most irreconcilable presentiments…

Old Man Nikolaev sat down again beside the Perminovs. The husband—an unusually loquacious and sentimental man—was full of all kinds of pieties.

"My brother you, I have never liked falseness. I can say I suffered and entered *katorga* for the truth. Yes! Wherever I went, commanders immediately singled me out. Otherwise, I'd be in Algacha right now. As soon as I'd show up with my wife I'd be kept in prison for just a day, because all my paperwork was in order… Now I'm going to the free command, and not for any dirty work but because I was assigned straight to the mining guards. 'Perminov,' they'd say, 'we can see you're an honest old man and haven't lost your conscience. So your place is there!'"

"Yer place should be in the burnin' fires, you damned Antip!…" suddenly groused the old man Timofeev, tattooed on his forehead (he called all other soldiers and any official "damned Antips"[7]). "You damned Antip!…" he repeated once more with unbelievable ferocity.

"You should shut up, you long-nosed crane," Perminov, face distorted, unexpectedly rooted him to the ground in one second, "God has already killed you, the tsar has marked you—so sit in the corner and chew your tobacco. If not, then lie where a horse can trample you."

"So you're the horse doin' the tramplin'? You're a damned Antip—that's what *you* are!"

"Crane! Marked man! Tobacco nose—that's who *you* are!"

"Who's insultin' our crane there?" Chinaman butted into the argument from the other side of the ward. "Ah! Is it Perminov? So it is, so it is, our own little crane! He's a damned Antip, the Antip!"

"He *is* a damned Antip!" the old man barked once more, suddenly stretching to his full soldier's height and glaring at his enemy menacingly.

But an instant after this he relaxed, settled down on the platform, and with a blissful expression on his face as if from acknowledgement of duty fulfilled, resumed as before chewing his tobacco, already paying no more attention to Perminov's grumbles and abuse. The latter, having cursed himself out and flung several more wicked looks at Timofeev and Chinaman, once more resumed his mellifluous discourse about his intellectual and moral virtues, now trying, however, to speak more quietly so that, except for Nikolaev and his wife, no one could hear him anymore. But his wife had long since fallen asleep; and Nikolaev was yawning. Evidently, he'd been listening more to what was happening beside him among the Jewish family than to his neighbor's words.

There the tea had already been consumed. The little children had calmed and lain down to sleep. You couldn't even tell how many there were beneath the sheepskins, cassocks, and various clothes. Little children's heads were all bunched together, like flowers in a garland. The two youngest daughters, red-haired Surele and black-haired Rukheniu, had lovingly wrapped their little arms around each other and were sleeping face to face. Only the father and mother were still not asleep, and lay quietly talking; in the wife's speech could sometimes be heard a jargon and particular words and expressions that denoted a Jewess from the western region, but her husband spoke only Russian and evidently sincerely regarded himself as completely "Rushim." He even liked to emphasize this by appropriately and inappropriately using purely Russian sayings and expressions, at times hilariously mangling them. Enta, frequently coughing and repeatedly putting a hand to her hollow, withered breasts, bemoaned her fate; her husband was trying to console her.

"No, you won't be bringing me to your free command, Moisha. Your term is big and I won't be alive long."

"How you talk, Enta! You don't know what you're saying! Can this really be said? You'll live longer than me. I really can't serve my family sitting in prison! What will happen to them without you? No, you're not gonna die, Enta, you'll see… You'll see, you'll live another hundred and twenty years! It wasn't for nothing we applied for Ze*l*entui—it's 'cause it's better there. The older children will be put in the shelter and learn a trade and to read. Abrashka, Khasia, and Brukhe will—presto—become peoples… In three or four years Khasia will be marriageable. Why are you shaking your head? I'm speaking the truth, Entale. A horse that's married won't eat you out of house and home—don't you know the Rushim saying? Where's the harm if our Khasia finds herself a *zooter*? A good man. I'm just a convict, but she's a free, honorable young woman and the *dofter* of an honorable mother. Abrashka is also a big chap now. He only has to learn a trade to be a cobbler or a smith or a turner. He's got his father's hands—and he could turn out to be a good earner. What do you say?"

"I'm saying I'll never live in freedom with you!"

"Why do you talk like this? Why won't you live, Enta? In Ze*l*entui we'll be nearer the leadership. We'll apply… When I see the commandant, I'll beg him on my knees. He refuses, goes to another ward, then I'll run there and get on my knees. He goes to a third, I'll go to the third… He comes another day, and once again I'll beg him that other day: 'Your Excellency! My sick wife is smaller than a child's little mill sack. I'm an honest craftsman. I want to work with my hands to provide for my family. Let me into the free command!' So what do you think, Enta? *I* think the commandant will up and decide to let me."

"Very well, he'll let you; but what if you're ordered into the isolator?"

"But what are you on about, Enta? I'm coming from one direction, but you're coming from the other… I'm sorry, but you're more… Khasia, Brukhe, Surele, Abrashka, Rukheniu—they'll all be bowing and shouting… You'll see, I'll pester him into listening, and he'll say: 'Ah, what a matter indeed! Let Moisha Borukhovich into the free command.' You'll see, Enta: if you don't see him saying so, then I'm not Moisha. Well, and then we'll be living! You'll see, Enta, how we'll be living! I'll be able to do whatever job. You'll see I won't look like a sick horse. I won't gosh-darn put up with less than hard work… My hands'll earn money so fast… You'll go around as my baroness. If I'm lying, don't let me in my spot, Enta: yer gonna be a baroness!…"

"What am I hearin' you go on about, Vorokhovich?" a voice near the sleeping platform suddenly blurted out unexpectedly.

Enta and Moisha suddenly jumped from their spots in fear. But they quickly relaxed as soon as they recognized Old Man Nikolaev's kindly face in the weak glow of the tallow candle illuminating the ward.

During the march he alone out of the entire party was respected. Regardless of his sharp tongue and tendency to intrude on others' business, the old man made the impression of a kind soul and inspired trust.

"Shettle down here, old man," Moisha looked at him, "be our guest. My Enta here is grieving that I'm far from being in the free command, but I'm telling her that no one but God knows. Isn't that right, old man, no one but God knows? God sent us here to *katorga*, and he may free us from here."

"She's way too skinny. I'm-a lookin'—what's keepin' her soul together? She dies—who's gonna get that horde o' kids? Well, you Yids are productive, 'tis truly said you're productive!"

"Once again, there is a God, old man. A Zid is a human being, y'know. What do you think: *is* a Zid a human being?"

"A human bein's a human bein'. Only, why'd you crucify Christ? That's why He's pushin' you all o'er the world!"

"But what's he punishing you for, if you're not a Zid?"

"Us? For our sins… Oh-oh-oh! Our terrible sins! Pity me, Vorokhovich. I see you're a simple fellow, without cunnin'. Him there, he's a Russian, one of us Orthodox" (Nikolaev motioned with his beard toward the cheerfully chattering Chinaman), "but so what? He'll sell 'n' buy ya for a copper kopek. But why'd you go about gettin' into *katorga* with your *family*?"

"God sees what for grandpa, what for. They mixed me up with someone else. Out of everyone—'it's that Zid.' A church in our village was robbed. Who'd they decide did it? The Zid, of course. My place was searched and some kind of church shawl was found, it was summoned out of thin air… Obviously, the Devil himself ruined us! To this day, Enta and I don't know how it ended up with us. But in the meantime—that was the evidence! So I got seventeen years' *katorga*."

"A pity for you, if'n you ain't lyin'. Yes! Lissen to one or to all of us, seems no one turns out to be guilty… Perminov o'er there says as well he came 'cause o' the truth… But, go on! 'Tis clear to the eye he either raped a girl or was runnin' a bandits' den."

"But you, grandpa, what'd you end up here for?"

"Me-uh?… Let's s'pose I'm-a really innocent… But who'd believe this? Who'd believe? Court didn't believe, so why would *you* believe any ol' thing? That's why I don't like talkin' 'bout the bad. Nowadays, 'tis better to look ahead. If'n later don't come, will you still blame *katorga*?"

"It's very simple," underscored Borukhovich, who also loved to philosophize at times. "A truthful Rushim saying goes: 'lost clothes are what we have but do not hold!'…"

Having conversed in such manner for half an hour, Nikolaev, yawning widely and crossing his mouth and noticing that the talking was beginning to quiet in all corners, finally went to his own spot as well. There, he spread a narrow felt mattress on the platform, found room for a sack at the head of his bed, and then, having prayed loudly on his knees and banged his forehead several times on the station's filthy floor, stretched out beneath his prisoner's jacket, pulling it over his head peasant-fashion. But sleep did not come to him for a long time.

"O Lord, Lord, will you forgive our weakness?" pondered the old man in genuine distress. "Weren't enough that the spirit was aware of its guilt from the first, but so it goes, so it will until the end. This Yid here—he must be lyin' as well. He robbed this church without a second thought, 'tis likely he was hardly scared. Oh-ho-ho! He wants any of ours' riches most of all, 'n' we're here on the ground readyin' ourselves for Heaven or the Inferno. Well, ain't there a Hell? It'll take me, then. I was livin' well, drinkin' a bit, dressin' meself like the good people, was respected by others, was obeyed by me children—'n' suddenly ka-boom! What an abyss I got myself into! Head shaved for several years, bracelets on my ankles, 'appened to live 'mongst folk who see 'n' hear nuthin'... Now, let's s'pose all that's past 'n' I'se goin' free... Well, but ever'thin' sure won't be what it was! I'll ne'er see my birthplace, I'll die in humiliation in a foreign land, cursed 'n' forgot by me children... Yes. Where'll I get a crust o' bread in my old age? If there's a bit o' money at my waist or hidden in my boots, then there'll be some hope... But these various throats 'n' snorters, like Chinaman, is callin' me an Asmodei. But what if you was luggin' around sixty-three years yerself—would ya be singin' then? That Chinaman's a crank: 'Set up a *maidan*,' he says. 'The party,' says he, 'is full o' money.' Well, 'n' jus' where am I, an ol' man, s'posed to carry on this business? You'll jus' ruin yerself—nuthin' more. Granted, I can read 'n' my sight's still clear. Ain't seein' anythin' specially strange: a supply o' several decks of cards, that's indeed a sign—certainly, at night the party gambles as much as your percentage o' fate lets you. No, indeed! Phooey-phooey, forgive me, Lord! Let 'em set 'emselves up, me, I think it's a sin!..."

The day after the new party was processed both barracks were opened and prisoners allowed to mix together in their wards as they pleased. Instantly, a whole crowd of those who did not have spots on the sleeping platforms surged from the large ward into the small and made everywhere as crowded as way-stations usually are. On the floor and even beneath the platforms—everywhere, folks jostled each other. The din became unimaginable. *Makhorka* smoke and steam from people's breath (regardless of the overpopulation, it was quite cold) suffused the atmosphere from floor to ceiling. The large party that arrived on the steamer from Blagoveshchensk was of the most various and variable composition: in it were simple passengers returning home via the way-stations, and those sentenced to *katorga* for different reasons now going to mines; and then there were the twenty men who were to be sentenced in Irkutsk. The latter group, consisting of rich and brazen people, clearly lorded it over the party. The eloquent speaker whom the returnees met the day before through a chink in the door, Krasnoperov by name, turned out to be a thirty year-old gentleman of short height with a very pale face and bulging brown eyes; he was dressed in a gray jacket with a waistcoat on which he flaunted a gold chain without a watch. He, too, was going to be sentenced for the case of the caravan robbery, and declared with obvious pride that he was facing the noose...

Behind their backs he cursed as worthless heathens his five or six comrades, who were no less proudly prepared for their fate. Among other things, Krasnoperov had brought with him a small boy of seven, very spirited and insouciant, who had one hand stuffed in his trousers pocket but was constantly shelling pine nuts with the other.

"Here's our Rinaldo-Rinaldini,[8] our gang's ataman!" our acquaintance loudly introduced the boy to Nikolaev, Chinaman, and the rest.

The boy looked brazenly and self-assuredly at everyone, moving his inquisitive gray eyes from one face to the next, and then sat down like a grown-up on the platform.

"Whose is he? He yer son, or what?" Nikolaev inquired.

"No, he's son o' the famous Jew Pento. You 'member several years ago he was hanged in Chita with the merchant Alekseev for robbin' the mail? Now his mother's gone with another, a Jew as well, who's goin' to Irkutsk to be sentenced in our case."

"But shouldn't *they* be takin' care of 'im?"

"They should, that's so. What surprisin' luck for a youngster, eh? To have two fathers both sent to the gallows! But you prob'ly wouldn't believe what a mature boy he is. Not yet seven—'n' he understands ever'thin' like an adult. So we call him the ataman of our gang!"

"A good beatin' 'n' he wouldn't be called that," Nikolaev enunciated with indignation.

"Ha-ha-ha! Misha, ya hear what grandpa's sayin' 'bout you?"

"Jus' try," snapped the gang's ataman, glaring impudently at grandpa and spitting shells out of his mouth. "Ya playin' cards t'day?" he then inquired of his patron.

But the latter had already gone over to Chinaman, having managed to establish a close relationship with him, and was now carrying on some sort of secret conversation.

After several minutes they approached Nikolaev as a pair.

"Well, Pavel Nikolaev! Yesserday I didn't advise you to set up a *maidan* outta spite. Jus' lissen to what the man says."

"Yes, I can tell you this business is jus' right. Keep in view that the Jew Levenshtein is aimin' for this prize. From this, you can unnerstand what a good little job it is."

"Well, let 'im set it up. Whatzit to me?… My view, that's a Tatar's job! I don't wanna take anyone's bread; we're all here without father 'n' mother, so fend fer yerself."

"That's not the point, ol' man. For us, as Russians, it's an offense if the Yids get hold o'er the whole party. You can see how much they got. It's gettin' bad."

"No one can offend me. I get my daily stipend—that's fine. Well, but if'n you wanna earn so much, then you should set up a *maidan* fer yerselves."

"You're a brainless idiot, Nikolaev, a true idiot! If'n we had money, then why would we be comin' to you? I wanna be good to ya, like a fellow countryman. All them years together in Shelai 'n' I never sinned 'gainst ya, ya ol' devil, so stand up for us!"

"'N' what'm I s'posed ta stand up with? Where do I buy what I need to set up a *maidan*? Don't I gotta pay fer it?"

"It's a trifle. Get 'em started for two rubles. Well, it could go up to six."

"So, a lotta needed capital! I don't got such money. 'N' if'n I did, I wouldn't pay it. Here you're jus' sayin' how rich your party is, 'n' lookie-now what some senators 'ave lain down nexta me… I daresay that is indeed a coonskin coat? Very, very costly, I'm a-thinkin'!"

"Well, if you please, it coulda been an honor. I'll come up with the money myself. I jus' didn't wanna dirty my hands with this business. All the same, I will not give in, won't give in for nuthin', to that Yid Levenshtein."

The newfound friends walked away from the old man, having however sown within him a nettlesome idea. Folding his arms across his chest, he tottered into the big ward to meander among folks, listen to conversations, and observe new faces.

The impression made on him by this stroll was evidently pleasant. Folks had actually seemed wealthy. During the rest of the day he approached Chinaman several times to talk about the *maidan*.

"Yer sayin', Chinaman, a *maidan*, as they say… I'm old, how I'm gonna manage such a business…"

"But whaddya gotta manage? Trade, buy—that's it. 'Member, you ol' blockhead, that no one aroun' ya in the whole party's gonna be dealin'! Trust me, yer gonna be the only dealer for what yer sellin'. 'N' cards? Jus' think whatta game there'll be. I'll have a hand to play ahead o' time, brother… That's the point, idiot. You'll march with us two months up to Verkhneudinsk 'n' pay us all six rubles."

"'Tis only six bein' said now, but I know that'll go up to ten."

"Well, it could indeed go to ten. Loosen up yer purse strings, snake."

"I don't got none o' that kinda money, I'm tellin' ya—none. 'N' here's another thing: I gotta find a comrade, an assistant."

"So find one."

"Who *can* ya find? A conscientious man is necessary. If'n it were Oska Nepomniashchii, I'd lose me grub. You'd be much better, Chinaman. I know yer a scoundrel 'n' a crook; well, but I know you wouldn't harm me, an ol' man…"

"That's obverous… Start buyin'!"

"No, God damn them 'n' the *maidan*… No, no! Get away from me, temptin' Satan! King David 'n' his gentleness, deliver me!"

"Blinded agin… Damn you, yer soul, 'n' yer David! Phoeey! Git far 'way from me, ya demon, ya soulless Asmodei! The hell with yer money, ya can choke on it, ya stinkin' mutt!"

"Such nonsense yer talkin'! Such nonsense yer singin'!" Nikolaev reproachfully shook his head, and slowly walked away once more.

Any business has its costs. The Perminovs were carrying on quite exclusively and oddly. Both were evidently worrying about something, because they were arguing about something, though this was all on the quiet and the dirty laundry hadn't left the hut. The husband was whisperingly reproving his wife. Finally, she couldn't restrain herself and broke down in tears.

"It's always like this, always… What'd I do wrong now? A man I know showed up, so why not talk? Why not invite him to tea? You yourself found some friends, 'n' you also spent a whole hour sittin' in that barracks—so I'm nuthin'."

Upset, she kept raising her voice, attracting everyone's attention.

"Shush!" her husband tried to stop her with an irate whisper, shaking all over from pent-up rage and seeming to swallow her with his eyes.

This family scene could not escape Chinaman's attention.

"Bah! Look, boys, at 'im shoutin' from the other end o' the ward—Perminov's jealous, natur'ly, of his wife again. Whatsa matter with our old holy man? A problem with the woman, 'n' how! He puts their sacks round 'em at night, as if someone couldn't manage to creep under 'em, but come daytime, permit me to say, 'e ain't missin' one. Ah, little woman! Spit on 'im, the ol' fogey. There's youngsters here a bit better'n him. She shoulda chose me to love."

"That is indeed what he's jealous of, little uncle… Livin' ain't gettin' easy," responded the little woman, beside herself. "He's shamed hisself in front o' people! *Now* someone's hankerin' for me. Fifty-two years, y'know…"

"You're a wolf in sheep's skin, a wolf," her husband, eyes gleaming wickedly, screamed at her, "I'll thrash you to death, to death, then you'll know how an honest woman should behave!"

"But why ain't I behavin' right?"

"'Cause you're ready to be spun by any passing cock!"

"Where'm I bein' spun by a cock?"

"You know where… You stinker!"

Following these words there was the sound of a loud slap. The woman began crying loudly. The whole ward, as one man, took up arms against such arbitrariness (solely because, of course, everyone was united in their hatred of Perminov); Chinaman even gave an entire speech in defense of humanitarianism in general and feminine weakness in particular and nearly came to blows with Perminov. Finally, the latter, spitting heartily, left for the neighboring ward. His wife continued to sit and cry for a long time. Old Man Nikolaev approached her with questions. Her face, despite the fifty-two years she'd just announced about, was still quite young-looking and pretty. Evidently, there had been a time when she knew a better life. In her heart, this meek and ravaged heart, there must have been a hard-boiled fury and resentment: glancing continually at the door, she told Nikolaev in a rapid undertone all about her life.

"Don't lissen, grandpa, to what he tells you 'bout my honesty. He was a brigand, a real brigand! 'N' the more he's nailed me—true, I myself ain't makin' sense—he's neither handsome, nor rich, nor reasonable… He's a stub-of-a-stump! He's my second, y'know. I got an already grown-up daughter from my first husband. I pity Sashenka most of all. What's become of her now, my little dove? Whatta good little one she was, if you'd seen her, delicate, tender, like a lady… Can you believe: he coveted her as well… made threats… 'n' weren't ashamed 'fore me!"

"But why didn't ya stop him from bein' such a barbarian?"

"For sure, I ain't free, y'know. I been deprived o' my rights as well, y'know. He dragged me into them deals of his… That's why I didn't report him 'n' covered up for him… For this, I got convicted. Now, it's said, the amnesty should apply to me, but I don't know the actual how 'n' way this notion applies. He himself should know, but he don't tell me 'n' won't let me ask people."

"What, ya mean 'e's 'oldin' ya back with force?"

"With threats, grandpa… All I want is to confer with good people if it's better to leave, but it's absolutely impossible—he's watchin' me. 'N' y'know what else he wants, is that I summon Sashenka to us!"

But then the speaker suddenly bit her tongue because Perminov once again appeared at the door, gazing suspiciously at Nikolaev, who was sitting beside his wife, red-faced and clearly upset.

"I'm askin' grandpa here to write a little letter to Sashenka," she hurriedly explained to her husband with a forced, ingratiating smile.

Perminov immediately assumed his usual thoughtful aspect and began asking Nikolaev to compose a letter and not put it on the shelf. The old man could not force himself to speak and, having laid out a sheet of gray paper, a quill and ink, and armed himself with an enormous pair of antique spectacles from a tortoise-shell case, he slowly began the composition. First, there followed the usual greetings to all relatives and friends, then there was the usual: "I am sending you, my beloved daughter Sashenka, my motherly blessing, which may avail you until the burial plaque." Further on, the advantages of life in Transbaikal District were described in vivid, charming strokes and, in conclusion, Sashenka was advised to abandon her thankless homeland and join her loving parents in a new, more fortuitous life.

The old woman shed tears the entire time the letter was being written, though did not dare say anything against what her husband was dictating. His green eyes apparently weakened any resolve she might have had to oppose him. And Nikolaev had no doubt that her dreams of leaving this man would thus always remain lost, unrealized dreams…

After evening roll call and the corridor was locked, the wards were kept open for a time because someone was shouting in a stentorian voice for everyone to gather in one place to choose the collective's administrators. Prisoners immediately flowed into the large ward, some moving out of communitarian instincts, others out of simple curiosity. In the smaller ward remained only the Borukhoviches, the Perminovs, and the madman Bova, sitting immovably in his corner in his cap and sheepskin, twisting some rope and muttering various incantations. Even the seventy-six-year-old Timofeev, with his long tobacco nose and tattoo on his wrinkled forehead, dragged himself along with the rest. But ahead of everyone moved with unhurried steps Old Man Nikolaev, in his white shirt belted below the waist, with hands folded across his chest and a rather sarcastic smile.

"Well, 'ave ya decided, Asmodei?" a bustling Chinaman clapped him on the shoulder and, not waiting for an answer, ran ahead to find Krasnoperov. But Krasnoperov had already made himself known. Having clambered on top of the sleeping platform, he was shouting to the assembled throng:

"We can't waste time, gentlemen! With regard to a headman, we all here may safely assure the returnee party that no better headman can be wished for than our own Svistunov. Indeed, there's no one else to choose."

"Whaddya mean no one? We could choose Sokolov, if'n not Ivanov," someone's voice came from the back.

"What's bein' said there? Stick with Svistunov! The returnee party's agreed!" Chinaman, who had already reached an understanding with Svistunov, shouted over him.

"Svistunov! Svistunov!"

"Sokolov!"

"Well, so that means we're keepin' Svistunov, gentlemen," Krasnoperov concluded, as if he'd not heard the other voices. "There now remains the most important matter—the concession for the *maidan*. Otherwise, we'll all be on the road sittin' with no tea, sugar, or tobacco. How much will you pay for the *maidan*, ol' men?"

Everyone was silent.

"I myself am ready to pay three rubles," Krasnoperov then announced.

"Three rubles! Who'll give more?" shouted the headman Svistunov—a peasant of athletic build with roseate swollen cheeks and a long, ginger-colored mustache—suddenly appearing on the same platform and grabbing the reins of government.

"I'll pay four rubles," a handsome brunet with smoothly shaven cheeks, dressed in a black frock-coat and gray checkered trousers, called out. Evidently, this was the Jew Levenshtein, about whom Krasnoperov had warned.

"I hear four! Who'll give more?"

Krasnoperov offered six rubles, Levenshtein eight. After that, Krasnoperov fell silent. Svistunov was about to declare that the *maidan* would go to Levenshtein, when suddenly from the other side of the crowd came a not loud and seemingly rather hoarse voice that made everyone turn:

"I'll add fifty k'peks."

"Bah! Countryman? Is that you?" a joyous Chinaman said in surprise. "Don't let the Yid git us, brother, don't let 'im!"

Everyone burst out laughing and pushed Nikolaev forward to the platform, where the contest continued.

"I'll add fifty k'peks," he repeated once more, clearing his throat and brazenly looking at his opponent with penetrating gray eyes.

"I'll pay ten rubles," announced Levenshtein.

"I'll add fifty k'peks," Nikolaev calmly called out.

"Twelve rubles!"

"Twelve 'n' a half…"

"Fourteen."

"Fourteen 'n' a half…"

"Oho-ho! *Very* good, ol' man. He ain't lettin' 'im! He ain't scared!"

"Aye, yes, Pavel Nikolaev. Help us Shelaians!"

"I surely won't let 'im… What was ya thinkin'?" Having assumed a dignified air and turning grandly to the crowd, Nikolaev elicited from it a burst of sympathetic laughter.

"That means there's fourteen 'n' a half. Anyone pay more?"

Levenshtein was conferring with a cabal of comrades. Krasnoperov appeared beside them and also whispered something to him.

"Fourteen 'n' a half for the second time… Who'll pay more?"

"Sixteen rubles," said Levenshtein.

"Sixteen 'n' a half," responded Nikolaev, like an echo.

He was red as a boiled crab from excitement, but a hard determination was written on his face. Chinaman was in utter rapture and kept sending him loud approvals.

"Don't be scared, good friend, roll o'er 'im! *Roll* o'er 'im!"

"But what're ya thinkin'? I ain't gittin' scared!" the worked-up old timer boasted. "I'll push straight on to a hunnerd."

The throng greeted these words with more joy-filled guffaws.

"Ain't no old-timer, but a straight-on double-dealer!"

However, one of the prudent ones approached and kindly warned that the *maidan* was hardly worth such money.

"I *said*: I'm pushin' to a hunnerd!" Nikolaev, without listening, shouted and impatiently waved his hand.

Levenshtein looked at him inquiringly.

"Twenty rubles," he grandiloquently proclaimed.

"Twenty 'n' a half," Nikolaev delivered his usual repost, pushing the crowd's joy into hysterics.

Levenshtein conceded… Svistunov pounded a fist on the platform.

"*Maidan*'s yours, ol' man! Pay half the money right now."

There wasn't time to complete the sale of the *maidan* because the players began tidying up. They gathered in the smaller ward, where along one of the walls there seemed the only spot in the entire station free from the convoy command's prying eyes. Participating were Chinaman and Krasnoperov and the Jew Levenshtein, having just tried to best Nikolaev for the *maidan*, and many other lovers of strong sensations. A stirrup was already standing at his post and the only hold-up was for the *maidanshchik*, who was obliged to provide cards and candles and to oversee the gambling. Nikolaev was impossible to recognize. The probity, stolidity, and serene contentment that had until recently so well distinguished him from the prison herd had disappeared. Inexperienced, utterly confused, drenched in sweat, and bright red, he comically threw himself from side to side, pitiful and helpless as a wet chicken, not knowing what to do or how to begin. The mare mocked and cut him down pitilessly. He finally succeeded in recruiting as his assistant the Tatar Ravilov, who had realized a profit at gambling and agreed to hire himself out for a certain fee. A rug was spread on the floor, a tallow candle lighted, and cards put down. Ravilov wended among the gamblers, intent on writing down the number of players in the party from whom the *maidan* would receive an income of ten percent. Nikolaev, amusing the gathered throng of curiosity seekers, walked around and kept anxiously slapping himself on the thigh and saying:

"Whatta mess I gotten meself into! This darn fool of an ol' man should be thrashed! I coulda been lyin' on my side in the clover without a care, but no! I hadda take up such a burden on my shoulders. Well, ain't it a wonder, good people, eh? 'N' now twenty 'n' a half's been thrown away, eh?"

"Ya done lost yer head, ol' man!" prisoners mocked him. "Wait a bit more, 'n' you'll be eatin' Cap'm Petrovskii's boot scraps!"

"Whaddya mean?!"

But he had hardly been able to utter this question, filled with the most genuine but at the same time comical horror, when something unusual happened. Something somewhere suddenly jangled in the distance, as if a door bolt had been quickly pulled; hearing the sound, they quickly jumped to their feet, everywhere the flames were extinguished, and the prisoners, even those who weren't guilty, flung themselves onto platforms, darted under their cassocks, and feigned sleep. But soldiers with their rifles leveled were already running down the corridor, the orderly's lantern had been lit, and someone was urgently screaming:

"Beat 'em, the scoundrels! I'll swear they got cards!"

Then they overtook someone in the corridor: there was the sound of a slap on a face and the knock of a rifle-butt, followed by a squealing exactly like that of a hunted hare caught between teeth.

"Mercy, schave me!… Your Excellency, I'm not… Let me go in peace!"

"Well, they've caught our Yid Vorokhovich," Chinaman muttered from beneath his cassock, "—the hell with 'im!"

A woman's hysterical scream prolonged this scene: this was the sick Enta rushing to help her ill-starred husband. She was answered by the crying of waking babes.

"You the stirrup? You protectin' gamblers?" the officer shouted, stamping his feet.

"Not at all, Your Honor, I'm honesht Jew, I was going do my biznish in the night tub."

"He's my husband, Your Honor… We have a big family… We're poor Jews…"

"But if so, there's no loafin' about at night. Hurry to the platforms this very instant."

The angry captain's small, unprepossessing figure, in the company of an entire horde of soldiers armed with rifles and lanterns, appeared in the ward. He slowly walked around it in a circle, gazing fixedly at the figures of prisoners lying on the platforms as motionless as corpses.

"Suddenly ever'one's asleep," he turned with irony to the soldiers. "Next time anyone's caught bein' a stirrup or with cards, you're goin' to the bathhouse."

And with these enigmatic words, Captain Petrovskii proceeded to the other ward. Four hours later, a sliding bolt sounded again, and finally everything was silent.

Awakening from their temporary torpor, the prisoners began little-by-little to emerge from their burrows. There was the sound of conversations, muted and quiet at first, then mocking and jovial.

"Damned Antips!" bellowed Zhuravl.

Chinaman laughed at the beaten Borukhovich.

"What, brother Moisha? I daresay yer side's hurtin', eh?"

"That's what must happen to demons… they get it good!"

"Ha-ha-ha! Whattabout that cap'm? Brother, 'e don't give a hang 'bout thrashin' 'n' beatin' a fallen one. Did you beg pardon?"

"You should beg… But what did he say about the bathhouse?"

"A pity you wasn't brought there. You should be cleansed with some Berëzov twigs till yer Jewess 'n' Jew-kids couldn't know ya… There also shouldn't be a thing standin' in the way of our stirrup gittin' a beatin'. Don't gape, you scoundrel, or don't ya want yer money?"

"Of course I do."

"But where's our *maidanshchik*, boys? Honestly, he weren't brought to the bathhouse, was 'e?"

"Yes, nuthin' worse'n the bathhouse, brother!" the voice of Nikolaev, for whom there was a burst of laughter in the ward, called from beneath his cassock. "'Twas a very-very narrow 'scape… 'ere's life for ya, ya Kolyvansk birch-box! Ya know what, Chinaman? Buy my *maidan*, honest word, buy it. I'll sell it fer fifteen coins, gosh darnit."

"A fool's been found. Ya think that ol' simpleton Levenshtein honestly wanted ta buy it? We jus' teased 'n' 'cited you like an Indian rooster on purpose, ya snake."

"Oy?"

"'Oy' is damn right. See, fer half a year ya didn't pull out yer twenty rubles so strict-like. What does that make of a returnee party? There's only one name for when twenty of our good men go straight to the pegs."

"So what'm I gonna do nowsie? Whatta kasha, whatta fix, what pitch darkness I'm in! Ain't you ashamed, li'l Chinaman. Mockin' yer ol' comrade? Why'd ya entice me? What harm did I do ya?"

"Don't fear a thing, old timer. Ever'thin' can still turn out right. No harm in gittin' beat once or twice. Look at Vorokhovich: e'en though 'e's a Yid, 'e's a good fellow. 'E was bleatin' like a sheep-bein'-shaved, but now 'e's jokin' with us. I love such people. C'mon, boys, let's get back to work. Hey, *maidanshchik*, give us the cards 'n' a candle!"

"Nope, e'en if ya murder me, I ain't budgin' from this spot."

"You're committed ta lyin', ol' man. We can make ya!"

But the tall Ravilov had already arisen as if from beneath the ground to run things. Hanging a cassock over the window to cut the light from the yard, he again spread out the rug, laid a deck of cards on it, and lit a candle. Gamblers once more appeared out of nowhere.

Old Man Nikolaev sat on the platform scratching the back of his head, muttering on and on and shaking his head in disapproval of himself.

The man had lived entire years as a skinflint—and he'd suddenly lost control and torn himself apart!... That such a mistake had happened to him was something marvelous, as if not to be believed...

On a gray, autumnal day the families' party was dragging itself in a long procession along the route from Sretensk to Zerentui Mountain. A distance of twenty to thirty versts separating one way-station from another is easily accomplished in four or five hours by the most bedraggled nag, yet, setting off at dawn, they would reach their destination only at twilight.

In front, as usual, clanked the fetters of the prisoners marching on foot—the healthier and younger members of the party, or those habituated to walking or wandering and who could not relax no matter their age. They marched "sharply," trying to keep up with the convoy soldiers; but from behind moved tortoise-like the long procession of two-wheeled wagons crammed with women, children, the weak, and the crippled. The monotonous, slow horror that seemed to be pulling the traffic forward presented something inexpressibly grim and pathetic!

And so it was, day after day, for a week, a month, and—for some—whole years! Flying past were lively troikas, a string of carts, walking people, but the party—sluggishly, tiredly, sleepily—was most certainly not hurrying... However, this is not completely true: a party does indeed still hurry itself. "The mare is always hurrying"—prisoners say of themselves with irony; but as a result of this hurrying their serious activity comes to naught: in a single day they may proceed no further than one stop, and are obliged to spend every third day in a way-station "to rest."[9] And where, in essence, are they hurrying to? Most certainly not to the Motherland, they're going to *katorga*...

The present is now not a returnee, but a transferee, party, and of all those we've met there is now in it only Moisha Borukhovich. All others from Sretensk left in the direction of Chita or were put on trial or were released to the countryside. Moisha is walking in the party's very first row, bitterly cursing his heavy chains. He seems to have gotten thinner and more emaciated; his wedge-shaped beard appears to have become still sharper, his eyes more haunted and restless, and the expression on his face has taken on an entirely new quality—not that of bitter determination but of utter despair. Is it any wonder? Two weeks ago, all in that same Sretensk, Enta, his faithful wife, mother of his large brood, sole supporter and buttress of all his hopes, plans, and dreams, died... What is there in life for him now? What matters the free command to him? Isn't it all the same, being in prison and how long you'll live? The administration is taking the babes to the shelter, of course, but as for Moisha... Who needs him now? What in the whole wide world interests or is needed by him now?

Nonetheless, from time to time he runs from the party's front rows and waits along the road for the much-lagging wagons to catch up. He is utterly intoxicated by the scent of one of the very crowded carts. Five children, one smaller than the next, wrapped in sheepskins, cassocks, and all sorts of rags, hugging each other closely, hail their father with loud cries, having once again been given to see his abject thin-as-a-rake figure.

"Aren't you ashamed of yourself, Abrashka, sitting along the way in the trouble?"[10] Moisha severely castigates his first-born and future progenitor of the Borukhovich name. "I'll lash you so you move quicker than my Eniseisk runner. Get down!"

Abrashka obediently climbs from the cart and skips ahead, yielding his spot to his exhausted father. Moisha climbs grandly into the wagon, takes his favorite, Rukheniu, into his lap, and with his daughters begins a conversation indistinguishable from that he'd had with them yesterday and the day before that and which would, in all probability, be carried on tomorrow, God willing him life and good health.

"Well, sthen, children? Is it hard to live without momma? You say: 'Oh, hard, hard... We're probably done for!' Well, done for or not, we're seeing much grief. You, Khasia, have to be master and momma for all of us. You're already a young woman. Now you can't get married and have your own children, and you'll do the sewing, mending, cooking, and wiping of snot for us. Yes. Momma was such a womensch, such a womensch... No, Khasia, no Brukhe, you never were and never in this world will be more than such a womensch! I'm speaking the truth. And so you all must try to be just like her."

"But are we getting to the way-station soon, papa?" asks the spry redhead Surele.

"Soon, soon, dofter. The way-station's said to be there, around that hill."

"But there's another way-station tomorrow?"

"Tomorrow another way-station."

"And what then?"

"Then? There's a day off."

"But after the day off?"

"Well... then another way-station."

"And what then?"

"Then? You're very quick, Surka… Then you'll see for yourself. As soon as we get to Zelentui Mountain, all you tchildren will be taken to the shelter. It's such a good home, so good, that you'll never see another so… You'll wear little clean aprons, little white bonnets. There'll be lots of other boys and girls there with you. It'll be cheerful and very nice. Comfy and warm. Only, you must study hard and obey the administration."

"But what will we be fed there?"

"You'll be fed very well. Bread and beef and cabbish soup and such sthings."

"And milk, too?"

"Well, milk on holidays."

"And thea?"

"See what you want, greedy-bird! Well, thea or no thea, there'll be plenty of Berëzov kasha."

Amid such conversations the time passed unnoticed, and the party finally reached the way-station. Fortunately for Moisha, the party was not especially large or rambunctious, and getting spots on the sleeping platforms was sometimes achieved without great trouble. But at times it nevertheless became tense. Way-stations between Sretensk and Zerentui are some of the most murderous… Dark, cold, and filthy, they have few equals along the entire stretch of the great Siberian "line of march." These stations' very names are somehow evil, troubling the imagination beforehand: Undinskie Kavýkuchi, Gazimurskie Kavýkuchi ("From Kavýkuchi to Kavýkuchi yer eyes'll git loosey," unbowed prisoners sarcastically appraise the forty-verst distance between these way-stations). Further on—Shalopugino, Tainá, Solntsy, Poperechnyi Zerentui, Mount Zerentui, or, as penal laborers call it, Bitter Zerentui.[11]

Certain of these way-stations are of the type that might render it impossible to regard as capable of human thought or feeling any of those who arrive in parties by the dozens and are put under lock and key during a long night. But, in actuality, and more so in Siberian actuality, this human herd does indeed not feel or reason in a human way, for the impossible turns out to be so possible for it that a hundred and fifty head will sometimes herd themselves into tight, suffocating, filthy little pig-pens! The mare bellows, the mare gets indignant and even protests, summoning the junior officer and trying to inspire in him a notion of good will and fairness; but, needless to say, the matter ends instead with the mare submitting to its fate: it is driven into the pig-pen, where at night a reeking tub is set up—the waste vat—and the lock is shut. Convoy guards are always terrible cowards and will not for anything agree to put the tub in the corridor, though there might be watchmen next to the door. Wishful thinking means more than the lock: playing cards all night in the guardhouse, soldiers feel safe from prisoners attacking them with a "hurrah" and scattering and beating them. Whereto and why would prisoners run into the cold dark of a winter or autumn night, when there still stands around the way-station a menacing palisade and watchmen clutching rifles? Clearly, these horrors are but nightmarish fantasies in the secret depths of each man's soul, but it was officially considered necessary to treat them in the most serious manner.

It was already getting dark when the party, famished and chilled to the marrow, came running into one of these way-stations. With the inevitable squabbling, confusion, and occasional blows, prisoners distributed themselves inside their allotted stall. Borukhovich and his creatures (so being in such cases) acquired a spot on the floor beneath the sleeping platform, near the waste vat, where a draft of cold air passed over them like an icy shower every time the door opened. All the little children were coughing terribly, yet, had it not been for their many years of tempering, they would have died from colds long ago. But, for God's sake, what a place this turned out to be: the present way-station was the glory and model of all way-stations! Folks were packed together in this little closet like herring in a cask. It was terrible to see what was happening there in the depths: the clanking of chains accompanied by the no less terrible curses, women's shrill cries, children's whining, body on top of body, head over head… It was agonizingly hot and stuffy above and cold and damp below, accompanied by an unbearable stench from underneath the platforms, where in the darkness living beings also writhed, a mass of children, men, and women…

"We're lucky we got a spot near the door today, children," Borukhovich, deep in thought, tried to console himself and his young ones, "you can suffocate over there, honest word, you can… But no worries here…"

The children were asking to eat, but the stipend had not yet been dispensed. A good two hours passed before the headman finally received it from the junior officer and distributed it to the party. Moisha managed to buy several unleavened breads with curds and potatoes from a trading woman, and to heat up the kettle and boil some tea in it. The latter was accomplished, however, at the cost of a big argument with the prisoners and even a few jabs in the chest, since there was a bunch of folks clustered around the only stove and every inch was nearly a life or death struggle…

"Where're ya climbin', ya lousy Yid? Cantcha see there's peoples 'ere 'fore ya?"

"And I'm not a personsh? My children aren't like yoursh? They also don't want to eat and drink?"

"Akh, ya Yid monster! How ya talk! How ya climb o'er folks!"

But Moisha didn't give in, and stubbornly insisted on his rights as a human being. He paid no attention to the punches, less to the curses. Hence his "childrensch" were given to drink, given to feed. The little ones were now propped up and sleeping, arms woven together and wrapped up in various prison rags, the older ones were still pottering about, disordering their various domestic possessions. Having collapsed into his sheepskin, Borukhovich lay in acknowledgement of having honorably completed his day's duty, and dreamed. What did he dream about? About his dead wife, a happy past, about his children, about their impending future? Or was he simply listening to the multivocal racket issuing from the inferno that this ward constituted? Often, lying on his back with arms crossed behind his head (his favorite position during evening rests), he sang beneath his breath a kind of long, monotonous, doleful prisoner song, the only one he knew and in which it was possible to make out only a single, oft-repeated phrase:

Mine's an unforshunate fate…

"Hey, Yid!" someone shouted at him from the darkness beneath the platform. "Why're ya singin' a song like ya been driven outta the land of Egypt?"

"That'd make you pharaoh, eh?" Borukhovich glibly shot back, and sometimes, in a sign of high disdain, he would add as if for himself his favorite saying: "Clearly, this cow wantsh to kick the bucketsch."

"See, the stinker's still lyin'," answered the unknown man, for some reason especially aggrieved at having been named pharaoh. "But didja hear, boys, how Yids swear 'mongst themselves? I've heard. One tell t'other: 'Ta hell wid yer dad!' But t'other answers: 'Yer lyin', take yer grandpa!' First goes: 'Take yer pa, grandpa, 'n' great-grandpa!' Then t'other gits mad 'n' shouts: 'I want that you got a house, 'n' in yer house there's forty rooms, 'n' in ev'ry room there's forty beds. 'N' let ya suffer the evil shakes forty days, so's yer bounced from bed ta bed, room ta room.' That there, boys, is how Yids curse each other."

"Well go to sleep, demon!" the storyteller's wife shoved him, and silence returned beneath the platforms.

At last Mount Zerentui, the end point of the party's road, appeared. Having ascended the mountain, the prisoners saw in the distance a white stone prison and, beside it, a village with a church in its midst. Each one's heart clenched from insane joy that the long, way-station ordeal was over, but in its place came anxiety over the imminent but unknown future. There it was, *katorga*! What would it be like? Better or worse than the march? Well, there's no one like God anywhere.

For Borukhovich *katorga* was nothing new, he was simply transferring from one prison to another. Nonetheless, his heart pounded in his chest. Only his children felt not the least anxiety, and joyfully pointed out to each other the central prison's shining, white-washed walls. They'd heard so much about Mount Zerentui, their parents had so mused about transfer to the prison, that in their imagination it appeared as an earthly paradise or at least a place where there would be neither cold nor hunger.

The walking prisoners put on speed; horses, sensing the proximity of the stall, began neighing and moving at a happy trot. Here came the homes of the prison department's officials, the post office, the *katorga* administration; here came the prison itself, a large, beautiful, clean building, its white stone border dazzlingly radiant. With its towers, embrasures, battlements, and drawbridges it wasn't so much a prison as some fantastical key to chivalrous times… Everything was new and unbeknown to gazes accustomed to Siberian way-stations' filth and unsightliness. The party halted at the gates in anticipation of processing.

There appeared the assistant warden, still a young man, short, round, stolid, affable, and obviously carefree about his duties. He proceeded to quickly read off prisoners' names, adding in the meantime inoffensive wisecracks and making a fleeting examination of their regulation items. Guards led the men one by one through the prison gates, the women with children were let into the freemen's barracks, and certain of the little ones were also put on a list of candidates for accommodation in the shelter. Then Borukhovich's turn came.

"Well, brother, you're a twenty-yearer? Through the gates! You're a prison resident!" the assistant, smiling, shouted at him.

"But you'll move my children to the shelter?" Moisha timidly asked, submissively clutching his cap and bowing his shaven head.

"What children?"

"But these five children here… My son Abram, eleven years old, and four dofters: ten, eight, six, and four."

"But where's their mother?"

"Mother's in the other world. My dearest died."

"Well, that's sterling! How can this be?" the carefree official grew flustered. "They can't go to the shelter right now… And stop, brother, stop: are you a Jew?"

"A Jew, Your Honor."

"There-there, I see the cat's *not* got your tongue," the assistant turned to him, as if having suddenly reached the desired conclusion. "Well, so your children won't be taken to the shelter, old man."

"Why not?"

"Because. A regulation came from the shelter's administrator saying there's to be only a certain percentage of Jewish children; their numbers are already over the limit. What can be done? Hey, Trofimov!," he turned to one of the guards. "Chap, run straight to the warden and tell him I need to ask him about an important matter. Well, and you, dear man, go to the prison, there's nothing more you can do here."

"Your Honor, how can I leave? Please let me wait for the gentleman warden. Let him decide the matter."

The assistant did not object, and turning from Borukhovich continued processing the other prisoners. After half an hour there appeared from out of a corner of the prison, proceeding with slow steps and leaning on a cane, the prison warden himself, a respectable gentleman with a thick black beard, gazing unkindly from beneath his brows. He was no closer to the party than thirty paces when a guard loudly shouted:

"Attention, caps off!"

The assistant quickly went up to the warden, saluted, gave his report, and explained why he needed to call him.

"It is absolutely impossible to accept the Jewish children," the black-bearded gentleman curtly replied, having cast a sidelong glance at Borukhovich standing humbly before him, and at the tight group of children off to the side. Moisha fell to his knees.

"Your Excellency, Your!… *Where* can they go now? They're little ones!…"

"Stand up, stand up, that isn't necessary… I'm not God or the tsar," the warden turned to him. "And all of you," he addressed the herd, as if having just noticed their bared heads, "put your caps back on."

"Your Excellency, what now?…"

"Just that you stop talking and get into the prison."

"But the children?…"

"But what can I do? What, are you deaf? They're forbidden to go to the shelter. It's the law!"

"Couldn't we ask the *katorga* director?" the assistant warden tentatively suggested.

"About what?"

"Why, about the children… That they'll be on the street, as they say… The father's in prison, the mother's died."

"Just yesterday morning the *katorga* director mentioned there's already a total of nine Jewish boys in the shelter. Soon the whole shelter will be filled with little Yids."

"So that's how it is?"

"*That's* how it is! We're not serving as your charitable institution. Kindly do your job. Guards, take the prisoner to the prison!"

Two guards slowly began to carry out their commander's order and tried to drag Borukhovich away; but he seemed to go insane: he tore himself from their grip and began looking around with such a terrible face that the guards stopped themselves…

"How, Your Excellency?" he screamed, flinging himself once more before the warden, who took two steps back and instinctively pointed his cane. "How! Jewish children are whelping cubs that can be tossed into the frost without a mother or father to stop it? They're not allowed to eat and drink, to cry, like other children? Jews aren't quite people? No! I'm not going into the prison, I'm not throwing them into the street—better you kill me, order your soldiers to shoot me… Would I have a soul if I abandon my own blood to save my skin? Gentlemen commanders! God watches over you… And you, the people."

Something strange had taken place inside Borukhovich. He spoke not as he always did, timidly and submissively, but powerfully, grandiloquently, even contrary to his normally almost whispering voice, filled with tears and imbued with the utmost soulfulness… And at that moment his face was as if transformed: gone was the ridiculous Moisha Borukhovich everyone had earlier known and recognized, the little man with the wedge-shaped beard, hook nose, roving eyes, and pitiable physique. His spine had somehow suddenly straightened, his flaming eyes were terribly open, and his whole face had become different, impressive, nearly beautiful…

To universal surprise the warden, instead of becoming infuriated and shouting, listened to his speech somehow ashamedly and with dismay.

"But what can *I* do? Goodness you, chap… I'd be happy, y'know…," he muttered, looking around helplessly.

At that very moment a tall, bony old man with a long gray beard, in simple prisoner dress but with unusual dignity on his face and possessed of all his capacities, forced his way from the back of the crowd.

This was a Jewish resident of the free command, a jeweler and watchmaker by profession, who enjoyed great renown and even respect among the local populace.

"What are you about, Goldberg?" the warden addressed him, as if anticipating salvation.

"I'll raise two of the little ones myself!" explained the old man, grabbing his ill-fated fellow tribesman by the arm.

"Well, that's wonderful," the warden brightened, "and I myself will probably take the youngster… I need a delivery boy right now."

"I'll also take the youngest girl," put in the young assistant, red as a peony, "we've no children and my wife will be very glad."

"Even better. This means only the young woman remains. What if you, Goldberg, agree to take the two middle ones so that the Oladins could probably take the eldest—they need a nursemaid for their baby. Well, that solves everything. But, God knows that was quite a racket over a broken egg! Everything's turned out humanely, and for the better… Well, have you completed the processing, Pavel Iakovlevich? And you… what's-your-name?… You're a dunderhead… A Yid—my, he's such a Yid! You'll now farewell your kahal and march into prison. It's long past due. The yard's completely dark and the convoy guards need to rest."

And with these words the warden turned smartly toward his house; but, having gone a few paces, he stopped suddenly and half-turned to shout:

"And you, boy, as for you, get in step behind me!"

In the meantime Moisha, having completely collapsed and shaking as if in a fever, showered with innumerable kisses the cold little faces of his children, frightened and even mortally pale after the terrible scene that had just passed but they'd little understood. They bade their father farewell somehow mechanically, dully, without tears. Finally, Moisha hoisted his bag onto his shoulder and quietly dragged himself toward the prison gates, into which he disappeared without once looking back.

And so he was again pathetic, not beautiful, and ridiculous in his impoverished prison wear, with his bag of regulation items on his crooked back!…

AMONG THE HILLS

I'm sitting next to a guard in a rocking one-horse cabriolet completing the easy trot from Mount Zerentui to Kadaia,[1] where I've been assigned to the so called free command. The guard, moreover, is completely unarmed and sooner relates to me in the manner of a tour guide; in addition, he bears my papers for delivery to Kadaia's warden.

As if celebrating the day of my release, sunlight gazes brightly down from the heavens today, and all the past is covered in cold, gray obscurity… There is not a cloud overhead; this marvelous autumn morning is so clear, blue, and sweet! Outside, the air feels of a warm, enchanting spring, and you can forget it's already late autumn (the first of November). But why is there such a terrible, occluded sensation approaching grief in my soul? I'm neither happy and light nor pitying something inexpressible, and want to laugh a child's unsaddened laugh, but bitter tears catch in my throat and I'm choked by a tourniquet…

Everywhere along the thirty-six-verst road from Mount Zerentui to Kadaia my gaze is met by a grandly monotonous, pathetic picture. Behind and ahead, and along both sides of the winding road, simply anywhere you look, stretches a sea of hills—conical risers, resembling one another just like drops of water and seeming to awaken in the soul of the newly arriving stranger a melancholy, sickeningly worrisome, feeling. It's as if the doleful, bare heaps with their yellowed grass and browned shrubbery have enclosed the horizon in an iron ring… There is an entire host of hills—group after group, row after row; clustering together, jostling one another, they gaze from all sides; but there, at the edge of the sky, is a fantastic outline of mountains mingling with the swirls spilling from out of their clouds and disappearing into the baby-blue haze of an autumn morning… There is not a brook, not a sapling, around! Colors are faded, life's sounds have died… You begin thinking—and it seems as though you've fallen into an enormous fabulist ocean: its iron-yellow waves having arisen and fallen into a magical sleep, petrified into gigantic troughs…

"How boring your place is!" I finally turn to my fellow traveler, interrupting the weighty silence. "In Shelai, the hills are covered with trees, but here—there's a desert, death…"

"Why're ya puttin' down our eastern Dauriia?"[2] answered the guard, evidently wishing to enlighten me. "Jus' wait—perhaps it'll get lovely. If you look, that's our springtime comin'! The hell with your Raseya!"

"But have you been to Russia?"

"Ain't managed, for sure, howe'er, we knows from all them books 'n' 'ave heard from Raseyan people. Your birthplace's a field inside o' all them woods—so what around here could be pleasin' to ya?"

"But what did you mean, springtime's 'coming'?"

"First off, the *palý* is a-comin'… For our brother peasants—'tis true—this is a dangerous joke, well, but if nature's beauty's to be found, then I report to you—it's first rate!"

"Please explain what this *palý* is."

It turned out to mean grass fires. Something passingly ignites last year's dry grass and fire begins spreading unconstrainedly. A great spectacle then presents itself in the dark of night; you can discern a bright glow for dozens of versts, and the closer burning hills, strikingly whipping their gigantic fiery tongues from place to place, do indeed produce an eerie illusion of erupting volcanoes…

"But then how many flowers we's got!" continued the garrulous patriot-guard. "You can find 'em so full nowhere else. First, there's the buttercups… The snow still ain't managed to melt, but e'en then, y'see, they're beautiful 'cause o' the sunlight offa the snow. Then the Mary's roots[3] come out…"

"Can they be eaten?"

"Why eat 'em! They're *flowers*… They blossom exactly like big goblets, white, red. Whole field's white. Air gets sweety-sweet from 'em! Then, too, there's the vales dotted with lilies-o'-the-valley. Well, then the *saraná*[4] also gallantly blooms, the wild rosemary… If you're a hunter, then you can prob'ly find no better place for birds in all o' Siberia: we got tons o' duck, hazel-grouse, field-hen. 'N' in the summertime, the larks alone'll sing till you groan! I got no truck for the cuckoos. Can't stand the bastards: there ain't a hillock ain't got its cuckoo, callin' o'er there, then rushin' at each other. Our spring 'n' summer's grand!"

The brief day had died when, having crossed Borzia Stream, we finally reached our journey's destination. Our eyes were met by a rather large village of three long streets running parallel to each other; but Kadaia lay in such a narrow, dark basin, both its sides enveloped by such terrible slag heaps, that it made the impression of something pitiful, worn-down, weak… The right side of the village lay on a rise—it extended to the very top of a hill, where it met a rich mine of silver veins; the left, by contrast, presented a low, swampy valley, though behind this narrow swamp arose a gigantic and nearly sheer cliff ruling over all the dwellers. It seemed suspended in air and threatening to fall and bury beneath its debris the settlement sheltering at its feet. Indeed, there had in actuality been an avalanche at one time, and it was even artistic: evident around it was a bare, rough cliff-side hanging above the village and a pile of broken blocks of granite lying beneath. Wilderness and cold emerged from this tumbledown and completely inaccessible stronghold. I unwillingly looked at it the whole time we were riding up into the village toward the prison.

"But d'you see that cross there?" asked the guard, pointing toward a small hillock to the left of the cliff.

I couldn't distinguish anything in the gathering dusk.

"Is it a graveyard?"

"No, the peasant graveyard's o'er there, on the other side o' the village. But here, the Poles is buried."[5]

"What Poles?"

"Criminals… They was amazin', y'know. Howe'er, there's one Russian there, a Mikhailov."

"Mikhailov?…"

I suddenly recalled that there had indeed lived and died there in banishment a famous poet and publicist of the sixties, a talented translator of Heine, Mikhail Larionovich Mikhailov. I also recalled that at one time there lived in Kadaia mine the still more famous author of *Essays on the Gogol Era.*[6] With alacrity, I began asking my talkative interlocutor about those times and about those people, but it transpired that he knew absolutely nothing except their names and the bare facts.

"It's likely them ol' men were what ever'one's ended up tellin' you they was," he consoled me, seeing my curiosity and chagrin.

Straining my eyes, I continued gazing into the gray evening distance, and it suddenly occurred to me that I was also looking at a kind of tall pole on top of one of the small hills… My heart began beating faster and my head raised higher thinking that these places where I, an unknown wanderer, was now being sent to live were distinguished by the lives of people from one of the most significant epochs in Russian history, and what people! My lips involuntarily whispered the lines of the latter famous poet to his friends:

In a gloomy haze of banishment
I will the world with difficulty await
And my soul will only wish,
As in prayer, to repeat:
"Your struggle will be successful,
Success in battle you will meet,
And we pass our cup
Forward to you!"[7]

I didn't notice how we got to the apartment of Warden Kostrov. The latter couldn't wait, and ran to the foyer in slippers and a colored nightgown with tassels. He was a short, shaven gentleman of middle age, with a fat, sagging belly and a round, kind-hearted face, rather preternaturally rosy. From his mouth came the reek not of onions but something more suspicious…

"Aha!" Kostrov, seeing us, cheerfully exclaimed. "Is it you, Egorov? But I was expecting you yesterday."

And having given a hand to the guard and me, he led us into a spacious, tall room distinguished by its near complete absence of furniture; except for a small table in the corner, its only other creature comforts were a decanter and some snacks.

"Gentlemen, don't you want to try a little glass of the nation's own? Sit right here. I'm living on a bachelor's foot—see what emptiness surrounds me? This is only on account"—the fat man, laughing, clapped his belly—"of my not liking to be empty… Now that there's a good chap and a guard as my guest, well, there's not so few of us… Have you met?"

Having refused the vodka, I sat down on a stool in curiosity. Addressing me, Kostrov continued to blather:

"There's been no prisoners like you in our Palestine for a good while. Everyone's the herd, you know! I'll tell you, those artists can only be dealt with through the rod and the isolator."

"What, you still believe in the birch rod?" I inquired.

"Well, little father, you should live with these folks!"

"I have lived with them."

"Eh, your life was a special matter… No, here, they would from the start give you three or four hundred such rogues and the high command would ask you to keep order in the prison and for success in the worksites, and then I daresay you would be singing something different. You'd understand what it means to be in a warden's skin! These devilish women especially weary me, may a bear grab 'em, the bitches… You must excuse me… But, tell me, please: why must I accept such rudeness or some other artistry from her? Y'know, it's now forbidden to flog their sister. Ha-ha-ha! Our love for humanity, our education, is now on a roll… But I'll be open with you: honestly, as I spoke earlier—honestly, I wish it, although I'm afraid I'll be called… Whatzit called? A reti–… a renegade, is that it? Mercy, gentlemen! I'd be putting myself in chains—you know, for depravity… So has she, as you can imagine, been pulling one over on me? 'I don't care,' she says, ''bout your chains! I'll take the chains!' You understand?! Well, what can you do with such a shameless creature, when it's forbidden to flog the filthy thing?"

"But surely everyone's not that way," I tried to point out.

"Everyone becomes that way in the end, so, please, don't defend them. Indeed, Egorov, you know that Mashka Dergunova?" he suddenly addressed my accompanying guard. "She's sitting in my isolator again."

"Still can't drive the stupidity outta her noggin?" Egorov inquired sympathetically.

"No, you might simply know"—Kostrov, growing hotter, returned to me once again—"she, the bitch, dares to curse me… The warden of a *katorga* prison!"

"To your face?" I asked.

"Well, this has still not been established… Indeed, I should spit all over her! But the mare'll learn about it and, as everyone knows, I'll be turned over…"

"You know the proverb: behind the eyes…"

"Well, no way, I'm not going to release her! That a prison warden… some *katorga* trollop?… She thinks that if she's got a pretty mug she can't go to hell with her razor tongue, don't you see? No, come off it. While you're good—we're good to you; but she wanted to have a go with everyone in the mine…"

Kostrov bit his tongue, having felt, as he should have, that he might be speaking out of place.

"Of course," he suddenly turned to the other side, "I'm not saying you have to be a barbarian, like, for example, Gribanov, who was Zerentui's warden not long ago—haven't you heard? Strictly speaking, he wasn't a complete barbarian, and the prisoners even loved him; well, you can only maintain yourself by knocking back a splash of the Fatherland's little water from the Brothers Eliseev or Popov,[8] as it were! He turns into the Devil, ready to kill his mother and father. Here's the story that was told about him… He's going around the prison drunk and bumps into a prisoner. 'And where're you goin'?' 'To the medic, Your Honor, to have a tooth pulled, it hurts so badly.' 'Ah, it aches?' And all of a sudden he punches him, punches him in the teeth. Of course, the prisoner screams like a crazy mother. 'Ah! you're rebelling against me?! Guard, the r-rod!!' The guard turns out to be a numbskull—runs and gets the birch rod. Right there, Gribanov laid the prisoner out in the middle of the yard, flogs him with his own hand. Mark this: without charges and without a conviction, in broad daylight in the yard of a major *katorga* prison, ten paces from the director's quarters!…"

"But wasn't he brought up on charges for this?"

"Hm… No! He was already too powerful throughout the territory. We felt sorry for Gribanov, that's the truth, even the director pitied him, but he had to be retired immediately. So, here's what I'm saying: even drunk, I'm not in a state to forget myself to that extent! Or, would you prefer to take your Luchezarov? It's said *katorga* moaned and groaned because of him, and at the time he didn't fret over using the rod… Now, he's turned up his nose, although—what is he on about, strictly speaking? He's nothing more than a little Armenian captain, y'know, and never finished seminary… Well, but I… I won't hide: I'm a man completely without education, didn't finish mining school… Well, but then again, I don't hold a high opinion of myself! So just ask me about the mare here… except, needless to say, about the women… go ahead and ask: I'll bet you won't listen to the word of a fool! Although I grab the birch rod, I in fact use it rarely and never more than what the regulation allows. I'm a simple man—frankly speaking, a peasant… So I'll speak to you again without cunning: it'd be an entirely different business were I to thrash the women… Well, I wouldn't hold back then! Ha-ha-ha! He-he! You wouldn't need any investigation to see I'd be innocent or guilty… Because woman—please excuse my candor—woman… she is, I will inform you, my weakness."

I hastily interrupted this drunken candor with a question as to whether there were people of higher education in the *katorga* administration.

"With higher? Oh, that's what they want! Ho-ho-ho! But you'd better ask whether there are people of middle education. You can count them on your fingers. Luchezarov, the seminarian, didn't finish his education. I didn't finish mining school. Ust-Kara's warden is simply a barely literate junior officer, a good fellow, but still a soldier of the Nicolaevan Era. True, he's a splendid old-timer and isn't a fool distinguished by drinking, but he scrawls his name with difficulty… Algacha's— some little Pole, like myself—was in the police, it turns out, before he served as a guard; the warden of Aleksandrovsk's almshouse is also some rascal without the least education. Well, who else is there? The director of the Zerentui region just barely completed mining school; only, he has connections, and his wife a gold mine… Yes, that's the region's director! Take it higher, little father: the assistant director of *katorga* began as a simple chancery scribe… In a word, were I to speak the truth, it's only our *katorga* director who can stand beyond us all!"

"But what about him?"

"He's from the Academy… He is, little father, a principal!… So aren't we all, ha-ha-ha! Well, I'll just inform you that none of us, not even your Luchezarov, has the determination, the bravery, of the late Bobrovskii, who actually managed to make *katorga* toe the line, but how? The birch rod, of course. As it were, everyone trembled like a leaf at just a hint he was coming! And did much happen in those days? I served under the director and I distinctly know that Inokentii Pavlovich was in general a man with a very soft heart, and was at the time quite opposed to corporal punishment. He told Bobrovskii more than once: 'You should, as they say, lighten up… If this is completely impossible, then don't touch the women.' But he didn't put a gun to his head, and the thrashings went on and on. Because that was the law: 'you're permitted to thrash the women just like the men'—well, frankly, no one could prevent him from this."

"But why did the director, a soft man, as you say, support such an assistant?"

"He had to support Bobrovskii, and probably couldn't see for the softness in his little head."

"However, now Bobrovskii's not—it doesn't matter…"

"I can say times have changed! I'd like to tear Mashka apart, but I'm told: 'Don't touch!…' Ha-ha-ha! Ho-ho-ho! You can put 'em in the isolator as long as you want, but can't flog a woman, 'cause now we have education, from Europe… Ho-ho-ho!"

I began to take my leave.

"Well, but how about the work?" Kostrov stammered.

"What work?"

"Why, yours… We're strict on this account, you'll know: soon as a new prisoner's gotten here, whoever he might've been there, we invite him to the mine the next day!"

I explained that a physician had long ago released me from labor owing to my painful condition.

"Aha, that means you have medical evidence," the warden rejoiced, "this is a splendid affair! With a medical we can't lay a finger on you and you can live at Christ's side."

"But where, permit me to ask, will I be settling?"

"Where indeed? I doubt you'll want to live in the prisoners' barracks with the herd? If you have the means, you can rent an apartment from any of the peasants in the village there. Egorov! Can you take anyone into your fraternity? Doesn't its building have a couple rooms?"

Egorov gave his consent and, having bid farewell to the unique warden, we went out onto the porch. I stood in the dark, starless evening. Suddenly, the door behind us swung open once more and I heard Kostrov's voice:

"Come back here, come back here for just a little minute! I forgot: there's a letter for you… Oh, what a memory!"

I quickly went back into the room. Rifling through a messy pile of papers in a box on his table, the warden finally pulled out a letter and opened it in front of me.

"Such formality, little father, shouldn't be required… However, permit me, more out of curiosity, to skim through it. Hm! hm! from your sister… received your telegram, is glad you've been sent to the free command… So, so, she can't be too glad! Well, *you* be glad: getting ready for you is… springtime!"

My breath was taken away. I almost snatched the letter out of Kostrov's hands and ran off with it, unable for my joyful confusion to hear the sound of my own feet. I vaguely remember we proceeded through utter darkness to some peasant hut and entered a tight, close space where we encountered a pure Babel of tongues: a baby was crying in a cradle, around a dozen little piglets were squealing in a corner seconded by their fond mother's basso grunts, a new-born calf lowed in another corner, and from behind it came the ceaseless rustlings of half-a-dozen chickens… I vaguely remember the details of my first meeting and conversation with the homeowners; it was decided I'd spend my first night there, in the company of suckling pigs and the homeowners themselves, but next morning they would clean and heat a "chamber" over which I would take command for five rubles a month. Weary and at the same time anxious, I was very little interested by any of this and, taking advantage of the first opportunity, hastened with trembling hands to open in the light of a tallow candle the aforementioned missive.

Without sleep, almost until dawn, I muttered to myself inside my hard loge, powerless to master my racing mind…

Kind, glorious, dear one! Wherefrom your tenderness and love for a distant brother, whom you only barely knew from childhood memories and according to his pitiful fate? What infinite kindness and sympathetic responsiveness for another's grief and suffering, what a lack of worry about your personal fate, for your young, blossoming life always flowed from your sweet, naïvely enthusiastic letters, those marvelous, crystal-pure letters that encouraged and consoled me in my grim years of banishment!…

I remember Tania as an unprepossessing ten-year-old girl with dreamy blue eyes and an un-childlike, serious, and nearly tragic expression for a thin, little face. But I was essentially unconcerned about my little sister's inner world (I was significantly older than she); we each lived our separate lives beneath the same roof and were unfamiliar acquaintances to each other. Then, being away from home for so long, I somehow lost track of her completely. We never corresponded with each other.

The first letter from my sister reached me while on the way to Siberia, and I cannot relate what an impression was made upon me by this fourteen-year-old girl's ardent, inchoately loving babble. She vowed to remain connected to her wretched, stigmatized brother until her last dying breath; and for many years afterward, not a week passed without my receiving new tidings of hope and light in the form of a small envelope imprinted with nervous, semi-childish handwriting, and each time all the more personal, kind, and intimate…

However, for a long time I gave no special credence to Tania's dreams of meeting with me, dreams she unfailingly brought up in all her letters: what don't juvenile girls dream about! And my transfer to the free command, to which these golden dreams were timed, was still so far off!

But now freedom's hour had imperceptibly struck. I was unable to seriously explicate to my sister the utter foolhardiness of her plan to volunteer to travel into *katorga*, since she'd already informed me of her firm, irreversible decision to depart upon the long journey at the beginning of spring. In another time and under different circumstances this letter would probably have distressed me, but at that moment, to my shame, I felt only mindless, limitless joy! A clear light shone through the murkiness ahead and dazzled a tired journeyman… What inexpressible, novel bliss! There would still be several months of bitter loneliness—and then the golden dream would be realized… After several years of continuous nightmare, of insults, sufferings, and all sorts of debasement, I would finally press to my chest a selflessly devoted friend upon whom I could focus all the tears welling inside my heart, and I would tell her everything retained and proudly withheld from a stranger's view.

However, my first Kadaia winter did not fall on me lightly. Even now, I cannot recall it without trembling… My quarters proved terribly cold because, in the manner of most peasant huts in Transbaikalia, its windows were not double-framed, and so an inconceivable hoarfrost covered them from top to bottom; an abominable, hardly warming, and terribly smoky little stove harmonized completely with the poorly caulked walls. But why didn't I rent another, better, apartment? Perhaps this is funny, but for some reason it seemed awkward and disgraceful to tell the owners that I almost literally turned into an icicle at night and that the stove wouldn't hold any more wood; my separation from people and a life that had led to my being a savage bore down on me especially at first… My landlady's experienced eye saw, of course, the deplorable quality of my place and often, bringing me an armful of logs, she said to me in consolation:

"How is it you ain't died? Sittin' here all by yerself, them books ain't gonna warm ya, y'know… If'n you had a family, people in the hut would git crackin'—'n' then it'd be another matter. Them there piglets is *our* children…"

The politics of over-exaggerated delicacy soon bore fruit—my returning rheumatism knocked me off my feet and for several weeks nearly rooted me to the bed. These were terrible weeks, when for entire days I saw no one and had no one to turn to for help. I'm amazed that I nevertheless survived and once again stood on my own feet. The cold began to subside only in late March, and with the arrival of warmer weather my health returned. Along with physical strength came good spirits and dreams about my soon-to-be-arriving guest… I diligently undertook to put my quarters in order, trying to make them cozier and brighter. Walls and ceiling were smartly whitewashed, the little stove repaired; the necessary appurtenances of a household—some furniture—appeared. Now and then I ran to the prisoners' barracks where the free command's bachelors lived and had conversations with the joiners, metal workers, and other craftsmen.

Once, on a clear bright day, I was walking past the prisoners' smithy with a joyous light in my soul and could not keep from looking inside. A readily familiar picture presented itself to me. The bellows was loudly wheezing, small hammers were smartly pounding, glowing sparks of iron were flying around… A smith and striker greeted me with gracious bows (all Kadaia's penal laborers had now long known my face). My attention was instantly riveted to a tall, handsome smith with jet-black hair and a sadly thoughtful expression in his dark, velvet eyes. All this man's movements appeared unusually smooth, almost graceful, but his beautifully defined thin lips were tightly compressed. I accordingly decided some Georgian or Lezgin was standing before me, and was very surprised when made aware he was a most typical Russian peasant from Tula Province named Andrei Busov. Then again, his comrades called him a Gypsy.

"Ever'one's a snore 'cordin' to his Duniashka,"[9] the young chap next to him pushing the bellows—and who'd noticed, as he must have, that I could not tear my eyes away from Busov—jokingly nodded toward him.

The latter's lips slightly contorted into a contemptuous smile, but he remained silent.

"Do you have a girl back in Tula?" I asked, wishing to draw the handsome smith into conversation, but the unduly easygoing striker answered on his behalf:

"Why Tula! Here, in the mine… Avdotia Finogenovna—the beauty of our entire community! Struts like a pea-hen, swims like a white swan, glows like beauteous sunlight. You'll see, if you ain't seen her already. Kostrov himself was starin' with his Popov peepers, but no, brother—back off, I daresay, no tastin'! I'll admit, as a sinful act, I also crept up: 'You're ours, Avdotia Finogenovna! We, too, as they say, weren't born yesterday, 'n' you'll gimme your love…' 'Get lost! I ain't the type you are, stinker… I'm Andriushenka's darlin', 'n' I ain't tradin' him for no one in the world!'"

"Vanka, you do jabber!" a blushing Busov shouted at him. "Ain't you cursed by that petty little tongue? Jus' think: why would *he* be innerested in hearin' 'bout our stupidities?"

And looking at neither me nor Vanka, he began heartily pounding the small hammer on a cold piece of iron. Feeling somewhat awkward, I was getting ready to leave when he suddenly turned to me and, having kindheartedly relaxed, said:

"There's no secrets here whate'er. Don't think somethin' foolish, sir, 'bout the lass… She really is my girl. Only, the leadership won't let us marry; them lazy-bones gotta jus' grin at me…"

Vanka grabbed his belly and let loose a most overjoyed laugh.

"Why won't the leadership let you marry?" I asked Busov.

"Y'see, I *was* married… 'fore *katorga*, that is. It means now there's gotta be proof o' my first wife's death."

"Ho-ho-ho! Ha-ha-ha!" Vanka began laughing harder than before. "Proof o' the wife's death… Oh, that's killingly funny, no more! Won't you explain anythin'? Y'know, he… ha-ha-ha! He bumped off his first wife, y'know! He came to labor 'cause o' this!"

Busov was blushing red.

"That's true," he said very quietly, "for deception, for depravity, I killed."

"Well, so what proof is needed," I wondered, "if you came here precisely for…"

But such a paroxysm of joy suddenly overcame Vanka-the-Striker that he, not thinking long, spilled onto the ground and began splitting his sides with convulsions of the most profound, irrepressible laughter. Busov didn't even glance at him.

"In this matter," he answered with bitterness in his voice, "that's a cavil. These proceedin's 'as been draggin' on for a year 'n' a half. To my misfortune, I'm illiterate: they say a mistake's been made in my file—it's written as if I'm married…"

"Married to a corpse, ho-ho-ho!" Vanka had in the meantime not calmed down. "That's killingly funny… You didn't kill the hag in a real way, 'n' she's kickin' up quite a row for you from the other world. Fool! Fool! You still call yourself a Gypsy—you gotta poke her with a shakin' stick."

Upon leaving the smithy I once more admired the beautiful physique of the smith, who was thoughtfully pushing a shovel into the brightly glowing furnace and was, as before, paying not the slightest attention to his mocking comrade's foolish barbs and jabs.

Serendipity soon introduced me to an epic *katorga* romance. I was tracking down a laundress for myself and peasants directed me to the so called mud huts where prisoner families lived, maintaining their own households. A verst from the village, at the foot of one of the hills, had been assigned the command post for these pitiable human dwellings, distinguishable by purely primordial simplicity and modesty. A deep, square hole was dug in the ground; what appeared to be a network of sticks and branches of various sizes strengthened the sides and cover of this pit, and thick layers of mud containing all sorts of forest materials were packed in between them. There then remained to build the inside stove, which, needless to say, occupied a good half, if not two-thirds, of the space. After this, the palazzo was ready. Judging by its grandeur, the structure cost fifteen to thirty rubles to make, and wealthy prisoners even had very spacious and beautiful wattle huts with windows at ground level; but the paupers, that is, the majority, huddled together in veritable subterranean burrows more suitable for moles than people. In Mount Zerentui such mud huts have formed an entire little city, with straight streets and several hundred little prisoner homes; in my day, there were no more than ten of these in Kadaia.

As to the question of a laundress, the first prisoner who came into view told me:

"Visit Poduzdikha, sir, Poduzdikha. Small hut there on the edge."

"Who is this Poduzdikha?"

"Well, she's the little ol' woman there, but she's got a daughter—a healthy, strappin' lass—named Duniashka. She'll prob'ly be glad to hire herself out to wash your laundry. 'Cause she's in need, to put it frankly—they're livin' in dire straits."

"And mother and daughter—both are convicts?"

"How can I tell you, sir, so's not to lie? Y'see, the ol' lady kilt her husband—he, certainly, was paternally related to Duniashka. A cruel man, a drunk, a barbarian—got what he deserved! Fought the ol' lady many years; she was very patient, but towards the end, the woman got mad, turned 'gainst him. She took an axe 'n' buried it in his sleepin' head! Took care o' the business very simply. O' course, the woman was a fool. Didn't know how to hide the crime, 'n' moreo'er, implicated her daughter. She got twenty years labor, but Duniashka's term—I can't tell you precisely—still ain't over, 'n' won't be till this autumn."

Of course, I immediately realized that none other than the smith's girl was being talked about, and I went with great interest to the designated mud hut. Unfortunately, I found there only old lady Poduzdova, sick and lying on the stove and moaning loudly. The usual laments about the prisoner's grief-stricken life began.

"How are you getting on?" I'd asked, among other things.

"But why can't state rations be bigger, little father? Ten pounds o' beef per person per month, five pounds o' buckwheat 'n' a pood o' rye flour… Well, 'n' a bunch o' salt—'n' that's it. That's how you're to fatten up! 'Tis said you can earn money in the free command. But how, I ask, can an ol' woman earn money? Where? Who's gonna gimme work? Now 'n' again you hafta go beggin' in the real world—but how can you go, 'n' when? 'N', y'know, you gotta work your quota 'n' pay the state. My legs are gone, I can't crawl to the door, but the guard comes runnin' more'n once: 'Bitch,' he says, 'git goin' to the medic! Ain't your luck to be free from labor—we're puttin' you in the isolator fer loafin'.' Akh, you asps are suckin' our blood! Were you to loaf like me 'n' my daughter! I daresay your belly'd swell up from hunger, not gluttony, like now! 'They say yer daughter's young 'n' beautiful—she can earn money.' Certainly, speakin' directly, she can go earn money as the warden's beautiful concubine… Well, we jus' won't agree to this! Duniakha 'n' I'll die like animals, but give away her maiden honor, no! Lordship, we got a suitor, y'know—a very good man."

"I've heard… The smith Busov?"

"Exactly. You've seen him? No one compares. Our chap makes a picture, but his morals are as humble as a beautiful maiden's. Certainly, he's observin' my rules 'bout Duniakha 'n' him, since there's no signs of consummation."

"And where is your Avdotia now?"

"At work, little father, where she mostly is. Wadin' through clay, moldin' bricks for a new prison."

"What! Isn't that the hardest men's work?"

Poduzdikha began sighing and sobbing.

"On our mountain here, little father, that is a convict's work… Outta spite they assigned my breadwinner Duniashka to it, outta spite!"

"Out of what spite? Who assigned her?"

"*Kostrov…*" (My interlocutor's voice fell nearly to a whisper.) "Believe me, ev'ry devil startin' with the least ward attendant is tryin' to get his dirty hands on the lass—all the guards, Cossacks, 'n' the warden hisself… He's our great woman-hunter, that warden! Well, my Avdotia, as she should, jus' pushes him away. She told me for real what happened 'twixt 'em… Only, ai-ai, my God, how cross Kostrov was! 'Twas said he promised to let her rot to dust in the isolator! The mare heard ever'thin'. He's been tryin' to get Avdotia into a secret tryst from the very first. Well, not a thing can be said 'gainst her, ever'thin's certainly always been 'cordin' to the law. The lass is most humble, dutiful, 'n' burnin' to keep her hands busy. Kostrov sees her situation's bad, 'n' assigns her to make bricks. 'If you submit,' he says, 'see me, and I'll give you the easy work I want to, and I'll free you from work completely, but if you don't submit, I'll work you to death in the brick factory!'"

"But how long has she been at this job?"

"Seems it's now the third week. Our life before was glorious, but somethin' angered God. At that time, Dunka was workin' a lot—sewin', other things. Well, now you prob'ly won't find anyone in the mine worse off'n us. The lass comes home, 'n' used to be she'd pick up a sewin' needle or straighten up the place, but now she's jus' a dummy 'n' drops straight into bed 'n' falls asleep. She's completely worn herself out, though earlier she was the picture o' health 'n' weren't at all 'fraid there'd be work. How many tears we've shed! Clearly, the Lord's decided, yes, He's decidin' to abandon us. 'Mama,' Duniakha says to me the other day, 'you're my kin! Clearly, God is not in this world, there's no deeper truth… Clearly, it's only left to die…' My dearie's musin' 'bout death, she can't stand it no more… Now 'n' then I'm e'en terrified: what that lass might do to herself! Kostrov—so he must—is blockin' the marriage."

"This is with the smith?"

"Indeed!… I confess I'm quite 'fraid what'll be if'n the authorities transfer Andrei to a dif'rent mine."

"So what are you waiting for? You should complain…"

Poduzdikha only wrung her hands in response.

"That won't do anythin', m'lord! They're all related 'n' the same, so is a crow really gonna jabber to a crow? No! But there's word the very toppest of all prison gen'rals—from Raseya, 'e is—will come to the mine soon, 'n' all our hopes are now on him. We'll complain to 'im."

The garrulous old woman promised to send her daughter for my laundry the next day. Avdotia did indeed turn up during the workday lunch break. After all I'd heard about her beauty I expected to see something special, astounding, and so in the first instance was a bit surprised when my eyes were presented with an ordinary peasant girl of twenty-two, with thick rosy lips and a broad, as if rather flattened, nose. Yet, I was instantly struck by her health, freshness, and strength: they resonated from the entirety of her youthful, sprite, well-endowed body… Duniasha was half a head taller than I and her large, solid, utterly masculine hand could seriously have replaced my own… However, I repeat, it seemed impossible to speak about any kind of beauty in the true sense. But I had barely decided this when I nearly shivered: staring me in the face were large, gray eyes, peaceful and sadly reflective, and their profound, tragic look suddenly altered the expression of her face, relieved it of all shortcomings, and granted to her unbeautifully broad nose and thick rosy lips a certain charm…

I wanted to talk with the young woman; handing her my bundle of laundry, I asked the first question that popped into my head:

"So it's too bad you've been assigned to state labor, Duniasha?"

"What pleases you to ask?" she shyly and wonderingly asked in return.

"Your mother told me yesterday that Kostrov's cornering you… I recommended she file a complaint. In my opinion, prohibiting you for so long from getting married is illegal!" I blurted out in one breath, for some reason getting embarrassed and blushing.

The young woman did not reply and only covered her face with her apron, as if she were going to blow her nose.

"Don't you want to speak to the director? Won't he be here?"

She remained as silent as before… Feeling awkward, I continued standing there expecting some answer, and suddenly the sound of quiet sobbing reached me…

Embarrassed, I turned away; in a second, Duniasha had disappeared.

Since my dear pilgrim was not hurrying to complete her long and difficult journey, it dragged on and on, encountering all possible delays—due now to the vernal washing out of roads, now to the laziness or caprice of fellow travelers, now to various other circumstances unforeseen. There's nothing much to say about my concerns and worries. Imagination sketched out innumerable terrible dangers for Tania on the road—steep mountains, maddened horses, attacks by robbers, fording wide rivers, blizzards on Baikal… Hearing the merest tap that might signal the late arrival of the prisoner Vasilii who usually brought my letters and telegrams from the warden, I would from my bed shout in a feverish chill into the night.

One day, the *katorga* director visited Kadaia, and it occurred to me, having received a telegram from my sister from the nearest point, to appeal to him with a request to go meet her at the last station. The request was, truly, very ticklish, its success extremely doubtful, but I decided to take a chance. Here was my first opportunity to speak to the director face to face. He took me in private into Kostrov's cabinet and, although he did not offer me a seat, himself continued the conversation standing. Lying inside the intelligent, almost cunning, face of this thin, unprepossessing but battle-seasoned man was a permanent mask of cold impenetrability; you could never have said what he thought about himself or anything else; with candor, some ulterior motive, or otherwise, he spoke the same way. Whether it included words of mercy or a death sentence his voice was always indifferently soft, even almost affectionate.

Beyond all expectations, the director reacted to my request without any surprise, even with evident solicitude, and merely tried to dissuade me from going.

"I'm absolutely convinced you won't escape," he said with a slight shade of a smile on his stony face, "and I'm willingly prepared to let you go without any guard, but… undertaking this journey is not in your interests. You'll probably miss your sister. You say she's got a traveling companion, but if he in all probability is a state industry official, then they may be traveling overland on horseback. You'll be waiting at the postal station, but they'll be staying in the land assemblyman's quarters."

"Such an instance is easily prevented," I parried this consideration, "I can in any case announce myself in the land assemblyman's quarters."

The director dryly nodded his head.

"Very well. But… I don't have the authority to release you for longer than one full day without a guard."

I bowed.

"I hope that will be a complete enough time."

However, when after a total of five days I'd received no news whatsoever from Tania, who had long ago reached Chita, I became terribly worried. A suspicion even arose in my mind that the director had ordered my latest telegrams withheld, so as to stymie the journey he wished me not to take…

Late one evening, the first thunderstorm of the year erupted over Kadaia… Rain poured down in a ferocious deluge, thunder boomed almost non-stop, and lightning so often lit up various places in the sky that the atmosphere was filled by an almost solid bright light, interrupted for only brief seconds by the thick black murk. Sitting alone at the window in my dark room, I distinctly made out all the surrounding hills, standing at their posts like watchmen in fearsome silence and immobility. I was in grief and pain beyond expression; I felt more than ever the solitude of the banished…

Suddenly, a hand's decisive, impatient knock on the door interrupted my melancholy thoughts, and after this came the sound of a familiar voice:

"Ivan Nikolaevich, you sleepin'?… Open up, I'm absolutely drownin'! There's a telegram!…"

It was the deliveryman Vasilii holding in his hands my longed for telegram, which included only these simple words: "I am coming."

One thought, one emotion, seized me: "At last!…" I ran with joyous excitement to my landlord, who'd earlier told me to call anytime I needed him, night or day. However, at that moment it proved not so easy to roust the Siberian and drag him from his spot. Master Ivan Grigorevich had, as usual, gotten drunk that evening and was now sleeping like a lord, so it was not a little difficult for me with the help of his entire family to get him up and making articulate sounds. But at first these sounds were hardly consoling.

"What's this? This is really… Y'see how dark it is outside… How it's thund'rin'!"

But I implacably and persuasively appealed to my sense of faith in his once-given word. Then, having meditatively scratched his still snoring nose for a bit, Ivan Grigorevich suddenly gathered himself up from his spot and, like a bullet, was outside to conduct the necessary meteorological observations. The rain was now ending, and furiously streaming rivers of water rumbled only here and there in the nighttime quiet; they were deeply seconded by the distant thunder, now dying down; the lightning flared decidedly weaker and more rarely, but, contrarily, it was now so dark that it was difficult to see a few feet in front of you.

"The principal thing, it's so confounded dark!" a befuddled Ivan Grigorevich, hopelessly slapping a hand on his thigh, turned to me. "I'm princ'p'ly all confused 'bout the road. Say we bumble into a pothole 'n' end up breakin' the horse's ribs. That would be a principal thing! Why must it rain under a new moon?"

"But won't the new moon be up soon?"

"In an hour or two we should be able to see much more… 'cause the principal thing is the darkness makes the water-filled potholes terrible! O' course, I'd get surprised…"

We ended up resigned to wait for the new moon. Having fed his horse and straightened out his driver (a wagon), Ivan Grigorevich went for another little nap, but I could not close my eyes for a second. A pleasing, sweet quiver constantly ran through my entire body… I went out to the street a dozen times, and there was probably no loved one in the world who lost greater patience at not finding a light on the nighttime horizon. Darkness reigned all around as before, and the ever rarer summer lightning, now silent, still glistened. I glanced at my watch every minute and, finally, at nearly two o'clock at night, a faint light began climbing the sky's edge…

"Ivan Grigorevich, the moon's coming!" I rushed to my sleeping driver.

We flew at top speed for half an hour with a pair of fattened and lively horses between endless series of mute hills, through the flood of enchanting silver light. This night was so captivatingly beautiful after the first storm! Such bright cheer was evident in all living things, and as if feverishly greedy, I gazed into the blue distance, cut here and there by the mountains' black shadows!

By around noon the following day we were already at the post station fifty versts from Kadaia. There'd been no lady with a gentleman that day, yesterday, or in the past few days. This news nearly instantly unnerved me, since the danger arose that my one-day furlough would expire before Tania arrived… This danger grew with every hour, and when night arrived and my driver, having emptied into himself his twentieth cup of tea, peacefully stretched out on the floor and soon began filling the entire station with his loud snores, it was no laughing matter. Finding no spot for myself, I moved from side to side in a sick melancholia, ran out to the porch, listened to the nighttime quiet, reentered the room, sat down, and in a minute was once more on my feet. It seemed to me that if my sister was for some reason late and I were not waiting for her at the post station, then this would be an irreparable misfortune for us both; that the supreme joy of a meeting, although this would take place several hours later, would then be incomplete, poisoned!

I don't know how I nevertheless finally fell asleep: I must have been overcome by nervous exhaustion. But my sleep was troubled and a little sickened. Strange, confusingly sad, vague visions mixed one after the other—and suddenly, it was as if an electric shock passed through me from my head to my toes… A sharp, metallic sound burst through the window along with a rush of nighttime wind…

I leapt up—it was the coach bell… Here she came!

I ran doubletime toward the door, barely managing to grab my hat and nearly stumbling over Ivan Grigorevich, who rolled over in picturesque disarray until he was practically on the threshold.

Dissipating under gusty winds, the rain clouds were strolling through the skies, and from underneath them, like the yellow eyes of an enormous ghost, dancingly gazed the silently gliding moon. I listened—the bell clanged once more, then in a second dropped off into a continuous drone. There could be no doubt: this was the post horses nearing the station. I ran in a frenzy to meet her at the gates… A troika and the covered mail wagon finally appeared coming down from the heights. Here it was coming alongside me… I strained my eyes and made out inside, among the pillows, the vague silhouette of a person, evidently a man. However, a quiet voice told me that Tania had to be there… I ran behind the covered wagon to the station. When, exhausted from anticipation and excitement, I reached the porch, the horses had already been in place for several minutes and an unfamiliar, mustachioed gentleman was standing beside the wagon's footboard with an expensive bag over his shoulder.

"Time to wake up, we've arrived!" he said, turning to someone still deep inside the carriage.

"Really?" came a sleepy voice, and this slender, silvery voice belonged, without doubt, to a very youthful woman.

Holding a hand over my chest, in which my heart beat wildly, and unable to make myself speak for anxiety, I stood right next to the driver, who several times glanced sideways at me.

"Tatiana Nikolaevna, d'you intend to luxuriate for long?" he once more peeked inside the vehicle.

In a single instant I pushed the mustachioed gentleman aside without further ceremony, hopped onto the footboard, and pulled into an embrace the utterly astonished young woman just emerging.

"Tania, my sister…"[10]

Cheerful, overjoyed laughter and non-stop youthful chatter filled my small apartment in Kadaia. It was as if a bright beam of sunlight burst into my despondent life and illuminated and warmed my frozen soul with a caress.

Tania was absolutely enraptured by everything—my apartment, the owners, and the Kadaia countryside. While still on the way from the station, disregarding the gray, overcast day, she constantly cried, turning to Ivan Grigorevich:

"Stop! Look at what a glorious little flower that is! I'm getting down to pick it."

And we'd both climb out of the wagon like children and run pell-mell toward the flower. Tania did not tire of admiring the surrounding landscape. I myself was gazing round as if only just awaking from a deep sleep. During my intractable melancholia I'd felt true hatred for these grim hills shaming the horizon and oppressing the soul; this territory of banishment seemed cursed by God Himself to be forever and always cold and covered in snow! Waiting for Tania's arrival, amid troubles and cares of all sorts, I hadn't noticed the surrounding countryside abruptly and magically change and now, almost not believing my eyes, I saw nearby these bare, gloomily icy summits suddenly blooming, greening, and exploding with sweet, magical aromas. A unique, austere, grand beauty appeared to me in the awesome, empty sea of green hills…

"But I imagined I'd see something very, very different!" my young woman cheerfully prattled.

"But what did you imagine, Tania? That people here have dogs' heads and instead of the sky there's a black hole?"

"No need to get cheeky with me, dear, but, honestly, I'm experiencing the most pleasant disappointment. For example, until now I'd imagined you had chains on your ankles and wrists, that in the free command you were always guarded by an armed sentinel, and that the free command itself was something like a huge, dark barracks, where day and night prisoners are forced to march like soldiers to a drumbeat… I'll confess I also imagined that, save for soldiers and penal laborers, there were no other people here!"

Tania said all this confused and embarrassed by her youthful inexperience. She did not now physically appear to be the young woman of my reveries and memories: she was well and sufficiently un-foolishly herself, an assuredly composed young woman with luxuriant blond locks and large cornflower eyes, and only in these eyes, always serious and thoughtful, was evident the former, naïvely dreaming child.

"The primary evil is not in the chains, Tania," I answered with a smile, "of course, I wouldn't want to distract you from your pleasant 'disappointment,' and I wish from the heart that you never be disappointed a second time; but I'll say one thing. People here are perhaps no worse than those elsewhere, yet hanging over them is the continual nightmare of evil, inhumane regulations, customs, and habits. Several times I've seen here how the most naturally kind person commits disgracefully bestial acts simply because they can be committed, and are often committed!"

But I saw that my cool comments went into one of my interlocutor's ears and out the other. In order to darken her rosy mood facts, not words, were needed, and the former were not soon forthcoming: we were living some distance from the Kadaia mare's veritable *katorga* existence, with all its usual joylessness, and I was also trying to conceal much from my sister, and only much later did some dark dissonance, echoing out of dark activities, begin burrowing into our peaceful corner.

With regard to the prisoners, it goes without saying that they initially made only a pleasing, winning impression on her; her acquaintance with them was (like mine in Kadaia) limited to an acknowledging bow on the street. At times, Tania would ardently turn to me:

"Are these not people just like you and I, just like everyone? Quiet, kind people, were they only not affected by misfortune. Gentlemen, though in Russia, they're depicted as convicts. Had I met one of them on Moscow's streets, I would have run away like mad!"

Needless to say, rather than greeting Duniasha Poduzdova (whose unfortunate romance I'd already sketched out for Tania) as having been reduced by indescribable circumstances to a penal savage, my sister embraced and showered her with kisses without a second thought.

"Duniasha, sweetheart," Tania said, sitting beside her, "don't be depressed, dear, be steadfast… Everything will clear up—it'll work out in the end. I'm firmly convinced all this is just a stupid misunderstanding, which won't be hard to clear up. You know, quite a plan has popped into my head: the first time I go to Zerentui I'll walk up to the director and tell him myself about your case. He'll look into it immediately—I've already thought this out!—and all your troubles and cares will soon end… You'll be surprised! But I won't be if you marry your groom this autumn… Relax a little for me, gather yourself—and I'll straighten everything out right away!"

My guest happened to become acquainted with Kostrov, to whom, upon arriving in his jurisdiction, she was personally obligated.

"I do not think," she equably said upon returning home, "he is an evil man consciously doing stupid things. At least, he was, in my presence, talking so casually with a prisoner it was like they were equals."

I was convinced that the pathetic sight of prisoners' mud huts would make an overwhelming impression on Tania, and with a certain timidity I brought her one bright Sunday to meet the elder Poduzdikha; but, to my surprise, the visit couldn't have gone better. That is to say: the surroundings were so seductively green and gleaming, the June sun so fantastically golden with all its warm, caressing beams, that the poorest gazed upon that day as more beautiful and satisfying than usual.

"These paupers are, of course, living poorly," my sister thus pondered her viewing of the mud huts, "however, so many people in Rus who are completely free and not experiencing any kind of punishment are having it not the least bit easier or sweeter. And if your stories about prison are true, they don't make me consolingly wish they be brushed over, since the life you've pictured there is not as terrible as it once was…"

"Well, in a word, Tania," I joked in conclusion, "you came here to console and encourage the suffering, but found a grease-fattened bourgeoisie who need to read the teachings of their younger brother's sufferings!"

With a friendly smile she covered my mouth with her hand and, putting on my cap, dragged me for a walk among the hills. Roaming the environs, we tried in vain to find shelter from the sun's scorching rays. The gaunt bushes of hawthorn and willow spread along the elevated right side of Kadaia offered only the merest semblance of shade, and if we nevertheless loved to wander among them, then this was mainly due to the lilies-of-the-valley that ran there in surprising abundance. Without end, without pity, as if in a kind of intoxication, we picked these sweet-scented flowers and hauled entire baskets of them back to our room. Sometimes, having awoken early at dawn when my sister was still soundly asleep, I held these enormous bouquets of lilies sprinkled with fresh dew and strewed flowers on her to wake her. Then, having barely managed to drink our tea, hurrying and excited, we rushed to gather them up…

Tania only disliked that part of the mountain where the mine went crazy with its caps, watch houses, and other structures. She was horrorstruck and filled with pain at the notion that in these places lay subterranean burrows where, in the dark and damp, people gouged out the cold, inanimate rock. Having seen from even a distance these wicked constructions, she forgot all her recent ratiocinations about people living significantly easier in *katorga* than free workers in factories, and dragged me as far away from them as possible. Yet, once, when a suspicious sound that seemed like the clanging of fetters reached her, she turned completely pale and, with a shriek of genuine terror, hurtled into a run away from the mountain, stumbling over rocks and brush roots. For my part, I vainly shouted that she was making a mistake, that fettered prisoners were not being taken to the mine—but she wasn't listening to my assertions and, without stopping, ran full-speed ahead.

"Well, you're as nervous as a prim young lady," I tried to chide her, after I finally caught up to her and we slowed our paces and were walking together.

She said nothing.

We did not manage to remain long on top of the gigantic cliff perched along Kadaia's left side and from which, according to the stories of local residents, could be seen a range of mountains stretching beyond the Argun River and on into China. We had left home too late and were risking being caught on the road by the darkness and encountering on the way a sharp, piercingly cold wind or some other misfortune. Unsatisfied curiosity only roused us further; we began jokingly fantasizing that from the summit of this mysterious mountain there might prove to be a view of an Edenic, unknown corner, completely unlike the gloomy depths of the Kadaia basin, with its impoverished, pathetic little village, scraggy meadows, and uniform hills… Then, going one day further than usual, we decided for no reason at all to reach that enigmatic borderline. The closer we got to it, the more excited we became; trampling withering buttercups, red lilies, and other flowers scenting the air, we practically ran headlong forward… What would we see now?

I ran first to the top, and died in rapture: deep below my feet spread a beautiful, wide valley… In the blue-gray mist of evening, the twilight of sunset, chains of mountains turned blue and red in the distance, and farther behind them, like a strand of gray hair, there dimly appeared the ribbon of the Argun… In an instant, my soul sensed something native and excruciatingly near in the free air of this scene…

"Look, is that… is that a cross down there?" Tania suddenly shouted, interrupting the magnificent silence and pointing to one of the hillocks lying below our feet to the right: "Look, there's not just one, but several!…"

Two or three tall crosses could indeed be discerned, and I instantly remembered their origin. I immediately told Tania everything I knew about Kadaia's lonely graves, and confessed I had until then not tried to visit them.

"So let's go down there now!" my passionate travelling companion insisted. But it was already too late for such an undertaking, and we didn't know a direct route to the hill. The sun was already setting, and it was time to think about returning home. We both plucked up our courage and decided to go back to the village along the steep side of the cliff, as it offered the shortest way. We imagined the descent would be much easier than the ascent. But we hadn't gone more than a fifth of the way down the trail before realizing our mistake: the path proved unusually steep and dangerous for such inexperienced tourists, and we were merely lucky we hadn't happened to pick the most difficult spot. In the meantime, I practically had to jump from ledge to ledge, and so I carried Tania through there in my arms; prickly dogrose bushes frequently obscured my line of sight and, miscalculating a ledge's height and stability, I went flying head-over-heels into a bunch of rocks as a scream of terror issued from my sister's mouth. I managed with difficulty to grab onto a bush or a rock, groped my way onto solid ground, and made out where we needed to keep going. It was terrifying to go down, but going back up seemed even worse, and I—now bathed in sweat, with torn and frayed clothes and my fellow traveler—continued to descend, pale and silently frightened… Within a mere fifteen minutes we found ourselves at the foot of the gloomy cliff amid its pile of debris, and, crossing ourselves again, we laughed joyfully and shouted triumphantly!

Very soon after that day, before going to the poet's grave, we went to see the domicile in which he'd lived and died and which, as I mentioned earlier, existed still in a dilapidated state. Having learned that the house belonged to the village headman, we'd decided upon a pretext for our viewing: an intention to purchase the house.

The owner himself, an athletic peasant with an intelligent, well-meaning face, brought us to the abandoned dwelling. The lock growled, the door creaked on rusty hinges, and we found ourselves inside a spacious, half-darkened room where light fought through a single half-opened shutter (the rest were hammered tight). The shack had long had no foyer. The bare log walls were dank and rotted through. We sensed a sepulchral dampness, and from all sides poured the grim traditions of the past…

"How much are you asking for this ruin?"

"Sixty rubles. This is where Mikhail Larionovich Mikhailov lived, 'n' this is where he died…," added the owner, obviously well comprehending the actual point of our visit.

"What, you even remember his name and patronymic?"

"As if I see 'im alive in front o' me! The lord was hon'rable 'n' kind, though personally unattractive… I was ten years old when he died; he was like a brother to me, 'n' I dug his grave."

We assailed our interlocutor with every possible question, but his answers, as to be expected, proved hardly interesting, possessing only a general character. He'd been a kind lord… He'd not begrudged money and never locked his desk, in which he placed "heaps 'n' heaps o' money!"… More than anything, he read or wrote… There'd been "lotsa" books.

Later, other village old-timers could tell us no more. Among them were grasped rather vaguely memories of those still comparatively recent times, when Razgildeev's infamous stooge Kabakov ruled Kadaia mine, and Chernyshevskii, Mikhailov, and the Polish insurgents of '63[11] found themselves beneath his ferule. That is to say: they had lived here insulated from the outside world, passing time for the most part in the company of books, and so what could our peasants have known of their characters?

I'd not known about the poet's health prior to his resettlement to Siberia; in Irkutsk, it seems, he contracted typhoid fever; but consumption was what eventually led him to the grave after only a year in Kadaia (1865), and local residents exclusively blamed this on the day of the funeral for the insane exile Karol, when Mikhail Larionovich either injured or exposed his foot to the cold.[12] From that point on, the illness proceeded quickly and a fatal end became unavoidable…

The path to his grave lay past our now familiar gigantic cliff. Here, among the granite debris, we encountered an entire forest of freshly blossoming Mary's root; blooming watermilfoil was also showing itself in abundance. Our voices scaring off a family of hawks, they arose with worried cries from a cleft in the rock face and began hovering overhead; in the distance, cuckoos cooed longingly and forlornly, and up above, in the blue sky, the grandiloquent song of the lark unfolded ceaselessly. Having grabbed along the way a huge bunch of flowers, Tania settled herself onto a granite block, and I watched without surprise how, beneath her nimble and expert hands, there grew from out of these modest, plain flowers of lily-of-the-valley, red lily, Mary's root, and watermilfoil a beautiful, luxuriant garland. After that, we continued on our way.

The hill, barely noticeable from afar, turned out to be near the high cliff, clambering onto which did not prove very difficult. We ran breathlessly toward the huge cross standing on the summit. There were three there, but one was lying on the ground, probably knocked down long ago by a blizzard, and had been eaten through by worms…

A Polish inscription said that here lay the dust of the "expellee" of 1863 Voloszinskij… One of the upright crosses belonged to the aforementioned Karol, and another—the tallest—said in Polish: "Wygnanieç polski 1831 goku Litynsky."[13]

"But where's Mikhailov?" we asked each other in one voice, and instinctively went toward the edge of the precipice, where a disorderly heap of fallen rocks (a sort of rough-hewn marble) apparently marked someone's unidentified grave. "Can he be here?"

Later, asking Kadaia's old folks and evaluating their testimony, we satisfied ourselves of this conjecture's certainty. In this spot there had at some point also stood a cross erected by the poet's kin, but it was now ten years since it had fallen and disappeared somewhere—in all likelihood, some Kadaians stole it for firewood (owing to Kadaia's forestlessness it would have been a valuable commodity)…

Having laid a wreath on the grave, we wandered along the cliff for a long time with grievous thoughts, gazing around and becoming enamored of the views it afforded. The abundance there of forget-me-nots struck the eye most pleasantly: the entire hill was literally inundated by them, and turned blue as if an enormous azure carpet beneath our feet… Far away, in the distance along a dark hollow, stretched a gray band of trees, and from the other sides, along the edges of the horizon, rose doleful, sharpened hills, seemingly guarding the dead's imperturbable sleep.

It was sad and lonely there during the long Transbaikal winters; the cliff, from below to its summit, was covered in shifting snows, and "now and then was visited only by lupine starvation."[14] Then again, at other times of the year this was one of the best pictures in Kadaia. The proudly solitary graves, dug far away from shunning and hostile looks, exuded peacefulness and poetry. On clear sunny days the air resounded with the unceasing and innumerable warbles of larks free-floating in the heavenly azure, and beneath their triumphant calls I remembered a poem by M. L. Mikhailov that appeared in *Notes of the Fatherland*[15] in 1871 under the humble initials M. M.:

I was serving a prison term—
And through the mountains I ran!…
A soldier's bayonet
So close behind me.
Greater freedom… But do those
Mountain walls
Crowd me worse than
Those of the prison?

There, beneath the vault dark,
It was hard to breathe,
And my heart tired
Of beating and wishing.
Here, above my head,
Beneath the vault azure,
Hovers a lark
Singing—and calling…[16]

Like a golden, blessed dream, the summer passed!

One beautiful August morning, we were caught completely unawares by news that the mine was at last being visited by that top general whose visit the mare had for a year already awaited with such impatience. However, we were unable to ready ourselves for the event, because the business had already transpired… The evening before, at eleven o'clock, the general "came running" to Kadaia, and was already gone by the following noon. During this brief span of time he managed to accomplish a great deal: he had a good sleep, ate breakfast, familiarized himself on the spot with *katorga*'s problems, completed an inspection of the prison, and, finally, gave the local administration its required orders and instructions. The other mines were evidently inspected with the same speediness and fundamentality, and the important personage hastened to leave for Petersburg, having left an impression of himself as thunder, lightning, and fog. It was said that the *katorga* director himself spent those days with his head hanging down, and no wonder: every one of his remarks was followed by a stern, irritable response just out of prisoners' hearing:

"I've come not to sound out your advice, but to instruct!"

After all this, the petty *katorga* administration exulted.

"Thunder's passed—and we're out for a stroll!…" jubilantly shouted Kostrov, flying to somewhere past my apartment window in the steam behind a pair of his chestnuts and familiarly blowing me a kiss.

True, many of the prisoners who'd been ready to appeal to the general with various requests and complaints but were unable to do so looked chagrined, but soon found consolation in sophistry.

"Well, no luck this time—better luck next time. 'Tis said he's off to Kara now, but he'll be back to visit us soon. Primary danger was not to let 'im too close to them dogs—them little guards—should he look thoroughly into ev'ry matter, 'cause he's really an actual general: 'n' they say he's been given authority to go against the law! Such a kind face on our brother!… But the little warden didn't worship him. So he's fibbin' 'bout us, m'boys, he's fibbin'. He'll be back—then we won't let 'im go on so."

But then one day, early in the morning—Tania and I had only just gotten out of bed—word came from our landlords that, for a long time, some woman had been waiting in the vestibule for us to wake up. We flew to invite her in immediately. Barely crossing the threshold, the woman collapsed at our feet in tears. With difficulty, I recognized in the little wrinkled old lady our friend Poduzdikha.

"What's going on? What's happened?"

"Oh, blessed little father, oh, my sweet dearies!" the old woman cried out, "sendin' away, exilin'!… Oh, I'm ill-fated, grief-stricken!"

"Who's being sent away? Where to?"

"Yes, Duniakha, my little girl… To Sokolin Island!"

"By what statute? This can't be. Please stand up and talk plainly. Why is she being sent away? Isn't her term ending in a month? This is some kind of nonsense, a stupid prison rumor."

"No, ain't no rumor, little father. There's already word"—Poduzdikha objected, choking on bitter tears—"the warden counted on paper at evenin' roll call another three water transports. They say the gen'ral ordered all single women under forty sent to Sakhalin… 'n' they're sendin' 'em off at eleven o'clock t'day!"

"What is this?" whispered Tania, blanching terribly and convulsively grabbing at me as if she feared collapsing. "Is she lying?…"

I suddenly recalled how the Prison Department had long been striving to colonize what would turn out to be the island of Sakhalin, and recalled that in previous years there'd been similar deportations of convict women; therefore, since I wasn't baffled by this unforeseen news, I kept silent.

"But she has a suitor, she has a mother!" Tania wrung her hands. "This is inconceivable, this is inhuman!"

"O mother, Pelageia Kontsova gots three children with a man who ain't her husband, but they read her name offa the paper 'cause, 'cordin' to the law, they say, she's single."

"No, this cannot be allowed! Ivan Nikolaevich is going to see Kostrov this second. If not, I better see him myself… There must be some strange misunderstanding… Just think, given all that I've done! Lord, Lord, how many times I've tried, and now—this!…"

"You're our ben'factors," Poduzdikha once more collapsed onto her knees, "intervene for us orphans. Ain't no one else we got more faith in!"

But I didn't budge from my spot. Tania sighed.

"Why're you standing there like an inanimate stump?" she said, casting me an angry look. "Hurry, let's go this minute!"

But I was unable to express my opinion regarding the uselessness of any intervention, especially on our part (and before whom? Before a warden who had no say in these matters!), because the door opened with a bang and into the room flew, not walked, in a disarrayed state with unbuttoned blouse and no hat, an extremely pale and breathless man. I didn't recognize Busov at first, and taking him for some intoxicated peasant, I instinctively hurried to confront him.

"Ivan Nikolaevich, ain't this your place?!" Busov wheezily yelled in a terror-filled voice, and, after looking at those present, collapsed helplessly onto the floor and, sobbing, began tearing his hair.

Staggered by the outburst of despair from a full-grown and powerful man, and still not fully comprehending what was happening, I tried to console him and told him to stand up and tell everything in order.

"Andrei, what is it that's got you so mortified and crying like a maiden? She's not being sent to Hell. After all, won't you be able to request a transfer to Sakhalin? With your craftsmanship there's nowhere you can't earn heaps of money. You should be ashamed of being so faint-hearted!"

"Faint-hearted?" Busov, who suddenly stopped crying and threw me a nearly malevolent look, took up my words. "She's already not 'mong the livin'! You get this! Or do you, like Mister Kostrov, say: 'She's run off'? Gentlemen, that's enough to make folks laugh. She ain't gonna escape, she ain't that kind. But I know where I gotta look for her: in the ol' mine shafts—that's where!…"

And, quickly rising, he readied to leave; old Poduzdikha barely managed to grab his hands.

"Lord be with you, Andriushka, come to your senses! I saw Duniakha a minute ago."

Busov sternly hesitated at the threshold.

"When'd you see her? Where?"

"Jus' as I was runnin' 'ere, to Ivan Mikolaich's… Yes, I'm thinkin', I'll go—they're educated people, not our stupid darkness, 'n' perhaps they'll advise me… But at that same time Duniakha was goin' toward the mine: 'I'm goin' to the smithy,' she says, 'to see Andrei'—that is, to see you."

"Well, she weren't in the smithy, not at all! 'N' some o' the mare's sayin' she went up the mountain… They're sayin' the watchman saw her: 'Where're ya goin', Avdotia?' he asks. 'To the flowerbeds,' she says, ' to ask Andriushka to pick me.' With that, she headed for the hill. I ain't believed this at the time: the mare's jabberin', I'm thinkin', 'n' wants to have a laugh at my expense… I ran o'er here first… Well, but it's clear…"

Poduzdikha shrieked and wailed… Having hurriedly dressed and told Tania to stay home, I left for the prison. Busov was by then gone from the street.

I found unusual activity in the warden's quarters. The voice of Kostrov, furious as a wild animal, roared throughout the house. Even after he saw me he continued shouting unprintable words at the guards.

"Swine, devils! I'll put all of you in chains! I'll let you rot in the isolator, I will fla-a-ail you!… Akh, don't come near me now," he rudely gestured in my direction, raising his nonetheless hoarse voice and not looking at me. "You don't know what's going on here. Good-for-nothings wanna haul me into court! I, y'see, in honest innocence, announced the deportation to Sakhalin too early. Deportation was supposed to be this morning and the order announced today, and so after this someone's gotta be arrested. To speak the truth, this is what's been ordered to happen to me… But I'm thinking to myself: there's other people as well… I must get ready, gather my wits… Acting humanely would be better… But how humanely the scoundrels here have been toward me! Just imagine, two tarts ran off with their lovers last night! Well, and now who, permit me to ask, is to answer for this? I, I alone! In the sea's depths I only find a good-for-nothing and a wolf in sheep's skin and I lose myself with the swine! I'm starting to talk nonsense in my own head!… God sakes, I'll flog myself to death with my own hands!

"But you're so good!" Kostrov suddenly ran up to the intimidated throng of guards standing round. "What were you looking at? Whaddya you want? I'll turn you all over to the court, so there! I'll send you to Siberia!…"

Kostrov, however, then considered that his tongue had run away with him by threatening Siberians with exile to Siberia, and hurriedly corrected himself:

"I'm dismissing all of you to a man! Devils, swine!"

"Permit me to point out, Mister Warden...," there came from one of the guards, stammering out of fear, but Kostrov roared at the top of his voice:

"Silence!" (As a Siberian, he pronounced the word "silen*ts*.") "Silence, if you haven't been spoken to!"

Then, in curiosity, he added:

"What's the matter?"

"Permit me to point out, Mister Warden, Andrei Busov has *not* escaped."

"Busov? Don't talk nonsense. I'm absolutely convinced that cunning Gypsy's mug has run off with Dunka."

I then seized the opportunity to interrupt the conversation and report my meeting with the smith and about his misgivings. Kostrov cut me off with a sardonic laugh:

"Ha-ha-ha! The rogue smartly decided, I say, to toss her into the old mine. He's found his little fool! That's what I think! I'll believe my own eyes. He hid her away so they can leave together later, after the party leaves for Sakhalin and the manhunt subsides. Well, y'know, they'll come down on the simpleton then... Let me arrest this stinker now and hold him under strict arrest! Better yet, take 'em all to prison. You'll answer for him with your own heads. But keep looking for Dunka. If Busov's here, that means she's not far off. Well, but what's been heard about the other couple? Where's Senka and Katka?"

"We dunno, Mister Warden," the guards answered, "it must be reported they really did escape..."

"'Really did, really did'...," Kostrov maliciously mimicked. "Based on your big fat face someone should really get a thrashing. So why're you sticking around here? Do what you've been ordered to!"

The guards vanished in an instant.

"However, what'll happen now?" the warden, turning to me, now began pathetically moaning. "What'll I tell the director? Of the five women I was supposed to deport today, a whole two are missing... What the hell! And the other three—you can imagine how sweet they are!—have suddenly come down with fever... I myself am being scammed. Some good-for-nothing's splitting her sides—they can do this. They're masters of all kinds of deceit! Only, this won't happen to me. I'll send every one of these ladies to the mining administration, and the doctor there can examine them..."

I finally abandoned Kostrov as well. I wanted to see Busov immediately.

It had turned into a clear, warm morning. The hills, dressed in their incipiently fading greenery, basked in the sunshine. The reddish-brown glass windows of the mine watch house sparkled dazzlingly. By some instinct, I went up the mountain. There, in the distance, the sun was glinting off the bayonets of a company of quickly moving Cossacks.

Suddenly, I heard someone's voice calling loudly from out of the mine:

"Here! Come here!"

I accelerated my pace and noticed on one of the crags a human figure, furiously waving a red flag. Farther behind me the Cossacks obviously spotted him as well: they came to a sudden halt, as if communicating something among themselves; the bayonets flashed once more, and the company turned again toward the ceaselessly shouting individual. It was Busov. I quickly ran up to him. He was soaked head to toe in a flowing river of perspiration, and it even seemed to me that the smith's jet-black hair was lightly spotted by a white foam, like lather from long- and fast-running horses.

"Andrei, what's going on?" I asked, out of breath.

"I found her… Here! Come here!" he shouted again, excitedly waving his flag.

I was at a loss: if he'd located Avdotia alive, why was he summoning the guards?…

"What're ya yellin' 'bout?" sternly asked, having come close, an *uriadnik* (a Cossack officer) with an unpleasant, purplish face covered in black-heads. "Who'd you find there?"

"Come, I've found Avdotia."

The Cossacks silently looked at each other, and we all followed Busov. Through prickly hawthorn and dogrose bushes, via tall heaps of pyrites and slag iron brightly twinkling in the sun, he finally brought us to a large earthen hollow covered with stones and weeds. Into their midst old, half-rotten planks had been tossed, and alongside yawned the black opening of a shaft with collapsed wooden framing. This was the old mine…

The *uriadnik* was the first to break the silence.

"You, dog's hair, don't be foolish," he turned on Busov, energetically shaking a huge fist in front of his nose, "don't lead the leadership off the trail! What'd you find lyin' in there? Where'd you see it?"

"You'll see what's lyin' there," the smith calmly replied.

"You'll be lyin' there yourself, you soul-of-a-convict! You've really found some dupes… I'm 'fraid your busy hand'll push me down in there … That's some rotten stuff, y'know… 'n' it's darkly in there! Maybe you saw nuthin' there? I daresay, it's gotta be seventy feet? 'N' there's prob'ly water down there?"

The Cossacks began making a row; threats and curses began pouring onto the prisoner's head from all sides.

"This is what I say to you, gentlemen servicemen," Busov began with his previously even voice (despite being terribly pale, he was, as the guards approached, surprisingly calm at that moment), "it's better not to get mad, but to hear me out. I've known since early this mornin' that Avdotia ain't livin' in this world; but now you can see for yourselves where to look for the deceased. First off, here's her kerchief I picked up next to this shaft."

Everyone's gaze fastened onto the red kerchief in his hands and which he'd earlier been waving like a flag over his head.

"Well, there's prob'ly nuthin' to find," the *uriadnik* began after a minute of general silence, "she coulda dropped her kerchief 'n' gone away…"

"But the planks? Are you blind?" In a sudden frenzy, Busov rushed toward the shaft beside the boards. "I daresay, y'know the shaft was covered… What uncovered the old mine?"

Everyone again fell silent a moment, struggling with the weighty argument.

"It's a diversion!" a beardless Cossack with a small, quivering nose and wispy-white hair suddenly shouted in a reedy voice. "This has been done for a diversion!"

"This does necessitate an inspection," the *uriadnik* decided, "but if it *is* a diversion, then you, old chap, is gonna answer 'cordin' to the law, but if not… Well, boys, someone quick-run to the watch house for a rope. 'N' don't forget a lantern. 'N' you, Pugovkin, hurry for the cornet! A gentleman officer is needed for this matter right now."

Pugovkin, that same beardless Cossack with a small, quivering nose who insisted this was a diversion, shouldered his Berdan and rushed headlong down the mountain; behind him ran two other Cossacks to the watch house. The rest began discussing the plan's finer points. However indecisive, they ran around the shaft, stepping close to the opening, testing the soil's firmness, unintelligibly shouting and swearing at each other. Busov, apathetic and seemingly somnolent, stood off to the side, taking absolutely no part in the general commotion. I sat on a rock a ways off and observed.

Not a half hour had passed when those who'd been dispatched returned with a rope, and behind them appeared the young cornet, riding a white horse. Tall, ruddy, with a round, still beardless, face that twitched incessantly from involuntary grimaces, he heard with cultured movements and intonation of voice the *uriadnik*'s report about the situation and what was unfolding.

"Well, let's go, lads… You there, wrap the rope over your shoulders… then what's-his-name, put it round his torso. And you others, hold tight!"

But the enthusiasts proved unable to tie up the rope or to climb down.

"How can you cowards be screwing this up?" the cornet grew cross. "You must go through fire and water if an officer orders you! Pretend the enemy is positioned in front of you."

"They're 'fraid, Your Honor," interrupted the *uriadnik*, "that the air is suffocatin' down there. They're sayin' they might not be able to breathe…"

"Nonsense, old boy… But, maybe it is," the officer suddenly agreed, and the skinny ambler beneath him began stamping out an angry fidget. "So, what now?"

"But he should go first," the *uriadnik* pointed at Busov, "'cause *he* ain't married… 'n' he's testifyin' 'bout this mine."

"What a business, what a business!" the commander ejaculated. "Well, then, it's you, old chap… Be so pleased as to let yourself down there… and allow my men to live! Don't dare refuse!"

But Busov did not consider refusing. He dexterously wrapped the rope around himself, grabbed the lantern—the Cossacks just managed to remember to hold the free end of the rope—and dropped headlong into the dark shaft.

"What a mumblin' idiot," the *uriadnik* muttered beneath his breath.

"Well done, he's certainly got spirit!" the cornet, prancing around handsomely, loudly praised him.

The rope played out rapidly and lengthily.

"It's already eighty-five feet, if not more," those holding the rope said to themselves.

During this, two guards who'd been dispatched by Kostrov breathlessly joined the group. The *uriadnik* whisperingly conferred with them about the situation.

"Hold up!" He stood on the hard ground, and the rope slackened.

Everyone held his breath.

"Well, what's there?" the *uriadnik* carefully approached the mine's edge and barked.

At that moment even the dashing cornet interrupted his prances and grimaces.

"Well?" he stretched forward impatiently.

Inside the mine's depths, silence reigned. The *uriadnik* shouted into it several more times, but received no response. Thus passed ten minutes of wearying waiting.

"Apparently, he's tyin' the rope to her."

"To who?..."

"Why, the deceased... So's she can be raised, 'n' then he'll come up hisself."

"Grab that rope! Is that swine taking the day off down there or what?" the officer finally complained.

The Cossacks began frenziedly pulling on the rope... From below, as if in response, the rope slackly flickered.

"He's orderin' you to pull, pull! Go on, boys, pour it on!" Five Cossacks, having seized the rope, began pulling with all their might; the guards joined them.

"Oo, whatta hard-a-nutter, whatta convicture!"

"Ain't for nuthin' they say she blostered off your Kostrov."

The authors of these crude jokes had evidently come up with their own strange words: they were obviously thoroughly scared, expecting they were just about to drag up a suicide's disfigured corpse... The cornet, indicating that for his part he couldn't stand his subordinates' talk, rakishly folded his arms akimbo and danced as before on his horse.

"Well-well-well, lads, once more again... Oo-ookh!"

And from out of the black opening surfaced Busov's head. Everyone screamed in surprise. The cornet turned purple with rage, and his ruddy, well-fed face contorted into a childishly capricious grimace.

"What're you doing, old chap, huh? Must you get cheeky with me, is that it? I'll have you flogged with my whip right now, you sonofabitch. I'm wasting time here because of you... Why didn't you pull her out if you found her?"

"You'll hafta pull her out yourselves," Busov vaguely said to himself, as if not having heard. And, without casting off the rope encircling his waist, he settled down on the mine's framing.

This reply stunned everyone for a moment; but then the young officer, having forgotten all caution, made an angry lurch toward the mine and, bending down from his horse, whipped the prisoner across the face. A bright crimson mark suddenly appeared on his cheek, and his lower lip began oozing blood...

"Is that how you answer an officer, you scoundrel? Going to tell me what you saw?"

But Busov didn't even glance at his tormentor. Without moving a muscle, head lowered, he continued to sit on the framing as if sunk deep in thought. Having during this time abandoned my observation post and come quite close to the activity, I once again turned my attention to the smith's hair, covered, as it had earlier seemed to me, with a white foam such as on exhausted horses: this proved to be gray strands, his jet-black hair having just distinctly become silvered!...

"Your Honor," one the prison guards, saluting, approached the cornet, "this artist has been ordered arrested."

"Serves him right, the scoundrel!" the cornet angrily replied, riding off.

The guards went up to Busov, loosened him from the rope, and began leading him away. He put up no resistance.

"Andrei, did you see her?" I quietly asked, gently holding the smith by the hands.

He started, lifted his deeply hollowed, lusterless eyes to me, and shook his head affirmatively. At that moment I saw before me not the young, handsome, powerful man I'd known days earlier as Busov, but a pitiable, bent old man…

"Whatta bother this criminal seed here has been to the whole world!" the guard who was arresting Busov turned to me, as if finding sympathy.

I shrugged my shoulders silently and, having interrupted the pathetic procession, hurried home.

Toward evening fever and delirium overtook Tania. Fugitive prisoners, hiding in the corners of our room, were haunting her, and soldiers, bayonets gleaming in the sun, were roaming throughout the village and shouting menacingly. Agitated and angrily waving her arms, she was off somewhere imploring and begging me, crying, cursing, praying… I was seized with horror at the notion that she might be commencing a nervous fever and I wouldn't know what to do. I bitterly imprecated myself, cursing my egoism and lazy-mindedness, and made an ardent promise that, as soon as the winter route was open, I would immediately send my sister off to Russia. Fortunately, I did not give myself over to fruitless self-reproach: I ended up bustling about day and night, executing what impoverished medical knowledge I possessed. Fate took pity on my helplessness: her fever gradually subsided, and after three days the patient, albeit still terribly pale and weak, was able to sit up in bed. All danger had apparently passed.

But when, joyful and happy, I went up to Tania and smilingly took her by the hand, she immediately collapsed into my chest and began sobbing grievous tears:

"My sweet dear! Will death really spare one this horror?..."

EPILOGUE

Years passed. Everything in the world has its end, and my *katorga* term ended. Much, very much, has already been blotted from my memory, and when now and then that or another image, that or another event, surfaces from oblivion and into my soul, I ask myself: "Was that real, or am I remembering some dream?…" Then again, these notes, half of which were set down while still in *katorga*, will forever contain for me the most important, significant, and—when I reread them—*all* the things I lived through, down to the petty details distinctly arising once more from the dark depths of the past. Standing so close again are all those "unfortunates"—those "know-nothings," "little rabbits," "mites," all those starving, wild, ignorant, angry, endlessly wretched people—the most grievously unfortunate of all! Once more my heart groans and aches excruciatingly! Occasionally, I want to be among them again, to share once more their bitter lot, to try to find in the depths of their spiritual gloom a spark of light… What shame to be for yourself, living once more in the camp of the "triumphant," of the "idle chatterers"!

Terrible nightmares often visit me at night, and amid the horror, pain, and suffering, familiar ghosts of all sorts flicker through my fevered brain. Hence, one night I dreamt of the unlucky escape from prison of several prisoners including Petin-the-Elk. Brutal soldiers were assaulting him with bayonets and rifle-butts and, dying before my eyes, he was moaning quietly and beseechingly, stretched along the ground to his full, gigantic length. An unknown physician was bending over him with a gutta-percha hammer, tapping for something along the hollow of his chest, counting off his broken ribs… The circling soldiers kept joking and savagely waving their Berdans in the air…

Rare and sparse rumors reach me about my cohabitants remaining in *katorga*. Chirok finally completed his term and was settled in the city of Chita, where he became a water deliveryman. Bashurov wrote me about a particular meeting with him. Chirok was in foppish blackened boots with funnel-shaped openings and a red calico blouse; meeting an old acquaintance brought him to ecstasy, and his entire face was beaming from the wide smile that spread across it. There was no end to his questions about me: "Where was I? Had I married? Would I be going to Raseya soon?" Bashurov in the meantime informed him that I would soon "expose" all we'd lived through together in Shelai. Chirok is enduring this news completely graciously…

I'll tell a little something that I learned about the subsequent fate of Old Man Pavel Nikolaev. Here's what Valerian—who after separating from me at Sretensk continued on the return trip to Verkhneudinsk with him—wrote about him:

> His dream was to sing on holidays in the choir at the Troitskii Monastery,[1] and on weekdays to collect alms in the name of Christ. True, he was disturbed by the very

idea that he'd gotten mixed up with such a dirty thing as cards, but in moments of calm he hoped to maintain his innocence (by atoning for his sins through prayer) and to acquire capital. Unfortunately, even in an enterprise for agreed upon remuneration fear has for the most part oppressed and not helped him. Twenty times a day he starts calculating how much he's spent on the *maidan* and gets terrified at how little he's gotten in return. And he still gets asked for credit—someone for a kopek for sugar, someone for a sheet of rolling paper, someone for a whole five kopeks of tobacco… "What're you gonna give?…" "I'm done for!…" They start quarreling. Sufficiently cursed and ridiculed, Nikolaev finally goes into debt, and as a result everyone's unhappy: he himself, insofar as he didn't maintain his role and gave things away and insofar as he received so much grief because of his prison of words. The others are cheeky and yell at him, and then he immediately gives away entire rubles but is afterwards, in some perplexity, bitter with me, positively bewildered at how he gave things away, and he remains a hopeless man… Ultimately, Nikolaev becomes a universal laughingstock; in the party, only the lazy fail to jeer him. Nothing can be said of any sort of thriftiness or efficient practicality. For example, it was impossible to persuade him to buy meat and fish for everyone. He once made such an attempt (at the very beginning of our trek), when the party encountered a flock of sheep on the road, and after considerable uncertainty and waffling, he purchased one. But upon arriving at the way-station, with the sheep slaughtered and skinned and a crowd of buyers surging forth, Nikolaev was at an impasse: how do you sell without a measuring scale? Wouldn't he go bust ("without a shirt there's no stopping") selling meat by the eye? His mutton was practically torn out of his hands, and the poor man probably never in his life heard so many insults and so much venomous mockery as on that rueful day; however, it must be said to his credit, that this time he stoutly defended himself well. Utterly red, bathed in sweat, hoarse from shouting, he indefatigably sent in all directions crossly amused rejoinders and his own veritable judgments and wouldn't begin selling until such time as a bismar turned up. A bismar wasn't located until the next morning, when the meat was grabbed so quickly that Nikolaev wasn't even able to remember or think through who owed what or how much. There was not even a speck of mutton left over for the master himself. Everyone was accusing him of hoarding, and now the old man was again ridiculed for not selling the fat, since it hadn't been added to or bumped up the price. However, he kept this fat in a birch box for so long (ever ready to have a "sumptuous feast" for himself) that it finally began reeking and had to be tossed away along with its vessel… Under the influence of this mockery, Nikolaev one day bought himself some pretzels and milk for his tea. You should've seen with what smug pride he drank the tea ("Now, here we go!"), a pride combining honesty with regret: "There's nothing, they say, you won't do… *Noblesse oblige.*"

But the principal test for him was cards. This sphere so exceeded his powers of comprehension that he did not even try to understand it. During games the old man remained vigilant, praying that he would win back the money he'd appropriated for the game, and under the tension of waiting he usually finally fell into vacant despair. No matter who won, he was paid the same measly amount. Even then, when he could clearly see he was being cheated, he was powerless to do anything. So it happened that, after he received his agreed-upon fees, he had someone in the other ward look after what he bought for himself with these monies. However, the next morning it came to light that his hired spy had unscrupulously cheated him, keeping for himself, besides his extra clothes, just as much again… Yet, that evening, when this fellow once more proffered his services, Nikolaev, not daring to refuse, accepted them again. Apart from periodic suspiciousness, he was dissatisfied with his assistant Ravilov as being too submissive, so when Ravilov was set free in Chita, he took as his assistant for the rest of the journey the boisterous and clever Chinaman, whom he rather feared, among other things. But Chinaman—a silly man, essentially—took to the business so zealously and thoroughly that the gamblers soon decided to emancipate themselves from him: they ripped cards and returned packs incomplete. What a catastrophe!… You can imagine what Nikolaev went through during those days. Open rebellion finally erupted, and Chinaman had to step down, but Nikolaev—I can't even explain to myself how this happened—now found he was no longer full master of the *maidan* but merely an equal partner with one of the heroes of the Amur gang known to you as Krasnoperov. This partnership consisted of Nikolaev having to manage the chest of goods and Krasnoperov the cards and is why, were there some kind of deception during a deal, the first was duty-bound to compensate the second… It should be added that Krasnoperov did not invest a single kopek in this affair.

This time, the confused, dispirited old man aroused my pity, though at the same time he pestered me, giving me no peace with his moaning and eternal talk about the *maidan*. His infantile stupidity and complete inability to stand up for himself against the herd's persistent insolence quite annoyed me. Thus, in Chita (in the capacity of an old man, and moreover one afflicted by a hernia), he was given a cart, but he barely used this cart: he was hounded to get out of it—and he got out, resignedly giving up his spot to a healthy young smart aleck. His practical naïvety and muddle-headedness, but especially his comrades' swindling provisos that kind-hearted Pavel Nikolaev, in essence, could not understand (otherwise, given his niggardliness, he would have died from horror!), finally compelled me to insist that he recuse himself from the *maidan* entirely. He agreed, only on condition that the new *maidanshchiki* secure a spot for him in the way-stations and make, in my presence, a solemn promise to pay him everything as agreed. Against all expectations, the liquidation of his affairs did not have bad results: Nikolaev had brought twenty-three rubles from Shelai, and it turns out he now has thirty-one rubles (not counting his expenses for three months on the road). He gave this money to me to hold, and since that moment the old man has been revivified: he placidly sings the blessed psalms in the evening, philosophizes aloud about the decay of everything earthly, and apparently feels not the slightest envy toward his successors, whose businesses are going decidedly otherwise. He only now and then jokingly expresses amazement that his business didn't turn a profit… But, more often, he expresses joy that he liberated himself from a terrible disaster, from claws he couldn't expect to escape alive! And how blissfully he smiles at the idea that he's survived all this, that he has, you know, willy-nilly proved his worth!…

"In the beginning, it was mostly thanks to Ivan Nikolaevich that I landed in the kasha, and during our goodbye I was thinking to amuse him a bit… Well, but then I tried to show off my power!"

I'm sorry I cannot depict in sufficient detail the various characteristic particularities that have so enriched this tragicomic episode. I can't even remember those amusing little words that Nikolaev, it seemed to me, used with special pleasure when he saw they tickled you and me. Only a vague representation is left in my memory.

Bashurov's kind letter is all that I know of Pavel Nikolaev's subsequent life. The old man promised to write me and was given my address, but for some reason did not keep his promise. Where is he now, and what's become of him?…

Shelai's escapees, to universal astonishment, did not receive any punishment: evidently, the brave captain's fall and the defeat of the model regime he'd established redounded to their benefit.

But this, it turns out, exhausts the happy news from the world of the outcasts.

Word is that the poor convict-poet Bear's Ears has been assigned for removal to Sakhalin Island, but is bearing this assignment with such disinterestedness that it's like he's received an order to become a cleaner or to dig potatoes from the garden. He is as silent and shut up inside himself as before, and, as before, he walks about with his head hanging down. But the poor man's health is now shattered: his chest hurts, he suffers insomnia; a dry, staccato cough gives neighbors no peace…

Days ooze by for the fat man Nogaitsev: he has dropsy. His legs have swollen like tree-limbs, and now the wretched "Mikhailo Ivanovich" can't leave the infirmary.

The stormy, gloomy career of Sokoltsev has also ended completely unexpectedly. Not having reached his "limit," not having broken out of the *katorga* regime's claws, he suddenly died of a heart attack while working in the joiner's shop. In the same place where lay the ashes of Marazgali and the tiny old bones of Goldy, near the road along which Shelai's convicts march to the mine, this indefatigable man, this prison sophist and Mephistopheles, has found eternal peace.

I've also been hearing that among the mines are spread the heroics of a well-built old man with a lion's mane of gray hair and a pock-marked face. The old man is a big phrase-monger, and he knows me and refers to me in each instance with a bow.

"Jus' tell Ivan Nikolaevich 'bout me, he'll know right away who it is!…"

I really have almost no doubt that this is Goncharov—my old acquaintance and friend… And my heart seizes painfully at the thought that the old rabble-rouser will to the very end be considered guilty and will nevermore see freedom or home!

1895–1898

FROM THE AUTHOR (*POSTSCRIPTUM*)[1]

The story of "Ivan Nikolaevich" is finished and, in conclusion, I want to tell the reader a few words about myself. The whole time I was writing this book, my cherished wish was that this true story about the life of the outcasts would be understood as the voice of their friend and defender; an appreciation of such immediate significance would, for me, of course, be the highest and best reward. I hope I've actually managed to show how "the inhabitants of this terrible world, these crippled, benighted, occasionally crazy people, were, like all of us, capable not only of hating, but of loving passionately and profoundly, of falling but of rising, of thirsting for light and truth, and suffering no less than we from all that is a barrier on the path to human happiness" (v. 1). To be honest, I planned from the start to present in all possible ways an unvarnished reflection of the truth; believing that it was possible to assist in the resurrection of a sick and criminal soul not with false idealism but, most of all, with a complete and impartial study—truthful and only truthful—I didn't want to hide the feelings of indignation and revulsion my very heroes sometimes called forth from me. However, was this the reason that some readers could draw mistaken and pernicious—I'm firmly convinced—conclusions from my book?

Although it may not be literary custom to comment on one's own work, I consider it within my rights to violate this norm in the present instance. The issues I broach in these essays hold least of all an abstract-artistic interest for me, since I cannot for one minute renounce myself from that concrete, absolutely years-long nightmare reality on which I terribly wanted rays of warmth and light, however minute, to shine. Not once have I happened to express in print my general thoughts and conclusions concerning the complex issues of "crime and punishment," which are like a sum total of all that I lived through, and here I want only to repeat something of what's been said in my previous journalistic essays, having abjured there everything that was incidental or controversial.

Among other things, my essays provided a certain former professor and psychiatrist Mr. P. Kovalevskii material for judging criminals, "based on their organization, their natural characteristics, and the unique structure of their central nervous system, to be as such criminals by birth, who account for the principal [!] *katorga* contingent and are by character the most inveterate malefactors." In the professor's opinion, such are "almost all [?] Dostoevskii's and Melshin's[2] protagonists."

It goes without saying that I can in no way delineate such an interpretation of my writings… In fact, what "objective" evidence shows that our *principal katorga* contingent and *almost all* of Dostoevskii's and Melshin's protagonists consist of natural-born criminals?

It should first of all be firmly understood that it is neither general amorality nor depravity nor viciousness leading people into prison and *katorga*, but rather certain and completely demonstrable violations existent in a state of laws. However, we all know (and the professor all the more) that, for example, fifty years ago, during the time of *Notes from a Dead House*, a law existed in Russia by which one man commanded another as if he were a thing, a chattel, and violations of this past law often led to one's being exiled to Siberia or even penal labor. There also existed another law on the strength of which a man, having been "called up" to become a soldier, essentially became a dead man, only in rare instances returning to his earlier, free life (service under Nicholas lasted a quarter-century), and it is no wonder that, in the words of the poet, "the people's terror before the word 'recruitment' was a terror of the death sentence."[3] Nowadays, for us all, these are merely historical reminders of the pre-Reform life's brutality to the point of inhumanity, with which we, people of the current generation, cannot imagine reconciling ourselves in any case; but during Dostoevskii's time, such was the *existing life*, and on the basis of his timeless essays it can be documentarily proved that a good half of those protagonists condemned to *katorga* went there precisely due to violations of slaveholding's and twenty-five-year soldiery's anti-humanitarian laws... Certainly, all those Sirotkins, Petrovs, Martynovs, Baklushins, Sushilovs,[4] etc. were nothing other than victims of that terrible spiritual torpor that all hearts even barely alive and beating necessarily experienced during those gloomy days; indeed, this most vivacious element of the Russian people was actually the *most gifted*, as Dostoevskii put it, and if the scholarly professor's opinion about his "natural-born criminality" is accepted, then what a grim conclusion we shall reach regarding the Russian people!... Torpor was the outgrowth of abnormal living conditions, and it set ignorant, intellectually and morally dissolute, Petrovs and Baklushins on the path of vice and drunkenness and on to senseless outbursts of criminality; yet, did not the people of higher breeding, the Dostoevskiis, the Belinskiis, the Herzens,[5] led by this very same torpor down a different path, bear in their unquestioning orthodox contemporaries' eyes the very same stigma of criminal deviation? Martynov, from *Dead House*, came to *katorga* for the "pretense" of calculating his battalion's kasha ration; but what, *in essence*, was the difference between him and, for example, Herzen, who, because of his pretenses regarding not only kasha but the entire pre-Reform structure, had to flee abroad permanently? In this regard, the Lombrosian School is utterly consistent: for it, there is no special difference between highly principled criminals and criminals opposed to general welfare. But herein lies the school's most vulnerable spot: on one hand, it is obviously clambering onto the heights of social probity and humanitarianism, is beginning to view the criminal as a sick individual, and is therefore banning from the penitentiary system the principal of retribution, yet, on the other, it crawls amid the ashes of its own inveterate conservatism. The more moderate among these scholarly objectivists reason thus: "Criminality amounts to an inability to live according to a given society's acknowledged standards. The criminal is a person for whom, owing to his organism, it is difficult or impossible to live consensually with these standards and who casually risks punishment through anti-social acts. Due to whatever accidental circumstances of his development, due to whatever insufficiencies in his heredity, birth, or upbringing, he is as if condemned to a lower and more obsolete societal order than that in which he moves.

It may even be that our criminals approximate the physiques and psyches of typical representatives of a lower race."

I've drawn these words from a book by the English criminologist Havelock Ellis (*The Criminal*, translated under the direction of Dr. Grinberg), a writer and, in general, very temperate and sympathetic.[6] Ellis still grants much to development and education; yet, the abovementioned Russian scholar does not cogitate for a moment, of course, that *whosoever* merely steps away from these standards comes to be seen as a natural-born criminal… Without the slightest hesitation be labels "criminals by nature" nearly all Dostoevskii's protagonists and nearly all of today's penal laborers, solely in the conceit that they cannot live within boundaries recognized as compulsory for contemporary society and determined by law. It is unimportant that these people, according to Dostoevskii's testimony, "may be the most gifted of all the Russian people," unimportant that outside *katorga* prison walls, advantaging themselves of all freedom's goods, might live tens of thousands of cretins in the literal sense of the word, ideal representatives of some sort of lower race: it *is* important that these cretins are nevertheless able to measure up to these standards—consequently, they are the normal people; those others, the most gifted, cannot measure up—consequently, they are the natural-born criminals. Thus would "objective science" speak, projecting today's knowledge fully armed…

Here, a proviso is necessary. It may be that some readers will recall and point out a certain contradiction on my part, that I repeatedly asserted in my essays the profound difference between contemporary *katorga* and the *katorga* of Dostoevskii's time. I have always placed the latter as incomparably greater, and consider his psychology very close to the normal type; contrarily, the population of today's *katorga*, *for the most part*, I have acknowledged as "the scum of the human sea" (*In the World of the Outcasts*, v. 1). In another place, observing the difference between *katorga* and the people, I said more distinctly: "The Russian people is not itself a collection of murderers, maniacs, thieves, rapists, and debauchees. Allow these individuals to depart from that same people, and allow most of them to be personally completely innocent about how they have so become; allow still many to find in themselves the strength to rise again, to again enter the great human sea, so allow them… And yet, the criminal soul will nevertheless not be the soul of the Russian people! With all the power of my words I protest such an identification" ("Sweetened Love for the People," *Russian Wealth*, January 1898).[7]

I will of course not take back any of these words. But I have never asserted nor will I agree to assert that today's Russian *katorga*, though for the most part representing the moral scum of the human sea, is nothing other than garbage produced by *nature itself*. I am profoundly convinced that nature does not matter *as much* as modern society and the social conditions resulting from our legal, economic, religious, and exclusionary relations, and also (and this is a huge factor!) the incomplete composition of our ethical understanding. I've intentionally said "not as much" so as to nevertheless credit something to nature. Theoretically speaking, immoral monsters undoubtedly may exist, carrying within themselves even inside their mothers' wombs the elements of criminality, but the point is, does this or that science with the help of such indisputable arguments show me criminals X, Y, and Z to have been designed by nature to be conceived as prison candidates? I exclude madmen and idiots, who are hauled before a jury only out of misunderstanding; there is talk about such criminals, who are not in any way distinguished from healthy and normal people by decisively evident peculiarities. I think such "natural-born criminals," victims of their own exclusively terrible heredity, ultimately amount to the most insignificant percentage. For example, it is *possible* (albeit not provable) that my Semënov was one such exception (v. 1, ch. XI).

When Dostoevskii talked in *Notes from a Dead House* about a certain nobleman who was a patricide, he was convinced the man was abnormal (in those days, the term "natural-born criminal" was unknown, though Dostoevskii would probably have used it) and could not be held responsible for his crime. He based his opinion on the proposed patricide's complete lack of remorse. "Once, speaking with me about his family's heredity of a healthy constitution, he [the murderer] added: 'So, *my parent*, until his very end, never complained about any illness whatsoever.'" These words' naïve cynicism struck Dostoevskii profoundly. In other regards the criminal seemed the most typical individual—true, he was eccentric and lazy-minded, but all the same neither stupid nor cruel; yet in the meantime, he could talk so astoundingly coolly about the very same "parent" he murdered! Such beastly unfeeling seemed impossible to the author of *Dead House*: "this is a phenomenon, for here is a kind of complete constitution, a kind of physical and moral deformity, still unknown to science, and not simply a crime."

Pausing without further commentary on this page from *Notes from a Dead House*, gentlemen scholars of criminology would, needless to say, hurriedly enter it into the annals of their "objective" science: here, they'd say, is testimonial fact from one of the greatest artists of the word! Isn't this a classic example of a natural-born criminal, whose nature consists of amoral refuse! But, to truth's good fortune, Dostoevskii was not only a great artist but an honest writer of life. In the conclusion of his book, he said that he'd only just learned that the patricide had been proven innocent: the actual murderer had been found, and the innocent man who lived so many years in *katorga* was released. A strange fact, leading the great writer to the bitterest misgivings…

Well, but how does Mr. Kovalevskii relate to this case? Does he simply fail to mention it, since it's not grist for his mill? No, incomparably worse: he fails to mention *only the proviso* by Dostoevskii that the patricide turned out to be innocent, and cites all the other circumstances… Such is his heartless clerical pedantry[8] that, for him, the elegance and structure of his "system" is incomparably more important than truth and a living human life!

For my part, I'm firmly convinced that criminal science, searching the essays of *In the World of the Outcasts* for indisputable objective proof for its dubious hypothesis of the "natural-born criminal," will discover no such proof.

"Here's rich pablum for Lombrosian deductions!" Ivan Nikolaevich one day decided (v. 2, ch. II), "having seen in the bathhouse Iukhorev's naked back covered with thick, shaggy hair." Some straightforward Lombroso disciple could probably earnestly parse out this fleeting notion by my essays' protagonist, holding up Iukhorev's hairy back as proof of his natural-born criminality. However, it is clear from subsequent exposition that this specimen, this intelligent and energetic criminal, was originally exiled to Siberia through a sentence by fellow villagers in his community (the "cattle's way") because he was defending the interests of the village poor. True, Ivan Nikolaevich knew him as a man already embittered by life, spiritually crippled and depraved, but what role in all this was played by his natural constitution and what was owing to social environment and living conditions—this is the question that modern science is still helpless to dissemble. In any case, life is simply too complicated a thing to be put inside the narrow confines of a theory.

The most antipathetic and immoral of all the given prisoners presented by me is, in my eyes, a certain Tropin (v. 2, ch. VII). "Of all the various riff-raff I saw in the outcasts' world he was perhaps the sterling example, concerning which I'd be hard-pressed to say: did he have in the innermost depths of his soul, in those depths hardly known to the possessor himself, something nonetheless cherished and sacred? … At the height of my war with Iukhorev, I could be intrigued and even carried away by this man, such was his power; but not once during all of our acquaintanceship, nor even during a single brief moment, did Tropin manage to inspire in me the smallest feeling of sympathy or accord…" However, following these lines, there also appears the following proviso: "I fear that in painting my portrait of this youth I've layered on some rather dark colors… Who knows, maybe I'm to blame for a lack of insight and consideration on my part? Maybe another, more indulgent and impartial, observer would have been able to discover in Tropin the holy spark without which it is somehow difficult to imagine an intelligent being—a human… But I'm simply writing what I myself saw and felt."

The latter is most significant. A person finding himself in the position of the protagonist of *Notes from a Dead House* or of my essays can portray only what he himself sees and *feels*. His portrayal, of necessity, is distinguished by enormous subjectivity, and any serious scientific generalization that may be built on it or even simply shown by it is at the least strange and naïve. Living in Shelai Prison and listening to various murderers' stories, the individual under whose name my notes appear says that he himself, as it happened, decided that Lombroso was right. "My entire body was trembling as I looked in horror at these people, wondering how they could laugh at such things. I clearly remember feeling at that moment [during a certain Andriushka Povar's talk] as if I were in a madhouse, and I was reminded of a certain criminal theory that had at one time powerfully disturbed me and that acknowledges all 'criminals' as people with abnormal mental capabilities" (v. 1, "Solitude," ch. I). But "to think" is still a long way from being persuaded. And it is clear from my subsequent account that, for example, his listeners were making fun of Andriushka's cynical talks: hardly sympathizing with his speeches, they were marveling at their stupidity… And Andriushka himself proved to be an imbecilic chap, as well as a great enthusiast for braggadocio and exaggeration. As such, this apparently favorably material does not, like water or fog running through the hands, permit so definite a conclusion, and only very casual people would not be embarrassed by such pettifoggery.

Proceeding in his brochure toward determining the "characteristic traits of the criminal family," Mr. Kovalevskii tries to lean upon Dostoevskii: his penal laborers are a people embittered, taciturn, envious, vainglorious, boastful, and prickly; they are terribly suspicious, and among them rules constant gossip and slander… True, Melshin's penal laborers seem less gloomy and more sociable, but is such a minor contrast dwelt upon, and does it explain him and, for example, the unsociable and mistrustful character of the author of *Notes from a Dead House* himself?[9]

Signed and sealed: the natural-born criminal (he *is* the penal laborer) is bitter and silent.

Mr. Kovalevskii should, however, perhaps remember: these wretched people are after all in a *katorga* prison! They are deprived not only of all the emoluments and joys of a free life, but even the right to human dignity! They're degraded at every step like cattle, made to perform forced and often completely mindless labor… They're shut up in prison walls like spiders in a jar… What remains for them if not to be gloomy, to devour each other, engage in gossip and judgments, wallow in all sorts of triviality and meanness? Place in the same situation not only criminals (completely uncultured people, in the main) but scholarly professors, and it would have to be seen whether even they remain in the loftiness of their scholarly grandiosity… As such, are the prisoner's foolish characteristics enumerated by Dostoevskii indisputably provable to be the "character traits" of the natural-born criminal?

Incidentally, Mr. Kovalevskii especially emphasizes prisoners' stubborn unrepentance, insofar as they apparently never suffer from a guilty conscience and don't want to think about: before whom are they to suffer, to whom are they to repent, and of whom are they to be ashamed? To be ashamed of their no less criminal and corrupt comrades? To repent before malicious representatives of the local administration, who for the most part are incapable of inspiring either respect or sympathy for themselves?

Melshin talks—Mr. Kovalevskii further points out—about penal laborers' monstrous moral vacuity, especially graphically manifest in their stories about exquisitely savage murders and bestial acts. There follows a quotation: "The crowd was evidently always on the side of the torturer and not the victim, and in its eyes there's always some excuse for the first of these." In the midst of an example of heartless cynicism and exquisitely voluptuous beastliness you may find yourself able to say whatever you like; but you should nevertheless not exaggerate and, principally, not generalize so ferociously. With regard to the above phrase, did I really say that prisoners *always and everywhere* sympathize expressly with the torturer but not the victim? What I'm saying concerns merely how they relate to their comrades' *stories* about their pasts. In *katorga*'s eyes each such storyteller, owing *in the given moment* to the fact of his stay in prison, in captivity, seems a victim, regardless of the horrors he's told about himself; living at *that* moment a trying existence, he inspires in comrades more sympathy than those he destroyed with his own hands and who have long since been lying in their graves… Philosophy, it is true, is odd and one-sidedly humane, but it is anyhow necessary to take into consideration the instant you want to judge impartially these uncultured, deeply corrupted, and so profoundly unfortunate people. In my essays, there are no few facts proving that the Russian prisoner is not at all devoid of a tender, loving heart and the ability to sympathize with another's suffering, an ability at times achieving self-renunciation.

Of the natural-born criminal's other "character traits" Mr. Kovalevskii notes his hatred "toward all other forms of humanity," without demonstrating, however, what he's based this charge upon. Apparently, this has been quoted from my biography of Semënov. Actually, he's an ultra-malicious individual, "deep-rootedly evil," as the scholarly professor puts it. But it goes without saying that to judge all the thousands of penal laborers by this lone example is unfair and unworthy of scholarly people, who should be fair regarding my Semënov. Reject the highhanded and clearly exaggerated pathos in his words about evil (and what little can be said in evil!), and left clearly before us is that Semënov by no means hates *all forms of humanity* but only that portion known to him—namely, the wealthy and self-satisfied. And this, I suggest, is an enormous difference! Regarding the other inhabitants of the outcasts' world (figures for the most part pettier and at the same time closer to normal human types), I could however go on with the chapter "Demons of Evil and Destruction" (v. 1), where conversations "on broad social themes" are depicted. It turns out that these "dreamers" never had a shred of doubt that the "people" and the inhabitants of *katorga* are completely one and the same… And what naïve plans—in truth, wild, terrible, nightmarishly bloody, but, all the same, instinctual (it must be admitted)—they concoct for attaining universal good fortune *in love* and not in any kind of indiscriminate "hatred toward all human sorts."

"Non-criminal society seemed for them nothing but a collection of mortal enemies whom they hated and [against whom (?)] they committed all possible evil [they did this, sitting in prison?]. Vengeance, unforgiving vengeance, threatens all enemies of the *katorga* cohort, and many have made this vengeance their principal object for freedom and exiting from jail." This is a generalization of a completely fantastical character… Neither Dostoevskii nor any other chronicler of prison and *katorga* life ever says that some prisoner made as his principal object for freedom and exiting from jail "vengeance against all enemies of the *katorga* cohort." For me, at least, a good deal has been penned about the vindication of Russian prisoners with regard to *personal* enemies, and so this assertion appears to be an absolute novelty, the baselessness of which I surely cannot doubt in the least.

Regarding another charge against the "natural-born criminal," that it is in the "basis of his existence" to be inclined to be lazy and opposed to work, especially if this work is mandatory, there emerges the unsought-for question: does a completely normal person really greet mandatory labor with joy, delight, inspiration?…

Finally, there is a still more surprising scholarly conclusion about the natural-born criminal's relationship to literacy. "Very many criminals are literate," says the former professor, "but the literacy they have acquired is not so much an expression of the mind's curiosity and inquisitiveness as it is *a means of concealing and abetting criminality*." One asks—where's this come from?… Naturally, you'll first of all remember my own words, my own stories. "Mikolaich, what's lit'racy to us?"—Nikifor Burenkov, in despair over his own inability, sometimes asked his teacher.

"I tried, in answering this question, to explain literacy's usefulness, saying that it makes a person intelligent and therefore honest; but, while asserting this, I now and then doubted myself: what did it, all this literacy, mean for them, the prisoners? In subsequent instances I several times became convinced that many of my best students, who had studied and read and written conscientiously, very quickly forgot this and that upon release to the free command, and a bitter vexation sometimes whispered in my soul, a conviction that so much of my gift of labor and time had been squandered. More than once I also happened to hear from prisoners themselves that literacy is actually harmful for them, that a swindler can become a bigger swindler with it, whereas an honest man, having dreamt of the easy work of a clerk and acquired an aversion to physical labor, can be corrupted thanks to it. *I well understood, of course, the utter superficiality and perniciousness of such generalizations on the basis of salient, exclusionary facts*, but I do confess I was often seized by all sorts of doubt, and would then abandon my school for a long time… However, a certain time passed, and I returned to it with love. My 'pedagogical' activity was strewn with bitterness and poison from all sorts of brambles and thorns that bled my soul, nevertheless, there was something kind, blessed, and warm in it that illuminated and comforted not only me but, it seemed, the entire ward. Prisoners somehow unwittingly became accustomed to regard paper and book with respect, and the ideas attuned them to a higher tone and harmony…" (v. 1, "The Shelai Mine," ch. X).

Those are the only corresponding sentences in my essays; and yet, how my intention was altered and so frankly misconstrued! Or perhaps Mr. Kovalevskii has made use of some other source here? But, in any case, it is difficult to tolerate that, in quoting me continually and treating me as an author of a certain type, he did not read through or devote sustained attention to those chapters of *World of the Outcasts* where I describe "student" prisoners and all their incalculably candid enthusiasm—at first in the study of grammar, and subsequently of composition (v. 1, "The Shelai Mine," ch. VIII, X; "Solitude," ch. IV; v. 2, ch. XIII, XVI). On the issue of how prisoners regard the recitation of books, Mr. Kovalevskii writes: "These people do not like to read [!], and if they do read, then it is mostly collections harmonizing and satisfying their base animal motives, their filthy fantasies, and their carnal inclinations." Permit me to recollect what I wrote concerning this: "These evenings devoted to recitation comprise the best and most gratifying part of my memories of Shelai Prison, and, regardless of all the personal disappointments accompanying my dreams about the humanitarian impact of artistic literati on *katorga*'s residents, I personally stick to my opinion to this day" (v. 1). In another spot, in reference to the prisoners' own compositions: "There was one universal similarity among them. Their authors were concerned and tormented by one and the same question—why they'd been pushed onto the path of criminality and debauchery—and all simultaneously complained they were incapable of living honestly among non-dissolute, good people, or did not know how to do so, and—what was most important—their grief, these thoughts, always produced an indubitable, profound candor" (v. 2).

It stands to reason that my opinions and stories, like any others, are subject to controversy and debate, but it's a fact that Mr. Kovalevskii, so lavish in his quotations from Melshin in other circumstances, treats them with silence when they quite characteristically contradict his theories. He set himself the goal, *at all costs*, of proving that the majority of our penal laborers are natural-born criminals. It seems to me that among the ideas about "natural-born criminals" there is but one step to the idea of the "criminal beast." And this step has been taken, also by a representative of the scholarly corporation, and it has also, to my chagrin, been referenced to my essays…

"Certain categories of prisoners are true beasts," insisted a representative of a certain provincial association of physicians, "and the only means of restraining them appears to be chains and canes." Once they're beasts, then, of course, there's nothing surprising in such a conclusion…

There should be more energetic protest against such dubiously scientific positions. Gentlemen scholars generally have a tendency to forget, or perhaps they don't want to remember, that their theories do not circumscribe a vacuum and that life is not just material for their speculative conclusions: beyond theory there stands a living human being, and any erroneous or simply unfairly stipulated idea founded on it is often bought at the price of blood and tears…

1900

NOTES

With Comrades

1 *Chernaia nemoch′*—a colloquialism for epilepsy.
2 Iakubovich did, in fact, work as a striker at Akatui.
3 Mispronunciation of "Petersburg."
4 Shteinhart and Bashurov resemble several of Iakubovich's real-life comrades in prison. Bashurov most resembles M. V. Stoianovskii (1867–1908); Shteinhart bears similarities to L. V. Freifel′d (1863–after 1934), M. A. Ufliand (1862–1922), and R. M. Gots (1866–1906).
5 A reference to the theories of Italian criminologist Cesare Lombroso (1835–1909), who purported to be able to identify criminals according to physical traits. Iukhorev's real-life analog was named Iudintsev and was similarly the headman at Akatui. He was reportedly a huge, muscular, red-bearded man whose gaze exerted a hypnotic effect over other prisoners. He was also said to intimidate the guards and commandant.
6 His mother was a *meshchanka*, i.e., a member of the *meshchane*—a social estate roughly equivalent to the petty bourgeoisie. His father was a *chinovnik*, who through state service had evidently advanced far enough through the ranks (*chiny*) to acquire nobiliary status.
7 Another word for everyday black tea.
8 A curious phrase: *chizholovatyi vozdukh.*
9 This following story is autobiographical, insofar as it concerns Iakubovich and his fiancée R. F. Frank. In a letter of March 1887 to N. K. Mikhailovskii, Iakubovich was unapologetic for including what he acknowledged is a "romantic monologue… somewhat sharply dissonant to the essays' general background."
10 This phrase appears in Scene Five of the lyrical comedy *Medvezh′ia okhota* (The Bear Hunt) (1864), by N. A. Nekrasov.
11 A town approximately 15 miles southwest of St Petersburg.
12 Line from the poem "Fortunata," by Apollon Nikolaevich Maikov (1821–1897).
13 Peter-Paul Fortress in St Petersburg.
14 Destinations for many exiles, Tomsk and Tiumen′ are located approximately 600 miles from each other in western Siberia. Tiumen′ was the location of the Exile Bureau (*Ekspeditsiia o ssyl′nykh*), which would have had to approve Elena's telegram before forwarding it to Shteinhart.
15 At that time, telegraphers hand-wrote, rather than typed, telegrams.
16 I.e., 30 miles east of Tomsk.
17 A town 220 miles eastward along the march route from Khaldeev Station.
18 Modern-day Daugavpils, Latvia's second-largest city.
19 A reference to Italian revolutionary Giuseppe Garibaldi (1807–1882).
20 Village and urban communal associations possessed the authority to administratively deport their members to Siberia. However, only serious criminal offenders were assigned to Olëkminsk, and then only by judicial, not administrative, measures. Bashurov, in other words, is unintentionally revealing that he's been duped by Iukhorev.
21 A subtle reference to Iakutsk's community of political exiles.
22 Low-grade tobacco.

23 An interesting suggestion, given that Orthodox Christianity forbids the consumption of meat on fast days.

24 Afterward, however, when the prison's material circumstances became more tenuous, our tobacco began to be distributed only to smokers through a similar agreement between prisoners and headmen. [Author's note.]

25 In deep, subterranean worksites the majority of prisoners regard whistling and singing as disgraceful. In our Shelai, as it turned out, they sang in the shafts, but their depths did not exceed thirty-five to sixty feet. [Author's note.]

26 From the poem "V rudnike" (In the Mine), by Fëdor F. Filimonov (1862–1920).

27 Pierre-Jean de Béranger (1780–1857), French poet and composer of especially satirical lyrics.

28 I.e., "different." [Author's note.]

29 It's possible, of course, that this is two different songs, though as a matter of fact I heard from the best prison singers, like Iukhorev, that they're always united without the slightest break, and everyone assured me it's a single song. [Author's note.]

30 A posse. Another meaning for "stirrup" is a secret lookout. [Author's note.]

31 As a matter of fact, penal laborers in categories II and III, sentenced to terms of up to twelve years in a factory or fortress and, given the lack of the latter, typically assigned as well to mines (which assignment is according to law the harshest punishment), take advantage of the so called mining reduction, whereby four months are subtracted from each year. Penal laborers in category I do not get this reduction. [Author's note.]

32 The manifesto of 14 November 1894 (coincident with Nicholas II's ascent to the throne) reduced the terms of those assigned to *katorga* by one-third. The prisoners had been read not the manifesto but the governor's circular, which contained an error.

33 A remote town in northeast Siberia.

34 A large *katorga* site and prison near Irkutsk.

35 Penal laborers' prison terms depended on the total number of years of their sentences. Thus, for lifers it amounted to eleven years; for those sentenced to 16, 17, 18, 19, or 20 years, it was seven years; to 13, 14, or 15 years—five years; 10, 11, or 12 years—three and a half, etc. Penal laborers having more than 12 years total were considered to be in the *first*, or mining, category, and did not usually have the benefit of any reductions, save for two months off each year for good behavior. Thanks to the large "mountain" reduction, *katorga* for short-termers was usually reduced by almost half. As such, the longer a penal laborer's term, the worse his behavior in all respects. [Author's note.]

36 *Kniga zhivota*—log of prisoners' behavior.

37 Apropos this, I'm so far not in a position to identify this flower. It is owing to me that in the first part of *World of the Outcasts* such singularly contradictory terms as "violet" and "red" rosemary flowers are to be encountered. But I think there's no contradiction at all: normally violet, this flower assumes under new light a reddish hue. [Author's note.]

38 A character in N. V. Gogol's *Dead Souls* who engages in sophistry.

39 The Russian word for "cucumber" is *ogurets*.

40 Mark Matveevich Antokol′skii (1843–1902) was a Jewish-Russian sculptor. However, given the description of Iukhorev's stance, with arm extended, Iakubovich appears to have mistakenly credited to Antokol′skii the sculpture of Peter that was in fact made by Étienne Maurice Falconet (1716–1791)—i.e., the Petersburg sculpture popularly known as the "Bronze Horseman" that portrays Peter pointing with outstretched arm astride a rearing stallion. By contrast, Antokol′skii's sculpture of Peter (which was moreover located in Taganrog) is sedate.

41 *Karas′* is Russian for "carp."

42 "Tropin" roughly translates as "Pathbreaker."

43 In southern Ukraine. Today called Myoklaiv.

44 A fictional character in novels by French writer Émile Gaboriau (1832–1873), who modeled Lecoq after the real-life Eugène Vidocq (1775–1857), a former-criminal-turned-policeman who eventually became director of the French National Police.

45 Word designating the Polish parliament and used derogatorily in this context.

46 Boris Godunov was first the de facto and then the official ruler of Russia between 1584 and 1605. Pushkin's play *Boris Godunov* was completed in 1825, and like other post hoc treatments it portrays the Tatar as a scheming, backstabbing manipulator.

47 *Les Exploits de Rocambole ou les dramas de Paris* was an internationally popular adventure series by Pierre Alexis Ponson du Terrail (1829–1871) published between 1859 and 1884.

48 These derived from standard replies expected of soldiers in response to officers' greetings.

49 A play on words: in this case "Lomov" has been delexicalized from the verb *lomit'*—"to break."

50 There is more wordplay in this paragraph: the adjective *lomovoi* means "draught."

51 Marcus Porcius Cato Uticensis (95–46 BC), political opponent of Julius Caesar renowned for his moral integrity. After learning of Caesar's victory over the opposition, he killed himself rather than submit to his rule.

52 *Russian Olden Times* (*Russkaia starina*) was a popular history journal of the late tsarist era.

53 A reference to a passage in the Book of Daniel about three young men ordered to be thrown into a furnace by King Nebuchadnezzar. They miraculously survived.

54 At the present time, when for me Shelai (Akatui) is now fifteen years past, it's possible, I think, to reveal Lomov's "pseudonym." With this name I've tried to portray Chita's Police Chief Somov, who was eventually tragically killed at his post. By nature and character this man was suited to policing. It's said that Chita, whose sanitation was improved and whose number of robberies and thefts was reduced, benefited significantly from his zeal and assiduity; but on the other hand, this Siberian tsarnik's enormous, peremptory power intoxicated him, igniting in his soul an innate, voluptuary cruelty and a love for mocking the disfranchised, defenseless victims who fell into his hands. Somov's favorite pastime in Chita was cutting down exile-settlers, which he practiced on the merest occasion and for the most insignificant offense… But human dignity finally arose in those dark, outcast souls—and so, one foul autumn evening in 1899, as he sat surrounded by his family and illuminated by a lamp, Somov was murdered on the spot by a shot fired from a rifle through his room's window…

Intense suspicion fell immediately on several exile-settlers. A military court from Irkutsk determined that the shot that felled Somov had come from a rifle fired by Parfenov, after which a certain Grishko fired again from a revolver; Taran and another unarmed accomplice were standing watch at the door. Gudkov had supplied the evil-doers with a horse and wagon; Doll managed to hide the evidence of the crime. The principal instigator to murder appeared to have been a certain Iashagashvili. Of those found guilty, only Taran confessed, and he slandered the others. All charges were based on Taran's testimony, and there was not one shred of material evidence. All the same, this proved enough for a Siberian military court, and three men (Parfenov, Grishko, and Iashagashvili) were hanged and the rest sent to *katorga*… [Author's note.]

55 A reference to Éduard Drumont (1844–1917) and Victor Henri Rochefort (1830–1913), publicists renowned for their antisemitic screeds published during France's Dreyfus Affair.

56 "Lastochka," by Apollon Maikov (1821–1897).

57 *Bachok* (sing.)—a large serving vessel from which several persons ate at once.

58 A food resembling ravioli.

59 "ѣ," from the old Russian orthography.

60 Iakubovich betrays some ignorance here regarding Judaism. The *Shema* actually denotes the central prayer that would be included in these "beat-up" books and papers.

61 A *Yahrzeit* candle burns for twenty-four hours on the anniversary of one's death.

62 Person who assists the rabbi in operating a synagogue.

63 *Chetvertnoi bilet*—bill worth twenty-five rubles.

64 Generally speaking, unless they had official permission to live elsewhere Jews were restricted to residing in what was called the Pale of Settlement. This region did not include Staraia Russa. Shuster seems to be implying that the policeman identified him as a Jew from his facial features and, therefore, as a non-resident.

65 *Bednost′ ne porok*, a comedy by Aleksandr N. Ostrovskii (1823–1886).

66 Inmate jargon for what seem to have been either sandals or slippers issued by the authorities.

67 In criminals' speech, a "full-on" signifies a theft of a home carried out very quickly in broad daylight. Thefts "on a good morning" are committed in summertime, at daybreak, while the masters are deep in morning slumbers. If the latter nevertheless awake because of the noise, the thief takes to his heels and avoids a fight. "Zips" are done on autumn and winter nights; weapons are often involved. [Author's note.]

68 A misspelling of "social," by which the author intended to mean "socialism."

69 All names in this book have been concocted or altered; Lavrentii Pomiakshev is, apparently, a singular exception, since—I don't recall for what reasons—I retained his real name. Many years later, I encountered his name in Mr. Doroshevich's book *Sakhalin*: having turned up in one of Sakhalin's prisons, Pomiakshev, it turned out, was now suffering from what the administration certified as genuine insanity. [Author's note.]

70 A poem by the Siberian poet and regionalist Dmitrii P. Davydov (1811–1888) that first appeared in 1858 in the newspaper *Zolotoe runo* (Golden Fleece) under the title "Dumy begletsa na Baikale" (Meditations of a Fugitive on Baikal). It later became the basis for a folksong, the words of which were first published by Iakubovich.

71 Type of fish found in Lake Baikal.

72 Siberian term for a northwest wind on Baikal.

73 River near Nerchinsk.

74 Sergei M. Solov′ëv (1820–1879) was the author of *Istorii Rossii s drevneishikh vremen* (A History of Russia since Antiquity) in *twenty* (not twenty-nine) volumes. Friedrich Christoph Schlosser (1776–1861) was a German historian and author of the uncompleted eighteen-volume *Weltgeschichte in zusammenhängender Erzählung* (World History).

75 A reference to two contemporaneous literary genres: Decadence and Symbolism.

76 Joséphin Péladan (1858–1918), French novelist and occultist.

77 Entitled "The Borers' Song" ("Pesnia buril′shchikov"), this poem by Iakubovich was composed at Akatui in 1892. Its final lines were not included in the first edition of *In the World of the Outcasts*.

78 Iakubovich suffered from severe rheumatism, which led to his premature death.

79 "Zalata" sounds like *zoloto* ("gold").

80 There are several villages in southern Ukraine called Poltavshchina ("Little Poltava"). Iakubovich's spelling is meant to express Zalata's pronunciation of this name in Ukrainian.

81 Government documents published during this period show that for just a span of several years escapes both attempted and successful were exponentially higher than the figures Luchezarov gives. It is interesting that Iakubovich poses Luchezarov's numbers as questionable rather than just simply wrong, since these publications would have been readily available to him when he was composing this account. Fears of official censorship may account for his not contradicting Luchezarov's figures outright.

82 Tatar for "young man."

83 A bread-filled rag called a *soska* was traditionally used as a pacifier in Russia.

84 After nine years incarceration, Iakubovich was transferred in September 1893 to the free command at Kadaia. In 1895 he was released to a settlement in Kurgan.

85 A clever name that puns on both *zausenitsa* ("hangnail") and *za usa* ("behind a moustache").

86 Brand name of an Italian shoe sold in metropolitan Russia.

87 This break is in the original publication. It does not seem to serve much of a narrative function, but may indicate that a portion of Iakubovich's account was officially censored.

88 Siberia's under-staffed administration often hired penal laborers as guards.

Mare on the Road

1 The present essay describes part of the march route from Shelai (Akatui) mine to Kadaia. I will here abandon for a time the memoir form of narrative. [Author's note.]
2 A title that originated in Germany and was established by Peter I to designate a senior military official.
3 A town on the Amur River, in what was then called Priamur Territory.
4 I.e., this prisoner had been convicted and branded during Nicholas I's reign (1825–1855).
5 This may be an ironic allusion to Bova Korolevich, a hero of Russian folklore.
6 The stipend (*kormovye den'gi*) to which Nikolaev refers was the food stipend disbursed to prisoners by the administration on a daily or weekly basis to buy food from peasant vendors.
7 Timofeev's "Antip" probably refers to the cock "Antipka," who according to Russian fairy tales brings his owner bad luck, death, or eternal damnation.
8 Character created by German writer Christian August Vulpius (1762–1827) in his penny dreadful novel *Rinaldo-Rinaldini, Robber Captain* (1797).
9 *Dnevat'*—lit., "to spend the day."
10 In Transbaikalia, a two-wheeled cart is called a "trouble" (*beda*). [Author's note.]
11 A pun on the words *gornyi* ("mount") and *gor'kii* ("bitter").

Among the Hills

1 The syllable "ia" is emphasized in the word "Kadaia." [Author's note]
2 Traditional name for eastern Transbaikalia.
3 Genus *Melampyrum*.
4 *Hemerocallis fulva*.
5 A reference to those Poles exiled after the uprisings of 1830 and 1863.
6 *Ocherki gogolovskogo perioda*. Iakubovich is referring to the radical publicist Nikolai Gavrilovich Chernyshevskii (1828–1889), whose far more well-known and influential work was *Chto delat'?* (What is to be Done?), a book that greatly influenced Lenin.
7 Excerpt from the poem "Krepko, druzhno vas v ob''iat'ia..." (Embrace You Friendly and Strong), by M. L. Mikhailov (1829–1865).
8 Vodka distillers.
9 This is a diminutive of Avdotia, a character to be introduced momentarily.
10 This chapter has fictionalized the real life arrival, after fifteen years' separation, of Iakubovich's fiancée R. F. Frank. They were married in Mount Zerentui.
11 Following the 1863 Polish Uprising some twenty thousand Poles and other insurgents were exiled to Siberia.
12 This association between Mikhailov's tuberculosis, or "consumption," and physical injury or exposure reflects the general ignorance in Iakubovich's day about this disease's bacterial origins.
13 "The Polish exile of 1831 Litynsky."
14 From a poem by Iakubovich entitled "Pamiati Pavla Osipovich Ivanova" (Memories of Pavel Osipovich Ivanov). (See note below.)
15 *Zapiski otechestva*, a "thick" journal popular during the late imperial period.
16 Since autumn 1894, the picture drawn above has changed. A fifth grave was added for Pavel Osipovich Ivanov, who perished in a most terrible struggle with the typhoid fever epidemic that mowed down Kadaia's population that same year (Ivanov was a medical student sentenced to *katorga* in 1882 in one of the political trials). Apropos the happenstance of those burials, my comrades and I managed to repair the other graves: a collective cross was raised, a new one erected over Mikhailov, and an entire family of crosses formed on the cliff-top... The local *katorga* administration ranted and raved about this with a pointed question: on what basis was

Ivanov allowed not to be interred in the common prison graveyard? At one point, we even feared they'd dig up his grave and transfer the coffin… This didn't happen, but if someone else of us had died he wouldn't have been brought to the noted cliff to lie beside the poet's remains… Now, twelve years later, has this picture changed? Have the crosses fallen once again? Have they disappeared entirely?… [Note added by the author in 1906.]

Epilogue

1 One of Siberia's oldest monasteries, near the city of Eniseisk.

From the Author (*Postscriptum*)

1 This postscript was written in 1900 and first published in 1902. It was largely intended as a rebuttal to the physician and psychiatrist Pavel Ivanovich Kovalevskii (1849–1923) who, based on what Iakubovich contended was his misreading of his book (as well as other prison literature), posited the existence of "natural-born criminals." (Cf. P. I. Kovalevskii, *Psikhologiia prestupnika po russkoi literature o katorga*, S.-Peterburg: n. p., 1900.)

2 Pseudonym under which Iakubovich published his essays.

3 From Nekrasov's poem "Komu na Rusi zhit′ khorosho."

4 Characters in Dostoevskii's *Dead House.*

5 Vissarion Grigor′evich Belinskii (1811–1848) was a literary critic and publisher who promoted a liberalizing social agenda generally associated with the "Westernizers." He was among the first to praise a young Dostoevskii's work. Alexander Ivanovich Herzen (transliterated from the Russian as: Aleksandr Ivanovich Gertsen) (1812–1870) was, like Belinksii, a Westernizer. In 1835, Herzen was banished to his country estate for having been present when poetic verses supposedly critical of the tsar were recited. Five years later, his banishment over, Herzen returned to Moscow and came under Belinskii's influence. In 1847, he left Russia, never to return. He lived in Zurich, Paris, and London, publishing the émigré newspaper *Kolokol* (The Bell), which was smuggled in large numbers into Russia and which even the tsars reportedly read. Herzen vociferously promoted serf emancipation. His writings laid the basis for the populist socialist movement to which Iakubovich adhered.

6 Havelock Ellis (1859–1939) was a British physician and psychologist best known for his pioneering studies on human sexuality. He was also president of the British Eugenics Society (today called the Galton Institute). His *The Criminal* was published in 1890 and was his first book. The Russian translation to which Iakubovich refers is titled *Prestupnik* (Kiev: F. A. Ioganson, 1898). However, Iakubovich is mistaken in characterizing A. M. Grinberg as supervising the book's translation. Grinberg was in fact the translator; his supervisor was named I. A. Sikorskii.

7 In Russian: "Pereslashchennoe narodoliubie," *Russkoe bogatsvo. Russkoe bogatsvo* was another "thick journal" of the late imperial period.

8 Here Iakubovich coins the conceptual noun *gelerterstvo*, based on the German word *Gelehrter* ("learned one").

9 I'm personally inclined to give a different explanation for this distinction. Between the 1850s and 1890s lay not only just a huge interval of time but an entire series of greatly significant events in the life of the people, altering not just old understandings but, perhaps, the very social character, and having established much greater joyfulness than earlier… [Author's note.]

www.ingramcontent.com/pod-product-compliance
Lightning Source LLC
LaVergne TN
LVHW091029080826
845145LV00002B/417